Praise for
Dark Lie

"A page-turner of a thriller with a truly unique and fascinating heroine."

—Alison Gaylin, national bestselling author of *And She Was*

"Nancy Springer's first foray into suspense is a darkly riveting read. . . . The pages swiftly fall away, along with layers of secrets and lies, to reveal the pulsing heart of this compelling thriller: the primal bonds between parent and child, between man and woman—and the fine line between love and hate."

—Wendy Corsi Staub, national bestselling author of *Nightwatcher* and *Sleepwalker*

"A fast-paced, edge-of-your-seat thriller that will have you reading late into the night."

—Heather Gudenkauf, *New York Times* bestselling author of *The Weight of Silence* and *These Things Hidden*

"If you're looking for something very different and gripping in a noir thriller, you won't go wrong with *Dark Lie*."   —BookLoons

"[Springer] captures the fear of the women and the sickness of their captor with precision and the resolution of the kidnapping with unforeseen irony."   —*RT Book Reviews* (Top Pick)

"A page-turner that is gripping, scary, and filled with twists and turns . . . one you don't want to miss."   —Fiction Addict

"A compulsive page-turner that will have readers cheering on the decidedly unglamorous heroine, this thriller gets points for making the suburban mom type the one who saves the day."

—*Kirkus Reviews*

ALSO BY NANCY SPRINGER

Dark Lie

DRAWN INTO
DARKNESS

NANCY SPRINGER

New American Library
Published by the Penguin Group
Penguin Group (USA) LLC, 375 Hudson Street,
New York, New York 10014

USA | Canada | UK | Ireland | Australia | New Zealand | India | South Africa | China
penguin.com
A Penguin Random House Company

First published by New American Library,
a division of Penguin Group (USA) LLC

First Printing, November 2013

LIBRARY OF CONGRESS CATALOGING-IN-PUBLICATION DATA:

Springer, Nancy.
Drawn into darkness/Nancy Springer.
pages cm.
ISBN 978-0-451-23976-1 (pbk.)
I. Title.
PS3569.P685D73 2013
813'.54—dc23   2013020023

Printed in the United States of America
1 3 5 7 9 10 8 6 4 2

Set in Janson Text

PUBLISHER'S NOTE
This is a work of fiction. Names, characters, places, and incidents either are the product of the
author's imagination or are used fictitiously, and any resemblance to actual persons, living or
dead, business establishments, events, or locales is entirely coincidental.

To Ellen Edwards and Jennifer Weltz

DRAWN INTO DARKNESS

ONE

I am one of those women with a high IQ, a good education, scads of arcane data in my brain, yet I seem to have no common sense when it comes to making personal decisions. I aced my college courses, with a double major, no less—but in philosophy and world literature, subjects so broad I came out with no practical knowledge except that I could never know anything for certain. Hello? Who would hire me? It didn't matter, because, being me, I dropped out of college three months shy of graduation to marry Georg with no *e*. Maybe God the mother of us all remembers why it seemed so urgent to get married; I don't. In hindsight, I think I did it to hurt my parents, fulfilling their low expectations of me, blowing all the money they had spent on my tuition while smugly letting them think I was knocked up.

Pregnant? Ha. I was *so* not pregnant, and after marriage it became apparent that I was going to have to work hard to get that way. Georg lacked a lot of normal attributes besides an *e*, as I found out over the next two and a half decades. Perversely, he turned out to be so much like Mom and Dad that they took him to their bosoms, giving him their unconditional approval even when he dealt with midlife by dumping me.

Divorce did nothing to improve my judgment. I dyed my hair

ridiculously red. I thrust cherished possessions into the Goodwill bin. Pausing only to retain a lawyer, cutting off all communications with Georg, I moved far away in search of long ago, to a place where I had been happy visiting my grandparents as a child, a place Georg would have loathed, short on culture but long on snakes and alligators: the Alabama border hinterlands of the Florida Panhandle.

All this against the advice of the friends I left behind along with anything else familiar and comforting except my dog.

"Schweitzer," I told the dog a week after we had moved into a rented shack wreathed with mimosa trees, "Grandma and Grandpa are so not here anymore, and this is not even their house, just something in the general vicinity, and I am so not a butterfly-chasing child anymore. I'm almost fifty. You'd think by now I would have a clue."

Schweitzer, an animal shelter graduate with a double major in dachshund and something else, kept gnawing on his teddy bear's nose. Schweitzer scorned all designated dog toys, preferring stuffed animals.

"But trust me to screw up. I go and move south at the beginning of summer, never mind global warming," I continued, "to the Bible Belt, where there's nothing but church open on Sunday, and 'church' does not include Universalist Unitarian."

Already I regretted my impulsive and idealistic retreat to my childhood Eden. Sure, I still loved the mimosas, the live oaks furred with ivy, ferns, and Spanish moss, the flocks of white ibis flying, and the wildflowers everywhere—but those reminders of childhood happiness made my heart ache. I was an adult now, and in the mood for extensive retail therapy, thanks to all the weight I'd lost. There's no diet as effective as divorce. I was a hot mama with my new red hair, but a lot of good it would do me here in

Maypop, Florida, where the nearest shopping mall was up in Alabama, eighty miles away. Ten miles from my shack, Maypop had
a Piggly Wiggly but not much else, and Maypop County was
mostly a wilderness.

Schweitzer started sucking on his teddy bear's nose rather
than gnawing it. I refrained from sucking my thumb. In every
corner of my small house stood stacks of cardboard boxes I had
not yet unpacked, but I felt too bummed to work. This was, of
course, on a God-it's-a-hundred-'n'-three-degrees-in-the-shade
Sunday as I sat in front of the huge old window air conditioner
while my personal ghosts floated in its blast. I had tried shopping
online, but this was slow-modem country, where the Internet was
like Chinese water torture. The only thing I succeeded in pur-
chasing was a set of bug-proof storage containers for the kitchen,
not very satisfying emotionally.

I had called both of my sons, twentysomethings busy in the
Big Apple or vicinity thereof, probably at a Yankees game. I had
left Hi-this-is-Mom messages on their voice mails requesting that
they call back, but I knew that neither of them would. While unlikely to admit it, they were both traumatized by the divorce, and
running away from it just as I was.

"I didn't want to be a clinging vine," I told Schweitzer, "so now
I'm rootless."

This was punny. My parents, Deborah and Gerald Clymer,
had named me Liana Clymer because they thought it was clever—
subtle enough that only smart people would get it, and sweetly
feminine. Our relationship had gone pretty much downhill from
there. I could not phone them, could not get past the knowledge
that Georg was likely at their Pennsylvania George-Washington-
slept-here fieldstone home for Sunday dinner, and probably Mom
was doing his laundry for him.

Schweitzer was licking his front paws now, in his usual philosophical manner. I wished I were a dog, so content with so little. My loneliness, as tangible as if I had painted the room indigo, felt so heavy that suddenly I knew I had to get out of there or develop existential nausea.

I stood up. "Schweitzer," I told my only friend in miles and miles, "this is the South, and a person is allowed to drop in on strangers, for God's sake. I'm going to get acquainted with the neighbors."

By "neighbors" I meant whoever lived in the shack diagonally across the road from mine, almost far enough away to justify taking the car. Nobody else lived anywhere within sight of either that shack or mine. One thing I liked about this part of Florida was its frontier feeling of spaciousness, small towns spread out enough so that people kept horses in their backyards. Another thing I liked was the tasteless colors. My shack—it really was a three-room wood-frame shack squatting on concrete blocks—was painted fuchsia, or at least that was what I called it, because "pink" didn't do it justice and I don't like magenta. Definitely fuchsia, and a good match for the fuzzy mimosa blossoms all around it. The shack I planned to visit was painted peacock blue, almost turquoise. Peeking from the edge of my front window, I could see parts of it and a generic white van parked alongside it. Somebody was home.

Defiant of the heat, I would walk there. Mad dogs and Englishmen, yeah, whatever, five minutes in the sun wouldn't kill me.

Shoving my keys into the pocket of my shorts and heading for the door, I said, "Schweitzer, be good. Stay out of the trash."

Schweitzer did not take this philosophically. The moment I stepped outside into the broiling heat, he started barking frantically, almost hysterically, almost as if he knew he would never see me again.

. . .

About an hour's drive away, across the state line in Alabama, another middle-aged woman, named Amy Bradley, sat on a sofa overdue for replacement, hugging the cat, a hefty brown tabby she and her daughter had rescued and named Meatloaf. There was plenty of room on the sofa for her husband to sit beside her, but he lounged separate and silent in a recliner even more decrepit than the sofa.

Amy sensed the presence of a large elephant in the room, and decided to stop ignoring it. Careful to keep her voice level and quiet, she asked, "Honey, are you still pissed?"

Chad—his actual name was Charles Stuart Bradley, but everybody called him Chad—gave an exaggerated sigh before answering, "I have a right to be pissed."

"Then, so do I." She tried to maintain the same neutral tone and did not quite succeed. Yes, she felt as angry as he did, but for a different reason. She was tired of being nice. For the first year after the unbearable had happened, Amy had borne it with all the nobility seemingly expected of women since long before Michelangelo had created the *Pietà*, feminine exemplar of tragedy faced with saintly calm. It seemed to Amy that the carved-in-marble Mary should have been screaming with grief and rage. Surely crying out loud was the more fitting reaction for a mother so unfairly bereft.

"Tell me again why you're pissed with me for trying to get our son back," she said.

Chad did not answer.

Amy hugged Meatloaf so tightly that he stopped purring and tried to squirm away. "I'm angry too," she said. "I'm angry at God for letting this happen. I'm angry at people who know where their children are. I'm angry at people who can have normal lives and aren't over their heads in debt. But above all I'm angry at that creep who stole Justin and I want him punished and I—I want our son back! Even if it's only his body, or his bones!" Her voice wobbled; the cat scratched her arm, drawing blood, and she had to let him go.

Meatloaf complained at her, but otherwise there was silence. Amy grabbed a tissue for her arm and surreptitiously applied it to her eyes as well. Chad still did not look at her. She stared at the side of his head as he lounged in his recliner, distanced from her as had become usual, front and center to the flat-screen TV, watching a nationally rated rodeo taking place in Alabama's Peanut Capital Arena. Amy ached to go over there and hug him and kiss him. But she couldn't, because Chad would mistake love for capitulation. She wished their ten-year-old twins, Kyle and Kayla, were there to cuddle with her on the sofa. But as so often happened those days, she had sent them to play at a friend's house to spare them the tension at home.

After an uncomprehending glance, Chad had silently turned his attention back to the TV. Amy decided silence might be best; she settled back to watch, sort of. She had no interest in bull riding or calf roping. Nor did Chad; Amy knew he would rather have been enjoying almost any other sport, especially NASCAR. But both of them knew that all the Bubbas and Bubbettes within five hundred miles of here, meaning pretty much the entire population of Alabama and upper Florida, would be tuned in—which was why, despite Chad's opposition, Amy had gone ahead and taken out a second mortgage to pay for the ad they were waiting to see aired.

Which was why, yes, he, the wage earner, was still pissed at her. Because of the additional financial burden, yes, but more because he thought it was time to move on. Just because he said so. The dickhead thought it was all about him—

No, Amy told herself. Chad was a good man. Certainly neither he nor she would ever have chosen this trouble that threatened to tear them apart.

Back when it had first happened, her husband had been with her two hundred percent, both of them intent on getting Justin back. Poor Chad, God, he had *seen* it happen, had seen their son pedaling his bike down the peaceful road to spend Saturday afternoon with a friend; Chad had been out front, mowing the lawn. According to what he'd told her, he remembered waving at the white van as it passed, but without paying much attention; in Alabama everybody waves at everybody. Reaching the edge of the yard, Chad had turned the mower just in time to see, toward the end of the road, the van deliberately bump into Justin's bike, knocking him to the ground. Chad had yelled, of course, quite futilely, "Hey!" as a quick, slim person—probably a man, but could it possibly have been a woman?—someone in a gray hoodie, sprang out of the van and grabbed Justin. Chad did not see the boy kick or resist. Justin had seemed limp, maybe unconscious, as the stranger threw him into the van, slammed the door, ran back to the driver's seat, and drove away fast. Still yelling "Hey! HEY!" in disbelief, Chad had jumped off the mower and "like a lunatic," as he said afterward, he had run after the van as it sped away, turned onto Wiregrass Widow Road, then disappeared from sight between the slash pine trees. Gone.

With Justin in it.

Their son, gone.

Chad and Amy's firstborn, abducted in broad daylight.

Almost two years ago now.

Amy remembered she had been folding laundry in the kitchen with Kayla, then an eight-year-old, when she heard the drone of the lawn mower stop for some reason. She did not yet know that the mower had turned itself off because Chad had ejected himself from the seat. But she remembered the exact item of clothing—Justin's NASCAR T-shirt, the red, white, and blue cotton tee—she laid down when Chad burst into the house, shouting incoherently, to phone 911.

During the panicky blur afterward, Amy had found strength she had never previously known she possessed, crying with Chad and Kayla and Kyle, trying to comfort all of them, trying to support Chad through long hours with the cops—local, then state, then all over again with the FBI. She had stood by as Chad identified the bicycle still lying at the side of the road with a dent and some white paint on its rear mudguard. Side by side, she and Chad had cried for the TV cameras, pleading with the abductor for Justin's return. She had spent as many sleepless nights as he did, had searched endless pine forests along with swarms of volunteers, had placed uncounted numbers of MISSING, ENDANGERED posters on telephone posts and light poles and in storefront windows, had answered too many phone calls, had comforted her husband in her arms at least as much as he had ever comforted her.

When it became financially necessary for Chad to return to work at Dixieland Trucking, the torch had mostly passed to Amy. She had quit her job as a dietitian at Delaine Assisted Living to search for Justin. She had spent her days on the phone, prodding the police, getting billboards put up, and sometimes going on talk radio or to a TV interview or a fund-raiser or a conference about missing children. Mostly for that first year she had sat with her computer, searching the Internet for yet more sites on which she could post pictures and descriptions of her missing son.

Yet, despite all this practice, how could she possibly describe Justin, really? He had more than his share of the mercurial, puckish quality of most children, which meant that, almost day by day, he had changed. His passions when she knew him had been

NASCAR racing and Taylor Swift, but were they still? Did he still turn to hide tears in his eyes when he saw a road-killed dog or cat? Did he still get that impish smile when he had a secret agenda? Was he still an adorable little squirt who looked and sounded prepubescent, or had he shot up, was his voice changing, was—if he was alive, was he okay, was he still Justin?

Would she know him if she saw him now, almost two years later?

It didn't matter. She would search for him twenty years if that was what it took. For the rest of her life if she had to.

But Chad was beginning to feel differently.

He had endured the first anniversary of the abduction hand in hand with her, through the sad ceremony, the painful emotions, the candlelight vigil. But no more than a week later he had turned over in bed and said the words of a practical-minded man, the words of a realist, the words Amy was not sure she could ever forgive him for saying.

"Pretty soon," Chad had said, "there's going to come a tipping point when we will have to stop."

In bed, in darkness. Pillow talk. How long had it been now since pillow talk, or since they had even slept together?

Sleepy and not paying much attention, Amy had mumbled, "Stop what?"

"Stop trying to believe Justin might be alive when common sense says he's dead."

Common sense and experts: statistically speaking, most children abducted by strangers are killed within the first seventy-two hours after they disappear, and most of *those* are dead even before the searches start. Amy knew this and she knew Chad knew it.

"Chad, you've got to be kidding." Amy felt wide-awake now. More than just awake. Palpitating. Panicked. "We can't give up on Justin!"

"How long are we supposed to live a nightmare? How long are we supposed to keep hoping when there's hardly any hope? And don't you think you should spend more time with the twins?"

"I keep them involved—"

"Posting their brother's picture on the Internet? Bullshit. You're neglecting them to chase an unrealistic dream—"

"Stop it, Chad!" Amy tried to keep her voice low so as not to disturb the children's sleep. She and Chad never made any kind of noise that might wake up the twins.

Chad said just as quietly, "I can't stop. This thing is killing us, deep-sixing our marriage. We have to move on."

"I'm Justin's mother! I can't give up on him!"

"You were my wife before you were anybody's mother."

Silence. Amy could not reply to that. Or not in any way that Chad could bear to hear. She had known since the moment Justin was born that motherhood came before anything else. It was a mother's instinct to protect her children, and if that meant protecting them from their own father, so be it. Amy put her children ahead of her husband. If she had to choose between Chad and her babies, Chad would have to go.

But she could not say this to him. And she felt pregnant with the knowledge, felt it kicking inside her, causing her to spend a mostly sleepless night.

A few days later Chad tried again, this time using the mundane argument of money, expenses, numbers on the bank statements. He said they had to cut back on their efforts to find Justin, which had almost buried them financially despite donations from hordes of sympathetic people. He thought Amy should help out by going back to work at Delaine Assisted Living. And they both should pay more attention to the twins. They should make an effort to become an untroubled family again. They should get back to normal. A new normal.

Amy could not help feeling horrified at her husband's "common sense." They quarreled. And a day or two later, again. And so on. It had been months now.

Chad wanted her back at work? Amy found herself barely able to do any kind of work at all. There had been a time, before Justin's disappearance, when Amy had gone to both yoga and Zumba classes after a full day at her job, when she had gotten up extra early some mornings to go jogging with friends, when she had created delicate, gift-worthy jewelry out of wire and beads, when she had started to weave (not crochet or knit) a colorful afghan for the sofa. Now, discouraged by Chad, she no longer spent all her time searching for Justin, yet she could not take up any of her hobbies again. Instead, she found herself wistfully bringing home angel figurines she picked up at yard sales, thrift shops, and dollar stores. Wasting more money, Chad complained, and she did not even try to tell him that placing angels throughout the house was the only way she could bear living in her own home. A lot of the time she moped around, feeling desolate. More so after each quarrel with her husband.

And each fight got worse than the last, until now when Amy had really pissed Chad off, spending their last dime for a television commercial about Justin. "It might make all the difference," Amy had argued. "Look how many people *America's Most Wanted* has located."

"John Walsh," Chad had retorted in stinging tones. "Let me remind you, Amy, his missing son is dead, always was dead, and always will be dead."

"But he never gave up."

"So now he's your hero instead of me?"

True enough, Amy thought, sitting uncomfortably on what should have been a comfy sofa, watching the rodeo on TV and feeling the knowledge that she could never give up still kicking like an overdue baby in her belly. Sensing another elephant in the room, Amy almost let herself think she stood to lose more than her son. She almost let herself think that pretty soon, if things went on this way, there was going to come a tipping point—make that a ripping point. The taut fabric of her marriage would soon tear apart.

TWO

Despite the heat, which sent my mind searching for quotes from Milton or Dante as I walked along the shoulder of the road, still this place did not qualify as hell, only a fantastically weird limbo of sprawling vines thick with the largest, most grotesque and barbaric wildflower I had ever seen: circular blossoms wider than my hand, each made of twelve creamy bracts upon which lay wriggly purple tentacle-like petals radiating from an erect and somewhat cruciform yellow center. The Spaniards had called it "passionflower" because it had made them think of the passion of Christ on the cross. Dumbidity only knew why Floridians called the magnificently weird blossom "maypop." And how ironic, I found, that the down-home place in which I now lived had been named after the most strikingly fantastic wildflower I had ever seen.

Amid the passionflower vines, a giant seashell lay in the sand—although sixty miles inland from the Gulf, still this place was almost as sandy as a beach—but the shell was part of a dead armadillo, really. Wacko things like them lived in my local limbo. Blue-tailed lizards, for instance. Walking fast to get out of the heat, I saw one scuttle away, its tail even more electric in color than the shack I was going to visit. I heard mockingbirds ranting

almost loud enough to compete with the sound of Schweitzer's
stubborn barking.

The blue shack lacked much by way of a porch. Its old wooden
steps were not painted any peacock color; they were not painted at
all. But at least they looked solid. I climbed them to the narrow
stoop in front of the door and looked for a doorbell. There wasn't
any. I knocked.

Waited a minute, self-conscious in my shorts—of course I wore
shorts; everybody down here wore shorts, but my legs needed to be
shaved. Every female down here seemed naturally hairless. And
they all, men, women, and children, wore flip-flops. Everywhere.
Dressy flip-flops for church, weddings, and funerals. But I couldn't
stand the feel of the things, the thong between my toes. I wore
socks and sneakers. Momentarily I wished I could have pulled up
my pink socks far enough to cover the hair on my legs. But then,
mentally, I shrugged. Who the hell cared how I looked?

Just as I was lifting my hand to tap again, the door opened. A
pale teenage boy with long bleached hair in cornrows stood there
raising his blond eyebrows at me. Immediately I felt absurd; I
might as well have been carrying a placard that said DIVORCED,
EMOTIONALLY NEEDY. "Um, hi," I blurted. "I'm your new neighbor
in the pink house, so I came over to meet my neighbors in the blue
house. We should get along, huh? Pink and blue?"

God, I was babbling. I blushed. But the kid smiled, a small
smile, but its shy generosity, not typically teenage, diverted my
attention from his rather extreme hair with its many cornrows and
braids to his face. Without a possibility of ever being handsome in
a chiseled-chin/cheekbone way, he was a total cutie. Wide, sensitive mouth, short nose, liquid brown calf eyes, soft smooth tawny
skin without a blemish.

"What's going on, Justin?" yelled a male voice from somewhere in the back of the shack.

"Visitor, Uncle Steve," he yelled back. "Come on in," he invited, holding the door open for me. Gratefully I stepped into a dim and blessedly cool living room where an air conditioner's hum competed with babble from Dish TV. As my eyes adjusted to the light, I looked around the room and saw its personality as being a bit anal, with sofa, lounge chair, end tables, and lamps arranged with rectilinear precision and spotlessly clean.

I heard Uncle Steve approaching, but saw him only as a silhouette against window light from the back door, quick and slim.

"Have a seat." The teenage boy gestured me toward one end of the impeccable sofa. The carpet, too, I saw, was innocent of dirt in any form. Yet nothing looked new, and nobody had decorated. No throw pillows, no color scheme, and nothing worth noticing hanging on the walls. All the essentials were in evidence, yet the place felt oddly incomplete, as if it were a motel room, as if nobody lived here.

And the man hurrying in gave every impression of being exactly that: nobody. Not very tall and not well built, narrow-shouldered and hollow-chested and stooping, he was a gray man, by which I mean more than the color of his goatee and his thin hair pulled back into an aging-hippie ponytail and maybe his pebble eyes set too close together, shrinking into his cork-colored face like a turtle into its shell. Pinched, beak-nosed, and weaselly, he looked like the result of centuries of inbreeding. "Steven Stoat," he said tonelessly, standing over me as I perched on his sofa but not offering his hand. "And you are?"

"Um, Liana Clymer." I wasn't legally, not yet, but I was using my birth name. The cutesy-poo alliteration of my married name, Liana Leppo, had always annoyed me.

"She lives in the pink house, Uncle Steve." The kid sat down on the opposite end of the sofa from me, where he could watch TV.

"I just moved in last week, so I thought I'd introduce myself.

Actually, I came looking for somebody to talk with. Another woman," I added quickly so he wouldn't get the wrong idea. I really had assumed there would be a woman in the house, a wife or a girlfriend. But if there were, the place would have had the pillows and tchotchkes it lacked. I couldn't imagine any woman living here and not wanting to pretty the place up. "But there isn't any, is there?"

The man's inhospitable scrutiny had begun to irk me. Having asked a direct question, I made myself wait for an answer.

He backed off and sat down in an armchair, but he didn't say a word.

I tried again. "Is your name Steven with a *v* or with a *ph*?"

Even though he did not actually roll his eyes, something in his silent stare made me feel as if he had.

"Are you the one who keeps this house so neat and tidy?"

Nothing. Not even a frown.

Screw him. I would get out of here soon, but I would stay long enough to show him that he didn't faze me. I turned my attention to Justin. "What's that on your T-shirt?" Like me and also like his uncle, he wore a tee with something printed on the front. Mine said, "Bad Spellers of the Wrold, Untie."

Justin readily turned his attention away from the TV to answer me. "It's supposed to be a dolphin." He had a pleasant, husky voice, not quite a child's voice yet far from being a rebellious weird-haired teen's. "But it got kind of messed up, see?" Turning toward me, he tugged the tee straight, stretching it like a canvas.

I would not have been able to tell that the broken, smeared image was a dolphin. "I see," I said. "Dolphin by Picasso."

Justin laughed, and his grin seemed to light up the dim room. "Dolphin by jammed screen print machine," he said. "Uncle Steve works at this business that makes T-shirts for tourists, and he brings home the ones that get screwed up."

"That's nice. Unless he screws them up on purpose," I added, trying for another laugh.

"No, he'd never do that," Justin said quickly, no smile, his voice stressed. "Uncle Steve's a perfectionist." But I heard no pride in the words, only smothered anxiety.

"Just kidding." I glanced at the Stoat man, his nearly fleshless face still blank, a muddle on his T-shirt that looked like it might have been a skull and crossbones. If so, it suited him, the parchment skin of his head pitted with acne and etched with lines from being stretched too tight over his own skull. He was the sort of person who made me wonder whether *anyone* loved him. I looked away again, deciding to be interested in the TV.

"What are you watching?" I scooted along the sofa toward Justin.

"Rodeo. There's nothing else on."

"What would you rather be watching?"

"NASCAR."

"What's that?"

"You never heard of NASCAR racing?" His genuine and ingenuous astonishment touched off an unexpected ache in my chest; something about him reminded me of my own boys when they were that age, of how much they had still been children even though they looked like young men. "Children are still children for a long, long time," my grandmother used to say before she died, and I had found out how true that was by my sons' reaction to the divorce.

"Course, you come from up north, right?" Worried eyes on me, afraid he'd been rude, Justin tried to excuse my ignorance.

I smiled at him. "Do I have a Yankee accent?"

"Um, sort of." Now he was even more afraid of offending me. "But it's okay, you know? Nice. Just a little different."

Peripherally I could see Uncle Steve, aka Steven Stoat, leaning back in his chair, but I sensed more than saw that he was not re-laxed at all. Too bad for him that he didn't like company. I'd leave in a minute, when I was ready. "Oh, look!" I said of the picture on the TV screen. "Barrel racing!" and I paid close attention as a girl in a huge pink cowboy hat and matching outfit spurred a black horse toward a barrel and skidded him around it. As she com-pleted the course, her time was announced by a deep, drawling voice, which went on to say, "Now, while we wait for the next rider, folks, please listen up to this important appeal."

A picture of a dark-haired boy with shining brown eyes and a winsome smile appeared on the TV.

I gasped, recognizing him instantly, although he looked a cou-ple of years younger and he had done radical things to his hair. "Justin, that's you!"

"No, it's not!" He grabbed for the remote, his voice a fright-ened squeak, but it was too late. The words MISSING, ENDANGERED, plus a phone number, had appeared on the screen, and the an-nouncer was saying, "Justin Bradley, shown here at the age of twelve, was last seen riding his bike away from his Delaine, Ala-bama, home—"

Justin killed the TV, and as for me, fear preceded rational thought, but what was the use of that when I didn't have a scream-and-run reaction? I was brought up to be civilized, and to freeze like a baby bunny when the shadow of the hawk passes over. Now, still mentally struggling to define what sort of faux pas I had com-mitted, I said, "Well, I guess I'll be going," in a voice that com-pletely failed to sound casual, and I started to stand up.

As if I could unring a bell? It had been all over the moment I gasped.

"I guess you'd better not," the Stoat man said tonelessly. "Sit down." On his feet, pushing me back into the depths of the sofa, he stood over me, and although his only weapons were his hands and his stare, I might have felt less intimidated if he had been a stereotypical bad guy with a snarl and a handgun. Truly, I might have felt less freaked-out if he had looked mean and cruel. Or dangerous and panicky, or anything except blank like a reptile, the way he was watching me. "Justin," he said without shifting his attention from me, "have you seen that ad on TV before?" His voice, although not loud at all and not very deep, nevertheless made me start to tremble.

"No, sir." Not Uncle Steve, but "sir." Justin was afraid of him too.

"You sure?"

"Positive, sir."

"Just the same, you shouldn't have left the TV on in front of her. And you shouldn't have answered the door. You think just because it's been a while, now it's okay to take chances? It's not. The rules are still the rules. Don't *you* go to the door if anybody knocks. You hear me?"

"Yes, sir."

"And you shouldn't have let her in. You know you don't let anybody in unless I say, you hear?"

"Yes, sir." He sounded wretched. Even though I sat trapped in the corner of the sofa shaking like a rabbit in a snare, I felt for him.

"All right." He snapped his fingers at Justin. "Get me a bottle of beer."

Only sometime after I woke up did I appreciate how clever he was. If he had asked Justin to bring him his gun, there was a slight chance that the boy, even as thoroughly indoctrinated as he was, might have reverted to being the kid his parents had raised, might have tried to use the weapon to save me. If he had said bring him the baseball bat, there was still the same remote chance. But by demanding a beer, he sounded as if he wanted to relax.

Justin jumped up to get him a cold bottle of Coors from the

fridge. And even I unfroze enough to whisper, "Listen, you don't have to worry about me. I won't tell anybody. If you say Justin is your nephew, I believe you. I—"

Didn't get to say any more. Justin handed Stoat the beer, and without opening it he swung the bottle hard at my head.

Blackness.

Regaining consciousness felt visually and mentally like being in a kaleidoscope, needing to put the shifting pieces together. At first I thought I was back in my longtime home in Pennsylvania, and then with a jolt of heartache I remembered the divorce, and my own parents siding with my ex, damn them, and my new fuchsia cottage in the weirdest part of Florida, where I had spent many hours miserably lying on the bed looking up at the ceiling—but there was something different about this ceiling, and who—my double vision was trying to tell me—who was looking down at me?

My heart started pounding. I knew I was in trouble even before I managed to focus on the sparse man holding a handgun, a long-barreled revolver that seemed too big for him. But that was an illusion caused by his slim build. One look into his empty eyes showed that no weapon was too big for this—this psycho standing over me as I lay immodestly spread out on the bed.

My arms and legs jumped, jerked. Some instinct even more atavistic than fear made me want to curl up, roll away from him, drop off the bed onto the floor, crawl under it. But I couldn't. Only my left hand flew up. Hard, hurtful tethers bit my ankles and my right wrist. I squeaked, but shut up immediately as—what was his name?—Steven Stoat angled the gun barrel toward my head. At the same time an anomalously gentle hand gripped my left wrist, swung it back to the bed, and snapped something metallic around it. Then I felt the arm drawn straight by some force fastening it to the corner of the bed.

"Tighter, Justin," Stoat said.

I tilted my head and tried to look at Justin as he tied the rope to the bedpost, but he wouldn't meet my eyes. As soon as he'd completed the job, he left the room.

"You," Stoat said, gesturing at me with the gun, "what's your name again? Lee Anna something?"

I nodded, afraid that if I tried to speak, I would burst into pleas or tears.

"Now, Lee Anna, listen. You shouldn't have come here to my house. You put yourself in the wrong place at the wrong time. So now I got to keep you here till I figure out what to do about you. But I want you to understand I'm a logical man and I don't hurt people for no reason. You just lay still and—is that your dog yapping?"

Sure enough, in this bedroom away from the air conditioner I could hear Schweitzer steadily barking.

My mouth opened on its own. "He needs to be fed," I whispered. "Key to the house is in my pocket."

"I already got it." He held it up for me to see, the house key dangling from its Hello Kitty ring. "Dog needs to be fed, huh?"

"Please," I said.

Justin came back in carrying a grungy white pillowcase. Stoat stuck his gun into the front waistband of his cutoff jeans and, just as I began to exhale in relief, he pulled something out of a pocket and snapped it open into a vicious-looking knife. That's subjective. If I had seen the knife in a display case at a sporting goods store, I might have regarded it simply as a rather large folding army-style survival knife with a four-inch blade. But in the hand of—I couldn't yet face what Stoat really was—in his hand it terrified me, slashing through the pillowcase as if it were tissue. When he was done with the knife, he made a casual move so fast I didn't comprehend it until I saw the knife quivering with its dagger point stuck into the wall on the other side of the bed.

The man had thrown the knife right over top of me, just like that, zing. He was a knife thrower. Oh, great. Just wonderful.

He knotted the strip of cloth in his hands—those hands looked overlarge, ugly-knuckled, and very strong to me—and then he leaned over me.

"What's that?" I gasped.

He growled, "I don't like noise," as he none too gently tied it around my head.

"But I won't scream," I tried to protest, or promise. "There's nobody around to hear me anyway."

"I'm a careful man. Open up." He forced the knot into my mouth, then tightened everything, ending my side of the conversation. "I like things neat," he told me sourly, "and you have sure messed things up for me." Then he walked over, yanked his knife out of the wall, waved it at me with no expression at all on his crater face, and left.

I suppose it's odd, considering my situation, but I felt great relief when he left the room. Listening, I followed his footsteps to the front door, where it sounded like he went out of the shack. A moment later I heard an engine cough into reluctant life. The van I had seen parked at the side of the house.

Good. Good, this Stoat man was going to feed Schweitzer.

Lying on a bare mattress and looking at a boring, cheaply tiled ceiling, I tried to come to grips, listening to Schweitzer bark and considering my new reality one aspect at a time. Daylight came in through two windows, but from where I lay, I could see nothing but treetops through either of them. My head hurt and I felt something sticky on my face and neck. Beer. Beer bottle. Couldn't have injured me too badly if I remembered what had hit me.

Raising two sons, I had learned all about concussions. I didn't have one. And I had not been raped. Yet. One out of every four women is raped sometime in her life. If the posts around me were women, which one would have been raped? But what an unseemly thought about such a decorous bed, an antique four-poster, unusual for this kind of shack. Had the man Stoat acquired it on purpose for—for . . .

For Justin?

My thoughts, frightened, issued a gag order in a hurry. Back off. Justin was still alive after two years, I told myself. Stoat had kept him alive. Maybe Stoat would keep me alive. And Schweitzer. Stoat was going to feed Schweitzer. In fact, I could tell he had reached the door of my fuchsia shack, because I heard Schweitzer launch into a crescendo of barking—

And then an innocuous popping sound and a sickening scream, like nothing I had ever heard before, not human. Two more pops, then silence.

It took me a few heartbeats to get it.

The gun. Oh, my God, the gun.

"No!" I cried, or tried to cry out; with the knot of cloth in my mouth I managed only a muffled, distorted yawp. Frantically I thrashed against what must have been handcuffs around my wrists and ankles, trying to rip myself loose and run to my dog, for all the good that would do. Behind the gag of denial in my mind, I knew that Schweitzer, my "reverence for life" dog, lay bloody and dying. Yanking harder, I felt my restraints cut my skin; now I was bleeding too.

Justin came running in. "Stop it!" he exclaimed with no threat in his voice; he sounded frightened. Grabbing my shoulders to hold me down, his face hovering over mine, he begged, "Stop it, ma'am. Fighting only makes it worse. Believe me."

I looked up at him, and as if what had happened to Schweitzer were not bad enough, I saw something unspeakable shadowing his eyes. There was nothing blank about this boy. I stopped struggling, but my body still heaved, now with hurtful sobs. My ribs and belly ached, I cried so hard.

"I'm sorry," Justin said, "I'm sorry," as if it were all his fault. "Lie still." He disappeared someplace and came back with a box of tissues plus a moistened washcloth. Sitting on the edge of my bed, he wiped snot and tears from my face, pulled the knotted gag out of my mouth and tucked it under my chin, then helped me blow my nose. "Please try to calm down before Uncle Steve gets back," he urged, folding the washcloth to lay its cool, clean side on my forehead. "I have no idea what he'll do if you cry. He hates women."

That statement instantly stopped my bawling. It made a soldier of me. I am woman, hear me roar. I stared up at Justin. "He's not your uncle," I stated with barely a quiver in my voice.

"I've got to call him that."

"You're not a woman, but I bet he likes to make you cry too."

Justin did not reply except with shifting eyes. With a fresh tissue he swabbed my face like the deck of a storm-drenched ship.

I said, "Justin, what about your mother? Do you want her to keep crying?"

"Don't talk about my mother."

"Why are you still here? Your family wants you back. What are you waiting for?"

He shook his head, stood up, and went to look out a window toward my house. Then he disappeared into some other part of the shack and came back again with a roll of gauze. Moving quickly, he started wrapping my ankle where the handcuffs—I couldn't see the handcuffs, but that's what the metal things had to be—where they had cut and bloodied me.

"Justin—" I started to question him again.

"Don't talk." He shoved the gag back into my mouth. "I have to hurry and do this."

He had finished my ankles and was starting on one wrist when we heard the door open. I stiffened. Justin kept on wrapping gauze. I heard footsteps stop at the bedroom door. Stoat demanded, "Whatcha doing that for?"

"You want her to bleed all over the mattress?" Justin's soft, husky voice made this retort sound peaceable enough.

I could not see Stoat and did not want to look at him, but I imagined he'd decided in Justin's favor during a long, silent moment. He gave a raspy laugh. "She threw a fit when I shot her dog, huh?"

"Yes, sir," Justin said tonelessly, bandaging my other wrist.

"Well, I didn't do it out of meanness. You know that. She should know that. It was the only sensible way to take care of the dog, what with him yapping all the time till somebody might notice."

"Yes, sir."

"And if the damn dog would have stood still, it would only have taken one shot."

"Yes, sir." Justin finished my wrist and stood up.

Stoat told him, "Now get out of here, and I don't want you in here with her. I'll take care of her."

Sure, he would, I thought, forced to face it now. Same way he took care of Schweitzer.

I just wondered how soon.

THREE

By nightfall I almost did not care how soon. My back ached atrociously, and when I tried to ease my joints—hip, knee, elbow—the metal bit into my wrists and ankles. It would have hurt much worse if Justin hadn't wrapped them, but it still hurt some. And I had to keep flexing my feet and hands because even in the subtropical heat I felt them going cold and numb, losing blood circulation. Maybe because I couldn't move, or maybe because I was so scared. I had to be strong, I coached myself. Take care of myself. Flex my muscles, keep myself ready to move, watch my thoughts.

Trying to be more bored than frightened, I examined the perforated white tiles—what were those things made of, anyway, Styrofoam?—and I tried to see patterns in the squares on the ceiling. And in the overhead light fixture, but it was just the usual two bulbs covered with a frosted-glass square bug-catcher. The hermaphroditic positioning of the lightbulbs gave me mental fodder for a few moments but nothing uplifting. I felt my backache getting worse, plus discomfort from pressure points on the mattress; I began to understand how people got bedsores, and I badly wished somebody had thrown a blanket over me, covering me, if only for psychological comfort. But I didn't make a sound. Didn't want

Stoat's company. Neither he nor Justin—what was Justin's real last name? My memory had dropped it somewhere between here and the living room. Anyhow, neither of them came near me. I smelled macaroni and cheese, supper, but nobody offered me any, which made me feel starved and abused even though my knotted stomach would not possibly have let me eat it. When I thought divorce was the best way to lose weight quickly, I was wrong. Being a prisoner in fear of one's life looked even more effective.

And hopeless. Nobody was going to miss me or rescue me, least of all my family. My parents and I were barely speaking. My ex had no reason to want to phone me. My sons would not call, and it might take them a month or more to start worrying about me. I had two older brothers who kept in touch sporadically and might call if the spirit moved them, but I couldn't count on it. I had not yet met anybody down here who gave a damn, just dollar store and grocery store clerks. My friends from up north might call, leaving messages on my voice mail, and get pissed at me when I didn't call back. Nobody would come to my little fuchsia home to check on me.

Like my thoughts, the room darkened—nightfall—but my eyes stayed open.

The overhead light fixture flicked on.

I think my whole body winced like my startled eyes. Reflexively I turned my head. By the bed stood Stoat with his big pistol and his goatee, which did nothing for his undistinguished profile, just made him look like a goat. Stoat the Goat, that was what I would call him, although not to his face.

As I thought this, as if he were psychic and heard me, he turned to glare, pointing the pistol at me as Justin went around the bed releasing my wrists and ankles. Of their own accord, my arms and legs curled toward my midsection like those of a squashed spider.

"Get up," Stoat ordered, gesturing with the gun. "Potty time."

I realized I should have been afraid it was more than just potty time, but my mind had gone as numb as my toes. Awkwardly I swung my legs over the side of the bed to sit.

"The gag?" Justin asked.

"Yeah, take it off. Let her spit and get a drink."

I felt Justin fumbling at the back of my head to untie the thing. Maybe he didn't want his darling Uncle Steve to realize he could slip it in and out of my mouth. Finally he removed it.

"Stand up," ordered Stoat the Goat.

Clenching my teeth against the pain and stiffness in my lower back, I tottered to my unreliable feet.

"Move." Stoat nudged me in the ribs with the gun barrel.

I stepped out of the room and toward the back of the house as directed, and my brain got going also, starting to try to think. Escape. How? Bathroom window? Surely Stoat wouldn't come in there with me?

He didn't, but the bathroom offered no back exit. Its window was boarded up, and not just with plywood either. Two-by-fours. And not from the inside. Not so that the boards could be levered up, pried off, nails pulled out. They completely covered the window glass and screen from the outside. I saw not even a knothole to peek through.

This place had been altered to serve as a prison long before I came along.

"Hurry up!" yelled Stoat.

I decided to stall him as long as I could. Get my arms and legs back to life. "I need to wash," I called back. "There's beer all—"

All over me, I was going to say, but a loud bang interrupted me. The gun. Aimed low, the bullet ricocheted off the base of the toilet and zinged around the bathroom, so fast it was over by the time I jumped and screamed.

"Just pee in the damn pot," Stoat said with patience that

menaced worse than a shower of obscenities. If the man didn't mind putting a bullet hole in his bathroom door, he wouldn't mind kicking it in either.

I had peed, but not in the pot. Unfortunately, the bathroom was as obsessively tidy as the rest of the house. Using toilet paper, I cleaned up myself first, then started on the floor.

"What's taking so long!"

"Almost finished." I flushed the toilet I had not even sat on, ran water as if washing my hands (or maybe getting a drink and spitting), said "Oops" as if I had splashed myself, stalled by spraying with raspberry Glade, then discovered I could not take the next step. I could not open the door.

"I'm scared to come out," I said.

"You come out or I won't shoot low this time."

It's amazing how brave terror can make a person. I opened the door and stepped out. Justin was nowhere to be seen. Stoat motioned me back to my room and onto the bed with his oversized pistol. "Justin!" he hollered, and the kid came in and cuffed my wrists and ankles without looking at me. Stoat nodded and stuffed his weapon all too appropriately into the front waistband of his pants.

"Okay. Bedtime. Nighty-night, sleep tight," he said, and I thought he was tormenting me, but there was a sort of genuine warmth, maybe eagerness, in his tone, and he put his arm around Justin, pulled him close, and kissed him on the lips.

I gasped in shock. This was probably what Stoat wanted, because he looked straight into my horrified eyes and grinned. Justin's face, what I could see of it, had gone crimson, and he kept his head turned against Stoat's shoulder.

With his arm still around the boy, Stoat left the room and flicked off the light.

When people say they spent a sleepless night, usually they're exaggerating. Usually they have at least dozed a little.

I spent a sleepless night, no exaggeration. The dark hours became one long panic attack. My heart raced, and my mind, and I ached all over with sheer helplessness.

But I, myself, was not the only one I felt helpless about.

Of course I felt terribly afraid as the captive of a psycho. I didn't want to die. I needed to escape. But even more urgently I needed to rescue Justin.

Sometime in the dead of night—that's what they call it, the dead of night, uncomfortable thought—I thought I heard stealthy movements somewhere in the house. Holding my breath to listen, despite the blathering of summer insects all around the shack, that plus the pounding of my own pulse in my ears, I sensed someone was awake and up to something. Stoat, probably, paying me a visit to—rape me, kill me, the devil knew what. I would be too proud to cry out, but he would make me cry out anyway. Unmistakable soft footsteps approached my room. I tried to lie still and not tremble—

It was Justin.

I knew it the moment he reached the door, even though I could barely see a thing, with only a whisper of starlight coming in the windows. Maybe I recognized him from that awkward, ardent pubescent-boy smell I knew so well from my sons, a whisper of scent just at the edge of my conscious awareness. Or maybe my primal mothering instinct knew him, or maybe there is a sixth sense. Somehow I could tell that the shadow entering my room was youthful, frightened, and wretched and brave, trying to— atone?

He sat on the edge of the bed—I felt the mattress sag—and he fumbled at my face to find the gag and pull it out of my mouth. "Shhh," he told me in the softest of exhalations, and he reached for something and fumbled again to find my mouth, pressing what felt like wood shavings against my lips. But my nose told me otherwise. Cornflakes. I opened my mouth.

The cornflakes tasted sugary. Frosted Flakes. When I had chewed and swallowed, I opened my mouth again, waiting like a baby bird for Justin to feed me.

After a short while, however, my stomach started to rebel, and I closed my mouth, turned away, and shook my head.

"Eat," Justin whispered so softly I could barely hear him.

"Can't," I whispered back.

"Drink?" he asked. "Milk?"

I knew I should try to stay strong and hydrated. "Okay."

He slipped one hand under my head and lifted it in the cradle of his elbow. With the other hand he guided a glass to my mouth, tilting it until I tasted milk. I sipped a few swallows of it, then pulled away.

He took the hint, laying my head back on the mattress. "How about some more cereal?"

"No, thanks."

As if I might change my mind in a few moments, he stayed where he was.

"Go back to bed," I whispered, "before that pervert wakes up and wonders where you are. He makes you sleep with him, doesn't he?"

Justin might have nodded, but I couldn't tell. I felt his body sag heavy on the mattress, saw him, or the dark shape that was him, curl up and slump over.

"Better go," I breathed.

Without a good-bye he got up and left me.

I looked up into darkness and tears ran down across my temples and trickled into my ears. My stomach hurt, trying to process food amid bile and stress, but that wasn't the cause of my tears.

Nothing Stoat could do to me would ever make me weep; I promised myself that. I had a great deal of useless pride, even after the divorce had flattened me. Especially then. But Justin and a few Frosted Flakes made me want to bawl like a baby.

I shied away from thinking the word "kindness." It was treacherous. Even Stoat could be kind.

He demonstrated that in the morning. Striding into my room—my prison—he said, "Hey, there," just like a truly nice guy, pulled the gag out of my mouth, and asked without a hint of sarcasm, "Did you sleep well?"

His gently smiling face astonished me so much that instead of glaring at him, I gawked.

"You ain't speaking to me?" His smile waxed even more saintly. "I can understand that. Come on and use the bathroom." He released my feet first, and I could have kicked him in the head, but I just stared. After he released my hands, he did draw his omnipresent handgun from his waistband as I struggled to get up from the bed, but he stood back and gave me all the time in the world to get my stiffened body up and walking.

Oddly, his unexpected patience made me more afraid of him, not less. In the bathroom, even after I had pulled my pants back up, I still felt trembly all over. I took my time washing my hands and trying to finger-comb my hair, at which point I realized I had somehow become reluctant to look at myself in the mirror. I could not meet my own eyes.

I could not bear to see my own terror, I told myself. But then I realized I was rationalizing what was really—shame? Of all the stupid—what did I have to be ashamed of? I had done nothing to be ashamed of.

Yet facing the mirror and the look in my own eyes forced me to acknowledge damage beneath the skin. Physically, Stoat had not hurt me much—yet—but already I had been crippled. Stoat was in the process of diminishing my selfhood, taking away my spirit, reducing me to a joyless middle-aged child who was dependent upon him for life itself.

This was not good. He must not see it in me.

I stood in front of the mirror and stared at myself straight in the eye until I had to lift my chin and grin.

From right outside the doorway Stoat demanded, "What the hell is taking you so long?"

I let go of the grin but tried to keep my chin up as I went out to face him.

"Feeling better?" he asked viciously. Yet his gun barrel motioned me not back toward the bed but in another direction, and I found myself entering a small kitchen that seemed a lot like the rest of the house, everything orderly, everything impeccable, everything cheap and without character. "Have a seat," he said as we approached the generic tube-legged table topped with scrub-worn Formica. "I always say the key to a good day is a proper breakfast."

Good day?

Again he seemed absurdly serious. Justin, manning the stove, served up toast, fried Spam, and scrambled eggs without letting me meet his eyes.

"Eat up, Lee Anna. Enjoy it," said Stoat sincerely, almost compassionately, laying his revolver on the corner of the table beside him. Well out of my reach.

Because I wanted to stay on the tube-legs-and-plastic-seat chair, as opposed to the much more formidable bed, I did manage to eat. Slowly, but Stoat seemed all patience and goodwill this morning.

"Justin, you gotta stay home from school today, boy. One look at your face, people will be asking who pissed on your Cheerios."

School? Right, it was Monday, but—but normally Justin went to *school*? Why hadn't he told a teacher he was abducted? Why hadn't he contacted his parents?

Justin looked at Stoat and whispered, "You *gotta* go to work?" as if he was scared of being left home alone with me.

"Yes, boy, I gotta go to work because it's spring break down in Panama City, the T-shirts are flying off the shelves, and if I don't show, my ass is grass and my boss is the lawn mower." He grinned at his own trashy wit. Justin tried for a smile, appearing anxious to please, but Stoat leaned back, crossed his arms, and studied the boy. Then, to my unpleasant surprise, he turned to me.

He stared straight into my eyes, and my pride made me stare straight back at him even though there was nothing to see in there. He challenged me. "You think I'm lower than a snake's asshole, don't you?"

I couldn't truthfully say no, and I didn't feel safe saying yes, so I said, "You seem hollow."

"Huh. Well, maybe that's from spending nearly my whole life not able to be what I am. Ever since I was a teenager, I knew I wanted to do it with little boys, but I stayed celibate for my parents' sake till they passed away. Justin, here, he was just a cute little brat when I grabbed him. I thought he was eight or nine years old. How was I supposed to know he was a late bloomer? My mistake he only stayed prime a few months before he shot up on me, and now look at him. But it's not his fault I'm fixing to get me a replacement. See, I like to think straight about things, Miss Lee Anna. You being here and putting us all in this predicament is nobody's fault—it just happened and we got to deal with it. Now, I don't believe in no heaven or no hell or any of that afterlife crap, so I intend to get what pleasure I can out of the rest of my life. Do you understand?"

Did I understand? Hell, no, he was a pedophile. And things

were looking all too much like the rest of his life took precedence over the rest of my life, but I couldn't say that, because talking about it might make it too true too soon. I was having a lot of trouble coming up with an answer.

"Didn't you hear a word I said? Are you stupid?" Jeez, one silent moment and he'd flipped from chatty nice guy to threatening psycho.

"As you said, you're a thinker," I replied as calmly as I could. "You're way ahead of me. I need time to consider your point of view."

"Huh." He seemed somewhat mollified. "Well, you're gonna have all day." He picked up his pistol. "Back to bed with you, Miss Lee Anna."

FOUR

My request for a blanket had been denied. "What for? It ain't cold." Maybe Stoat was afraid I knew some kind of Houdini escape I could perform under cover of a blanket. Maybe he enjoyed making me lie there for hours on end, physically and emotionally uncomfortable with my legs immodestly spread. Maybe he just didn't want to be bothered.

Hell, he didn't matter. Justin mattered.

Staring at the ceiling again and feeling the age lines in my face deepen, I tried to think how best to approach Justin. Wanting to rescue him was just fine, but I couldn't do it until I'd rescued myself, which probably meant talking him into helping me. But in my experience, most teenage boys would rather sit on a fire ant hill than talk with a motherly woman.

I could hear Justin doing chores. First the breakfast dishes, judging by the sound of running water and the clatter of plates, and then—whump of pillows being plumped—making the bed he shared with "Uncle Steve," a thought that made me feel sick. *Don't go there*, I told myself; the anthill syndrome went double in regard to talking about personal things. If I ever got to talk to Justin at all. What would be the best way to lure him into my room and get him talking? I could start fussing through my gag—

Justin walked in, sat down on the side of my bed, pulled the gag out of my mouth, and slipped it down beneath my chin. "How are you doing?" he asked. "Can I get you anything?"

So much for fire ant hills and most teenage boys. My mouth and throat felt strangely dry. "Um, I'm okay," I managed to croak.

Justin nodded. "I know it's not real comfortable. Uncle Steve kept me tied to this same bed for the first month."

The first *month*!

"He would come home in the middle of the day to check on me," Justin added. "He told his boss he was taking care of a sick dog. He's not a bad guy, really."

What? If Stoat wasn't a bad guy, then would somebody please define—

But I didn't say that. I felt eggshells under my verbal feet. One false step, one wrong word, and I'd lose Justin. Even clearing my dry throat would be a bad idea at this point.

In the lightest tone I could possibly manage, I asked, "How do you figure that?"

"Well, he lets me watch NASCAR. He brings me stuff I like to eat, like Oreos—he doesn't care about them, but he gets them for me. And the brand of cereal I like, and—and clothes and stuff. Last year he even got me a Christmas present. A PlayStation."

I wanted to scream or laugh or cry—he sounded so ludicrous, thankful for Oreos and a PlayStation while Stoat the insult to goats kept him as a sex slave. Needing time to contain my outrage and prompted by my raspy throat, I asked, "Could I have a glass of water?"

"Sure." Justin headed toward the kitchen. As soon as he had left the room, I aimed a silent, primal scream at the ceiling, then tried to think. I knew I would get nowhere unless I figured out Justin's point of view. Which wasn't easy. Why was he still living with the man who had abducted him?

Justin came back with a coffee mug with the Gators logo on it, and before giving me the water, he cautioned, "Just sip a little. If you wet the bed, Uncle Steve will beat . . . well, that's what he did to me if I couldn't hold it—he beat me. And sometimes he made me stand against the wall while he threw the knife at me like in the circus. But I don't know what he might do to you."

Justin's tone was so matter-of-fact that it rendered me speechless. He sat on the bed, lifted my head with one hand, and held the cup to my lips with the other. Heeding his advice, I drank only a little, then nodded, and he laid my head back on the mattress again.

Trying to keep my tone as no-drama as his had been, like, hey, I just want information, I asked, "Did he ever get you with the knife?"

"No. He has a real good aim. I know he meant to miss me, to scare me."

"And how did he beat you, with a belt?"

"No. He just beat me up, slammed me around, broke my ribs, knocked me out sometimes. I thought he would kill me."

Again, I enforced a no-fuss, conversational tone. "Why didn't he?"

"He planned to. He almost did." Justin set the cup on the bed-side table, his face turned away from me, and for a moment I thought he was going to leave. But he didn't. I don't flatter myself for any cleverness; I think he just really needed to tell his story. Two years, and who had he been able to tell? Nobody.

Still without looking at me, he said, "He kept me and messed with me until his boss got tired of him and his sick dog. No more taking off in the middle of the day, his boss said, or he'd lose his job. Kill the damn dog. So that night he got out the gun and told me to get in the truck. He took me way out in the swamps some-place and—and maybe I should have just let him kill me."

"It's not that simple, is it?" I said, remembering how it had felt after the divorce, the suicidal thoughts, some petty vengeful part of me wanting to die but no match for Schopenhauer's "irrational will to live," aka Darwin's "survival instinct." Whatever you call it, that invisible and unmeasurable phenomenon is amazingly strong.

"You got that right. Even though I knew all the things he'd keep on doing to me, I still begged him to let me live. I promised I'd never call the cops or contact my parents or run away. I promised I would take his name and be his family, and I told him he could—he could do whatever and I'd never tell. He took a big risk, believing me and letting me live. I'm grateful for that."

But the words sounded flat, and Justin still didn't face me.

"I can understand," I said, and at the moment it was true. I knew how grateful I was going to be if I got out of this mess alive. "But what about your parents?"

He shifted his gaze downward, plucking invisible bits of lint from the edge of the mattress. "They don't want me."

"You could have fooled me." I kept my voice as neutral as I possibly could; I mustn't argue with him. "It costs big money to advertise on TV—"

He interrupted with some force. "They want their sweet little boy back. They don't want *me*."

"I think you're sweet," I responded impulsively and quite truthfully. This was the boy who had risked a beating to come feed me Frosted Flakes in the middle of the night.

"You're crazy!" Deep and sudden anger blasted him up off the bed and out of the room, leaving me blinking.

Part of the reason I make stupid blunders in my personal life is that I use my mind to block my emotions. Most of the time when I was a kid and especially when I was a teenager, my parents didn't want any trouble out of me, trouble meaning door slamming, back talk, or blubbering. My father was an English teacher and an Anglophile; he wore brown tweeds and worshipped Kipling. Stiff upper lip, white man's burden, a rag and a bone and a hank of hair, the whole repressed, bigoted, misogynist charisma, and he never saw anything funny in my favorite joke: "Do you like Kipling? I don't know; I've never kippled." Father kippled constantly.

Mother, who was also a teacher—kindergarten—escaped being woman as enemy, a rag and a bone and a hank of hair, simply by externalizing her inner child of the past. Her existence was a strong argument for Descartes' essential self that does not change over time. Hers was the happy child of the ever and always. Her version of the stiff upper lip curved in a perpetual smile. Pollyanna, move over. There was no situation to which Mother couldn't find a bright side. Or, to put it another way, no dark sides were allowed, which made me yearn to go Goth. But as different as Mom and Dad seemed, they were essentially the same. Neither of them particularly approved of PMS or any other mood swings or fashion or mascara or hair.

So acting like a teenager was counterproductive and I didn't try, for the simple reason that I was chickenshit when it came to confronting my parents. On a conscious level I perceived myself as way smarter than other kids butting heads with their families because of their snits and crushes and fads. I detested girlish giggling and painted toenails. I cherished my high SAT score, my National Merit Scholar status. I eyed the dark side of existence, contemplating life on a distant and cosmic level. Rather than plan my own insignificant role in the great unknown, I let myself get drawn into a conventional marriage with a man who, I realized too late, might as well have been my mother with a penis. Rather than face the desolation and humiliation of the divorce, I moved away. Rather than embrace my loneliness, I went knocking at a peacock blue cottage, and now, shackled to a bare bed with a gag in my mouth, I did not want to feel panic anymore and I did not want to cry and above all I did not want to accept that I was probably going to die.

So I concentrated on remembering my college psychology courses, searching my mind for any insight into pedophilia. I found none. I did recall, however, something about laboratory rats and random reinforcement. Performing their task, sometimes they received a treat and sometimes an electric shock, but they kept at it, pathetic, subservient little beasts. Justin was experiencing random reinforcement, and Stoat had Justin right where he wanted him, scared stupid and eager to please.

I also remembered something-or-other syndrome, hostages bonding with their captors, although the only example I could call to mind was Jaycee Dugard, kept for years in her captors' backyard. Why hadn't she escaped? Too scared. And if the person who had the power of life and death over you was occasionally nice, wouldn't you want to make nice too? Become friends, stay alive? If Stoat offered me a deal, however sick, cleaning the toilet while dancing naked or whatever, wouldn't I go for it?

Yes and no. I'd agree, but every minute I'd be looking for a way to escape, even if I knew he would kill me in some very unpleasant manner if he caught me—

But what if I were just a child?

The thought made some visceral understanding move in me, because my salvation as a human had come from being a mom. Each birth had been baptism by my own blood, each baby a redemption by sudden, utter, overwhelming love—really, my only experience of ever falling in love. I had raised two sons, and I remembered what it was like for boys around thirteen, fourteen years old, still thinking in terms of absolute rules without compromise, still believing in a kind of magic whether white or black, still thinking the world revolved around them, that they were the axis of the universe. But that also meant everything that went wrong was somehow their fault. At that age a boy was still vulnerable, still very much a child, but trying to act like a macho man, to be one of the gang, and if he showed tender feelings, somebody was sure to call him a sissy—

Oh, my God.

All in a moment, and with a stab of pain as if the knowledge had raped my heart, I understood Justin. He couldn't contact his parents because he had not yet been a parent himself. He honestly thought he deserved punishment for having gotten into trouble, or even worse, that Mom and Dad must not love him or want him anymore. He felt smelly and slimy, like garbage, toilet paper, worse than worthless. He did not know that, even after the passing of time, he was still a victim. He knew only that the worst thing in his world was to be so fundamentally screwed.

Immediately after she saw Justin's face on the TV screen and heard the announcer respectfully airing the ad, Amy left Chad in front of the TV and ran upstairs to what used to be the guest bedroom but was now the Justin Bradley Search Headquarters. There, amid walls covered with posters for community rallies, she sat down at the computer flanked by gray metal file cabinets loaded with printouts, clippings, phone tips, leads, ideas for possible leads, contacts with the police, all the paperwork generated by the search for Justin, and, most recently, guardian angels hand carved from cypress knobs. She knew they freaked Chad out and she didn't expect him to come in. Even before the advent of the angels, he had often said he felt mildly claustrophobic in the small room with piles of scrap paper by the printer, boxes of flyers on the floor, folding tables for multiline telephones dedicated to

1-800-4JUSTIN. But to Amy it was the one room in the house where she felt most at home.

The phones started to ring even before she had grabbed a pen and a long pad of yellow legal-sized paper. Tips came in so fast that Amy had to put several people on hold. Fervidly she hoped they wouldn't hang up. Just as she thought, angrily, that Chad ought to be helping her no matter what he thought of her and the TV ad, she heard him coming up the stairs. Amy tried to catch his eye and smile a thank-you, but he wouldn't look at her; he just got to work. Talking to callers, he sounded plastic polite, like a telemarketer.

Within ten minutes, the spate of phone calls slowed to a stop. Amy sat back to review sheet after sheet of yellow paper scrawled with—with nothing of any use, really. Calls from people who thought they might have seen Justin someplace a month ago or six months ago if they could just remember where. Also there had been the vague insights of earnest self-proclaimed psychics, which she no longer bothered to write down.

She took a deep breath, then lifted her eyes to face the man who had always been her true love. "You got anything, honey?"

He shot her a look that said clearer than words, *No, are you kidding?* "Amy," he told her, "the only reason I'm here is if somebody had hung up, you would have thought for sure that call was the one."

"Well, it could have been," she retorted before she could stop herself. "Sweetie, it's not over. There could be more calls. If just one good lead comes in—"

He turned his back on her and walked out of the room.

"Just one person!" she shouted after him. "All it would take is just one person!"

FIVE

Feeding me a pink salami sandwich on cheap white bread for lunch, Justin wouldn't look at me or speak to me.

"There's no reason for you to be angry," I said.

He gave me no response except silence and averted eyes. Just the same, something about the stillness of his face told me he wasn't angry, not really. He just didn't want to talk to me anymore. Didn't want to get to know me as a friend. Didn't want to care about anything that happened to me.

Which meant he did care.

It also meant I had to shatter his silence so he would care more.

"Justin," I began, "did your parents beat you?"

"No!" Shocked, he not only yelled, but he faced me. "Hell, no, my parents are good people! They would never beat us. They—" His voice cracked.

Blandly, as if I hadn't noticed the emotion he didn't want to feel, I went on. "Us? You have brothers and sisters?"

"Yeah. Younger than me. Twins. Kyle and Kayla." I think he didn't want to say their names, but they forced their way out and made his face wince, his lips tremble. He was not used to thinking about his family.

I intuited that he had survived the past two years by not

thinking about his life before being abducted, not thinking about his family, and not thinking about his own future either. No goals or dreams or plans. Numbing his mind and emotions just to survive day to day. What had once been normal wasn't anymore, not for him; he had to survive in a new normal, and he did so by functioning like a robot.

My only chance—and *his* only chance—depended on coaxing or jolting him out of robot mode.

What should I say now? My mind raced. This wasn't any ordinary conversation, not with me lying shackled in a spread-eagle position and him hovering over me, poking a junk food sandwich into my face. Instead of saying something conventional, maybe asking whether his twin brother and sister looked alike or what color their hair and eyes were, I said, "I bet Kyle and Kayla are supersmart."

His hand about to offer more sandwich stopped in midair, his other hand lifted to his nose as if I had punched him, and he stared at me. "How'd you know that?"

"Because you're very intelligent."

"What makes you think that?"

"You're alive, aren't you?"

His hands slowly lowered. "I figure that's because I'm a wuss."

Kind of grinning, I shook my head. "I can be the biggest wuss in the world and Stoat's still going to kill me, isn't he?"

Justin's jaw dropped, I guess because I was willing to say it.

"Which will make you his accomplice," I added as an afterthought, "so then he'll have even more power over you."

"Shut up," Justin whispered.

"Why am I still alive? What's he waiting for?"

"Shut *up*."

"Tell me, Justin—what would you do if Stoat got his hands on your brother or your sister?"

His face reddened and contorted with such fury—accumulated fury he'd swallowed during the past two years, maybe—that he threw down the sandwich, lunged up from the bed, and for a heartbeat, as he loomed over me with his fists clenched, I thought he might hurt me, sparing Stoat the trouble.

Instead he rammed out of the room, slamming the door behind him. He had forgotten to put the gag back in my mouth, but I didn't yell anything after him. I stayed quiet all afternoon. I was still hungry, I was thirsty, I needed the bathroom but had hours to go before any hope of that; my body ached more each minute from its forced immobility; fear of death weighed stony on my chest and tried to make me weep; I could barely keep from sobbing. But I managed to stay as still as a windless day because I hoped that, somewhere in that peacock blue shack of a prison, Justin was thinking.

Extracting a dog hair from a crack in one of his ridged, splitting fingernails, Ned Bradley thought: *I'm getting old.* He used to be able to pat his dog, for God's sake, without getting hair stuck in his nails. He studied his own hands, dry and taupe like winter leaves, as he held Oliver and stroked him. Oliver, small enough to heft yet big enough to provide a warm and reassuring weight in his lap, felt like a grandchild—but Ned knew that was wistful thinking. What little family he had didn't want anything to do with him. That was what came of being an alcoholic, taking no responsibility, losing job after job, deserting his wife and kids. Going for a geographical cure instead of for sobriety.

Well, he finally had sobriety now, starting right after his ex-wife had died, shocking him into taking a hard look at his own mortality. He'd stayed at the same address in Birmingham, same apartment, for almost eight years now. He had a steady job, and he had Oliver, named after Oliver Twist because his puppy eyes had constantly begged, *Please, sir, may I have more?* That was last year, when Ned had found him shivering in an alley. Now Oliver had plenty to eat, and he was Ned Bradley's own very special spotted mutt and cherished companion.

"Time to get down, woofhead," Ned told the dog with a final pat, standing up. Lacking a lap, Oliver decamped. Ned took a few long-legged strides across his apartment to the computer, drawn like a moth at twilight to the white light of its screen. He never took part in Birmingham's Southern-fried bar scene anymore; now this was his evening ritual. Once online, he went directly to the Web site dedicated to the search for Justin Bradley.

His grandson.

Still missing.

There seemed to be no new developments, dammit. There hardly ever were anymore. So Ned lost himself in contemplation of the boy's captured-in-time face, absorbing it visually and viscerally, memorizing it in his gut, warming his heart in the cappuccino glow of the boy's eyes, more heartening to him than anyone else's best smile. Justin looked like a kid with his soul intact. Those openhearted eyes and the firm curves of the kid's chin reminded him of his son, Chad, when he had been that age, which was about the time that Ned had left for good.

Not that he had seen Chad much since, drunken ass that he, Ned, had been. But he did remember.

And he dearly remembered his few hours with Charles Stuart Bradley's children. Ned had gone to see his dying wife mostly to apologize. His apologies were accepted by her but not by their son, all grown up and pissed at him proportionately. It was meeting Justin and Kyle and Kayla that had really pushed Ned to change. He had three grandchildren. He had wasted too much of his life.

So he had done the hard work to get himself clean and sober. And then, just when he was getting up the nerve to approach his son and his family again, he started to see their faces nightly on the TV. Chad all choked up, and Amy crying alongside her husband and begging an unknown abductor to please bring back her child.

Justin. Taken away.

Ned had thought he could only make things worse for them by intruding. Or maybe, face it, he was a coward. But ever since then, Ned had dedicated himself as if he were a candle lit for Justin. Visiting the Web site daily. Anonymously donating all the financial help he could afford. Alert day after day, at the office building where he worked and around town, in case he might, just might, be the one to sight the boy, even though he knew that his chances were ridiculously, outrageously, infinitesimally small.

Ned explored the Web site and found nothing new except a few more sympathetic comments. No fresh hope. And with every day that passed, hope was harder to hold on to. With a kind of glum, muted anger Ned booted down the computer. The damn thing took its time, finally darkening like a blinded Cyclops, leaving the apartment shadowy; it was getting dark outside. Nightfall.

"Oliver," Ned said to the dog, "I want to get out of here."

Go to a bar, get a drink, be with other people escaping their misery? It was an old, familiar urge and one that Ned had learned he must acknowledge but refuse. The silence of the apartment enveloped him. Always around this time of day he found it paradoxical that this comfortable place, with his big Tree of Life tapestry on the wall, his Bev Doolittle prints, his chunky sofa with a genuine Navajo blanket thrown over it, his books and glossy Sierra Club magazines piled on every surface, could feel so empty.

Ned got up from the computer chair, turned on some lights, then stood studying the intricacies of the Tree of Life—a gift from his AA sponsor, handmade by her—until the difficult moment had passed. He knew that the apartment's smell of Budweiser and black bananas was in his imagination, an olfactory hallucination.

Sensing watchful eyes on him, he looked down at the dog, rendered almost shapeless by long white fur splotched with black patches.

"Oliver," Ned gravely addressed the presence, "this is not a dive and I am not a drunk anymore. Let's see what's on TV."

He would far rather have phoned his son. But he knew if Chad had felt too pissed to deal with his fuckup father after his mother's death, he sure as hell wasn't going to feel any better now, with his son missing. And maybe he never would.

Stoat arrived home from work in a mood as expansive as the aroma of the Popeyes fried chicken he carried in with him. At cheerful gunpoint he released me from my bondage, laughed as I ran to the bathroom, and invited me to join him and Justin at the supper table afterward.

Justin wasn't looking at me, and I let him alone. I did not talk either with him or with my jovial gun-toting host, but focused all my attention on getting spicy, Louisiana-style food I wouldn't normally eat into my very hungry stomach. Or I should say, almost all of my attention. I kept mental feelers reaching toward Justin, and sensed plenty of turmoil beneath his blank exterior.

"They didn't pack enough napkins," complained Stoat, snapping his fingers at Justin. "Go get some paper towels."

"Who was your slave before you got me?" Justin retorted, at the same time getting up to bring the paper towels.

Stoat flipped like a lightbulb from bright to dark, scowling. "That's exactly what you are, boy. My little sex slave."

Face afire as he returned to the table, Justin protested, "It was a joke, Uncle Steve!"

"You call me sir."

"Yes, sir."

"You are a slave and you can be replaced and don't you forget it."

Sitting down, Justin mumbled, "Yes, sir," to his plate.

"As a matter of fact you're too big and it's high time I oughta ditch you and get what I wanted in the first place." Stoat's fingers gave a pop like gunfire, he snapped them so hard. "Look at me!"

The boy obeyed with hatred well disguised but still just barely visible, at least to me.

"Are you my personal favorite asshole?"

"Yes, sir."

"Louder!"

"Yes, *sir*!"

Stoat transferred his glare to me. "What's this all about? You been making trouble?"

The pervert was no fool, damn him, but years of marriage and part-time jobs had made me a good liar when necessary. Motioning that my mouth was full but maintaining earnest eye contact, I shook my head.

His stare moderated from sharp to sour. "Damned if I know why I'm spending my hard-earned money feeding you."

Swallowing my mouthful of food, I said pleasantly if unwisely, "Because you are such a nice person."

I thought there was no trace of sarcasm in my voice, but Stoat stood up, glowering. "You got a mouth on you, bitch."

By which he meant a brain in my head, I suppose. "Just joking," I said meekly, and, like Justin, unsuccessfully.

"Shut up. That gag was out of your mouth when I come home. Who took it out?"

I said nothing.

He stepped toward me, fists menacing. "Who took it out?"

"You told me to shut up."

He struck so fast I didn't even see it coming. Next thing I knew, I hit the kitchen floor, sprawling and unable to move because things were spinning around and fireworks seemed to be going off inside my eyes. I took mental notes, because I'd never been clouted on the side of the head before. Or on any part of my body, for that matter.

Fist raised to strike again, Stoat yelled, "Who took the gag out of your mouth!"

"Nobody," I mumbled reflexively, like a child.

Stupid answer, when you think about it.

Certainly Stoat didn't care much for it. He punched my face again. "Who!" he shouted inches from my ear.

"I did, myself," I told him. "I pushed it out with my tongue. I have a very strong tongue. See?" I stuck it out at him.

Luckily I got it back inside my mouth and out of danger just before his fist struck so hard I felt my teeth loosen and my lip split. Stoat howled, "Damn it, don't bleed on my clean floor!"

Oddly, none of the above particularly hurt. Yet. Bemused, I explored my bloody face with my fingertips.

He kicked me in the gut. "Up! Get up!"

This made no sense. The man wore scruffy cowboy boots with metal doodads on their pointy toes. He kicked me, and then he kicked me again, in the ribs, and he expected me to get up?

I lay limp instead. Now, in a sort of delayed reaction, parts of me were starting to hurt badly enough so that playing possum wasn't hard, except I had to keep from moaning.

Swearing fluently, Stoat shoved a paper towel into my mouth, then ordered Justin to help him carry me back to the bed. The poor kid had seen the whole thing, of course, and as he lifted my shoulders, I felt him shaking. He slipped his elbows under my shoulders to lift me, and I felt his chest heaving as if he was trying not to cry. He had that kind of heart. I think it hurt him more to watch somebody else get clobbered than if he had taken the beating himself.

They dumped me on the bare mattress, shackled me—Stoat snarling orders, Justin mutely doing as he said—and left me there in the dark. After I heard the door close, I opened my eyes, spit out the paper towel, and tried to comfort my lips with my tongue. No gag. Ironically, Stoat had forgotten all about it. Even more ironically, now that I had more reason than ever to cry, I did not feel like weeping. Oddly, I felt triumphant.

SIX

Justin came for a stealth visit in the middle of the night, as I had expected he might. He brought plastic bags of ice, laid one on my swollen lips, and held the other against my cheek, whispering, "I'm sorry. I'm sorry."

What for? He hadn't done anything wrong. I shook my head emphatically, the ice bag slipped off my mouth, and I mumbled, "Did he beat you too?"

"No."

"Good."

"Why didn't you tell him I forgot about the gag, it was my fault?"

"Justin, none of this is your fault."

He put the ice back on my mouth, so I didn't say any more. But I wished I could get it through his head that he was the victim in this scenario, not the scapegoat. I wished I could sit up and demonstrate. I wished I could bash a bedpost into pieces, then ask him whether it was the bedpost's fault that it was broken, whether the bedpost had made me hurt it.

"How's your gut where he kicked you?" Justin whispered.

"Mmmm," I grunted dismissively, although the truth was I

hurt like hell. I shrugged, or tried to. It's hard to shrug with your arms stretched above your head.

"You're no wuss." Justin got up and padded out of the room without explanation. After a short time he came back, took the ice off my mouth, and dropped pills into it, whispering, "Ibuprofen."

I swallowed, with the help of some water from a glass he held to my bruised lips. And the kid was not just taking care of me out of the goodness of his heart, I sensed; I felt as if, for the moment at least, Justin was totally on my side against Stoat. So I said what I had not dared to say before.

"Justin, why not just call 911? Get us both out of here?"

"There's no phone."

I had kind of figured that, as I had never heard one ring. "There's my cell phone, in my house on the kitchen table. Or else maybe in my handbag."

"Stoat has the key to your house."

"He's asleep."

Justin sighed, kneeling beside the bed and leaning against it as if to explain life to a kindergartner. "It's not like he keeps it in his pants pocket. Maybe it's under his pillow with his gun. Maybe hidden in the suspended ceiling somewhere. He hides things. He already has your purse and your cell phone, but I don't know where he put them."

"Oh." I lay with hope leaching out of me.

"I would call 911 if I could, to get you out of here," Justin murmured after a while, "but if I did, Uncle Steve would take me someplace else and beat me silly, maybe kill me."

"No, he wouldn't! He'd go to jail and the police would take you back to your parents."

Justin said, very low, "I don't want to go back to my parents."

Aside from exhaustion, the reason I did not gasp in disbelief and protest was because Plato believed in timeless norms, but

Heraclitus had said nothing was constant except change, and Descartes could only just manage "I think, therefore I am." In other words, because philosophy had taught me no rules were absolute. If anybody believed all kidnapped children longed to go back to their parents, well, here was the kid to prove them wrong.

Trying to keep it light, I quipped, "I thought you said your parents didn't beat you."

"They didn't! There's nothing wrong with my parents."

"Then why—"

"They don't want me back! They just think they do."

"But, Justin—"

"Listen, Miss Lee Anna, just go to sleep, okay?" He left me.

I didn't think I could possibly sleep, yet I did. I awoke to see daylight at the windows. It had to be morning. Tuesday. I felt my face and ribs aching from having been beaten, I needed to go to the bathroom, and I truly with all my heart loathed that bed I was shackled onto.

The bastard had done the same thing to Justin for a month. A *month*. All alone, nobody to keep him company. How had the kid not gone crazy?

"Nothing wrong with my parents," Justin had said. Did it follow, then, that he thought there was something wrong with *him*?

Day looked kind of dim, my two useless windows showed wet spangles, and I heard the sound of rain falling on the roof, a sound I usually found pleasant. But at this point I didn't like it. You could have brought me lobster Newburg and I would not have liked it.

The door opened, and mentally I braced myself against the possibility of Stoat, but it was just Justin with a glass of milk in his hand. "Uncle Steve left for work already," he said, obviously reassuring me although I thought I had hidden my fear.

On his knees at my bedside, he lifted my head with one hand

and guided the glass to my mouth with the other. "All we have besides milk is Dr Pepper and Mountain Dew. Neither of those are good for you."

I sipped obediently, then said as best I could through my swollen lips, "I bet you also have Jack Daniel's."

"Not me. Uncle Steve. I'm not allowed to touch it." Justin did not seem to get that I was trying to joke.

"Well, it wouldn't go so great with milk anyway."

The kid remained utterly solemn but not blank, not expressionless; far from it. He looked completely human and nearly sick with concern.

Setting the milk aside and standing, he said, "You can't chew on cereal with your mouth messed up like that. Peanut butter sandwich?"

"Applesauce?" I suggested.

"Sure." Like an eager waiter at an upscale restaurant he strode off, and when he came back, he brought me an applesauce sandwich. Applesauce between two slices of insipid white bread.

I tried not to laugh, if only because my ribs hurt, but I guess he could see I was amused. "Duh. This isn't what you meant."

"I'll eat it. Looks good."

I managed to down part of the applesauce sandwich, after which he fed me more applesauce from a bowl with a spoon. Then he brought soap, water, and a terry cloth dish towel, very carefully washed and dried my face, and with a gentle finger spread Neosporin on the worst of the damage. "I'm glad you can't see yourself," he muttered.

"What? You're not going to bring me a mirror?"

"No!" Then, after a moment's thought he added, "You have a weird sense of humor, don't you?"

"Yeah. I do."

"Do you want me to change those wrappings on your wrists and ankles?"

"Are you joking?"

"No."

"Well, only if you feel like it."

Apparently he did feel like it, and as he went through the considerable trouble of gently soaking the gauze away from the scabs, I began to wonder why. Formulating some theories, none of them very pleasant, I began to feel the invisible leaden sensation on my chest gaining weight. But I said nothing to Justin until he had finished his self-assigned job with salve and fresh gauze. Then he left with the breakfast detritus, and I could hear him doing dishes in the sink. If he hadn't come back into my room—my prison—I would not have called him.

But he did come back in, to sit wordlessly on the edge of the bed.

"So why did Stoat skip my potty break this morning?" I asked. "Is he so mad at me he wants me to bust wide open?"

Justin shrugged, looked down, didn't answer.

Just for something to say I remarked, "It's raining like a cow pissing on a flat rock, isn't it?"

"Uh-huh." A barely audible answer.

"Is it supposed to go on like this all day?"

No question could have been more banal, so Justin's reaction took me completely by surprise. He opened his mouth but made no sound except a weak gasp. His face went chalk white, and he swayed as if he might faint.

"Justin!" Reflexively and of course quite unsuccessfully I tried to grab him, jangling my shackles.

"I'm all right," he whispered, both hands flat against the mattress to brace himself.

"Justin, what's wrong?"

"Nothing."

"Justin, tell me. I'm going to have to pee the bed and get beat up again, is that it?"

Startled, he looked at me with haunted eyes, then lowered them. "Sure, that's it."

"No, it's not." The lie was as transparent as a ghost. "Justin, tell me. *Look at me.* Whatever it is, just spit it out."

He faced me, his smooth skin nearly as gray as the day, and he forced out a few struggling words. "It—it's supposed to rain all day and night."

"So?"

"So—you asked what he's been waiting for."

Before I could respond with more than dumb shock, Justin ran from the room.

Charles Stuart "Chad" Bradley, driving from one prospective client to another in his red Ram pickup truck, felt profoundly alone, and not just because of the monotonous slash pine plantations for miles all around him, not just because of the immensity of the relentlessly blue sky, not just because of the long, straight, empty road before him. He felt alone and lost in his life. In the mornings Amy stayed in bed so she would not have to speak to him. Even Dixieland Trucking could no longer hold him steady during the long days. Driving gave him too much time to think, and his thoughts disturbed him. So much so that, impulsively, he pulled off the road beside a cotton field, took out his cell phone, and thumbed a number he normally called only once a year, at Christmastime.

"Yo." The old man sounded a bit blurry. Chad wondered whether his father had been drinking.

None too affectionately he asked, "You sober, Dad?"

"Chad! I was sleeping. I work nights now." Anxiously, as if he expected to hear that someone had died, Pop asked, "Is everything all right?"

Chad responded with a mirthless laugh.

"Okay, stupid question," said his father, sounding awake and focused now. "I thought maybe something happened, like maybe they found Justin."

"No such luck. I don't think they ever are going to find Justin, which is why I called you."

"Come again, son?"

To be so gentle, Dad had to be sober. Sure, he had been saying for years now that he had stopped drinking, but despite wanting to believe, Chad had sardonic thoughts. Hey, look at the pigs flying. Would wonders never cease?

He could not help sounding snide as he responded, "I called to ask you for advice in your area of expertise."

"Which is?"

"Forgetting about your son and leaving your family."

"Whoa. What the hell is going on, Chad?"

"Nothing. Same as before. Wearing me down." Chad figured his father knew the score, albeit long-distance; plenty of checks had arrived from Birmingham. Dad would probably have done more, like maybe come to lend a hand, if he'd thought Chad would let him. "I'm over my head in debt. Amy won't work at anything except spending money, mostly to find Justin, who is almost certainly dead—" Chad's voice broke up like a bad cell phone signal, but he turned the pickup truck back on for the sake of cold air-conditioning and forced himself to keep talking. "My son's gone, and I barely got a wife or a family anymore. All me 'n' Amy do is fight, and the twins keep to themselves. At least they've got each other. But I—I feel like I've got nothing anymore. Less than nothing. I just want to walk away. Like you did."

A pause. Then Dad drawled, "Now, don't that just take the cake? Ain't Kyle and Kayla the same age you were when I left? Which I have been told hurt you so bad you still haven't forgiven me?"

True enough. Chad still felt the same old pain and anger, and he still thought his father had some damn nerve trying to get back into his life decades later. Childish resentment edged his voice as he said, "Dad, I'm asking you for help now."

"I hear you. I'm just having trouble believing you."

Now, wasn't that just too damn perfect? His father didn't believe him either.

Chad hardened his voice. "Believe me. I want out. I want to know how you got the guts."

"It wasn't guts, Chad—it was rotgut whiskey. Liquid stupidity out of a bottle. Ruined my liver and my life, and you know damn well it was as wrong as wrong can be."

"Right or wrong, I got to do something to get out of this situation. If there was a cliff handy, I'd jump off it."

"I've felt the same way. It'll pass. Are you at work?"

"I was."

"You still are. Do as I say, not as I done, because I fucked up bad and it ain't no honor to either of us if you follow in my footsteps."

"Dad—"

"Son, it's taken me a lifetime, but now I have a chance to do right by you and I don't want to blow it. I need you to do as I say, not as I did. I haven't earned the right to say I love you, but goddamn, Charles, I care about you. Now, are you going to get back to work?"

After a long pause, Chad mumbled, "I guess."

"Good. And after work, you going home to your family?"

"Whatever."

"Whatever yes or whatever no?"

Chad raised his voice, peevish now. "Yes, I'll go home. Today."

"Good. Call me again tomorrow if you need to. One day at a time is the best anybody can do, ever. I promise I will not pray for you, son."

Chad actually laughed out loud. Damned if his father didn't share something in common with him besides a set of chromosomes. Both of them felt the same way about religion. Being prayed over was a bitch.

SEVEN

The rain pounded against the windows now and ran down in water snakes.

Rain like that would wash out tire tracks on a dirt road, footprints at the end of the dirt road, even blood. Even lots of blood.

Stoat, the obsessively tidy pedophile, had chosen his time to be a cautious, methodical murderer.

It made sense. It made so much sense that I sweated and clenched my hands and not quite voluntarily peed my pants, flooding the bed I hated with my own watery relief and revenge.

Feeling both worse and better, I wondered where Justin was, and what he was doing or thinking.

I badly wanted to talk with him, to coax him or persuade him or manipulate him or shame him, whatever it took, and somehow force him to rescue me. And himself.

I could have called, "Justin!" and he would have come into the bedroom to see what I wanted.

But I clenched my teeth against calling him and I did not do it.

Stoat had made him a victim. I would not, could not, must not victimize him yet more.

. . .

I cried a little, cursed under my breath, stared at the ceiling, and thought about Susan Sontag finding metaphor in fashionable forms of death, then of Socrates, examiner of the good life, hefting his cup of hemlock. How had he lived that legendary last day? How could I best live my last day, disregarding the outcome, thinking only in terms of doing a good job of it? Lying in urine put me at a disadvantage. I thought of my sons and hoped they would never find out that detail of my final hours, then worked out a tentative plan to make sure. Thinking of my children made me think of my ex-husband, and I found myself mildly pleased to discover that I no longer cared about him one way or the other. The opposite of love, quoth Confucius or somebody, is not hatred but indifference. With Stoat's help I'd gotten over my divorce in record time.

Big whoop, because now how much time did I have left?

Like unbleached muslin, time started pleating for me, moments stretching far too long yet passing far too soon.

After what seemed forever and was probably a couple of hours, Justin came into my room on his own, looking like a sleepwalker, as if his feet had brought him there involuntarily. He struggled to look at me and could not quite manage. He struggled to speak and hauled the words out, low and wretched. "Um, do you want some lunch?"

I considered carefully before responding. "I guess not. I'm hungry yet I don't think I could eat. Does that make any sense?"

"Oh, yeah. Been there."

"It's not a good place, but I'm from Missouri, you know?"

"Huh? I thought you were from Pennsylvania."

"Nope. Missouri, because Missouri loves company." Giving up on my weird sense of humor, I softened my voice. "Please stay awhile, Justin, if you can stand the smell of pee."

"Does it bother you? I could bring the spray from the bathroom."

"No. Don't go away."

He sat on a dry edge of the mattress near my head, looking not at me but at his hands lying curled and dormant on his cut-offs. His classically perfect hands had long oval fingernails; my fingernails grew wider than they were long, shaped like muffins, ridged like cupcake cups, crumby. To hell with Freud and penis envy; I had a lifelong case of fingernail envy, seeing so many men with absolutely perfect ones that nobody except me seemed to notice.

Justin had great fingernails. Justin had long, strong, capable hands and I should not, could not, must not suggest any action he might take with them.

He blurted, "Are you scared?"

"Hell, no. I'm too terrified to be scared. But Stoat's not going to mess around with me, is he?"

"Probably not. He's not into torture unless he's in a really bad mood. What I meant was, are you scared of maybe going to hell?"

Hell? Didn't Justin know he was already being tortured and living in hell? I very nearly laughed. A kind of snort escaped me, and Justin turned to see what was funny.

"There's more than enough hell in life," I explained, or tried to explain. "No, I don't believe in heaven or hell or any kind of an afterlife."

"You think there's nothing after we die?"

"Just the same poetry we share with any animal. We disintegrate—we mix back into the earth and nurture plants and trees, which drink sunlight and make air for our great-grandchildren. Somewhere down the line the earth, too, will die and disintegrate and maybe in zillions of years some of it will find another life. Someday some of my atoms might brighten the petal of a zinnia or the core of a nova. Everything's recycled as energy or matter. You're made of stardust, Justin."

His eyes had widened. "I never heard anything like that."

"Haven't you? To me it makes a lot more sense than resurrection or reincarnation." The rain pouring on the roof and slithering on the windowpanes sounded wondrous to me for a moment, cosmic. Heraclitus said that no one ever stepped into the same river twice. New rain nourished the soil or ran in rivers to the sea, returned to the sky by evaporation, gathered into clouds, and rained again, a vast symbol of—so much. Symbols by their nature cannot be fully named.

Justin had relaxed into fascination. "Did you make all that up, or do you really believe it?"

"I don't just believe it. I *know* it. Empirically."

"Right, like I understand what that means."

"It means from actual experience of physical fact. And here's another thing I know empirically, Justin. I know that your mother loves you."

That blindsided him. He stiffened but kept staring at me.

"Your mother loves you and she always will love you and she will never forget you and she will never stop searching for you."

He responded with anger to save him from tears. "Yeah, like you can prove that."

"I *know* it, because I'm a mom and I know what the love of a mother is like. It's a passion for the person who came out of your own body. Nobody male can imagine the strength of it. I have two sons. I love them with all my heart and I always will. Nothing they could ever do or say could make me not love them."

"Stop it." His voice husky, Justin slid off my bed to stand up, to flee.

"Okay, I'll stop. There's just one more thing, Justin."

He faced me narrow-eyed, on guard.

"Does Stoat ever tell you he loves you?"

His face hardened. "A few times. In bed."

"He's a liar. What he does to you in bed is not love."

"I figured."

"Yet I bet you feel something for him, don't you? You have a big heart. It's impossible for you to live with somebody and not get attached to him, right?"

Justin's rigid face contorted. "What are you trying to prove?" he yelled.

"Just that you're human."

"And what am I supposed to do about it?"

"If you do anything, it's completely up to you."

"Damn it, why aren't you begging me to cut the ropes off the bedposts or something?"

I took care to speak exact truth. "Because I am a mom and I am starting to love you too, Justin."

He gawked, gulped, then ran from the room.

Throughout history, female philosophers are few and far between. It would seem that women generally have had better things to do than ponder how many incorporeal bodies can caper on the head of a pin, or how many existentialists it takes to change a lightbulb. Searching my mind for a feminine Socrates to comfort me (Socrates himself wouldn't do; he, like Stoat, hated women), I found myself baffled. Raging Ayn Rand, hell no. Simone de Beauvoir, too hung up on Sartre. Mary Wollstonecraft probably wore a corset. Hypatia—

Hypatia might empathize.

In ancient times just as today, women were not supposed to be philosophers, of course, but Hypatia was, so a kind of exemption was made in her case. She was not a woman. She was something more, at one with the divine being she called the One. Her students, all male, were not allowed to fall in love with her. When one of them had the temerity to do so, she showed him a diaper stained with her menstrual blood and reminded him that earthly beauty is an illusion. And that took care of that, I'm sure. Talk about attitude.

Hypatia referred to the One as best discovered by "the Eye buried within us" and urged a return to the teachings of Plato and Aristotle. These tales of her survived; however, most of her thoughts did not, because the fourth-century Bishop of Alexandria put out a hit on her, ordering a group of fanatical monks to haul her from her chariot, divest her of the white cloak of a philosopher, strip her naked, and either beat her to death or, some accounts say, attack her with sharpened seashells. Then her writings were burned along with her body. In history as written by the Christian church, Hypatia never existed.

Whatever Stoat did to me, I reflected, would be mild compared with what had happened to Hypatia.

Nevertheless, dead is dead. Especially if one doesn't believe in the afterlife.

I doubted whether Hypatia had reached any deep philosophical insights during her last moments.

And I doubted whether I was going to reach any either, but all the rest of the day, lying on that mattress as if waiting to be stretched on a rack, I occupied my mind with a vain attempt. At wisdom. Or consolation. Or at least a worthy quotation upon which to hang my metaphorical shroud.

Death be not proud; carry my shroud.

Do not go gentle unto that good night . . . as if I had a choice?

"Though boys throw stones at frogs in sport, the frogs do not die in sport, but in earnest." Plutarch. Who the hell was Plutarch? I ought to remember. . . .

Something similar in Shakespeare. *King Lear*. "As flies to wanton boys are we to the gods; they kill us for their sport."

Ashes, ashes, all fall down.

Dust to dust. Dust in the wind; all we are is dust in the wind. . . .

Soughing outside my thoughts and my room I heard plenty of wind, but saw no dust. Just rain, lots of it. Rainsnakes on the windows.

Then came the familiar asthmatic roar of the generic white van. Cough of silence, in front of the house rather than alongside. Slam of doors, first vehicle, then house.

Stoat was home.

But darkness would not come for hours yet.

I hoped Stoat would ignore me until then. But my own hope made me so angry at myself, him, and fractal theory (ridiculously random, how I had gotten into this fix) that I would not go gentle after all. I yelled as loud as I could, "Stoat!"

I heard a thunk as his cowboy-booted feet fell off the coffee table. I heard him swear. I heard, then saw him run into my room. "Where's your gag?"

"How should I know? You never put it back on me."

"Phew!" Short attention span; he batted at the urine-scented air with one hand. "You wet the bed!"

"What did you expect? I understand you plan to kill me tonight."

Thoroughly distracted from the wet mattress, he blinked a few times, but kept the blank look on his face and in his eyes. "That's none of your business."

Although painfully aware of the utter absurdity of this statement, I managed to keep a straight face. "Yes, it is, because I'd like to write a letter to my sons first."

"What for?"

"Tell them I'm dead. You like things orderly, right? If your mother was dead all of a sudden, wouldn't you want to know?"

"I suppose so." The mention of a letter seemed to have swung him to the opposite extreme from the Stoat whose fist had split my lip only yesterday. He seemed slightly harried, like a fussy clerk troubled by a complicated business transaction. "But you can't tell them about me."

"Of course not. I wouldn't want to get you and Justin in trouble. I'll let you read what I write."

"Huh." He stalked off, but returned in a few minutes with his pistol, aiming it at me with one hand while he unshackled me with the other. "Okay, potty time, then supper. Tie a towel around your stinking self."

It did not surprise me that Stoat would not be distracted from suppertime routine no matter what the extraordinary circumstances.

Supper was canned beef stew, presumably bought by Stoat, who therefore should reproach no one, yet the man criticized Justin, saying he had failed to microwave it evenly to the proper temperature. I had no way to verify or disprove this because I did not taste any. The concept of imminent death had solidified and lodged in my throat, preventing me from eating. Stoat frowned at me as if I were being unreasonable.

"Now, why ain't you eating? You know I ain't gonna hurt you much," he said. "Like you noticed, I like things neat and tidy, so I don't mess up people more than is necessary. I don't want no fuss and I'll make it quick. I told you before, you was just in the wrong place at the wrong time, so it ain't nobody's fault. Even if you do have a big mouth and you did wet the bed."

I nodded soberly but did not trust myself to say anything lest I begin to laugh hysterically, his assurances seemed so ludicrous. Then I thought of the way he had fired the gun three times, killing Schweitzer, and how the dog had screamed, and my gut heaved, but there was nothing to retch.

Stoat frowned harder and took my bowl of stew away. "Put that back in the pot," he told Justin. "No use wasting good food."

Justin obeyed silently. He hadn't eaten much or said much and he wouldn't look at me. Common sense told me not to hope for any help from him. He had given up most of his selfhood in order to survive.

After the dishes were cleared away, it was still light outside. There was still a little time. I managed to move my mouth and form words. "A letter to my sons," I said slowly and laboriously. "I need to write my sons. I need paper, a pen, an envelope, and a stamp."

Seeming genuinely flummoxed, Stoat retorted, "What you think this is, some kind of office supplies store?"

Justin brought cheesy unbleached tablet paper from school. Stoat made me pull out a page from the back so Justin's fingerprints would not be on it. Justin supplied me with a school-issue wooden pencil. There were no pens in this house, and no envelopes, and certainly no postage stamps. "I'll take care of it next time we go to town, can't I, Uncle Steve?"

"Sure, Justin," Stoat said with expansive generosity. "I'll give you money to buy a stamp next week sometime."

Sitting to write, I discovered that my hands were clumsy, shaky, so I printed the mailing address first—c/o my ex-husband, the only address I could remember clearly, because for a long time it had been my own. Then, switching over to handwriting necessarily a bit larger and more childish than usual, I wrote, *Dear Forrest and Quinn*—

"Forrest and Quinn," said Justin, maybe as a weak attempt to joke or tease. "You gave them those names, Forrest and Quinn?"

Yes, I had, meaning only to prove them a bit different, when in fact they had turned out quite conventional. Quinn, my firstborn, had become a banker, of all things, and Forrest a civil engineer, which did not mean that he was polite but rather that he constructed efficient sewer systems. Neither of them had married yet, having too much head and not enough heart; being, I thought, too much like their father, Georg with no *e*.

"It's too bad babies are named at birth," I told Justin.

"Go do the dishes, Justin," growled Stoat.

I continued my letter.

> *Dear sons, please remember life has not been*
> *kind lately so this news is not terrible to me. I have*
> *encountered a man who needs to kill me. He promises to*
> *do so as quickly and painlessly as he can. By the time you*
> *receive this, I should be dead. This is my last will and*
> *testament in which I divide all my belongings equally*
> *between you. There is much I want to say but cannot,*
> *except that I wish you long and wonderful lives.*
>
> *With greatest love,*
> *Mom*

Stoat read this over my shoulder—revolver in hand, of course. When I had finished, he nodded. "I reckon that won't hurt anything. Leave it lay where it is. Justin can mail it next week."

I looked at Justin, who had just finished washing the dishes. Drying his hands on a dingy kitchen towel, he nodded, giving me a flickering glance of acknowledgment. I barely glimpsed his eyes, yet saw there a near replica of the blank terror that might have been in my own.

Maybe he realized, as I did, how extremely theoretical, almost fictitious, "next week" was for him; otherwise, Stoat would not have allowed me to write the letter. Logic told me that Justin was in as much danger of death as I was. Even before I came along, Stoat had wanted to replace him with a younger victim, and now would be the perfect time to kill him. Two for the price of one. Would Stoat leave Justin at home while he went to murder me? Of course not. He would keep Justin with him so the kid could not turn against him, run away, alert the police. And would he keep Justin alive after Justin had witnessed my murder? I doubted it.

"We can't go till deep dark." With a stab of his gun barrel, Stoat ordered me toward the living room. "Sit down and watch TV."

So I did. Wrapped in my towel as if in an overlarge diaper, I sat on the sofa and looked at some program without comprehension. After a while Justin joined me on the other end of the sofa, while Stoat slumped in his chair, keeping the gun aimed at me. All the while my mind trolled near and far, fishing for any possibility of escape, any improvised weapon, any plausible ploy, but came up with none. I remembered having heard once that, when held at gunpoint, one should run while dodging back and forth, the rationale being that most criminals neglect their target practice, are indifferent shots, and it is better to risk a flesh wound than to be killed. My body, however, felt watery after being punched and kicked and handcuffed to a bed—not that I had ever been an athlete, far from it. My memories of school phys ed class, dodgeball in particular, were dismal. And the decades since had not helped any. (Jogging? I have *never* seen a smiling jogger.) After just two days of Stoat's abuse, I felt incapable of jumping up and running to the door, much less dodging. Maybe later, once we got outside?

Maybe if adrenaline kicked in?

Maybe?

EIGHT

S toat showed no impatience, not even a jiggling leg, as the television babbled and the sky darkened outside the living room window. He had decided beforehand what time to proceed, I inferred, and his plans were not to be rushed even by himself. When the TV changed programs at exactly nine o'clock, he stood up. "Leave it on," he told Justin, who had reached for the remote. "If people drive by, it'll look like we're home. But they don't need to see me standing here with this pistol. Kill the lights."

Justin did so. Hardly anyone drove past in the daytime, much less at night, but Stoat took no chances.

"Go get a pair of handcuffs," he ordered Justin.

The boy returned almost at once. Obviously it had not been necessary for him to untie some cuffs from the bed. I wondered how many pairs of handcuffs Stoat kept around this place.

"And an extra towel. So she don't stink up the upholstery in the van."

Or leave evidence there either. As I had come to expect of him, he had planned down to the smallest detail.

With my hands cuffed behind my back, I gave up thoughts of possible escape, thus, unintentionally, freeing myself in a different way. Freeing myself to breathe deeply of the wet night-time air, to feel the raindrops with a perverse joy, to listen with a bittersweet pang to the frogs chiming, their croaking somehow as tuneful at a slight distance as a choir of angel bells. I had time to stand breathing and listening, for Stoat our goat man, so meticulous, would not turn on the porch light; someone might see us. So it took Justin a few minutes to feel his way down the steps before Stoat prodded me ahead of him with a hard little hollow circle pressed to my back.

I felt for the edge of the step with one foot. "Take your time so you don't fall," Stoat whispered. He sounded as if he meant it sincerely, frightening me worse than if he had cursed me. The scariest thing about Stoat was how normal-nice he could be. A little bit of good in the worst of us? A little bit of bad in the best of us? Bullshit. I knew then, as never before, that there is unfathomable capacity for both good and evil in every single one of us.

The rain poured down, drenching me to the bone, and I tilted my face up and opened my mouth, not because I was thirsty but because I needed to open myself and be cleansed. Rain, please wash away the stink of pee and sweat and fear. Rain, be my baptism into night, my last rite.

Across a stretch of darkness I heard the side door of the van slide open as Justin got in. No overhead lights came on; of course Stoat had disabled them. I heard him open what seemed to be the passenger seat door, feel around with his gun-free hand for something, then say, "In you go."

No. I wanted to keep standing in the rain, all night if it would help. I did not lift a foot to feel for a step.

"Get in." With his free hand he grasped my upper arm and hoisted, but I became limp and unhelpful.

"*Move*, or I'll kill you right here and now, ditch you afterward."

His voice remained quiet and steady but conveyed a remorseless logic, making me suddenly cooperative. I fumbled with my feet, he maneuvered my handcuffed arms, and I landed more or less on the passenger seat, which felt unaccountably, ever so kindly fluffy and soft. Dry, warm. As if the loving mother of my earliest memories had somehow reached out to embrace me from heaven on this hellish night. Even though I didn't believe in heaven or hell, not under normal circumstances, and even though I fully realized my comfort came from a towel meant to protect Stoat's upholstery from my personal pollution, still the touch of terry cloth wrenched sobs out of me, one after another.

Nothing Stoat could do to me would ever make me cry? Riiight.

Did Stoat get credit if fabric softener made me quake with tears?

On my shoulder I felt a touch, tentative and quickly withdrawn. Justin, in the backseat. Meanwhile, Stoat slammed doors, started the van, and told me, "Shut up." I saw no light, not even headlights as I felt the van begin to roll, but I did not need to look at Stoat's face to know I'd better stop crying. Not that his voice growled or menaced. Not at all. It was his starkness that terrified me. His hollowness.

I shut up.

Stoat drove without headlights onto the road, and accelerated even though the asphalt showed only as a shinier blackness in the night. Somehow Stoat kept us more or less on the pavement, and when we hit the shoulder by mistake, no one spoke, not even him. Not even swearing broke the silence inside that van and the susurration of rain outside. We encountered no other vehicles for some time, but when one appeared in the distance, Stoat turned on his low beams.

"We're far enough away from the house now, it don't matter," he remarked genially.

No one responded. Stoat turned off the paved road onto one of the gazillion dirt roads that I had not yet gotten around to exploring, meaning I had no idea—did people live back here? Since I could not lean back with my hands cuffed behind me, necessarily I perched on the edge of my seat and peered through the windshield. All I could see in the headlights, through a blur of rain, were trees and brush as oppressive as a tunnel, forest crowding the road into a single lane. Forest as thick as jungle, spiked with palmetto and slathered with Spanish moss like massive weeping cobwebs.

Since it had been raining hard all day, fervidly I hoped that Stoat, driving on a dirt road, would get his van stuck in the mud.

My mistake. Did I say dirt road? These roads were yellow sand plus maybe some orange clay. Sand roads don't make mud in the rain. They just get nice and hard. It's when they're dry and soft that people get stuck in them.

Stoat turned onto another one of them, and we slowed to go over—yikes. The bridge consisted of two spans of wooden planks, each just wide enough to accommodate a vehicle's tires, plus timber supports but no rail. Just below what should have been the middle of the bridge, I saw water rushing. I flinched and closed my eyes as Stoat sent the van across the bridge that was barely there.

We turned onto another narrow, serpentine sand road, crossed another two or three minimalist bridges, and duh, I realized we were driving not through forest, but through swamp. Or into swamp. Most of Maypop County consisted of forest or swamp, forest being trees plus undergrowth, and swamp being trees plus water. Through forest the yellow sand roads ran arrow straight. But in swamp they wriggled to find higher land.

Since we had left the paved road, we had not met up with another vehicle, not one single car, and it had been quite a while since I had noticed a shack or a trailer or even a mailbox to show that anybody lived back here. I supposed it was not the best place in the world to locate one's home, what with mosquitoes, flooding, and the omnipresence of the nastiest of all native poisonous snakes, the water moccasin. I gave up forlorn hopes of encountering anyone who might rescue me. These twisting roads ran deep into places where my body most likely would be eaten by alligators before it was ever found.

If Stoat had not handcuffed me, I would have made a move before now, grabbing the keys out of the ignition, twisting the wheel to send us into a creek, anything for one last chance. Now I thought about throwing myself bodily against Stoat the next time we came to one of those sketchy so-called bridges. All I had to do was send the tires off the planks and the van would drop—

"Where's that mouth of yours, Lee Anna?" Stoat drawled. "You're awful quiet."

I opened that mouth of mine. "I was just wondering who's going to miss me first, the Mormons or the Jehovah's Witnesses. I couldn't decide which to join, so I went to both, and—"

Stoat chuckled. "Good try. I like you, Lee Anna. Don't feel bad about what I'm fixing to do. It's nothing personal, just what has to happen, logically speaking."

Behind me, Justin hadn't said a word, and I could not think what on earth to say to him.

I watched and waited for another bare-bones bridge.

But I had missed my chance. We crossed no more bridges. Stoat turned the van onto another—not a road, really, but two tire tracks in the sand, weeds thick and tall between them, undergrowth scrubbing against the sides of the van, thick skeins of Spanish moss dragging, sodden, across the windows and windshield. In the wet night it was kind of like being in a car wash.

And this was a fine time for me to be thinking such clever

thoughts when, face it, I was running out of options. Next moment I heard no more brush, saw no more Spanish moss. Night opened into nothing I could see. The track sloped slightly downhill and ended. Or, really, I didn't know it ended, but Stoat did. He stopped the van and turned it off. Its headlights shone through rain amid darkness in which I heard a bedlam of frogs. All around us, they no longer seemed to sing so much as babble, bark, bleat, and belch.

"Get out," Stoat said, apparently to Justin; obviously I wasn't going anywhere without assistance. Stoat himself got out, but Justin didn't move. I watched Stoat, ghostly in the rain and headlights, cross in front of the van and come to open my door.

He snapped his fingers hard. "I told you to get out!"

I turned sideways on my seat and felt for a step with my feet before I realized he wasn't speaking to me.

Justin said, "No."

"What you mean, no?"

"No. I'm staying here."

"You get out of this van, boy, or I'll beat you like you never been beat before."

"No. I don't care what you do to me, I want no part of this. I'm not moving."

Shouting obscenities, Stoat snagged me by the shoulders and flung me straight down out of the van to sprawl with my face in wet sand. I didn't care. Somehow the flipped-out, raging Stoat was easier to handle than the marginally nice Stoat. I heard him rampaging inside the van, trying to grab Justin, but evidently Justin had lodged himself someplace impregnable, maybe under the backseat. Meanwhile I struggled to my feet—oddly, I seemed to be standing on open sand, because I felt no vegetation groping me—and I began to stumble away, blindly, into the unknown.

Sure, I felt a faint hope, but realistically I was trying not so much to save myself—with handcuffs on?—as to distract Stoat from Justin.

And maybe Justin was trying to distract him from me? How ironic.

"Hey! Hey, stupid woman!" Stoat caught up to me in seconds and whacked me on the side of the head with what felt like the butt of his gun. I saw stars and nearly fell, but he yanked me upright by the handcuffs and started marching me down a slight slope.

Behind us, the van headlights went out, dumping thick darkness as well as heavy rain all over us.

"That miserable ass-reamed snot-nosed punk thinks he's so smart!" Stoat sounded as if he might just possibly blow a major artery, which would have been wonderful. "Screw him. I got a flashlight." He demonstrated by turning it on, and its wavering circle of white, plus his own triumph, seemed to calm him down as suddenly as he had flipped out. Stoat, a man like a lightbulb, but cracked.

Now his hand on my elbow felt gentle and ceremonious as if we were going on a date. "This way, Miss Lee Anna." He had to raise his voice in order for me to hear him, there was so much noise in the night—the frogs twanging their soggy concert, and the patter of rain on leaves making the trees sound like an audience applauding. Stoat led me down an area of open sand between what sounded like two walls of forest. We seemed to be on a narrow beach of sorts, ending at some fairly large body of water.

"Is this a lake or what?" I asked, stopping as if to look, though I could see very little through rain so thoroughgoing it had already washed the sand off my face.

"Chatawachipolee River, running so high it's nearly covered

the boat ramp down yonder. Now stop stalling," he added in the kindest of voices. "My gun's right here in my belt. Move."

Crap. There seemed to be no point in delaying the inevitable. I walked on.

"Okay, this is close enough."

It certainly was. The beam of the flashlight showed the sand ending a scant two feet in front of me. Beyond that I saw swiftly running water.

Stoat let go of me and drew his gun. "Kneel down."

I started trembling, and not from cold. "Why?"

"Just do it." With the gun barrel poking my back and his gun hand gripping the handcuffs, he shoved me to my knees at the edge of the water, then stood back.

"Now, Miss Lee Anna," he told me in avuncular tones, "you are going into the river, but you'll be dead before your darlin' little face hits the water. You ain't gonna drown, and I promise you, you ain't going to feel a thing."

Not going to feel a thing? I felt sickening fear. I shook so hard my handcuffs rattled.

Maybe that reminded him. "No use wasting a good pair of cuffs," he remarked. Bending down to take them off, he set the flashlight aside, on the sand, since he was not about to relinquish hold of the gun and he did not have three hands.

The moment the handcuffs came off, my arms swung forward and I boosted myself to my feet.

"Hey! Crazy bitch!" Stoat barked, no longer sounding the least bit avuncular. "Stop right there!" I heard him backing away, presumably so I could not grab the gun. "I'll shoot you in the gut, slut! You want that?"

"I want you to look me in the *face*, you creep," I yelled, beginning to turn—

Wham.

. . .

A dull cracking noise, but to my gun-shy mind it sounded like a shot. I should have felt the pain; he couldn't have missed me. I didn't get it—until I swung around and saw Stoat crumpling to the ground.

"Justin!"

I grabbed the flashlight off the ground to verify. Yes. Standing over Stoat, Justin held a wooden baseball bat, and even in the downpour I could tell that the water running down his face was not entirely rain.

"Justin," I repeated, dumbfounded, and also weak in the knees with relief.

He spoke between sobs. "Is he—dead?"

I wanted to wrap my arms around the kid and weep on his shoulder, thank you oh thank you my hero—

"I—hit him—hard—but I didn't want to—kill—"

My knees still wobbled, but I started to get a grip. Justin didn't need a clinging vine right now. Like it or not, Stoat had been his family, sort of, for the past two years, and he felt as if he had just betrayed his word and maybe orphaned himself. He needed me to be strong.

I got strong. "You didn't kill him." Crouching over Stoat, I felt a pulse in his neck, and I could see him breathing. "You just conked him good." Stoat's gun lay near his limp hand. Standing up, I snatched the gun as if swinging a snake by the tail; grabbing it by the tip of its barrel, I winged it like a boomerang into the middle of the Chatawhatchimahoosim. The river.

Weapon gone, Stoat lay unconscious, yet my terror of the thin gray man only increased.

"We've got to get out of here, Justin!"

The boy hadn't moved from where he stood sobbing and shaking.

"Justin." I found that I lacked the guts to hop over Stoat, but I got to Justin roundabouts and gave him a solid hug. "Thanks for saving my ass. Now we have to save yours. Did he leave the key in the van?"

"I, um, I guess so." Justin's guess-so was hardly more than a whisper.

"Then come on. Run!" Still holding the flashlight, grabbing his wrist with one hand, I hauled him with me toward the van. Partway there he kicked out of neutral and got himself in gear, passing me. He yanked open the passenger's side door at the same time as I got to the driver's side and aimed the flashlight at the ignition.

No key.

"Sometimes he sticks it on top of the sun visor," Justin said, voice strained.

I flipped the visor. Papers fell down, but nothing with a metallic jingle. I scanned the dashboard, the seats, the floor. Nothing.

"Oh, shit." Justin sounded choked. "He must have put it in his pocket."

"Come on." I started running back toward where we had left Stoat, but after only a few strides I stopped dead, grabbed Justin by the wrist so I wouldn't lose him in the dark, and turned off the flashlight.

From where we had left Stoat, maybe thirty feet away, I heard the sounds of groans and fervid curses. Chillingly specific curses regarding the punk and the bitch and what he would do to them when he caught them.

"Run!" Justin sounded panicked, yet he had the good sense not to yell; he spoke just loud enough for me to hear him in the hullabaloo of rain, river, and frogs. No way had he betrayed us to Stoat.

Just the same I pulled him toward me and spoke close to his ear. "Run where?" Heading into the woods, thick with palmetto, would have been like running through razor wire in the night. And Stoat would catch us with the van if we tried to escape back up the road.

"I—I don't know!"

Stoat roared, "What the fuck? A baseball bat! I'll show them how to use a baseball bat." Damn. He didn't have his goddamn gun, but he did have a weapon.

I imagined him using the baseball bat like a walking stick, staggering to his feet.

In the total drenching darkness we could not see him and he could not see us. But to find the van, all he had to do was feel his way up the sand slope. And once he turned on the headlights, we were roadkill, if not worse.

Adrenaline is a remarkable stimulant of both body and mind. I said softly, "Justin, can you swim?"

"Of course. Why?"

"We're going into the river." I envisioned a Southern, sandy river with no rocks, no white water, and most certainly no waterfalls.

"That's crazy! Alligators, moccasins—"

Well, yes, there was that.

People down here called the poisonous cottonmouth viper, aka water moccasin, simply "moccasins." Indeed, some people called all snakes "moccasins," as if they were terrified by Native American footwear.

I declared, "I'd rather face a snake any day than *him*." By Stoat's constant swearing I could tell that, yes, he was on the move, feeling his way toward the van—and us. "The river, Justin. It's our only chance."

I felt his hand grip my wrist the way mine gripped his, so that we forged a strong link. "Okay." He sounded more brave than desperate. "Let's go."

"Quietly." Instinctively I crouched, keeping my head down. Justin did the same. Like a pair of soldiers under fire we scuttled past the noise pollution that was Stoat—I think we blundered within ten feet of him, and if he had shut his foul mouth, he might have heard us. But he kept stumbling toward the van. Quite blindly in the dark we dashed away from it, toward the hiding place we could not see.

NINE

First I felt water puddling around my ankles, and within a few steps, the river current shoving against my shins. Stumbling, I almost lost my balance, and Justin stood still, bracing his feet and hanging on to me. Now the water reached up to my knees—

Muffled by frogs and distance, I heard a slamming sound.

Slam. Door. Van.

"Down!" I hurled myself into darkness, pulling Justin with me.

We ducked just as the van's headlights blazed on, blindingly bright for an instant before our heads hit the water.

Had Stoat seen us? Would he see us now? Desperately hoping not, I held my breath and did a pretty good imitation of a log just by keeping still. Clutching my arm and taking his cue from me, Justin did the same. Meanwhile, the river current swirled us around and took charge of us, so by the time I had to raise my head and gasp for air, we were nicely downstream, away from the area where the van's headlights still shone across the surface of the water.

But not quite far enough downstream to suit me, because the van's lights also shone on the all-too-familiar figure of a quick, slim man near the flooded river's edge.

"Uncle Steve!" gasped Justin, bobbing alongside me.

"Stop calling him your uncle! He's a kidnapper and a pedophile and a rapist and he deserves—" I managed to cease firing from a sawed-off shotgun of rage I hadn't even realized I had in me. Words badly aimed, scattering, good for nothing. "Sorry, Justin. Are you okay?" I tried to reach for his hand, which had slipped out of mine, but I didn't find it.

"He knows where we went," Justin said in the dead voice of someone who has already given up.

Actually, bent over and pacing back and forth at the edge of the water, Stoat seemed to be hunting upstream and down like an old hound dog. And the river carried us farther away from him every moment.

"I don't think so," I told Justin. "Our tracks are rained out. He doesn't even know what he's looking for."

But he did. He found it, reached down to seize it, and turned it on.

The flashlight.

Justin gulped air and disappeared underwater at the same time I did. Holding my breath and hurrying myself along with the rushing river, I fired some angry mental bullets at myself. Damn flashlight, I didn't even remember dropping it. Stupid, clueless, what was I thinking, why hadn't I thrown it into the drink like the gun?

Really, rationally, I did not think it likely that Stoat had seen us when he had turned on the flashlight, but at the same time, I felt an irrational fear that he had, and I knew Justin would be feeling it a hundred times worse, would be absolutely sure his "uncle" knew exactly where he was and would come after him.

A burning feeling started in my lungs. I thrust myself to the surface and gasped for air while trying to clear my eyes of bleary water so I could see.

But there was nothing to see. Complete darkness. Either the river had taken us around a bend that hid everything from our view, or Stoat and his flashlight and his van were gone.

I asked the darkness, "Justin?"

No answer.

"Justin!"

Nothing. And it was high time to get out of this flooding river. At any moment it might conk me with a floating log or smash me against a fallen tree. Which, with my luck, would have snakes on it.

"Justin!" I called, uselessly, before I kicked, managing to lie more or less on top of the water, and by swimming across the river current, I aimed, I hoped, toward shore. The opposite shore from the one we had left Stoat on.

I was just getting into the rhythm of a pretty good Australian crawl—stroke, up and over, stroke—when my extended hand touched something that felt like a big tree. But when I tried to grab on to it, it lashed like a giant whip, threw me aside as if I were made of cork, and took off.

"Sorry, alligator," I said politely, treading water. Having never before in my life been in a situation like this, I found it impossible to predict my own reactions or even explain them. I reached out again, could not find the alligator, and promptly panicked because now it could be behind me, underneath me, anywhere.

"*Justin!*" Why not yell? Between the swoosh of the water and the gibbering of the frogs, he could be a few yards away from me and still not hear me.

No answer.

Anxiety kicked me from inside as if I were pregnant with worry. That boy might as well have been one of my sons. Getting myself drowned along with him would not help him. Once again I swam, trying hard not to thrash (were alligators, like sharks, attracted to thrashing?), and headed toward shore.

But where was my strength? I was only menopausal, dammit, not geriatric. I had been a lifeguard not so many years ago, which meant I had been a strong, fast swimmer. But I couldn't seem to make any progress muscling myself out of this damn pushy water—

Conk. The river bashed my shoulder against something rough and hard that could have been an alligator but didn't move and was therefore of the tree persuasion. Or so I surmised in the total darkness. The river immediately twisted me and tried to whirl me away from it, but I grabbed hold and managed to get a leg flung over the thing, which lay horizontal, partially above the waterline.

Definitely a tree, I found as I crawled onto it. A nice, round, fat, sturdy tree. Embracing it—I had always aligned myself with tree huggers, but never before had I actually thrown my arms around a trunk—I lay on my belly with the side of my face pressed against the bark and most of me at last out of the flooded river. Despite rain and darkness, I felt tension drain out of me; I lay limp, with no idea how exhausted I had been until strength began to return.

"Justin?" I called to the night.

No answer. I sighed, sat up, and began to inch toward shore. To make sure I hadn't gotten turned around in the darkness, I stuck a foot down into the river. The direction of the current reassured me, and I went on, feeling my way along the tree trunk on all fours until something, I suppose the stub of a branch, poked my collarbone. I tried to circumnavigate the obstacle, slipped, and ended up back in the water. But this time, mothers be praised, it wasn't wash-me-away water, only a quieter eddy in which I could stand on the bottom. In fact, the water reached not far above my waist.

But if I thought I was out of trouble, the notion was premature.

Blundering toward what I hoped was shore, I collided with tree branches, stumbled, fell, dunked myself in water over my head, fumbled my way upright, sneezed, stumbled only two steps before I dunked myself again, got up, and did it all again, muttering a few new words I had learned from Stoat, before I finally reached dry land.

Well, not dry land, exactly. It was still raining. But I did find a stretch of something that was not flooding river.

I sat. I panted. I called for Justin. I intended to sit and call for Justin until daybreak, but my body had other ideas. At some point I toppled sideways and, curled in the wet sand, fell sound asleep.

I awoke to find myself basking in bright sunshine, feeling pleasantly warmed, grateful that the rain had stopped and even more grateful that it was no longer dark. Seldom had I so ardently appreciated simply being able to see.

The only immediate problem was that I had company. I was not the only life-form basking on that stretch of sand. When I opened my eyes, they stared straight at a brown thing that looked a bit too much like a snake. I had to blink and focus right in front of my nose to see—whoa. It really was the head of a reptile. At first I tried to convince myself it was a lizard or something, not a snake, but I remembered all too clearly reading about the poisonous snakes of Florida, that vipers had eyes like those of a cat, unlike the beady eyes of harmless snakes, and I remembered laughing because who the heck was ever going to get close enough to a snake to check out the pupils of its eyes?

Well, here I was looking into a snake's eye, and even though a bony ridge like an eyebrow shadowed it, I could see quite clearly the vertical black slit of its pupil.

Water moccasin.

My heartbeat might have sped up somewhat, but I did not bother to panic. After all, things could have been a lot worse. It could have been Stoat.

I must not move or I might be bitten. Sheer inertia had kept me still when I awoke. The bliss of lying in a position other than spread-eagle had made me so lazy I hadn't even lifted my head. Now I realized that the only part of me I could safely move was my eyeballs.

I deployed them as best I could from where I lay sprawled in the sand. Focusing beyond a blur of mud-colored snake, I could see water sparkling, and some turtles basking on a log—doubtless the tree trunk I had grabbed on to last night—and beyond the river a solid wall of forest with mistletoe balls in the oaks and scraggly pines towering above all the other trees. Trying to make out the river's far bank, I thought I saw a sketchy line of yellow-tan sand between the gleaming brown water and the mostly green jumble of forest. Understandably, I was not certain, but I thought maybe the river level was beginning to go down.

I took another look at the log, really a long-dead fallen tree with its roots somewhere above my horizontal head. Yes, turtles and all, it seemed to slant a bit higher above the water than it had last night. If I could judge by what I had felt in the dark of the night.

Okay, so I couldn't really tell. Why did I care?

Justin, that was why. Floodwater going down could only be good for him if—if he was still out in this swamp somewhere, if Stoat hadn't gotten him.

Was he at least *alive*? Or had he bumped his head on something and drowned? Or had Stoat killed him?

Never once did I think in terms of Justin's recapture, because I felt certain Stoat had wanted to kill him even *before* Justin had conked him with a baseball bat last night, thereby totally and ir-revocably pissing him off.

God, where was Justin? I needed to get up, call for him, go looking for him, but here I lay helpless because of a damn poison-ous snake sleeping in front of my nose. Or at least I supposed it was sleeping. How could I tell? It didn't have eyelids, but I hadn't seen any movement in its eye, which seemed unnervingly fixated on me.

Probably just my imagination. And I remembered the book said snakes were deaf. What if I ever so slowly inched away—

No. The book also said that snakes made up for being deaf by sensing vibrations.

Besides which, I didn't know what was behind me. With my luck, there could be another snake cuddled up against my rear end.

Gaah. Creepy thought.

Well, sooner or later, it or they had to go away, right?

Right.

Meanwhile, I tried to pass the time by looking at anything and everything else. The turtles. Stumpy heads and legs striped with yellow.

Lichens on the log like green-gray rosettes with sprinkles of paprika—spores?

A turtle plunking into the water, showing its yellow-orange belly shell.

Beyond, a wading bird landing for a moment on the log—some kind of small heron or bittern with chartreuse legs—quickly gone again, flapping upriver.

Long wait.

Wait. I heard something. Not too far away, somebody trying to start a lawn mower. Stupid thing blustered, spit, and died, the way they always did. Again, and again. But finally, protesting, it was coaxed to continue, its loud gasps steadied into a regular chugging, and I heard it heading closer to me.

Lawn mower?

Boat motor. Already the boat had appeared, a shining aluminum savior perhaps twelve feet long, a rudimentary rectangle in which sat two burly trucker-hatted men. I did not dare move because of the snake, but surely they would see me.

". . . water this high, we should be able to get clear into Chipoluga Swamp, places we couldn't ordinarily," one of them was saying to the other.

"All right!" In the local Southern accent, this sounded like, "Aw, rat!" He went on, "That'll be a sat to see."

See me, I begged mentally, my heart pounding as they scudded past, hurried along by the high-running river. I couldn't move or yell because of the damn water moccasin, but there I lay like a corpse on the bank; how could they not see me?

But they didn't.

"We got the beer?"

"Damn straight we got the beer. You think I'd forget the beer?"

Idiots. Beer-swilling Bubbas. Still talking of beer, they disappeared downriver. The grumble of their motor blended into the distance.

"Meatloaf, please don't sit on my face." Still in bed, Amy Bradley shoved the cat off her forehead, only to feel him settling on her pillow as close as possible to her, on top of where her hair lay, with his blunt snout purring whisker-tickly feline secrets into her ear.

Since she and Chad had started quarreling, Amy had been finding it harder and harder to get herself out of bed and pointed in a direction in the morning. It had been weeks since she had made breakfast for Chad before he left for work, at first because they weren't speaking, and later because she couldn't get moving, not even to see the twins off to school. The kids took care of themselves, and every morning before leaving, Kayla climbed the stairs to say bye to her mom. Today, Amy had gathered enough energy to call her daughter over to her bedside, hug her, kiss her, and tell her she loved her. As always, Kayla had "forgotten" to close the bedroom door when she left. And as always, Meatloaf had come in to sprinkle Amy's bed with the cat litter caught between his paw pads. Meatloaf was never allowed outside the house. The Bradleys were too afraid something might happen to him.

"Meatloaf," Amy told the cat breathing in her ear, "I've been awake for hours, no thanks to you, so why can't I seem to get up?"

The phone rang.

Amy groaned, shoved the cat aside, and achieved rapid verticality. The urgent need to run and answer every single phone call had started the day Justin was abducted, and no amount of passing time could abate it.

Barefoot and in her nightgown, she sprinted across the upstairs hallway into the room devoted to 1-800-4JUSTIN. They had an ordinary landline in there as well. Amy snatched up the phone and shoved it against her head.

"Hello," she mumbled.

"Amy."

She woke up fast, recognizing her husband's voice. "Honey?"

"Yes." Chad sounded devoid of any honey; it had been a long time since he had called her anything sweet. "Amy, this is just to let you know I ditched work today—"

Amy gasped, "*What?*" Chad had taken personal days when Justin was abducted, but she had never known him to outright ditch work.

He went on speaking as if he hadn't heard her. "—and I'm driving up to Birmingham to see my dad—"

This was even more unheard of, so unlike Chad that Amy lost her breath and could not speak. She found herself clinging to the cordless phone for imaginary support.

"—so I don't know whether I'll be home tonight," Chad concluded. "Don't worry if I'm not."

Don't *worry*? Amy felt too scared to worry. Panic gave her the strength she needed to say, "Wait! Chad, what's this about?"

"Nothing."

"Nothing?" She smiled painfully; it was what Justin would have said when he was in trouble at school. She said now, "Don't 'nothing' me, Charles Stuart Bradley, and don't you dare hang up."

"No, ma'am. Yes, ma'am." Chad sounded a little more alive than before.

"Can you pull over?" She could tell by the whooshing and roaring background sounds of vehicles and semis that he was on the interstate. "So we can talk?"

"What for, Amy?" His voice had gone dull again. "I really don't have anything to tell you."

"Sure you do. There must be some reason—"

"I need—I don't know what I need. I just can't stand it anymore. Anything."

Terror more than courage helped her say it. "Chad, are you leaving me?" It was okay that her voice trembled. Let him hear how she felt.

Silence, except for the sounds of speed and distance in the phone. The sounds of someone running away.

"Chad?" Her voice shook even more.

His words so low she could barely hear them, he said, "I admit the thought has crossed my mind. But, Amy," he went on more forcefully, "Dad talked me out of it. He said the worst thing he ever did was to leave Mom and me. That's why I'm going to see him."

"Oh," Amy said, or exhaled, almost in a whisper.

"Amy?"

"I'm here."

"Okay. Don't worry. I'll call you."

"Chad, I—"

"Gotta go." He disconnected.

"I really do love you," said Amy to the lifeless phone.

TEN

Lying along the riverbank right beside an unfriendly neighborhood water moccasin, listening to the boat's motor dwindling way and fighting an impulse to cry, I forced my mind back to a contemplation of the glories of nature.

I saw another leggy bird beauty, this time white, skimming the opposite shore. Some kind of egret.

And a black vulture circling over the woods, soaring, its tapering wings forming a slight V. Why did buzzards get no respect when they were beautiful things in flight?

Long wait.

Flickers of songbird in the far trees.

Something moving on the far shore, maybe a deer? No, too golden, bobbing blond head—

Justin! Walking downstream along the other edge of the river.

The sight of him alive made me feel almost dizzy with happiness and—and he simply had to see me. I couldn't let him go past as the boaters had.

He disappeared from my view behind my snake-in-residence.

Lying with my right shoulder in the sand and my left one in the air, I took the risk of gingerly raising my left arm skyward and swinging it, waving.

The snake camped in front of me turned its head and sampled the air with its forked tongue.

And I saw Justin emerging from behind the visual obstruction, almost past me already, his eyes on his footing, his head not turned in my direction.

The incident of the two blind Bubbas had made me desperate enough to take risks. One of my few talents is whistling loudly enough to summon a taxi. Pretty sure the snake hadn't heard—I mean sensed—anything like that before, but with no idea how it would react, I put my tongue to my teeth and shrilled.

Justin's head snapped up. So did the snake's. Justin stood still and looked toward me. As soon as I was sure he had seen me waving, I froze with my hand in the air.

The snake shot its head up to loom over me like a cobra without the hood. Hissing, it opened its mouth wide, I mean really wide, showing off the startling interior seemingly upholstered in puffy white silk.

Justin walked into the river, heading toward me.

All the turtles evacuated the log. I didn't see them, not with my gaze fixed on the pristine lining of the snake's mouth, but I heard them plopping into the water. Nothing else made quite the same splash as a big turtle.

I also heard Justin splashing as he swam across the river. The rhythmic sound changed from splashing to sloshing when he reached shallower water and walked.

The snake swiveled its rearing head toward Justin.

I heard him say, "Whoa. Lee Anna, lie still."

I wanted to tell him no duh, but that would have involved moving my mouth. With my hand still straight up in the air I felt like some sort of ridiculous modern sculpture.

I heard the snap of a branch breaking and wondered whether

Justin had stepped on it or what. I heard his footsteps padding along the sand toward me.

The snake struck.

Faster than my eyes could follow.

I almost screamed. At first I thought it was biting Justin.

Launching almost its whole long burly body, it struck again. And again. And again. A little farther from me each time.

Forgetting all about the imaginary snake lying on the other side of me, I rolled away, sat up, and saw Justin holding the cottonmouth at bay with a long, dead stick. As I struggled to stand up, the snake struck the tip of the stick again and broke off a considerable piece of it, which fell into the edge of the river and floated.

Justin froze.

I did the same, in a most undignified pose, with my butt in the air and my hands on the ground.

The snake eyed the only moving thing, which was the stick in the water. Then with simple dignity it slithered into the river and swam away, its head gracefully raised as if it were an ugly brown swan.

I breathed out, staggered to my feet, and cried "Justin!" as he headed toward me to help me. Without permission I hugged him rather hard.

"Please get off," he begged, although he did hug me back. A little.

I backed off.

"God," he complained, "that was like being attacked by a giant dish sponge."

Finding myself shaky in the knees, I plopped my butt on the sand again and said, "Wow. That snake. Thank you for—"

"Forget it." Blushing, he looked upriver, not at me. "We don't have time. Uncle Steve has to be hunting for us."

"I told you, he is *so* not your uncle."

"What do you want me to call him?"

"Stoat the Goat."

He looked at me and cracked up. He actually fell down on the sand beside me, laughing. At first I was pleased, but then I realized he sounded a bit hysterical. I laid a hand on his forehead until he calmed down some, then demanded, "Justin. What happened?"

"Huh?" he mumbled, still giggling.

"What happened after we got separated last night?"

"Oh. That. He knew we went down the river." No more giggles, and no eye contact either. "He came after us with the flashlight."

I felt cold little lizard feet run down my spine at the thought of Stoat searching for us to kill us. As smoothly as I could, I said, "Since you're here, I take it he didn't find you?"

"He almost did find me. He waded right past me, but he didn't see me. I'd come up for air in the middle of a mess of brush and stuff the flood had piled up against something, and I guess it hid me pretty good. It was just dumb luck I happened to come up there."

"Dumb luck is as good as any other kind."

He tilted his head back in the sand to look at me upside down. "What the heck does that mean?"

"It means I read Nietzsche in college. In other words, it means nothing. How long did Stoat keep hunting?"

"Too damn long. After he gave up on the river, he went into the woods. From where I was, I could see the reflection of his flashlight in the water. Even when I couldn't see it anymore, I didn't dare come out."

"You mean you were still in the river?"

"Of course I was. All night. I finally heard the van drive away around dawn."

"Then he's not here now." Ridiculous, the tsunami of relief this assumption provided me, considering that I remained stranded in the wilderness.

"He probably just went home to eat something and grab another gun. He'll be back. Heck, he could already be back. When I heard that boat, I thought it was him, so I hid."

"It wasn't him. It was two men, but they went right past and didn't see me."

No comment. It occurred to me that Justin must have peeked at the boat himself, or he wouldn't know it wasn't Stoat and he'd still be hiding.

"Why didn't you yell?" I asked. "Flag them down?" I would have if I hadn't been situated too close to a snake.

Justin shrugged. Damn. In some ways he was so much a typical teenager.

"Well," I said, swallowing my irritation, "if they launched from that same boat ramp, their car will be there."

"Truck," Justin said. "You don't haul a boat with a car."

Teenager.

"Whatever." Acting far more brisk than I felt, I got on my feet. "Let's go have a look."

Justin didn't move. "What if Stoat's there?"

"It's a chance we'll have to take. Stoat thinks we're somewhere down the river, so we're better off heading back upstream, don't you think? Justin?"

He just shrugged again.

I swore to myself that I wasn't going to get parental with him. "We'd better get a move on," I said in a neutral tone, starting upstream along the riverbank. "Come on, Justin."

He didn't say a word, but he got up and followed me.

The river had taken away Justin's flip-flops.

There's an old saying my father liked to recite at annoying times: "For want of a nail the shoe was lost, for want of a shoe the horse was lost, for want of a horse the rider was lost, for want of a rider the kingdom was lost, and all for the want of a horseshoe nail." I guess Dad was a kind of philosopher on that subject. It's the little stuff that screws you good, like the *Columbia*'s O-ring or the Crocodile Hunter's stingray or, according to fractal theory, some butterfly in India fluttering its wings to eventually cause Superstorm Sandy.

I still had my socks and sneakers, sodden but intact on my feet, but with Justin barefoot, for a thousand sharp, pointy, and/or venomous reasons we couldn't slip into the woods to stay out of sight. We had to walk on the sandy bank of the river, where anybody could see us.

Which explained why, luckily for me, he had been on the riverbank to save my life a second time.

Progressing upriver, we discovered that we shared the bank with several snakes and four alligators, all of which slid into the water before we got anywhere near them.

They weren't what scared us.

The whole way back to the boat ramp, neither of us said a word. We kept pausing to listen. Warily we rounded a bend in the river, then stopped, glimpsing somebody's old blue pickup truck through a screen of leaves. If the river curve was the one that had hidden me from Stoat last night, then the blue pickup had to be sitting at the same boat ramp where he had taken us.

The problem was, what if Stoat was there too?

Justin and I stared at each other, silently discussing this. Then, gesturing for him to stay where he was, I headed into the woods to have a look at the boat ramp and its parking area from a hidden vantage point. The rain had soaked and muffled most of the noisy vegetation, so my main stealth problem was to keep my aforementioned big mouth from screaming or swearing as I edged between palmettos that tried to saw my legs off and knee-high Spanish

dagger—each long leaf might as well have been a switchblade—
and other things that tried to stick major thorns into me. What
the hell. My skin was just one big mosquito bite anyway; why
should I care if the vegetation now started sucking my blood?

Finally I got to where I had a clear view of the blue pickup,
which sat with its nose tilted upward and its rear end partway
down the boat ramp. In all the open space around it I could see no
other vehicle and no people, least of all Stoat.

Rather than ouching my way back to Justin, I broke into the
open, jogged down where he could see me, and beckoned forcefully. "Come on!" I snapped.

"What's your hurry?"

"I'm hungry! I want to raid their truck!"

By the time he joined me, I was already in the truck bed pushing aside fishing rods to open a tackle box with no idea what I
hoped to find. Bait? I didn't think Justin and I were quite ready to
eat worms, especially not plastic ones, which were the only kind I
found, along with fishhooks and sinkers and every conceivable
lure, including bright-colored tubular foam ones with a fringe,
kind of like Nerf squid.

"Get out!" Justin meant this as an expression of excitement, I
think, as he reached over my shoulder and picked up an
insignificant-looking rectangular object.

"What's that?"

"An everything tool!" He opened and explored it as he spoke.
"Pliers, file, knives, can opener—"

"Why would a guy keep condoms in his tackle box?" I had just
found some.

"Because his wife would never look there. Oh, my God!" Justin had opened the other tackle box, and he lifted out a can of
"Field's Pride Whole Kernel Sweet Corn." Feverishly he applied
his can opener to it.

"Okay, why would a guy keep a can of corn in his tackle box?" I asked, genuinely puzzled.

"Bait. Some people use corn on little hooks to catch bream."

Justin got the can's lid off, flung it aside, and lifted his find to his mouth with trembling hands. He poured corn into himself almost as if drinking it. Trickles of cloudy liquid ran down his chin.

When he had gulped all he could that way, and lowered the can to poke a grimy finger into it, he noticed me watching him and visibly startled. "I'm sorry! You said you were hungry. Do you want some?"

"No, thanks." I had to laugh at him even though my gut grumbled painfully. "No, I have the usual feminine fatty deposits to draw on."

He grubbed the remaining corn kernels out of the can with his finger to eat them, making sure he didn't miss a single one. Meanwhile, I felt insight forming. When Justin had set the empty corn can aside, I asked, "Did Stoat starve you?"

"Sometimes." He looked away from me. "Maybe you could find some food up front?"

While he rooted around the truck bed some more, I searched the cab, finding lottery tickets, old and new, cigarette butts in the drink holder, and a filthy greenish item lying on a seat like a road-killed turtle, actually a battered Maypop Goobers baseball cap. And country music CDs in the center console along with all the usual detritus: pennies, toothpicks, three cough drops, rubber bands, greasy terry cloth rags, and a stubby flashlight. With some vague idea it might prove useful, I stuck the flashlight into my shorts pocket, then continued pawing through the truck cab. In some fast-food rubbish on the floor I found a few stale french fries, which I ate with revulsion. With similar revulsion, but knowing what the sun could do to my unprotected face, I jammed

the greasy baseball hat onto my head. As an afterthought, I shoved
the cough drops into my mouth for the sake of the sugar in them.

Out of the cab and heading back toward Justin, I said, "Okay,
while we wait, let's use the fishing rods and those rubber
worms—"

Startled, he interrupted my hunger fantasy of food on the fin
in the swollen river. "Wait? What do you mean, wait?"

"Wait for these men to get back so they can take us to the police."

"We can't do that! What if Stoat—"

"We'll hear the van in plenty of time to hide. But if he was going to come here, he'd *be* here already, don't you think?"

"I think you're crazy! This is the first place Unc—Stoat is going to come, even if it's just to park the van!"

"Like I said, we'll hide. This blue truck is the first *vehicle* I've
seen in this godforsaken swamp and those two Bubbas in the boat
are the first *people* I've seen, and I'm not—"

Justin didn't hear me out. He turned and ran away.

"Wait till I leave them a *note* at least!" I screamed after him.

He showed no sign of hearing, but sprinted straight up the
weedy lane that ran down to the boat ramp.

Mail carrier Casey Fay Hummel pulled off the road and stopped at
the pink house's mailbox, which like all the rest of them faced in-
ward, with its back side to the road. Looked kind of weird to people who didn't come from around here, or so they said. Casey Fay
had lived in the area all her life, and having the mailbox face away
from the road made a lot more sense to her than having to stop on
the road to deliver or pick up mail. This way she pulled clear off
the pavement, nobody was likely to rear-end her, and she could sit

in the driver's seat, like a sane person, and put the mail into the box from there.

Huh. The new woman who lived in the pink house hadn't picked up her mail either Monday or yesterday, which was Tuesday. No big deal, just credit card applications. Casey Fay started to shove today's mail in on top—

Oops. Liana Clymer—or Leppo; judging by her mail, she seemed to go by both names—anyway, Liana had a big package that would not fit into the mailbox, something from Kookrite Kitchenware.

Retrieving the accumulated mail along with today's, Casey Fay steered onto the yard in front of the pink house—hardly anybody had "lawns" down here, let alone paved driveways; the whole world was for driving on. Well, except for pure swamp, but people didn't live there. Casey Fay stopped between two mimosa trees in front of the place where Liana Clymer lived, and beeped her horn.

She waited a minute, because rather than just dropping the mail at the door, she really wanted to have a look at the new woman who was renting the house where Old Lady Ingle had lived so many years before going into the nursing home. Like everybody else around here, Casey Fay kept track of, well, everybody. But if Liana Clymer/Leppo was a Yankee, maybe she thought honking your horn was rude and she wouldn't come to the door. The reason a little beep-beep was *not* rude was because it gave the person inside the house a chance to get some clothes on before somebody knocked on their door. Some people spent the summer days sitting butt naked in front of a fan, especially if they only had window air conditioners, when even central air couldn't keep up with the heat.

But the house door didn't open, so Casey Fay sighed, gathered all the mail plus the parcel, got out of her aging Chevy Cavalier, and walked up three wooden steps and across a small porch to the door.

Even before she knocked, she knew something was wrong. That strong odor, unmistakable. Something had died.

Why would anybody let something dead lie and stink in their house? Unless it was—the person herself?

Nose wrinkling, Casey Fay put the envelopes and the parcel into a transparent plastic bag she pulled from her pocket, knotted it to protect the contents against rain, then left the entire package on the porch by the door, as was policy when something wouldn't fit in the mailbox. Yet, after slowly retreating down the steps, she didn't leave. Not sure what she was looking for, she walked to the side windows and peeked in, seeing nothing except a shadowy bedroom. Still uneasy, she ventured around back—

Now, why in hell would anybody leave her car, in this case a metallic blue Toyota Matrix, parked in the backyard under the clothesline?

And if the car was here, why didn't the Clymer woman seem to be home? Unless she was lying dead inside the house . . .

Casey Fay knocked at the back door anyway, but when nobody opened it, she found she'd already made up her mind. She sure didn't like that smell coming from behind the front door. As she walked back to her old Chevy, she pulled out her cell phone and dialed 911.

ELEVEN

"Hey! Justin, damn it . . ." Given no choice—or it felt like no choice, as if Justin were a three-year-old chasing a rattlesnake and I were his mom—I ran after him.

I might never have caught up with him if it hadn't been for sandspurs. Those small weeds didn't look like much, but just as their name implied, they grew thick in sandy ground and had seeds that were—prickly was not the word. These things were vicious, like Mexican cowboy rowels.

"Ow!" Justin yelped, trying to run through them barefoot. Cursing fluently enough to show that he was indeed no longer the sweet little boy his parents remembered, he limped to a halt before he could reach the dirt road. He raised one foot to pull sandspurs out of it. Catching up with him, I glimpsed red; the little green devils had stuck him deep enough to draw blood. And he couldn't bear putting his weight on either foot for long. Swearing, he hopped from one to the other as if he were standing on hot coals.

"Sit down," I told him, trying to get hold of him somehow to help him ease the weight off his feet, but like a drowning person he grabbed me instead and nearly pulled me down with him. Yet his butt had barely touched the ground before he started protesting, "What if Stoat comes?"

It was a horribly real possibility with no solution. Sitting on the ground, I lifted one of Justin's feet into my lap and started pulling the sandspurs out of it with my fingernails as quickly as I could.

"What if he drove down here right now, what are we going to do?" Justin insisted.

"What if we're little pink seashells on a vast ocean beach and someone steps on us?" I grumbled, waxing existentialist at him. "What if the world is a flake of dandruff on a Titan's head, and he gets itchy?" I finished with one of his feet and grabbed the other. "Hold still!" I complained as he winced—whether from physical pain or from mental anguish, it was hard to tell. "What if Stoat the Goat *doesn't* drive down here right now?"

"You're loony," Justin said.

"Kierkegaard called it a leap of faith. Stay where you are a minute." Finished with his feet, I reached for my own to yank off my wet sneakers, then my equally soppy socks. "Put those on." I handed them to Justin.

"These?" He accepted them with two fingers. "How am I supposed to fit my feet into these?"

"However you can."

"They don't even reach past my heel," Justin complained, stretching my socks to their utmost.

I pushed my sneakers back onto my bare feet, but just as I started to stand up, I heard the growl of a vehicle approaching on the dirt road that passed not nearly far enough away from us. I lapsed back onto the ground, mutely terrified it might be Stoat.

Justin whimpered, "If they turn down here, they'll see us!"

Terror had made me memorize the sound of Stoat's van bone-marrow deep, and—I exhaled in relief—this vehicle wasn't it. "That's not Stoat," I said, lurching to my feet.

"Lee Anna, what're you *doing*?" Justin yelped.

I windmilled my arms. Trying to flag down some help for us, that's what I was doing, but the truck—spewing loud country music, it was one of those asinine jacked-up trucks with balls, literally, having a long antenna with tennis balls skewered on it arching over its cargo bed. Stained yellow by sand, ballsy whip bobbing, the overtall truck drove past the boat ramp entry without stopping.

To stifle a pang of hungry disappointment I said, "Well, at least now we know there are people back here."

"Who cares? We need to get out of here."

The restrained panic in Justin's voice echoed the fear I had felt when I heard the car, and helped me concede in my mind that we could not hang around to wait for the boating Bubbas to get back from Chipoluga Swamp. We were on the run from Stoat.

Looking back the way we had come, I noticed with dismay the clear prints of our feet in the sand. "Justin, may I borrow that knife you found?"

"Sure. Which blade?"

"Biggest."

He pried the blade into position with his thumbnail and handed the knife to me. "You're, like, really polite," he said as if I puzzled him. "If Uncle, um, Stoat wants something, he snaps his fingers."

"I noticed." I struggled to cut a low branch from a catalpa tree, succeeded, returned the knife to Justin, then backtracked to sweep the sand with it—catalpas, aka bean trees, have very broad leaves. My branch resembled a fan more than a broom, but did a pretty good job of erasing our tracks.

"Sweet," Justin remarked when I had made my way back to him.

"Like tupelo honey," I agreed. "Okay, let's go. Single file." He went first, and I followed, trailing the catalpa branch behind me.

Looking back, I saw to my satisfaction that my improvised drag was doing a pretty good job of erasing our footprints.

Weeds flourished around my ankles—wildflowers, really, and any other time I would have been exclaiming over their blossoms. But now all my attention was focused on listening for the sound of a certain vehicle approaching. Okay, Stoat was so anal that maybe he had reported to work and was putting screen prints of cats in bikinis on the front of T-shirts right now, in which case we had time. But what if he wasn't quite that anal? What if he was out here looking for us?

Still, we reached the dirt road safely and turned left, away from where Stoat would enter. Justin didn't need foot protection on the smooth, sandy road. Standing on one leg to pull off a pink sock, he remarked, "I feel like a flamingo."

He made me smile. "Okay, flamingo, keep walking."

"Just a minute." Balling my socks into his pockets, Justin deployed his knife and cut himself a tree branch to drag. Side by side, we hiked onward at the quickest pace I could manage.

Any other time I would have been fascinated, crossing the most rudimentary of wooden bridges and looking down between the boards at minnows, frogs, maybe a baby alligator in the water below, passing forests that were not forests, seeing the still green sheen of swamp water between trunks shaped like tepees. But under the circumstances all I could think was that we had to keep moving, find some kind of sanctuary before Stoat found us. Silent, we listened for the cough of the white van, or for any crackle of brush or outcry of birds in the muted midday swamp.

Time passed without any alarm. I decided to speak.

"You okay?" I asked Justin, wanting input but not wanting to ask the specific questions on my mind: How do you feel about me? Will you listen to me or do you think I am a pain? How about what I'm trying to accomplish, which is getting you home; are we on the same page at all?

Understandably puzzled by my question, Justin stared at me. "Okay? Compared to what?"

"Compared to yesterday or the day before."

"I am, like, floating, it feels so good to be away from Unc—uh, you know. I guess I sort of never saw how bad it was until I got away."

"Are you looking forward to calling your parents when we get out of here?"

Silence.

"Justin?"

Without turning to look at me, he said, "I kind of wish we could just be like this forever."

"Like what?"

"Like, just kind of be lost in the middle of nowhere. Walking in the sun. I don't care that I'm tired and hungry. That gives me something to think about, so it's okay, okay? I don't want to think about my parents yet."

"Okay," I lied, feeling a dark cloud sail into my personal sunny day. I did care that I was tired and hungry. I cared quite a bit.

And I cared about getting Justin back to his parents whether that was what he thought he wanted or not. I cared enormously.

But I'd deal with that once we got, quite literally, out of the woods.

If we got out. If Stoat didn't find us first.

"Oliver," said Ned Bradley to his dog, "dip me in cream and throw me to the kittens. I'll be licked."

He had been saying this, or variations of it, and walking around his apartment in circles ever since he had received the phone call from his son telling him that he was ditching work and driving up to Birmingham to see him. This had never happened before. In fact, he hadn't actually laid eyes on Chad in years.

"Laid eyes on." Odd expression. As if seeing were like touching, like the laying on of hands. Like a blessing.

Which was what Chad needed, the way Ned figured. He intuited that Chad was badly upset to be coming anywhere near him. He guessed he was Chad's last hope of—of something. An anchor. A family.

"What have we got to eat?" Ned crouched to confer with his dog nose to nose. "Or drink? Jeez, I wish I could offer him a beer." But Ned didn't have any beer in the fridge or whiskey in the cupboard. There was still time for him to run out and get some, but Chad would never believe Ned didn't keep it around all the time, that it was just for his visit.

Ned stood up to stare at his Tree of Life tapestry, telling himself that his son had every right to suspect the worst of him. It was up to him to prove to Chad that he was really, truly no longer drinking.

Snacks, then. What could he put together for snacks?

He was just about to head for the kitchen when the doorbell rang.

Heart thumping, Ned strode over and pressed the intercom. "Yes?"

"Dad." Ned thought this sounded curiously monotone, even for a single syllable.

"I'll be down." Chad had never been to the apartment and might have some difficulty finding it, so rather than just buzz him in, Ned headed for the elevator and pressed *G* for ground floor.

When the elevator doors opened, he got his first glimpse of his son standing behind a plate glass door. One look, and he could tell Chad was an emergency on feet. He wore his Dixieland Trucking uniform with his oval name patch on the shirt; he really had been driving to work when suddenly he couldn't go on. When Ned opened the door, Chad walked in without offering to hug or even shake hands. His face looked as hard and flat as his voice, saying, "Which way?"

"Tenth floor." Ned didn't try to make small talk in the elevator, even though the silence felt thick enough to choke him. Chad didn't speak until he got into the apartment and Oliver, fuzzy ears flapping, ran to meet them.

"Hey, dog!" Chad dropped to one knee to greet Oliver with both hands. "What's his name?"

"Oliver. Because he always wants more."

"I know how that is." Chad sounded morose again. "Where's your bathroom?"

Ned pointed the way. "Have a seat," he offered after Chad had returned. "Iced tea?"

Chad slumped on the sofa. "No, thanks."

"Something to eat?"

Chad shook his head.

"Winning Lotto tickets? Five thousand bucks a day for life?"

Although Chad didn't smile, he did focus on his father in a guarded way. Ned sat down on the chair closest to his son and said as neutrally as he could, "What's the matter?"

"Nothing."

"Bullshit."

"It's nothing, Dad!"

His tone kept Ned at a distance but not Oliver. He sat his furry butt in front of Chad, peering up at him with liquid-eyed canine concern. Chad glanced at the dog and quickly looked away again.

Ned coaxed, "Come on, son. You don't drive three hours for nothing. Why are you here?"

Chad puffed his lips in exasperation before saying, "I felt like, if I went to work, I'd punch somebody."

"Angry at the whole world, huh?" Ned let sympathy into his voice, but not too much. Chad wouldn't have liked too much. "What about if you went home to Amy?"

"She doesn't deserve to have me always pissed at her."

"But you are."

"Yes, goddamn it! If she'd just let go about Justin—"

Chad broke off, looking awkward.

Ned coaxed, "Go on. If Amy would just let go about Justin, then what?"

"Then—damn it, I don't know! But she won't, and I'm thinking about divorce, and it's your fault."

Chad had become loud enough to make Oliver change his mind about sitting in front of him. The dog retreated.

"Aahhh," said Ned to fill the moment it took him to process what Chad had said. "I understand." This was true. "You've brought your anger to me—"

"Well, if you hadn't left Mom and me, none of this would have happened!"

Ned accepted this absurd accusation without blinking. "You never had a chance to tell me off, did you?"

"No, and I don't want to."

"Yes, you do." Ned stood up. "You want to hit me."

"No, I *don't*."

"Yes, you do, Picklepuss." As a little boy, Chad had always hated to be called Picklepuss when he was having a snit fit. "Come on, snootface." He'd always hated that too. Ned picked up a sofa pillow by the corner and swung it at Chad's head.

That was all it took. Instantly the boy—no, a strong man now—was on his feet charging him like a bull with fists. Sidestepping, Ned grabbed a big square cushion from the sofa and deployed it like a shield. Chad's fist thudded into it.

"Ow," Ned said, more in acknowledgment than in mockery.

"Shut up!"

Ned did not shut up. "Ow," he repeated, "ow, ow, ow," as Chad punched the sofa cushion again and again. Ned noticed that Oliver was nowhere to be seen; most likely he was hiding under the bed. Sensible dog. Chad kept punching, harder and harder, but always at Ned's protective shield rather than at Ned himself. Watching his son closely, Ned saw trickles of sweat on his flushed forehead. Then, panting, Chad bent over with his hands on his knees.

Ned allowed him only a short rest. "More," he coached. "This time for the bastard who stole Justin."

"Fucking hell!" Chad slammed his fist into the cushion-cum-punching-bag, shouting profanities as he hammered, attacked, assaulted, hitting even harder than before. "Goddamn everything!" Once again he wore himself out and stopped, panting for breath.

"Any for Amy?" Ned asked, hoping he already knew the answer.

Chad shook his head hard and turned away. His anger at Amy didn't run very deep, then. Good. Ned put the cushion back on the sofa where it belonged. With his back turned, it took him a moment to realize that his son's labored breathing had turned to sobs.

"Hey! Chad, it's okay." Hurrying to him, Ned tried to put his arms around him.

Chad pulled away.

"Goddamn," Ned complained, "let me be a good father for once in my life, would you?" He hugged his son, and this time Chad let his head rest on his father's shoulder, let Ned rub his quaking back with his dry old hands. "It'll be okay."

"I don't see how." Chad straightened and stood back.

Ned handed him a box of Kleenex, then headed to the kitchen and came back with two tall glasses of iced tea that might as well have been an energy drink, there was so much sugar in it. Good and proper Alabama sweet tea. He handed Chad his, and they both sat down. They sipped. Chad wasn't looking at him. Ned gave him some time to regroup.

After the minutes had passed, he started making small talk. How old were the twins now, how were they doing in school, what did they like to do outside of school? Pretty soon he had Chad facing him, telling him Kyle was building a skateboard ramp in the backyard and Kayla liked to draw those big-eyed pointy-faced Japanese cartoon pictures. He described Kayla as popular but running with the right kind of kids and Kyle as more individualistic, having a few good friends. Ned watched Chad's face become more relaxed, sometimes even smiling, as he talked. He was careful not to mention Amy, not yet. After a while he turned on the TV, and under pretense of watching tennis, he and Chad both napped, Ned in the recliner with Oliver on his lap, Chad on the sofa. Ned saw Chad nodding off, and smiled to himself; good. Chad had to be feeling less angry, less tense, if he could sleep. Ned allowed himself to doze from sheer weariness; he had worked the night before.

After they had snoozed the afternoon away, they went out for supper at a steak house. Ned encouraged Chad to have a beer, asked him about his job, talked baseball with him, and tried not to show quite how much Chad's presence meant to him. He knew what he had to do, and he wasn't looking forward to it.

He waited until they were back in the apartment and had found Chad the stuff he needed in order to spend the night on the sofa. He waited until they sat down again and were talking some more.

He started small. "Is Amy still working at that nursing home?"

"No." Chad's tone turned curt, and watching his face, Ned thought of shutters closing over a window. "No, she doesn't have time for anything except trying to find our son."

"That one time I met Amy, she seemed like a good woman," Ned ventured.

"Good? She's so damn good I can't begin to keep up with her. She's dedicated her life to finding our son, and I—" Chad turned his face away, and his voice rasped. "Sometimes I hate myself, but I have got the shits of the whole thing."

"Nothing wrong with that. However you feel is how you feel."

"That's Zen, Dad," said Chad sarcastically.

"Whatever. Are you and Amy getting along together at all?"

"No."

"Sleeping together?"

"No."

"Are you and she equally pissed at each other?"

"I—actually, no, I don't think she's really pissed, but she won't cut me a break either."

"When's the last time you had some fun?"

"*Fun?*"

"Good time. Joy in life."

"With Justin gone?"

"You want to move on, right? When's the last time you had a vacation?"

"Vacation? What's that?"

Ned ignored the sarcasm. "When's the last time you went someplace?"

"Back before—back when we still had Justin, we took the kids to Disney World."

Ned refrained from snorting like a horse. "That's not what I mean. When's the last time you and Amy went someplace together? Just the two of you?"

Chad actually turned his head to look at him, a bit wide-eyed. "I don't recall ever doing that since the kids were born."

"Well, it's high time you did."

"We can't."

"Why not?"

"We're broke. We can't afford it."

Ned said, "You can't afford not to."

"Dad, get real."

"I am real. A trip to get you two started working things out would be a heck of a lot cheaper than a divorce."

"I can't just take off work."

"Why not? You already did. You're here, aren't you?"

"Well, I can't tear Amy away from her self-appointed job looking for Justin."

"Have you asked her nicely?"

Chad rolled his eyes. "What does it matter? We can't just leave the kids."

"Sure you can. Their grandpa will take care of them." Then, as Chad gawked at him without apparent comprehension, Ned added, "Me."

TWELVE

For me the day became a haze of hurry hurry hurry, trapped on a narrow serpentine of road in a jungle of dusky trees and things, whether animal, vegetable, or mineral, that bit. With my innards cramped by hunger, my skin in a mess of itchy lumps and bloody scratches, and Stoat a dark and evil goat-demon looming ever larger in my mind, I walked as fast as I could. Justin lagged a bit behind me. Given his longer legs and more resilient youth, this made no sense except in terms of ambivalence. He wasn't nearly as ready for his future, or as anxious to have one, as I was.

But there was nothing I could do about him except keep hustling and hoping for any kind of sanctuary or assistance. I had thought it would be simple to flag somebody down, but not a single vehicle had come our way since the dust-coated monstrosity of a pickup I had failed to alert. We had walked for several miles, yet I had not seen any human habitation, not even a trailer.

Sunlight slanted low through the moss and mistletoe of the treetops. If Stoat was not already on the hunt for us, he had come home from work by now and would be soon.

"Hey," Justin said, breaking a long silence, "what do you think's back here? I mean, besides mosquitoes?"

I lifted my despairing stare from the ground and looked. By "back here" he referred to a very overgrown track heading off the dirt road. No sandy ruts, just wildflowers. Okay, weeds.

"I have no idea, but we're going to find out," I said, immediately wading into the knee-high jungle. "Anything to get out of plain sight. Ow," I added as I encountered a bull thistle. "Put your socks on."

He did so and followed me. The grass and weeds, I noticed, looked bent or flattened where we had swished through them or stepped on them. I went back and whacked the verdure with my catalpa branch until I'd achieved a sort of parity, either flattening everything or making some of it spring back up. Justin picked a path forward while I walked backward, flailing away.

He started to laugh. "You look insane!"

"What makes you think I'm not?"

"Gimme the branch." Interesting that he had managed to lose his own. "I'll do it."

"Why? You want to look insane?" I had to smile as I handed him the catalpa branch.

"Just trying to lend a hand," he said in a manly tone. Back turned, swinging his new weapon as I led the way, Justin called, "Watch for snakes, Miss Lee Anna."

The "Miss," I knew by now, was a Southern honorific, usually affectionate but sometimes patronizing.

"Just call me Lee," I responded.

Typical of myself, I had chosen the oddest moment to decide that I did not want to be Liana the clinging vine ever again. Miss Lee of the Jungle, I stalked along, watching for snakes.

And seeing them. They sure grew big down here, all different kinds and colors, their thick coils pressing down the springy grass. Big and lazy, reluctant to relinquish the sun after too much chilling rain, they generally slipped away like water down a drain when I got close enough to really look at them. But a few played possum. One of these, a large but harmless gray and white oak snake, I grasped firmly around the middle, lifting it and taking possession of it.

I did this on impulse. When I was a little girl, I had often captured turtles, frogs, caterpillars, praying mantises, and, yes, snakes, to keep for a few hours, just long enough to get acquainted with them before I put them back where I had found them. My mother approved; she had helped me look up the various species in her twelve-volume nature encyclopedia. But my ex-husband, who didn't seem to like anything about nature, went postal if I so much as touched a hoppy-toad, vehemently insisting that I wash my hands at once, as if I were plotting to poison him with critter cooties. So I had been away from my truer self for a long time.

The oak snake came with me so docilely it felt almost as if he or she were welcoming me back. It tucked its head into the comforting cave of my shorts pocket, while the rest of it wrapped around my waist.

I walked on, and the next snake I saw, as if to restore antithesis to my life's dialectic, was a cottonmouth as thick as my arm, a snake only God the mother of us all could love. It reared its mud-colored head and gaped the puffy white lining of its mouth at me, threatening to use its fangs even though I stood a good ten feet away.

I called, "Justin, bring the stick, would you?"

He did, and by repeatedly swooshing the moccasin with its leafy end, he discomfited it enough so that it departed to find a more peaceful place. "Better stand still awhile till we're sure it's not coming at us," he said.

We did stand still, and the late afternoon light cast long shadows, and I noticed that the grassy way through the swamp we had been following, the opening between trees barely worthy to be called a lane, had broadened into a wider clearing. Was it ending? If so, why?

Before I had realized what I should start looking for, Justin spotted it. "Hey! There's a little fishing cabin under the live oaks!"

"Where?" I saw nothing at first. When he pointed it out, I understood why. I would not have called it a cabin, or even a shack; it was barely a shanty. Its gray and splintered never-painted planks blended into the swamp woods and the shade of the live oaks that stooped over it. Judging by the weeds everywhere, no one lived here or had been here for some time. Although a rickety gray outhouse stood by, the place seemed barely habitable overnight. Very likely we would find rats in there, and mice, and maybe snakes. But for me, and I thought I could speak for Justin too, only one thing mattered: was there by any chance some food?

Maypop County sheriff's deputy Bernardo "Bernie" Morales caught the call regarding a suspicious stench at a rental property on the state road north. Maypop PD took calls only in town; the Sheriff's Office took care of the county, and what the Staters did, Bernie often wondered.

Bernie had responded to many such calls, and usually they involved dead fish left under the front steps as a prank. Without hurry, he drove to the address in his much-abused old cruiser, which in his birthplace—Chile, South America—would have been called by an insulting name insinuating that it was a latrine on wheels. Although he was the only Latino cop in Maypop County, Bernie did not think of himself as Hispanic, but rather as a Chileno citizen of the U.S.A. Like many of his friends in the Chilean army, after discharge Bernie had gone on a work visa to Orlando, Florida, kingdom of a cartoon mouse and many good jobs. His plan had been to save his money, go home to Chile, buy a taxi, and be rich. Instead, too many beautiful gringas had spent his money for him, until he had fallen in love with Tammy Lou Steverson.

Tammy Lou was just passing through Orlando. Her home, her family, her roots, were in Maypop, Florida. Bernie had moved there to court her, working for McDonald's until he had married her, and they had lived there ever since. An uncle of Tammy Lou's served as a deputy in the Sheriff's Office. As soon as Bernie had obtained his citizenship papers, he had begun to do likewise. Now a balding, slightly overweight man who could have passed for an Italian if it were not for his accent, Bernie had grown to love the job. It seldom bored him, and sometimes it gave him a chance to help someone.

Pulling off the road at the address he had been given, Bernie blinked and shook his head at the gaudiness of the small house's neon pink paint job. But the moment he opened his car door to get out, the odor that assaulted his nostrils took up all his attention. He frowned. This was no mere case of dead fish.

There was no need to draw a weapon, he decided; whatever had happened here was in the past tense. Still, it would be better, he decided, to enter the pink house some way other than by the front door, where the odor stank strongest and where, he noted, a package had been left in a plastic bag by the mail carrier who had called this in. Ducking under mimosa trees, he walked around back, stopping to stare at the Toyota parked out of sight of the road and out of place; what was it doing there?

He tried the kitchen door, unsurprised when the knob turned in his hand. In the Maypop area, most people locked the front door to let friends know they were not home, but left the back one unlocked in case somebody needed to get in.

Bernie entered. He did not pull his gun to point it various directions while yelling "Police!" He just walked in.

What he noticed first in the kitchen was how the things on the table—saltshakers, napkin holder, a pink pottery catchall bowl, bottles of stool softener and Tylenol and Tums—how everything stood exactly centered, like soldiers ranked along an imaginary line. Yet in the sink he saw a heap of dirty, messily stacked dishes with bugs and cobwebs on them. Cobwebs on dishes—that said something. The dishes looked slimy, and they stank.

But something else smelled far worse. Proceeding to the living room, Bernie found an unpleasantly dead dog on the carpet near the door. It looked like it had been a miniature dachshund, poor little thing, somebody's pet.

This was not good.

Bending over it, careful not to touch, Bernie counted three bullet wounds.

So where was the gun?

Standing up, Bernie took a look around the room. He saw no weapon. Which was not a surprise, because Bernie very much doubted that the woman who lived here had shot her own pet and left it lying on the carpet.

Still scanning the living room, Bernie noticed that all the books and magazines on the coffee table and the sofa's end table were stacked exactly on top of one another, corners aligned, according to size.

Also he saw from marks in the carpet that the furniture had been moved. Straightened.

He shook his head and went to investigate his doubts, checking out the bedroom. There he found an unmade bed. And in the bathroom, talcum powder covered everything like that north Florida rarity, a thin snowfall.

Bernie recalled the report: the mail carrier said a single woman named Liana Clymer, aka Liana Leppo, lived here. The flowery sheets in the bedroom, the cosmetics in the bathroom, and the Hello Kitty artwork on the walls tended to confirm this. The kitchen sink plus the bedroom and bathroom showed she didn't care much about keeping things orderly. So who had rearranged the kitchen table, straightened the furniture, and put the mail-order catalogs in tidy stacks?

An intruder?

The same intruder who had shot the dog?

A compulsively tidy person who had let the dog bleed to death on the carpet?

Shaking his head, Bernie started muttering to himself in Spanish, as he often did when something stank figuratively even more than literally. Where was the woman who was supposed to live here, and why had she left her dog to rot? He needed to contact her or someone who knew her.

Bernie roamed the small house, pulling out drawers and checking shelves, searching for more information. Old enough to remember how things used to be, Bernie missed address books, landline telephones with important numbers posted next to them, piles of snail mail. What he needed to find was the Clymer woman's cell phone or, better yet, her handbag with a cell phone in it.

He found neither purse nor phone.

Which caused him to say something particularly profane in Spanish, because what the hell was going on? The Clymer woman took her purse and went somewhere, but without her car, and leaving her dog dead on the floor?

Bernie had reached the point at which he should have left the scene, gone to file a Missing Persons report, and turned it over to the chief sheriff. What happened after that would be none of his business.

What was most likely to happen was nothing. This woman had

no kin in Maypop to pressure for an investigation. It was no crime for adults to go missing.

Still swearing in his favorite language for that purpose, Bernie decided to fix one thing at least. He opened the front door, took what the mail carrier had left, and put it inside, so that it would not advertise the emptiness of the house. Then, not yet satisfied, Bernie headed back into the bedroom, where he had seen a laptop computer.

He booted it up, knees jiggling with guilty impatience as he sat on a chair that was too small for him. The laptop hummed into beaming compliance, requiring no password. Bernie invoked the Internet symbol, then the e-mail envelope. Again, no need for a password; it seemed Liana Clymer stayed logged on. Bernie searched her contacts list for people with the names Clymer or Leppo. There were several. He addressed a single e-mail to all of them, scowling as he struggled to compose a suitable message:

> Hello family of Liana Clymer, aka Liana Leppo. This is Deputy Bernardo Morales of the Maypop County (Florida) Sheriff's Office contacting you. I have been alerted by a mail carrier that Liana seems to be missing from her residence. She seems to have been gone for several days as there is a dachshund dead of bullet wounds and decaying in her living room, her car is parked out of sight in the backyard, and her purse and car keys

Bernie stopped to think, then saved the draft, headed out into the backyard, and tried the Toyota's driver's side door. It was locked. Shading his face from the sun with his hands, he peered in through the window, then went around to the passenger side and tried again. He saw no keys in the ignition or anywhere else. Satisfied, he walked back into the pink house and resumed his e-mail.

purse and car keys are unaccounted for. I will file a Missing Under Suspicious Circumstances report but beyond that I have no duty or authority. It is not in my job description to write this e-mail but where I come from it would be considered the honorable thing to do. How you respond is of course your business and not mine.

Sincerely,
Deputy Bernardo Morales

He added the Sheriff's Office's phone number, complete with area code, paused to think again whether he might get in trouble about this, then shrugged and clicked Send. Tammy Lou, still after twenty years the love of his life, told him often that he had a bigger heart than any other man she had ever met. Bernie considered this meant he was a true Chileno. By sending the e-mail, he had maybe broken a rule, but before being a deputy of the sheriff he was first a caballero, a gentleman.

THIRTEEN

"Make sure you hide all of our tracks," I told Justin, heading toward the pitiful hut we had found.

"Make sure you watch out for snakes," Justin retorted.

"Like this one?" Pausing, gently I unwound one end of the oak snake from around my waist and coaxed the other end out of my shorts pocket. As I held her up, she hung between my hands in a catenary curve like an overly thick, gray and white telephone wire.

Justin's jaw sagged. I realized I was showing off and tried to retract.

"You're not afraid of snakes," I stated, matter-of-fact, lowering my own specimen. "Not the way you took care of that cottonmouth that was looking up my nose."

He succeeded in moving his mouth, forming speech. "What are you going to do with that?"

"With *her*." Actually, no way could I tell the snake's gender, so I chose one. "Her name is Hypatia the Wise. If you don't mind, I'll take her inside to chase the mice away." The oak snake flicked its tongue, then oozed up my arm and into my T-shirt sleeve.

"Where is she going right now?" Justin inquired innocently.

"Ha-ha." Turning my back to preserve some dignity, I carried Hypatia to the shanty. Or hut. Whatever. Rudimentary and rotting. No problem opening the door; the knob and lock had long since fallen out of it. But I couldn't see a thing inside, it was so dark. I pulled out the flashlight I had toted all the way from the blue pickup truck, clicked it on, and used its rather dim beam to reconnoiter. I saw mouse turds, mostly, and scuttling toward the shadows were some of those huge insects euphemistically called palmetto roaches, a cockroach by another name, still icky all the same. I saw no snakes but did not doubt there might be some underneath the few furnishings. These consisted of a picnic table in the middle of the splintery plank floor and a bunk bed standing against the rickety wall, the mattresses wrapped in thick plastic so the mice wouldn't get into them, I surmised. Hefty Rubbermaid containers stacked in one corner probably served the same purpose, to protect the contents from varmints.

A deer mouse, not to be confused with a dear mouse, scuttled out from under one of the bunk beds and dived into some firewood stacked beside an honest-to-God potbellied stove. I carried Hypatia over there and set her down on the floor, exhorting her, "Enjoy." An oak snake, after all, is just a fancy-colored rat snake by another name.

Next, with my heart beating a little faster than before, I pried open the Rubbermaid containers.

Acute disappointment. The containers protected blankets and candles, not food.

There were no kitchen cupboards or counter space. No kitchen sink. What did the people who used this place do for water, let alone food?

Ah. I saw a screen door, much patched, leading to the backyard jungle, and toward the near side of the jungle stood an old-fashioned water pump.

I barely noticed the gallon plastic milk jug squatting on the floor inside the screen door. The flashlight battery seemed to be dying just in time for dark. Quickly I scanned the back steps in case of snakes other than Hypatia, then the floor under the picnic table and under the lower bunk—

I shrieked. Justin burst in at a run. "What? What's wrong?"

"What's *right*!" My flashlight had picked up words in thick black marker—CANNED GOODS. Plunging to my knees, I laid the flashlight on the floor and began pulling out flat cardboard boxes crowded with cans and jars. "Peanut butter! Do you like peanut butter, Justin?"

"At this point, who cares? Give it here!"

"Wash your hands first." Oh, how childbearing doth make mothers of us all.

"How? Should I spit on them?"

"Try the pump."

Then I had to show him how to prime the pump with the water in the plastic milk jug, left there for that purpose. As he scooped peanut butter with a relatively clean finger, the flashlight began to fade so rapidly I turned it off. It was getting dark outside, so I couldn't read the labels on the cans that I was hauling out from under the bunk. Then I remembered the candles I had seen in the Rubbermaid containers, and with them I found, along with a black marker, a dish towel, and some other things, matches.

That simply, like a butterfly fluttering its wings in India, the evening reversed itself and became nearly festive. By the light of candles stuck into the chinks of the picnic table, Justin and I used his handy-dandy multipurpose tool to open cans of Vienna sausage (which I loathed, but he wolfed down like a puppy), stewed tomatoes, baked beans, mixed vegetables, sauerkraut—at this point almost anything edible looked good, and wonder of wonders,

I found some Pringles! An acceptable starch on which to load the other things and gulp them down.

While Hypatia traced contented serpentines all over the cabin, Justin and I ate hard and fast. After we had gorged, we belched nearly in unison, laughed, and sat back to look at each other.

"You feel better?" we both asked at the same time, then laughed again.

This was, of course, too good to last. Every movie I had ever seen told me the bad guy should arrive this instant when we were off guard. I said, "We ought to douse the candles."

I saw a quick shadow of understanding cross Justin's face almost as if I had taken the black marker and written "STOAT" there. He nodded, yet said, "Before we do that, could you cut these Goldilocks cornrows and braids off of me?"

"You don't like them?"

"God, no, I hate them!"

"Stoat the Goat's idea, to draw attention to your hair and not your face, right?"

"Right." He handed me his pocket tool opened to rudimentary scissors. "He even made me dye my eyebrows."

"Now, that's extreme." As quickly as I could, listening all the time for the sound of any vehicle approaching in the night, I started shearing his bleached hair, proceeding at first around the base of his skull. As plaits of hair dropped away from the back of his neck, I saw two marks that wrenched my stomach.

Trying not to sound as sick as I felt, I asked, "What are these, cigarette burns?"

"Stun gun tracks. From when he first knocked my bike down and hauled me into his van."

Little kid. Stun gun.

"That consummate bastard," I said.

"Overkill," Justin agreed. "But effective. I didn't even try to run when he got me home."

"And *then* what did the son of a bitch do?"

He told me a little bit about it, not too much, and I did not press him with questions. By the time I'd cropped his dreads off, he'd fallen silent. I started on the cornrows, which were more difficult to cut off. After I'd been yanking and tugging for a good time, Justin complained, "Ow."

"It'll be worse than ow if we don't get our butts to the police station." I kept hacking, piling shorn yellow hair onto the table. Finished at last, I jammed the grubby green baseball cap onto him. "Wow. You look completely different." Then, quickly, I blew out the candles and at once felt safer.

Justin's voice spoke to me out of the darkness. "Lee, I don't want to go to any cops."

Damnation, I'd hoped we'd gotten past his hang-up, whatever it was. "Why aren't you in a lather to get home?"

Silence. I flicked on the flashlight, and in its feeble remaining illumination I saw an answer of sorts in his face. He looked down, then to the side, then turned away from the light.

More gently I asked, "Justin, what are you ashamed of? Nothing's your fault."

"Yes, it is!"

"Like what?"

"Like you said yourself, I could have called 911, or I could have told a teacher anytime I was in school, and—and now that I'm away from Stoat, I don't know why I didn't! I'm worthless. I—"

"Stop that, Justin. You got drawn into an appalling situation, that's all, and you dealt with it the best you could. You have to remember you're a good guy. You're a hero. You saved my life."

"But I let my parents down for two years. I'm a coward."

"No, you're a survivor. Lots of captured people do what you did."

"Sure they do."

"No, it's true. In order to go on living, people adapt to brutal situations and accept them as normal." Belatedly, my brain offered me the name on a platter. "It's called Stockholm syndrome," I told him as if having a labeled disorder might help him.

I think for a moment it did. He stopped looking at the ground; he looked at me instead. "You serious?"

"Yes. Totally."

He stared at me for a while before he asked, "So you think my parents will forgive me?"

"Justin, there's nothing to forgive! The whole world will welcome you back."

"Okay, but everybody will want to know—they'll ask questions—especially the cops." He sounded panicky. "Lee, I can't face it."

"Face what?"

"Just for starters, my—where he hurt me, Lee—I'm going to need to see a doctor."

"Not your fault. Are you scared?"

"Mostly embarrassed."

"If I got raped and needed a doctor, should I be embarrassed?"

"Lee, that didn't ever really happen, did it?"

Yes, it had. College. Date rape, although I didn't have sense enough to call it that at the time, and I hadn't reported the prick who did it, either. But this mustn't be about me. "It happens to one in every four women," I said. "Should we be embarrassed?"

"No! That's horrible!"

"Exactly. Horrible is the word. What else did that effing pervert do to you?"

Silence, and I thought I'd lost him, but finally he said very softly, "He—my body hair—he's been making me Nair myself all over. Even, you know, down there."

Unexpected, that hit me in the gut. I banged the table with my fist. "That total creep!"

"He wanted a little kid. He was going to find one soon. Replace me. You think I'm such a hero, listen to this: I snuck the baseball bat into the van because I was pretty sure that when he went to kill you, he was fixing to kill me too. Like, that letter you wrote, that was a farce. He would never have let me mail it. Which told me I wasn't going to live to mail it."

"I know," I said, my voice low.

"You know?" His adolescent voice creaked up an octave.

"I figured. Why would he bring you along to be a witness to murder? He meant to kill you too, and you're smart enough, you knew it."

"Kind of. I knew yet I kind of didn't know. Am I crazy?"

"Nope. You were just in denial. I've been there myself." I thought of the five wasted years before the divorce. Georg running around, chasing skirts, looking for his missing *e*. I had thought it was just his midlife crisis. Crapola. I should have dumped him before he dumped me. Way before.

In a very low voice Justin said, "I could have got away once he let me start going to school. Just a phone call. Now I feel like a total coward."

"Hell, no. It was incredibly brave, what you did, whacking him with that baseball bat to save me. To save *us*."

"But what if you hadn't come along? What am I supposed to tell people when they ask me why I didn't try to escape?"

"Tell them they should just try it once. Try being kidnapped by a psycho. Try being immobilized by a stun gun and raped and beaten and starved and chained to a bed and afraid of dying any minute."

Silence again. I kept my lips pressed shut to keep from saying any more. Thousands of his self-esteems could have danced on the head of a pin. The decision to contact his parents was one he had to make himself, if at all possible.

Bleakly Justin said, "Nobody's ever going to understand."

"*I* understand."

"And that's why I want to stay with you, Lee. Can't I just stay with you? I don't want to go home yet!"

"Stay with me? I don't know where I'm staying myself!"

"Here! What's wrong with right here?"

"How long?"

"Long enough for my hair to grow out." The flashlight beam was too dim to show me, but I bet he blushed. "The hair on my head, I mean."

"Justin, we can't risk it. What if Stoat finds us?"

"I just need a few days—"

"Justin, I can't handle a few days." It was no use; I had to take charge. "We have to get you to the cops. Tomorrow."

He blurted, "But they're gonna think I'm a faggot."

"No, they won't think any such thing. They'll understand."

"Lee, there's no way in hell *anybody* will ever understand what it's been like for me."

"Nobody ever understands anybody completely. But your parents love you." I pressed more than I should have. "You can't possibly understand what they've been going through, missing you, searching for you. They love you so much. That's all that matters. Don't you love them, Justin?"

Too late I remembered I was talking to a kid who, in addition to being terribly damaged, was a teenager. But he didn't roll his eyes, just narrowed them, wincing. "Look, can't we just go to sleep now?"

"Oh. Um." I realized I'd gone too far. "Sure, excellent idea."

Maybe in the morning he'd be more able to deal with his situation.

The dying flashlight helped us grab blankets out of the Rubbermaid containers. We took turns using the very primitive outhouse. Then Justin kicked off his pink socks and headed for the top bunk. "Good night," I told him.

He didn't answer. Typical kid. I took the flashlight with me to the bottom bunk, turned it off, lay on my side almost in the fetal position, nestled under my blanket, and tried to relax. I was so physically exhausted, this wasn't as impossible as it should have been. Within minutes, Justin and I were both asleep—or so I thought.

"Now, tickle my grits—just look at this."

The loud and unpleasantly familiar voice plus the glare of a Maglite in my eyes startled me from a deep sleep into—I wished it were just a nightmare.

Lying flat on my back in the flashlight's glare amid utter nighttime darkness, I could see only that the man steadied a long gun with his other hand, a double-barreled shotgun pointed at me. His head appeared only as a bobbing shadow, but by his gloating voice I knew well enough who he was: the bogeyman in person. Stoat. Come to get me. Us. Justin in the bunk above me—

At the thought of Justin, adrenaline bolted through me so that I reacted like lightning. Feeling Hypatia's weight coiled atop the warmth of my midsection, I grabbed the snake and flung her into Stoat's face.

He screeched and staggered back, arms flailing so that his Maglite showed me only mad flashes of shotgun out of control and snake convulsing as it fell. On my feet, I yelled, "Justin. Justin!" and grabbed at the top bunk where he should have been as the shotgun went off with a blast that traumatized my ears and my heart; what could Stoat be shooting if not the boy? "Justin!" My arms searching the top bunk found it flat and empty. Where was Justin? In a panic to find him and run from Stoat, I slewed around to look, then stood paralyzed by what I saw.

The Maglite lay on the floor, showing me Stoat with a contorted face and his shotgun shaking in his hands. He aimed the shotgun toward a biggish snake writhing at his feet, but it was not Hypatia. Its crisp markings, diamonds running down its spine, identified it unmistakably as a rattler. So did the raised, quivering tip of its tail, although I could barely hear it buzz through the clamor in my ears.

"The fucker *bit* me!" Stoat yelped, sounding incredulous just before his shotgun roared again, the second barrel blowing the rattlesnake into bits. Then, visibly shaken, he raised his unlovely face to glare at me. For the gray man that he was, he looked unusually white, and I didn't think it was the spotlight effect in the darkness. On his hollow cheek above his goatee, paired puncture wounds and trickles of blood showed garishly red against his pallor. He clenched his long yellow teeth as he said, "You threw a *rattlesnake* at me and it bit me."

"I'm sorry, I didn't realize!" I responded with spontaneous, genuine contrition. "You'd better sit down."

"The hell I will. Where's Justin?"

"I wish I knew!" Then, top volume, I called to the night, "Justin!" before I realized how stupid I was being, summoning him to where Stoat would kill him.

Or maybe not. Staggering to the back door, Stoat doubled over, vomiting.

I grabbed the Maglite and darted out the front door, running for my life yet yelling, "Justin? Justin!" because I didn't want to leave him behind. I tried to scan with the Maglite as I ran. The beam jumped like a demented flea but did show me something big and white: Stoat's van, left where he had stopped it in the middle of the tall grass. I surmised that he had rolled it down the hill with the engine and headlights off. Please, I mentally begged some unknown deity. Please, if only he had left the keys in it. I sprinted over to it and yanked at the driver's side door handle.

It didn't open.

With desperate, illogical persistence I shone the Maglite inside, pressing my face against the window to see the ignition. Like it would do me any good if Stoat had locked his keys in the van? Anyway, he hadn't. They were probably in his pocket, damn him. But if the rattlesnake venom killed him—

"Miss Lee Anna." I gasped at the sound of his voice, mean and mocking and not nearly far enough away. "I can see you and I got my gun reloaded and I will kill you if you don't git over here right now. MOVE."

I moved, but only to duck behind the van. He couldn't shoot me through it. Damn him, why wasn't he inside the cabin, lying on the floor, dying? Probably rattlesnakes died from biting *him*. But he had to be feeling weak, I thought as I fumbled madly at the Maglite, trying to get it turned off so maybe, just maybe, I could get away from Stoat in the darkness.

The Maglite shone on relentlessly, its dazzling bright bulb illuminating everything except its own handle, where I could not seem to find the on/off switch.

"Bitch, I told you git over here!"

Time was running out. Unable to turn off the damn Maglite, I swung it at the end of my arm and flung it—not nearly far enough away from me, damn everything. Nevertheless, still crouching behind the van, I scuttled toward that bulky vehicle's hind end.

"Goddamn you, Lee Anna. . . ." Stoat said several obscene things about me.

Damn absolutely everything. Now that I had thrown the Maglite away, I could see that darkness had turned disloyal to me. A sickly pallor of dawn had sneaked into the sky. It was Thursday fricking morning. I would be a clear target the minute I stood up.

But if I stayed behind the van, maybe Stoat wasn't strong enough to come after me.

"Bitch," he roared in what sounded like total exasperation, "git your fat ass over here and fetch me some water!"

Huh. He needed me to do things for him?

"On the count of three, I'm coming after you! One . . ."

Maybe if he wanted a nurse, he wouldn't kill me.

"Two . . ."

"All right," I called, standing up. "Don't shoot."

I walked toward him none too steadily. He cursed me every step of the way. And even in the persnickety dawn light I could see why. Half of his face had swollen hugely and turned a lurid purple. He could glare at me out of only one eye. His voice had gone hoarse. "Git me water right now!"

He looked tottery. Yet he managed to follow my every move with the shotgun as I walked into the fishing shack and out the back door to the pump, where I plied the handle long and hard before a gush of water saw fit to emerge.

He emptied the mug of water I gave him with one gulp while I stepped out of range in case he wanted to clout me. But hurting me seemed not to be foremost in his mind. As if he'd been through a fight, he panted with his mouth open, his breath rasping in his throat. "More water!" he ordered me, his voice a croak, and he menaced with the shotgun as if he would be watching me.

By the time I got back with his second mug of water, he had sat down at the picnic table and laid his shotgun on it kind of as if he had put it on a stand. He kept hold of it, swiveling it, finger on the trigger. But by now enough morning light had infiltrated the place so that I could see how ghastly Stoat looked, his forehead sweaty, his skin as gray as the shack's splintery unpainted walls. That place was so small I could take in everything with a single glance. Stoat swilling his water. Dead rattlesnake splattered on the floor. Stoat swiveling his shotgun toward me as if he could make me any more terrified than I was already. And under its double barrel, something on the plank surface of the table. Black block letters drawn in marker on the raw wood.

SORRY LEE

DON'T WORRY

I HAVE A PLAN

FOURTEEN

I stood owlishly blinking at those three lines like haiku, cryptic and profound, compressing worlds of hope and fear into a few syllables.

SORRY LEE

DON'T WORRY

I HAVE A PLAN

That note hadn't been there the night before. It could have been written—in the dark, in careful printing like that of a blind man—by only one person. Justin. He had been alive a short time ago.

"Justin," I blurted, staring at the message. "He ran away."

Stoat put down his mug, swiveled his head in his lizardlike way, and peered at me with the one flinty eye that wasn't swollen shut. "What you mean, Justin ran away?"

I felt like crying because Justin had sneaked away like the coward I knew he wasn't. I felt like laughing because Stoat wouldn't get to kill him today. I had to keep my voice very neutral so that

Stoat would not take offense and kill me instead. "Justin wrote that." I pointed. "He must have left right after I went to sleep."

"Gee, ain't that too bad." The water seemed to have lubricated Stoat's wheezing somewhat. "And you lying in wait for me with a rattlesnake in your hand. Fixing to kill me."

He gave me way too much credit. Me, some sort of super-woman wielding a rattlesnake instead of a zap gun? My mouth hung open but words failed me.

"Stupid bitch." Creepily calm, Stoat began to feel surreal to me, a horror-movie monster whose ballooning purple face might explode at any moment. "You think I'm going to die, don't you?" He pointed his shotgun at me. "Say it."

I stood there unable to say a thing.

Stoat said, "It so happens I got double vision right now, but if I shoot one of you, I guarantee I'll get you both." The shotgun's double barrel wavered, showing how weak he felt, and how dangerous. "Go ahead—say you mean for me to die."

Just in time I got my big mouth back. "I certainly hope so," I told him brightly.

"Huh." He put the shotgun down on the table as if it were too heavy for him. "Well, I ain't gonna oblige you," he lectured me. "See, I'm the kind of person that if you mess with me, *you* die, not me."

He paused to breathe heavily. Some sort of comment seemed expected. "I believe you," I said politely.

"I need you for a couple days, but soon as I can, I *will* kill you, tricky bitch. I—what the hell?"

His voice shot up and his single viable eye widened, staring past me. I turned to see what had spooked him.

"Hypatia!" I greeted the oak snake emerging from under my bunk with the absurd joy of seeing a friend during a difficult time. So graceful, the way she poured herself like a meandering stream—

BAM. Shotgun, so close, so loud, I jumped and screamed.

Hypatia disintegrated. I stood gulping and quaking. Stoat was a good shot.

"Git me some more water," he ordered, "then clean up them dead snakes."

Thomas Hart Benton murals distinguished the ballroom-sized lobby of the skyscraper where Quinn Leppo worked. Podunk people touring the Big Apple stood gawking, but Quinn strode through without hesitation, tall, reasonably handsome in a three-piece suit custom-tailored to give his long legs and narrow shoulders the most flattering fit, all banker. Or so he might appear, Quinn thought as the elevator lifted him to his office on the twenty-second floor. Hardly anyone ever looked closely at his tie or his socks. He wore plain socks today, but his tie featured a tiny print of Munch's *The Scream*. Tomorrow, Friday, he would wear his TGIF socks.

In his office—as midlevel management, Quinn had scored an office with a window—he immediately set down his Starbucks coffee and checked his e-mail. He could have done it on his iPhone during his subway ride, but he hated working before he got to work. He rolled his eyes when he saw, again, the e-mail from his mother that had been there since yesterday afternoon. Guiltily aware that he hadn't phoned her, sure it would be mama drama, he had left it unopened at the time, and again last night, and in the bright light of morning he felt inclined to leave it unopened yet once more. But if he did, he'd have to begin actual work. With a sigh, he clicked.

What the ruck?

> Hello family of Liana Clymer, aka Liana Leppo. This is
> Deputy Bernardo Morales of the Maypop County
> (Florida) Sheriff's Office contacting you.

Quinn read on with rapidly increasing consternation. Schweitzer, dead? *Shot?* Mom had to be heartbroken, especially at this bad time when she was still getting over Dad's defection. But Quinn had learned to distance himself from his mother's feelings, so this concerned him more: Mom would never willingly have gone away and left Schweitzer's dead body on the floor.

And who could have shot Schweitzer? Unbelievable.

Was this e-mail maybe a hoax? Mom was capable of doing outrageous things, such as the time she painted her car with quotes from her favorite philosophers interspersed with daisies, or another time when she had accumulated a variety of concrete animals on the front yard and dressed them up in fancy finds from Goodwill. Could she maybe have sent this e-mail herself as a weird kind of comeuppance to him for not answering her calls?

The reaction she desired from him being, of course, a phone call.

Damn. Trapped. He brought up his mother's name on his cell phone and, feeling doomed, he thumbed the green button with every expectation of hearing her answer ever so innocently, "Oh, hello, sweetie!"

But he didn't even get a ringtone. Just a recorded voice nasally informing him that the subscriber was unavailable.

Huh. Not good. Quinn pondered a moment, drumming his fingertips on his desktop, then swung into serious action. Stepping up to the plate was what had gotten him early promotion to the position he held. He looked at the e-mail's addressees and decided to call his brother first. Grandma and Grandpa might not have seen the e-mail yet; they didn't check every day. Uncle Hi (Hiram, the Hi Clymer) and Uncle Rocky (Rockwell, the Rock Clymer) were not likely to give a shit. For that matter, Grandma and Grandpa would dismiss the situation as "one of Liana's shenanigans" when they heard. Quinn called his brother, who lived on the fringes of the megalopolis in New Jersey.

Forrest answered his cell phone on the first ring. "What's up, Suit? Wait, I bet I can guess. You just got around to reading that weird e-mail from Mom. Or about Mom. Whichever."

"Yeah, well, when did *you* read it?"

"This morning. I put it off. Like you."

"Well, what do you think?"

"At first I figured maybe it was her trying to do a number on us."

"Same here. So I tried to call her—"

"And her phone seems to be shut off," Forrest finished for him. "Which would never happen. Unless maybe she let her battery funk out—"

"As has been known to happen."

"True."

"So what do we do about it?" Quinn asked with more than the usual New York City edge. He had always been quick, and his younger brother had always been—not slow, exactly, but in no damn hurry, and it had always annoyed him that Forrie seemed to do just fine in his lackadaisical way.

"I been thinking about that," Forrie drawled, and Quinn could have sworn his kid brother was intentionally trying to irritate him. "So I called the Sheriff's Office down there in Maypop."

"Did you?" For Forrest, this was an impressive show of initiative. "What did they say?"

"They say yeah, Mom seems to be missing, but they haven't done anything because they need a family member to request an investigation."

"I'm going down there," Quinn said. "Where are you now?" An oblique way of asking whether Forrest could go along, or even wanted to.

"Out at a bridge site in a hard hat," Forrie said, "but I can get to Newark Airport in a couple of hours."

"Have you spoken to Jeb and Derry?" Meaning Deb and Jerry: Mom's mom, Deborah, and Mom's dad, Gerald. Speaking of the Clymer grandparents so unceremoniously helped Quinn keep them safely distanced, emotionally if not geographically. Jeb and Derry's fieldstone farmhouse south of Philadelphia was not nearly far enough away. Even before the divorce, going to visit there had felt like walking into a thicker dimension in which his childhood, which he wanted to leave behind, hung somehow preserved as if caught in Jell-O.

Forrie said, "Hell, no. You think I'm going to tangle with those two old chain saws?"

"Well, one of us has to call them and tell them we're going to see about Mom."

"They won't care. They'll be glad they're off the hook."

Silence, because this was too true.

"All right," Quinn said finally, "I'll flip you for it when we get to the airport."

"Call me when you know which airline." Anyone else would have been concerned about tickets and airfare, but Forrie was content to leave everything up to Quinn.

"Right. Get moving."

Hanging up, Quinn knew he ought to get moving himself, arranging to take personal days, delegating his workload, finagling project extensions, persuading colleagues to cover for him, providing for the care and feeding of his job as if it were family. After which the biological family, his grandparents and his two uncles, would be happy to stay at home all smug and virtuous.

Quinn took a moment to lean back in his expensively comfortable desk chair, checking on his own emotional weather. It startled and gratified him that he and Forrie seemed to be on the same page for once. But it also gave him kind of a chill he didn't like. Forrie wouldn't be going anywhere unless he felt afraid, as Quinn felt afraid, that something serious had happened to Mom.

Down on my hands and knees on the rough wooden floor, at gunpoint, trying to gather goopy remnants of dead snake with a scrap of cardboard, I considered that Zeno or any other Stoic had nothing on me when it came to accepting the vicissitudes of life.

"Hurry up," Stoat said.

Why? It wasn't like we were going anywhere. "I need a Mr. Clean Magic Eraser," I said, thinking of the hypercivilized ads on TV and trying to joke.

"Just shut up and do it." Stoat sounded extra cranky. I realized he had to be in a great deal of pain, although he would never say it or show it. But surely he felt like killing something. While keeping his shotgun close at hand, he had his knife out also and was flicking it into the table over and over again, as if practicing to improve his short-range accuracy. Cold little lizard feet of fear scampered up my spine, and I hurried to collect the ophidian carnage and carry it outdoors, where, I had decided, I would just keep going. Starving in a wilderness would be way better than being terrorized by Stoat.

But it was as if he had read my mind. "Stop right there," he ordered as I reached the back door. "Stay where you are and pitch the stuff outside and come back here."

"But I need to go to the privy!" The moment I said this, it became suddenly and urgently true.

"Privy," he mocked. "What the hell is a privy?"

I tried again. "I need to pee."

"Too bad. Either hold it or else squat where I can see you."

"You've got to be kidding."

He raised the shotgun and thumbed back one of the hammers with a click.

"Okay, okay!" I threw my cardboard and its contents into the bushes, decided I was going to have to delay urination a little longer, and came back inside to look at the snake blood on the floor. No way could I get it up without a scrub brush and water.

"Would you like something to eat?" I asked Stoat as a diversion.

"Hell, no. I still feel like I'm gonna puke. You eat if you want to."

This was going to be a very long day. Unless it was shortened by death, either his or mine.

And if he was going to die from the snakebite, I would have thought he'd be doing it by now. Damn.

Although not really hungry, I decided to eat for the sake of something to do, or, more important, something for Stoat to watch me do. I needed to keep him occupied in ways that did not involve shooting me. Looking around our too-cozy hut, I found the multiple-purpose pocket tool. Had Justin intentionally left it for me? Was there any way I could use it to escape from Stoat? Both questions drowned, answerless, in my swampy mind as I looked over the selection of possible food. I saw no cans missing. If Justin hadn't taken the can opener and something to eat, what the heck kind of plan could he have? My whole body weakened with worry for him.

I made myself open a can of peaches and sit down at the table across from Stoat and his gun.

"I hope you don't really think I threw that rattlesnake at you on purpose," I told Stoat after a while. "I'm not crazy. It's just that you surprised me, that's all, and I thought it was the other snake."

It was difficult to interpret any expression on his grotesquely swollen face and in his one functional eye. But as far as I could tell, he was staring at me as if I were the freak.

"I didn't mean to hurt you," I said, which, strictly speaking, was true. I had meant only to escape from him. And looking at him gave me an extreme case of mixed feelings. Vengefully glad I had wreaked such damage. Appalled, shuddering, to know I had grabbed a rattlesnake with my bare hand. Sorry for him, sorry about his pain, and I couldn't believe my own empathy for this creep. Even more unbelievably, I felt grudging admiration for him; the bastard was so tough he wouldn't give in to the poison in his system. He refused to pass out or even lie down.

My face must have shown far too much. "Don't you dare pity me!" Stoat growled. I sensed he would have liked to shout, but his breathing was too shallow, his face pearled with sweat, and a pulse pounded in his temple. "I *thank* you for this goddamn pain because it means I can't sleep and you ain't got a chance in hell to get away until I feel better, at which point you're going to be the one to die, Miss Lee Anna. I advise you to keep that in mind."

He scared me. I very nearly peed my pants.

Wait a minute. He hadn't scared me that much. I just needed to go.

"Stoat," I said equably, "lookie here." I stood up, came around the table so he could see me, and toed my unlovely sneakers off. Standing on my bare, blistered feet, I said, "Please let me go to the privy like this. You're a fair man and you've got good sense. You don't want me stinking up this shack and you know I'm not going to run away in this swamp without any shoes."

I'm sure the "fair man" and "good sense" flatteries were key. Stoat hesitated, staring at my toes as if he found them repulsive, but finally he growled, "Fine. Just take them smelly shoes away from me."

"Okay!"

"Say, 'Yes, sir.'"

"Yes, sir!"

"Say, 'Thank you, sir.'"

"Thank you, sir."

"Go."

I picked up my much-abused shoes and placed them against the wall farthest from Stoat, where he could see them. Then I started toward the door, but I felt something whiz past my backside and turned to look. Stoat had thrown his big, vicious knife at my shoes. If he had double vision, like he said, it didn't seem to be slowing him down much. His knife had gone right through one sneaker and pinned it to the floor.

"Bring my buck knife back," Stoat ordered, but I headed out the door, pretending not to have heard.

"I said bring it back!"

The tone of his command stabbed me in the gut, and I knew he would kill me if I didn't obey. I scuttled back inside, yanked the knife out of my sneaker, and returned it to him, all the time trying to muster the will and strength to kill him with it instead. But I couldn't. Because I badly had to go pee. How humbling is that?

Finally out the back door, picking my way carefully toward the privy, I nevertheless cut my foot on something sharp hidden by old live oak leaves. It bled a little, and hurt. But not as much as my heart. How could I possibly survive Stoat? And what had become of Justin?

FIFTEEN

Seated beside his brother on the flight to Tallahassee, Forrest looked at Quinn and asked, "The iPad, is it really for work or just to keep me from talking at you?"

"Both," Quinn replied at once, without looking up from the tablet, but divulging just a hint of a smile.

"So what exactly is it that you don't want me to talk at you about?"

Quinn actually turned his head to answer. "Forrie," he chided, very dignified in his three-piece suit, "where's your grammar? You mean, 'What is it about which I do not wish you to talk?'"

" 'That is the sort of pedantry up with which I will not put,'" retorted Forrest promptly, quoting Winston Churchill. Both brothers enjoyed their verbal sparring, although it had been a lot more serious in their teen years, all about sibling rivalry—well, mostly on his part, Forrest admitted to himself. As always younger, shorter, chunkier, and grungier than his very successful brother, Forrest sat next to the Suit, wearing khakis and shirt-sleeves, uncomfortable in the airplane's narrow seat and also within himself. "Are you going to answer my question?"

"What do *you* think?" Quinn parried.

"I think, as usual, you do not want to talk about the dysfunctional family."

"You mean Jeb and Derry?"

"Them too." Their perennially married grandparents were at least as dysfunctional as their divorced parents. "What did they say?" Quinn had been the one to phone them.

Quinn looked away, checking out the cloudscape. Of course he had the window seat. All Forrie could see from his seat was a rather murky horizon.

Finally Quinn gave an oblique reply. "I think they're still mad at Mom."

Her own parents. Bummer. "What do they think is going on with her?"

"They have no clue and neither do I."

"And they don't care."

"They didn't say," Quinn hedged. "They're happy to leave it up to you and I."

"Grammar, Quinn." Forrie pounced on this unexpected opportunity. "Objective case."

Obedient to their longtime rules of verbal engagement, Quinn corrected himself. "Okay, they're happy to leave whatever's going on with our mother up to you and me."

"And what the heck *do* you think is going on with Mom?"

"It is a capital error, my dear Watson," lectured Quinn, waggling his eyebrows, "to theorize with insufficient data."

"Suit, come on." Tired of the game, knowing damn well Quinn used it to keep his family at a comfortable emotional distance, Forrest gave Quinn a long, level look that would not let go. "What do you think, really?"

"Hell, I don't know!" Quinn broke eye contact, studied his manicured cuticles, and said to his hands, "Maybe an irate neighbor shot Schweitzer because of his constant barking, and Mom lost it somehow, and—I just don't know. What's the worst that could have happened?"

"She could have murdered whoever shot Schweitzer."

"If she hasn't killed Dad by now, she's not likely to murder anybody."

This was a joke; therefore, Forrest answered it soberly. "True," he admitted. But something about his face or tone made Quinn laugh, and Forrest had always loved to laugh; he joined in.

"The real capital error," he told Quinn, chuckling, "is to try to figure out Mom."

"And yet we do."

"Yeah, well, how about those Yankees?"

An excellent diversion. A subject fascinating to both of them. One of their few mutual interests. Quinn put away his iPad and willingly discussed the Yankees during the rest of the flight to Tallahassee.

Deplaning took as long as ever, but lugging his carry-on duffel bag through the Tallahassee terminal, Forrest, to his surprise, saw the light of outdoors ahead. This was not as large a terminal as he had expected. A moment later they checked in at the one and only rental car desk, then stepped outside. Forrest looked back at a single brick building flanked by tall pine trees.

"This airport is tiny!"

"For a state capital, yes. There's our rental." Quinn stopped rolling his carry-on leather suitcase, tucked away its handle, and lifted it into the car's trunk. "Dorothy, we're not in Kansas anymore. Would you like to drive?"

"Sure, but don't call me Dorothy."

"I'll navigate." Belted into the passenger seat, Quinn deployed his iPad and pulled up a map app. "I'm hoping we can get to Mom's place before dark."

During the two-hour drive on I-10 that followed, Forrest

found himself and his brother in heartfelt agreement on a couple of sentiments not involving the Yankees. One, a Chevy Aveo had to be the Worst Rental Car Ever. "It was all I could get on short notice," Quinn said, genuinely apologetic. Two, the Florida Panhandle was the most alien place either of them had ever seen outside of a sci-fi movie. Miles and miles of nothing except tall forest standing in dark water. A road-killed bristly bloating black pig on the shoulder. At a rest stop, a hillbilly with a long beard that looked entirely too much like Spanish moss—only he couldn't rightly be called a hillbilly, because there were no hills in this flatland. Call him a swamp denizen, selling watermelons and boiled peanuts.

Adding to the surreal feel were Stetson-shaped billboards advertising a Western-wear outlet, and others, normal in their rectangular shape but not so normal in content: "Learn to Fly at Wiregrass Aviation," "Camp at Sinkhole Springs," "Enjoy Family Fun at Possum Park." Forrest slowed down to look at that last one.

"Dancing possums?" he reported doubtfully. "Tempting tasty possum soup?"

"Not in my lifetime."

Another billboard that caught their attention advertised Bucky Bob's Bait and Live Oyster Bar.

"I like oysters," Quinn mused aloud, "but not when they've been rubbing elbows with night crawlers."

"Since when do oysters have elbows?"

"Shut up and drive."

Late in the afternoon they exited I-10, and once they got past the small cluster of motels, gas stations, and fast-food restaurants by the interstate, they left behind civilization as they knew it. The rudimentary road on which they drove was a pencil-straight line punctuated by a few trailer parks and several small frame houses painted in rainbow colors. When they reached an ornate but faded sign, THE CHURCHES OF MAYPOP WELCOME YOU, Quinn told Forrest, "Keep going to the third traffic light, which happens also to be the last traffic light."

"Why does that not surprise me?" Forrest had slowed down not so much in obedience to the posted speed limit as to gawk at what might as well have been a Midwestern not-quite–ghost town with false fronts. PAWN SHOP, WE BUY GOLD. CHECK CASHING. Then he did a slight double take and read aloud, " 'Best Pharmacy and Hunting and Fishing Supplies. Gun Sale.' "

"Eek." Quinn gave an exaggerated shudder. "I'd be scared to go in there for Advil."

"Look what's right next door. 'Snell Furniture and Undertaking, Family Owned for Three Generations.' "

"We're in Oz, Forrie. Look over there at Cutzit Hairstyles."

"You've got to be kidding." But Forrie could see all too clearly the beauty salon's window display of conditioners, curling irons, and chain saws.

"If there's a doctor, I suppose they're also the vet."

"Why isn't there anybody on the sidewalks?" Forrest complained. "Is this a movie set for a bad Western?" The buildings, venerable but undistinguished, bothered Forrest; the way they stood scattered, oddly spaced, made no sense to his urban eyes. "Why is there a horse in a pasture right behind the People's Bank of Maypop?"

"Never mind the horse. Have a look at the church."

Forrest looked. "Holy crap."

"Yes, and a lot of it, I would say." Even with its rather squatty steeple, a concession to hurricane country, the church loomed by far as the most imposing structure in Maypop.

"Third light ahoy," said Quinn.

"First cypress swamp to the right and straight on toward Mom's place."

The swamp quip turned out to be prophetic, but Forrie saw that he should have added cotton fields, a dairy farm, several ponds, numerous pinto horses, and a scattering of very modest houses.

After a few miles, Quinn started watching the numbers on the mailboxes. "We're getting close."

Quinn sounded tense, and Forrie noticed because he felt tense. More than tense. Worried. Scared. What the heck was going on with Mom?

Trying to lighten the mood, he remarked, "Do you think she was serious when she said it was pink?"

"I'd say." Quinn pointed.

"Whoa!" Forrest pulled the rental car off the road, stopped it, and stared. Nestled amid clouds of fluffy pink mimosa blossoms glowing in the sunset light, Mom's shack looked like it belonged in a fuchsia fairy tale.

Quinn concurred with Forrie's unspoken sentiment. "That is so Mom it is eerie."

"I expect her to come flying out on her broom at any moment."

"Don't we wish." Quinn unbelted his seat belt. "Turn this pitiful car off and let's go see what's what."

A smell diametrically opposed to that of mimosa blossoms assaulted their nostrils the moment they got out of the car. Wordlessly they exchanged a shocked look. Forrie stared straight ahead and let Quinn lead the way to the back door. Pinching their nostrils against the stench, they let themselves inside.

It seemed much darker there. Who could think anything so aggressively pink could be so dark? Forrest groped for a light switch, but when he found one and flicked it, he wished he hadn't.

It would have been better not to see what the maggots were doing to Schweitzer.

Quinn made a retching noise, U-turned, and rushed out back to lean against Mom's car for support. Forrest retreated there too, staying a safe distance away from his brother. Quinn had not actually vomited—yet—and Forrest didn't want him to in case his own stomach responded accordingly. Grabbing Quinn's elbow, Forrest said, "Come on. Fresh air," and tugged his brother toward the portion of the yard farthest from the house. There, under the lovely low branches of a mimosa tree, both stood and breathed deeply.

"My God," Quinn burst out as if he had just that moment realized how seriously screwed things were. "My God, where the hell is Mom?"

Those good ol' boys drinking whiskey and rye in the "American Pie" song, singing "This'll be the day that I die!" had no idea what they were talking about. But I couldn't get that plangent song out of my head as I brought Stoat tepid water, drank some myself, offered to put a wet cloth on his face, and got no answer except the mean stare of his one eye and the even meaner twofold regard of the business end of his shotgun.

Fighting to remain conscious and in control of me, Stoat did not eat. Because I needed to stay physically strong, I made myself eat stuff out of cans, using my fingers as knife, fork, and spoon. Cold baked beans. Ick.

Very icky, because Stoat waited for that moment to pick up his big buck knife again and point it at me to gesture: *Come here.* Every movement cost him a gasp of pain, and he panted so badly that pity helped me overcome my fear. But as soon as I reached the picnic table bench where he sat, I was sorry. He grabbed me hard by one arm while he stretched his other hand up to my shoulder.

Golly gee whiz, had he put down his shotgun?

Golly gee nothing. I stopped trying to joke with myself when I felt Stoat place the edge of his knife against my neck.

"Help me up," he ordered, his voice thick. I wondered whether his tongue had swollen along with the purple half of his pockmarked face. I also wondered where the heck he thought he was going, but with his buck knife nudging my neck, I wasn't about to ask.

Making very sure to keep my hands above his waist and below his neck, I helped him up. With both of his arms on my shoulders he leaned on me hard, shuffling toward the front door. To the van?

"Where are we going?" I blurted.

He gave a single snort of ugly laughter. "Stupid bitch, you ain't the only one that's got to pee."

Oh. Great. Was he going to need me to help him unzip?

Of course he did, because he couldn't hold the knife on me and take care of himself at the same time. I tried not to look, but of course I saw glimpses. I tried to tell myself that nurses dealt with this kind of thing every day. I tried to tell myself it was just another wanker, but its proximity made my stomach spasm, threatening vomitive convulsions—not good, especially not while a snakebitten pervert held a big knife to my throat. I took a deep breath and closed my eyes.

"Shake it off," Stoat ordered, "and put it back."

It's fair to say that was the low point of the day, and things didn't get any worse once I had zipped Stoat up and helped him back to his seat, even though he took to throwing his knife at the knotholes on the wall and having me bring it back to him, over and over again, at gunpoint. Every time I fetched the knife, I felt like using it on him, and I knew he knew how I felt, and he was just daring me. He would have blown me full of buckshot the instant I made a wrong move.

Eventually, somehow, day turned into twilight, and Stoat ceased his knife play. Once it got pretty dark inside the shack, I asked Stoat whether he wanted me to light candles.

"Hell, no."

"Well, could I light one—"

"I said no!" His short temper was no act put on to keep me in line. It was real. Parts of his swollen face were starting to turn black, as if they would die and fall off. If that were happening to me, I would be cranky too.

"Permission to speak, sir," I said as lightly as I could. "I need the candle to find my way to the privy. You know I'm not going to run off barefoot at night, right? When I get back in—"

"Goddamn shut your mouth and just go!"

I hustled to do so, and never mind the candle; I managed to do what I had to in the dim light of dusk amid swarming mosquitoes, and I had never felt filthier, body and soul, in my life. Back inside and very likely making bloody tracks that I could not see on the splintery floor, I asked the shadowy form that was Stoat, "You all right?"

A remarkably stupid question, in retrospect. He literally sputtered—I heard him—before he retorted, "What the hell you mean, all right?"

"I mean, do you need anything else? Can I get some sleep?"

"Don't go thinking you'll catch me sleeping," he responded, his tone as dark as the nightfall. "I hurt too much to sleep. Don't go thinking you'll catch me lying down neither."

"Whatever you say."

"Call me 'sir,' you dumb cunt!"

"Sir, yes, sir."

"Git in the top bunk and shove the ladder away. You don't come down till I say so."

"Yes, sir." Amazingly, I felt almost grateful to him; sheer stress had made me that tired. Lying down in the sagging, lumpy top bunk felt so luxurious I didn't even mind the smell. Of myself, mostly.

I was already falling asleep when Stoat said sardonically, "Nighty-night."

SIXTEEN

S till at his desk in the Sheriff's Office after his shift was over, detained there by paperwork—they should hang by the nuts whoever had invented the spelling of the English language— keyboarding a report by the hunt-and-peck method, Bernie heard voices at the front desk, which was only ten feet away. The Sheriff's Office building, previously a shack, now occupied a double-wide trailer.

Bernie noticed a Yankee accent, unusual in this area. Starting to pay attention, he heard a young male saying, ". . . been going on too long already." He sounded upset yet civilized. "We demand to see a detective right away."

"First things first. We are required to follow proper procedure, gentlemen." The deputy at the desk sounded more than usually supercilious. "Your names?"

"Quinn Leppo."

"Forrest Leppo."

Bernie's stubby fingers stopped pecking and his head jerked up. From his cubicle he couldn't see the people at the front desk, but he saw the guy who manned the security equipment facing the wrong direction, grinning as if he was enjoying his colleague's interchange with the pushy strangers.

"Spell, please." The man at the desk managed to make "please" sound like an insult. "One at a time. You first."

But Bernie, on his feet, stepped out there and interrupted. "I got it." He took a quick, appraising look at what he had volunteered for: two young men, dark-haired, suntanned, and unmistakably brothers, one taller and slimmer but both good-looking in a citified way. Nobody in Maypop ever wore a three-piece suit, which was why the security guy was watching. Even the other one, dressed in creased khakis and a long-sleeved shirt, looked way upscale for Maypop, where people wore flip-flops, not Red Wing work boots.

Both skewered Bernie with their attention. "Are you a detective?" the taller one demanded.

Both the deputy at the desk and the one at security stifled snickers. Bernie took no notice. Straight-faced, he motioned for the Leppo brothers to follow him and returned to his desk in the back. "I'm Bernie Morales," he told them as he unfolded two metal chairs for them. "You are the sons of Liana Clymer, yes?"

"Yes. And you're the one who e-mailed," said the other brother, more soft-spoken and, Bernie guessed, the younger of the two. "We appreciate your doing that. Above and beyond, wasn't it?"

Seating himself behind his desk, Bernie shrugged and refrained from saying it was true; he should have been finishing his reports and going home right now instead of talking with these young men.

"There is not much more I can do for you," he cautioned them. "The chief will be in tomorrow—"

"My God, there has to be *something* we can do before tomorrow," said the softer-spoken one, his taut voice hinting at emotion he was trying to hide.

Buying time to think about this, Bernie asked, "You are which one, Forrest or Quinn?"

"Forrest. The Suit here is Quinn."

Forrest looked for a reaction from his brother, and the Suit obliged by rolling his eyes. Bernie found himself smiling. "And you are from where?"

"The Suit," said the Suit himself, Quinn, "is from the south end of Manhattan, and the Grunge is from the north end of Joisey."

With raised eyebrows Forrest asked, "Is that the best you can do? The Grunge?"

Brothers bickering: this was normal and good. Bernie put in, "Why your mother moved here?" Where Bernie came from, families stayed as close together as they could.

Both young men looked at the floor.

"To get away from Dad," Forrest said.

"Divorce," said Quinn.

Their pained reaction told him that they and their mother had perhaps quarreled about the divorce. Could it be that they had not spoken with their mother recently? Could the Clymer woman have gone missing to punish them, or to make them come to her new home? He felt sympathy for them, and glad this was not his case, so there was no need for him to question them further. Still making conversation, he asked, "You stay in your mother's house?"

Quinn reacted strongly. "No! God, no, with Schweitzer lying dead on the floor—"

"Schweitzer?"

"Mom's dog." Quinn Leppo might have been a rich New Yorker, but his voice hitched like that of a boy near tears.

In true Chilean fashion Bernie let his heart take charge. "You want to do something tonight, how about if we give burial to the dog?"

Swallowing repeatedly, Quinn seemed unable to speak, but Forrest responded, startled. *"We?"*

"Now?" Quinn added huskily. "In the dark?"

"Why not? The cars, they have headlights. I will go with you to take the bullets for evidence. We can bury the dog in the yard." Bernie stood up as if the matter was decided. "You have shovels?"

"I doubt it," Forrest said with something both warm and wry in his voice. "I can't imagine Mom buying anything so practical."

"Mom let Dad have the house and everything in it when she moved down here," Quinn added. "Supposedly the one who gets the house wins."

"Not in Dad's case," Forrest said.

Bernie sensed a fraught topic and interrupted. "I can borrow shovels from the maintenance shed. You go ahead; I will follow in ten minutes."

It took him more like fifteen or twenty minutes to gather everything he thought he might need. Then he headed out in his official vehicle on unofficial and unreimbursed business, what he called "missionary work." The Leppo boys, he sensed, could use some help.

When Bernie pulled up on the front yard of the pink shack, he saw lights on inside. That, and Quinn and Forrest opening all the windows. And the front door hanging ajar. Hefting a number of helpful items in a shoe box, Bernie went to the door, grimaced at the sight and smell of what was left of Schweitzer, and produced three air-filtering masks for mouth and nose. He put on his own before he actually stepped inside the house, then handed the other two to Quinn and Forrest. The Suit, he noticed, had put aside his jacket and vest, loosened his tie, and rolled his shirtsleeves up.

Bernie handed the brothers two powerful flashlights. "How about you go see where we bury this one?" He wanted them occupied elsewhere while he dug the bullets out of the dog.

"Just not too close to the well," he called after them as they headed out to explore the yard. Then he crouched over the decomposing canine corpse.

Even with a handheld metal detector and a forceps it was no easy matter finding the bullets. Bernie was just dropping the third one into an evidence bag when the Leppo boys came back in.

"The well's in the backyard," Forrest said, "so we guess we should put Schweitzer up front."

"Keeping it simple," Quinn added, "we can put him where the car headlights are already pointed."

"Okay." Bernie put the evidence bag into his shoe box and took out a utility knife, with which he began to slice into the carpet beside the dog's corpse. Focusing on the task, he sensed more than saw how the two brothers stiffened, looked question marks at each other, then relaxed in understanding. Their mother's carpet was ruined anyway; what did it matter if Bernie cut a hole in it? He freed up a neat rectangle of carpet around Schweitzer so that they could pick it up like a stretcher to carry the dog's corpse without touching it and in one piece.

"Okay," he said when he finished, standing up and flexing his aching knees—damn, arthritis starting already. "Shovels are in the trunk of the toilet."

"Huh?" both Leppos said.

"My vehicle."

Bernie's aged cruiser made no fuss about shining its headlights and depleting its battery. The rental car needed to be turned on and left with the motor running to do the same. In a place under the mimosa trees where the two cars' headlights intersected, Quinn and Forrest started to dig. Bernie had made sure to bring three shovels; he helped. He observed that Forrest knew how to tackle manual labor but Quinn not so much. Quinn stopped first.

"Deeper," Bernie instructed gently, "or the coyotes will get him. You have blisters? You want some work gloves?"

Quinn shook his head and resumed shoveling.

"This isn't so bad," Forrest remarked. "Sandy soil, no shale, no need for a pickax."

Quinn muttered, "Go to it, Grunge."

For a while there was silence except for the scrape and spatter of shoveling. Then Forrest asked, "Deep enough?"

Bernie nodded in agreement. "Let me stay here while you get the dog." He sensed that these two had little experience of death and they needed him to guide them, but also they needed some small time alone. He waited until they had returned, each of them holding two corners of the piece of carpet with the dead dog on top. He stood aside while they lowered the deceased into the grave.

"Is there anything else that should go in?" he asked after they had stood up again. "A blanket, a toy?"

Forrest and Quinn looked at each other for a few moments before Quinn replied, "We don't really know. I guess not."

"Anything to say, then?" Bernie asked. "A prayer? What would your mother want?"

"We don't really know that either," said Quinn bleakly.

Forrest blurted, "We don't know what Mom would do. We never talked with our own mother enough to have a clue!" His voice shredded more with each word. "And now she's gone."

"You'll get her back," said Bernie with unreasoning certainty. He had been raised to have faith. "She will come back. I know it." He took a shovelful of sandy dirt, let it fall, and saw both young men wince as they heard the thud of soil in the grave, that saddest of all sounds. But they said no more as they joined him in the task of shoveling until the earth formed a mound over the buried body.

After they had finished, he put his borrowed tools back into the trunk of his cruiser, then joined Quinn and Forrest in the house. "You stay here now?"

"No way." Quinn seemed shocked. "The smell, and the dirty dishes, and the place is so small—"

"What he really means," said Forrest with an effort at a grin, "is there's no way he's either sleeping on the sofa or sharing a bed with his brother."

"Damn right," Quinn retorted, then told Bernie more gently, "We'll find a motel out by the interstate."

"The Econo Lodge has the best rates. Come to the office in the morning any time after eight, ask for the chief, and he can put you in touch with detectives who work for the state."

He helped them turn off lights and lock the front door.

"Thanks, man," Forrest told him, shaking hands as they stood beside their cars ready to leave.

"Yes, thank you," Quinn concurred. "Above and beyond."

Bernie shrugged. "I wish you sleep good tonight."

"I sure hope we get some sleep. Where's the *best* place to stay?"

Bernie gave Quinn a puzzled look.

"I know you said the Econo Lodge, but we want a place with nice rooms, a good restaurant, a swimming pool—"

Bernie realized he had made a mistake, assuming they would want the Econo Lodge. The rich were different. "I don't know," he said with sober honesty.

"It's just that it's going to be hard to sleep, even in a cushy room," Quinn added.

Bernie told them to try the Maypop Inn and wished them good night. Maybe the rich were not after all so different.

I awoke with a lurch as if a fire alarm had gone off, then lay looking up at splintery gray rafters and a tin roof, unable to think for a moment where I was or why my heart was pounding or why I felt immobile beneath a weight of dread, as if a leaden vulture were perched on my chest.

Something smelled quite skanky, and it was me.

Lack of proper hygiene or sanitation, I remembered. Fishing shack. Top bunk. Justin—Justin! Where was he? Stoat would kill him—

Stoat. Nightmare. Here.

When I turned my head, I expected I would see him sitting with his shotgun, leering at me.

I took a breath, and arranged my face in a mildly pleasant mask. Clenching my teeth behind slightly smiling lips, I turned as silently as I could to take a look, and instantly forgot all about facial expression. I gawked.

Stoat was sitting where I had expected, all right, but he was slumped forward with his arms and head lying beside his shotgun on the picnic table. That explained why he had let me alone for so long that it was daylight again. He had fallen asleep.

Or could he be *dead*?

At the thought, my dread gave way to deplorable, barbaric joy. I studied Stoat sprawling there, head turned so that the less injured side lay pressed against the table planks, and all I could see was the swollen side like a bumpy black mushroom hiding his mouth; I could not tell whether he was breathing. I watched his shoulders for several moments and still could not tell. But Stoat, dead—I should be so lucky. A more honest sense of my own karma told me that Stoat was just sleeping.

The shotgun lay under his forearm, inches from his right hand.

My leaden vulture had given way to Emily Dickinson's feathered thing that sings. Maybe, just maybe, if I could secure the shotgun, I could live and take the van and get to the cops and they might find Justin. . . .

The thought of Justin gave me the nerve I needed. With great caution, as silently as possible, I started to move.

Of course I had to watch for snakes that might have settled in bed with me during the night. As if Stoat in the cabin were not snake enough.

And of course all my muscles ached, if only from sleeping in that despicable bunk, and various cuts on my hands and feet hurt, and so what? Ignoring all protests from my body, I had to get down from the top bunk without thumping to the floor. I did it by easing myself over the edge until I hung by my hands—something I had not done since phys ed class in college—and letting myself down slowly, easing my weight onto my bare feet. Finally I stood facing the bunk and listening.

I heard no reaction from Stoat.

My sense of balance felt uncertain, perhaps because of the heightened pulse pounding in my temples or perhaps because I hadn't had enough to eat. With one hand on the top bunk's bed rail for support, I turned around as silently as I could to look at Stoat, more than half expecting to see him sitting up and grinning at me. But he still slumped sprawling with his head on the table.

So far, so good.

Feeling a little more steady, I let go of the bed rail to stand on my own and take charge of my breathing. Slow, deep. Calm down. One step at a time.

Quite literally. I put one foot forward—not too far, half a step—then shifted my weight slowly to avoid making any sound, then paused like a bridesmaid in a wedding processional. I checked Stoat; he hadn't moved. I listened as if something might be sneaking up on me. Then I skimmed my other foot forward and balanced with just my big toe on the floor, trying to remember where the creaky floorboards were so I could avoid them. Then I took another stealthy half step, and another—who would think a tiny cabin could seem so huge? By increments I crossed the floor, watching out for things that bit—spiders, scorpions, snakes—and even more, watching Stoat.

Closer, closer. I was close enough now to hear him breathing—

Damn. Breathing meant that the freaking pervert was alive.

But he seemed to be sound asleep. Zonked, conked, somnolent. I stood within arm's reach of his shotgun, but on the wrong side of the table. The shotgun barrel projected over the edge of the plank surface toward me, easy to grasp, but if I failed to wrench the weapon away quickly enough, if he woke up and grabbed his end, he could still shoot me. Even if the gun went off by accident, buckshot was likely to get me.

I had to sneak around the table to stand right next to him before I dared to lunge for the gun.

I took a long breath and a short step.

A floorboard creaked under my weight. I froze.

Stoat kept sleeping without even a hitch in his breathing.

I ventured another slow, soft step, then another. Around the corner of the crude table and bench I crept. Just one more step. Noiseless, thank all the deities. Close enough at last, I tensed to try for the shotgun—

My fingers never touched it. I never even saw Stoat uncoil; the bastard must have struck like a rattlesnake, only harder. I felt his fist impact my eye and the back of my head impact the floor, equally hard. But I was not knocked out, which might have been preferable. I could see only something like sparklers on a very black Fourth of July night, and I could hear Stoat laughing.

SEVENTEEN

First thing Thursday morning, early enough to avoid Birmingham's rush hour traffic, Chad set off on his drive home, with Dad in the passenger seat and Oliver standing on the backseat, his big, shaggy head thrust happily over the console, between their shoulders.

Without taking his eyes from the road, Chad acknowledged the dog. "Oliver, I wish I had half your optimism." Amy had reacted better than he had expected when he had phoned her last night, but still, Chad didn't feel much hope that Dad's plan would help the marriage. Mostly because he didn't dare. Hope was scary.

Ned asked, "You sure Amy doesn't mind that I'm bringing the woofhead along?"

"Oliver? No problem. Amy loves animals."

"That's a sign of a good heart."

"You've got that right. Dad, I don't deserve her."

Peripherally, he saw his father stiffen as if he had struck a nerve. "Now listen here, son." The intensity with which the old man spoke would have compelled Chad to listen anyway. "You gotta stop thinking like that. Life isn't about what you deserve or what you don't deserve. Did you deserve to lose Justin that way? Do you deserve to get him back?" His father didn't pause for an answer to either question. "You take what you get, not what you deserve or don't deserve. That's just another way of being a self-centered jackass."

Self-centered? It was the last thing Chad would have thought of himself. On the other hand, he was definitely capable of being a jackass. Trying to define what he thought a jackass was, Chad didn't say a word, but Oliver whined as if he had been scolded.

In a much more subdued tone, Dad added, "I been there. Damn martyr who didn't deserve this and didn't deserve that. Just an excuse to keep drinking."

"Huh," Chad remarked, processing information that was entirely new to him.

His father rumpled the fur on Oliver's head, then patted it smooth, reassuring the dog that everything was okay. And maybe reassuring himself as well. "I'm nervous about meeting Amy," his father admitted.

"What the hell, Dad? So am I."

Stoat ordered me, "Git your fat butt the hell up off the floor and get me something to eat. I'm hungry."

I could hear him, all too loud and clear, but I could not see him. One of my eyes was swelling shut and the other had not yet made sense out of anything.

"Oh, hi, Stoat," I mumbled.

"Hi, hell," he barked. "I'm hungry."

"That's good. I'm glad you're feeling better."

"Bullshit. You were fixing to shoot me dead. Git me something to eat!"

"Well, what would you like?" I asked ever so politely, heaving myself to my feet and making a mighty effort to focus my one viable eye. "We have cold canned lima beans, cold canned okra, chunky peanut butter—"

He invoked his patriarchal deity loudly, at length, and by various names, while I stood watching his grotesque face come into focus, one side swollen like a football and turning black, the other side ugly enough to start with. "Jesus jumpin' on the water," he yelled in conclusion, "I want fried eggs and grits and coffee! Git going!"

In order to show my willingness to oblige, I wobbled over to the flat boxes in which the canned goods were stored. My legs buckled just as I got there, but I guess it looked as if I was kneeling in order to get at some food. I had to act as if I were catering to Stoat; my life depended on appeasing him. "There are some canned grits," I reported, "and instant coffee. I could make a campfire and heat some water in a can or something."

Only a foreboding silence answered. Pain from my insulted eye seemed to radiate through my skull; my head throbbed, and I noticed the taste of blood in my mouth from further damage not yet identified. I swiveled to check my whether report: whether Stoat was going to finish the job and kill me now. I saw what looked like two cartoon eyes, round and black, until I realized they were two shotgun barrels pointed straight at me. They held my attention so thoroughly that I barely saw Stoat behind them.

"Can or something my ass," he said. "Git over here."

Despite feeling weak, I obeyed almost quickly. It's amazing how fear can quake a person's gut one moment yet give strength the next.

"Stand there. Not like that. Put your back to me."

Thinking I was about to be executed, I balked, deploying my big mouth. "Why?" I asked as loudly as I could, which wasn't very.

"Just goddamn turn around!" The menace in his voice shook

me so much that I shuddered. I thought wildly that the rattlesnake venom, instead of killing him, seemed to have joined forces with his own spleen.

I turned around. Yes, sir.

With one hand he seized my shoulder and leaned on me for support while with the other he held the shotgun to the back of my neck. "Move," he ordered.

"Where?" I had to keep talking, make him think a black eye and a gun to my back meant nothing to me.

"Out the damn door."

"But where are we going?"

He sighed gustily like a horse. "There ain't no damn eggs or frying pan here, are there?"

"No."

"Then what do you think, dumbass? We're going to my place. You drive."

By midmorning, Quinn and Forrest had filed Missing Persons reports on Mom with the Maypop police and the Florida state troopers. But doing so had made Quinn feel worse, not better, because the authorities had given the distinct impression that they would not search seriously for an adult who had every right to go missing; how did they know she hadn't shot her own dog to death? *Assholes*, thought Quinn, driving the rental car, heading toward Mom's shack for lack of anything else to do. *Dickheads*. Although Quinn hadn't asked, he felt pretty sure Forrest felt the same way. Normally upbeat, Forrie looked remarkably glum.

"It's going to be hot as hell," he remarked dourly from the passenger's seat.

"Face it, Bro, we're *in* hell."

"Is it that bad," Forrest shot back, suddenly argumentative, "that we had to go on Facebook to find a photo of our mother? Or that we don't know her Social Security number? Or that we don't know her exact place of birth, or whether she has any friends down here, or a job, or a church, or a boyfriend, of all things—"

Quinn cut in. "Because we haven't talked with her for a month and a half?" He kept his tone angelic.

Slumping in the passenger seat, Forrest groaned. "Then, to top it off, we didn't open Bernie's e-mail for almost a day."

"They don't know that."

"But we do," Forrie muttered.

"Okay, okay." In a tuneless waltz rhythm Quinn sang, "We are bad, bad, sons, and we've been sent, to, hell—"

The Worst Rental Car Ever strayed off the road and onto the grassy shoulder. Forrest yelled, "Shut up and watch your driving!"

"Relax. We're almost there."

"Yeah. As if that's a reason to relax."

Quinn turned off the road and bumped across the sandy yard to park in the shade of the mimosa trees. Silently he and his brother went inside the pink shanty and had a look around as if their mother might somehow have turned up since yesterday. But except for where Bernie had cut a rectangle out of the carpet to carry Schweitzer to his grave, nothing had changed. The stench had abated slightly overnight, and now the heat seemed more objectionable. They went around closing windows so they could turn on the air conditioner. Mom's bed remained empty and unmade, her bathroom snowy with talcum powder, her dirty dishes stacked in the kitchen sink.

"These stink almost as bad as, you know," Forrest said of the dishes. "Howsabout if I wash them?"

Quinn nodded. "I'm going to have a look around."

Going back outside, he didn't look at Forrest, and Forrest

didn't look at him. They both knew that the only trace of Mom he was likely to find might be her body.

Not about to search randomly, Quinn visualized a grid pattern of the property and set off toward the handiest perimeter.

Walking slowly between mimosa trees and scanning mechanically up and down, then from side to side, Quinn felt his mind rebelling. There had to be some way to make sense out of this mess.

Time for data assessment.

His mother's car was here.

But Mom herself was very much not here.

Neither was her purse, cell phone, or keys.

Most logical explanation: someone—for instance, a new friend—had come to the house, picked her up, and taken her somewhere.

And shot her dog, and rearranged her furniture?

Try again, Sherlock.

Okay, an intruder seemed to be indicated in the picture.

But Mom had not called the cops. Of course, with Mom there was always a chance that she'd let her cell phone battery run down. But if she'd been able to flee, why on foot? Why not take the car?

Useless question. She had not taken the car.

More useful questions: On foot, where would she go? Where *could* she go?

Mulling, Quinn completed a circuit of the property. As he passed the house, Forrest came out to walk along with him. "AC's starting to take hold," he reported, then asked, "Find anything?"

"I hope I don't. Forrie, where would she go?"

"We've been through this with the cops. We have no idea."

"But now that we're here, look around. Where would she go on foot?"

Both of them stopped where they were, scanning, and both

finished by focusing on the bright blue shack a short distance down the road on the other side. Then they eyeballed each other.

"Come on," Forrest said. "What are we waiting for?"

Amy made a cow face at the mirror she was polishing, then laughed at her own reflection and herself inclusive because she could not stop housecleaning. She knew that neither Chad nor his father nor least of all his father's dog would give a rat's sphincter whether the mirrors and drinking glasses were spotless, yet here she was trying to put a shine on every possible surface. She had already dusted the house, including every angel figurine in her large collection that spread throughout every room, but next she planned to take porcelain angels into the kitchen and *wash* them. With Dawn dish detergent. Until each ceramic face and feather sparkled.

She was being ridiculous and she knew it and she humored her ludicrous self. While not exactly afraid, she felt as nervous as a cat having its whiskers shaved, and she could not sit still until Chad and his father arrived. Chad's sudden actions, not only visiting his dad but bringing him home for her to meet, signaled a huge shift of some kind in her husband. With no idea what to expect, Amy reminded herself that the marriage couldn't end up in much worse shape than it already was.

Downstairs again, finished with all the mirrors, she had just picked up the first cloud white porcelain angel when she heard the truck pull into the driveway.

"Jesus!" she cried more in prayer than in frustration. Then she put the angel down and headed for the front door. Allowing herself no more time to dither, she opened the door and went outside to meet her husband and his father, feeling as if she were greeting not just one stranger but two.

. . .

Because the day was heating up like a gas-fired barbecue grill, Quinn insisted on driving the short distance to the tastelessly blue house. He parked the dinky rental car in front. As he and his brother approached the door to make inquiries of whoever was home, Quinn felt as if he were stepping into a Hollywood melodrama: Did you by any chance notice what has become of our mother? You say three swarthy men in a black Cadillac stretch limo with tinted windows took her away? Did you happen to memorize the license plate?

Quinn knocked and got no reply. Forrest made a futile effort to turn the doorknob.

"Locked," he said unnecessarily.

"Nobody home," said Quinn just as unnecessarily. He felt an uncharacteristic desire to peek inside, but saw that the window blinds were drawn right down to the sills.

"Maybe they're out back."

"Taking a sweat bath?" said Quinn sarcastically. But in this outlandish area of what barely seemed to be the same country he lived in, Quinn couldn't rule out the possibility. Still, his feet felt nearly steam-cooked in their wing-tipped shoes, and he had to force himself to trudge around the corner of the blue house. Forrest, despite his heavy work boots, strode ahead, around the house and out of Quinn's sight.

When Quinn caught up, he found it easy to see that there was nobody in the backyard and no reason for anybody to be there—no aboveground swimming pool, no lawn chairs in the shade, and, for that matter, no shade. Only a rectangle of sand and/or grass. No fire pit or grill, but no need, Quinn thought. The sun might as well have been a flamethrower. Its blaze would sizzle anybody. It was sizzling him right now.

His brother stood staring at the back of the blue shack with an odd look on his face.

"What?" Quinn demanded.

"Why would anybody board up their window that way?"

Quinn stood beside him and looked. The small house's smallest window, set rather high in the wall, had been barricaded by a rank of two-by-fours so close-set they wouldn't let in the light.

"Left over from a hurricane?" he thought aloud, not convincing even himself.

Forrest said, "Don't they use plywood? Anyhow, none of the other windows—"

"I can see. I have eyes." The blue house's rear windows looked no different from the front windows, with their roller blinds pulled clear down.

Forrest said, "If those boards are meant to keep somebody out, they're stupid. Why block the highest, smallest window? Anyhow, a guy with a pry bar could—"

"Hey," Quinn interrupted, staring intently at a window with drapes instead of a roller blind. Kind of a picture window. He jogged toward it.

"Hey, what?"

Quinn did not reply. Crouching, hands cupped beside his eyes to lessen the outdoor glare, he pressed his nose to the glass. The drapery fabric had left a small space through which he could glimpse the shack's dim interior.

Beside him, Forrest repeated, "Hey, what?"

Not much, Quinn thought. From what he could see, the rigidly arranged rectilinear furnishings looked bare and sparse, indeed Spartan. The inhabitant or inhabitants had to be masculine, he assumed almost unconsciously, and when he glimpsed a discordant object, an instinctive part of his mind gave him a jolt before he consciously recognized it. Then he stiffened and stared.

"What?" reiterated Forrest patiently.

Quinn straightened, stepped back, and motioned for Forrest to take his place at the window. "Look at the bag tucked down beside the sofa."

"Bag?"

"Purse. Handbag."

"I don't see it."

"You will when your eyes adjust."

"Oh, okay, I see it now. What about it?"

"Does it look like a Mom bag to you?"

Quinn knew that his brother knew exactly what he meant. Women's handbags in general did not interest them, but they knew their mother's funky taste as exemplified by her Hello Kitty collectibles, and they knew she liked her purses colorful and capacious. If there were such a thing as a large Hello Kitty purse, Mom would have bought it. The purse Quinn had seen was comparable to a baby elephant except in color, or rather colors. It combined scarlet, turquoise, white, and black in a kind of checkerboard, or rather plaid, or perhaps quilt pattern? Quinn felt his fashion vocabulary inadequate to describe it, as usual when regarding his mother's choice of apparel.

Abruptly Forrest left the window and strode to the back door, where he seized the knob as if he would like to tear it off. "Locked." Judging by the tension in his voice, he agreed with Quinn about the handbag.

"We need some cops with a search warrant." Quinn started to reach for his cell phone.

"Are you crazy?" Forrest was the one who looked crazy, giving Quinn a demented stare. "Mom may be dying in there. We don't have time to fool around."

"But if we don't work with the police—"

"Look, they'd just hold us up. We don't know for sure that's

Mom's bag in there. We don't have, whatchacallit, probable cause."

"We could say we *are* sure—"

"Oh, for God's sake. The door's open." Forrest whirled on one foot and planted a hefty kick beside the doorknob with the other. "There, see? It's open."

It certainly was.

Speechless with the shock of watching his usually docile brother take charge, Quinn shot his hand out to halt Forrest from plunging through the doorway.

"*Now* what?" Forrest demanded.

With an effort Quinn spoke. "Now I expect somebody to pop out screaming, 'What the hell you think you're doing?'"

"And has that happened?"

"Excuse me. Let's just be a little careful, okay?"

"Sure. You first."

Quinn sighed forcefully and strode in without flinching at any shadows. He went over, set aside a tablet of cheap paper that had been parked on top of the purse, and picked up the massive handbag. He lifted the flap and peered within, but it was like looking into a well. He reached for a table lamp.

"No," Forrest said, "no lights," and he grabbed Quinn by the elbow, towed him across the room, and halted him at the back window, where he parted the drapes a few inches.

In bright daylight, it turned out that the black things on the purse were Scottie dogs cavorting on patches outlined in turquoise tartan plaid. "Mom," said Quinn with near certainty even before he pulled out her wallet, unsnapped it, and flipped it open. Yet at the sight of his mother's face smiling at him from her none-too-flattering driver's license photo, he felt an unexpected heat stinging his eyes.

"Damn," he said, his voice cracking. "What the hell is going on?"

EIGHTEEN

Little known fact: a rattlesnake can control the amount of venom it releases when it strikes. It doesn't want to waste venom on things it can't eat. So it can give you a warning with a dry bite. Or it can give you a punishment with a moderated bite. Or it can go all out and give you the works.

Standing in the fishing shack with Stoat's hand clawing my shoulder and his shotgun jabbing the back of my neck, I wished to all deities ever that the snake I had thrown at Stoat had gone all out and given him the works. Instead, it had bitten him just badly enough to make him somewhat dependent on me but extra mean. He marched me to the van through tall weeds hiding fire ants that stung my bare feet. He held me at gunpoint quite efficiently as he opened the van's sliding side door and reached inside for—a roll of duct tape?

Son of a bitch.

Wielding the duct tape expertly with one hand, he taped the shotgun barrel to the back of my neck. I couldn't see what he was doing, but I could feel it with wretched certainty and sickness in my gut. From time to time I heard him rip off another length of tape—with his teeth. His crooked, yellow, rotting teeth. I wished the duct tape would yank them right out of his foul mouth, but no such luck, apparently. I could hear Stoat go on ripping and taping for quite a while after he finished with my neck, and I wondered what he was up to.

At last my peripheral vision glimpsed a miniature UFO of silver gray, and I heard the roll of duct tape thump onto the seat of the van. "Now you listen, tricky bitch," Stoat crowed at me. "This here shotgun is not only stuck to your dumbass spine but also to my hand so there ain't no way my finger can slip off the trigger. So you ain't got *no* options, you hear?" He yanked open the passenger side door. "Get in."

With his shotgun connected to me like a long leech hanging from my neck, and with him at the other end of it, I did so.

"Head on over to the driver's seat."

I moved from one bucket seat to the other, and as I did so, Stoat climbed in after me, stepping as spryly as a goat over the console and gearshift and into the backseat. He sat behind me with the shotgun barrel between my seat and its headrest. There had been a few moments of slippage, but none of them long enough for me to rip free of the duct tape, and now I felt the shotgun barrel pressed against the back of my neck as firmly as ever.

As I thought of throwing my weight against the tape and taking a sort of suicide plunge out of the van onto the ground, Stoat commanded, "Fasten your seat belt."

Damn him.

Not until I was trapped in every conceivable way did he toss me the keys, describe in detail what he would do to me if I gave him any trouble, and then tell me, "Drive."

I turned the key in the ignition and cursed it mentally because it worked. The van started.

I said, "I need to move the seat forward." My feet barely reached the brake pedal and accelerator.

"No, you don't, slut. Drive."

Okay, okay, I could manage. I put the van into gear and drove up the narrow weedy lane to the dirt road—more accurately, the sand road. "Which way?"

"Left."

I turned, then accelerated, on the lookout for a good tree to crash into.

"And don't go wrecking my van," Stoat said as if prescient, "because the way I got my finger taped onto the trigger of this here shotgun, if you give me any kind of jolt, it'll go off and blow your stupid brains out."

Damn him.

Because sometimes he kind of liked my big mouth, I grumbled, "First I'm tricky, then I'm stupid."

"Shut up and drive."

So much for that.

In silence I drove along the narrow yellow-gray road in its green tangled tupelo-oak-magnolia tunnel, between sepia-toned swamp water, over wooden, barely there bridges. And then another swamp road to the right, and another to the left. It seemed too long yet not long enough before we reached the paved road. Stoat, who had not said a word except "Turn here," now jabbed the shotgun harder into my brain stem and said, "Go right and hit the cruise control, forty miles an hour. Not thirty-nine or forty-one. Forty."

As if he could even see the controls from where he was sitting in the back of the van. I fiddled with the cruise control but could not make it work, so with my right leg rather painfully stretched to toe the accelerator and one eye on the speedometer, I kept the van going around forty. The fact that Stoat did not say anything about my disobeying orders told me he was still feeling weak, and I allowed myself a chirp and twitter of hope. I tried to plan how I might escape when we got to Stoat's house, how there had to be an instant when the shotgun barrel slipped askew in the duct tape, and if I saw a passing car—

Damn. There it was already, his shack the color of a skink's neon blue tail—

My jaw dropped. I frankly gawked.

Stoat barked, "What the fuck?" He saw it too. A small, newish but nondescript car parked in front of his home.

He shoved the shotgun harder into the back of my long-suffering neck. "Keep driving. Don't you dare honk the horn."

Shucks, why hadn't that occurred to me?

Heading on up the road, I had only a glimpse of my own fuchsia home on the passenger side, because I did not dare to turn my head and look. A moment later, Stoat commanded, "Turn here!"

A very rutted and rudimentary lane ran off to the right.

With mental eyebrows raised, wondering what the crazy old pervert was up to now, I took the turn and sent the van into thick woods at a bumpy crawl. I remained terrified, of course, but after a person has been scared fit to pee her pants for long enough, fear becomes a chronic condition to be endured like arthritis or a bad back or the common cold.

The woods gave way to what had maybe once been a pasture but was growing up in scrub—scratchy bushes, shaggy junior pine trees, twisty vines with chalk white leaves. Judging from the crudest of all possible twin-rutted trails winding through the obstacles, I saw that kids had been riding four-wheelers here, cheerfully trespassing while risking their fool necks by crossing the road to jump the ditches on either side.

"Turn right," Stoat ordered.

Mine not to wonder why; mine but to do or die, or postpone death slightly. Anyway, it was his van that was going to be scratched silly and break an axle. I turned into a space so narrow that thorny branches skittered across the metal on both sides. Necessarily, I slowed the van from a crawl to a creep on terrain more appropriate for tank treads than tires. Plowing through ditches, trundling over logs, all the while I wondered what the heck Stoat was planning. Inwardly I trembled; was I driving him into this hinterland so that he could kill me and nobody would ever find my body?

The four-wheeler trail diminished, faded, then vanished altogether, leaving the van surrounded by privet so thick and tall I felt justified in taking my toes off the gas pedal, relieving my overstretched leg muscles.

Stoat barked, "Whatcha stopping for?"

"We can't go any farther."

Stoat actually chuckled. "You ain't never been no man. Sure you can. Just ram on through."

"You want me to ruin your van?"

"Go right ahead. You ruined my life already, ain't you?"

Interesting. I'd never thought of our unfortunate acquaintance in that way.

"Go!" Stoat barked.

Fine. Okay. Whatever. I extended my protesting leg and punched the gas pedal, sending the van crunching through and over the privet, which alternately lifted the vehicle clear off the ground, then set it down again with a wildly slewing vengeance. In the backseat, Stoat lurched and swayed, but I still felt his hand on the business end of the shotgun he had duct-taped to both of us, clever bastard. He could not have foreseen that we would go four-wheeling in a vehicle with two-wheel drive, and that I could have been out of the van and away, but there I still was, stuck to a shotgun stuck to him.

Out of the privet at last, the van struggled through brambles and saplings.

"Just aim between the big trees," Stoat instructed. "Don't bother about nothing else."

Following instructions, I ran the van like a bucking Bubba truck over crepe myrtle, but shied away from a thick catalpa, zigzagged through a grove of water oaks, trundled beneath pink-furred boughs of mimosa—

Mimosa?

"Stop here," Stoat commanded. But before my foot touched the brake, the van coughed, choked, gasped, exhaled a malodorous steamy cloud from beneath its hood, and died. The engine went shockingly silent.

"Punctured something," Stoat grumbled. "Don't matter. This is where we git out."

Quite illogically, I turned off the ignition, removed the key, and put the gearshift in park, discombobulated to see where "here" was: the woods immediately behind my so-called home. Between the pink fuzz-flowers and plumy kelly green leaves of drooping mimosa boughs, I could glimpse planks painted fuchsia.

"You better goddamn well hope you got some eggs that ain't gone rotten," Stoat said.

Trying to remember whether I had eggs in the refrigerator was like trying to revisit a previous life. As if through a glass darkly I recalled that, yes, there were eggs, but it all seemed so long ago, maybe they had gone rotten like Stoat.

"And some halfway decent bread," Stoat added.

Bread? Did I have any bread, and if so, was it decent or otherwise by Stoat's unpredictable standards? My brain froze like an overtaxed computer.

"Move your ass," Stoat growled far too close to my head; I jumped. He edged his way between the bucket seats, his duct-taped shotgun turning my head for me, forcibly. "Gimme them van keys," he demanded. "We get out the way we got in."

Sure thing, Mr. Stoat, sir, whatever you say. I handed him the keys, noticing that he was taking the duct tape with us; he had lodged it, an oversized silver bracelet, on his arm. Like a pair of mediocre contortionists linked by duct tape and a dangerous stick, we got out of the van and, hampered by trees, sticker vines, and armadillo holes, bumbled toward the house.

The sight of my own white aluminum back door, once we finally got there, seemed like the strangest, most bizarre and grotesque thing in the world to me, utterly alien. Hazy with anxiety about eggs and bread, I could not remember whether I had left the door locked. And the stench coming from inside the house didn't help. I knew what smelled but I did not want to see it or think about it. Poor Schweitzer. So much had happened since I'd left him yapping his cute little dachsie-moron bark, and almost none of it good.

Stoat prodded me with the shotgun from behind. I reached out to open the door and it gave way like an ulcerating wound beneath my touch. I walked into my own home a stranger and a hostage. I saw the items lined up, Stoat-fashion, on my kitchen table. I knew what else Stoat had done in my house. I tried not to look for Schweitzer, but my eyes refused to obey me. They forced my mind to focus on the place where Schweitzer must have met Stoat at the front door—

My dead pet wasn't there. Instead, I saw a rectangle of carpet cut away.

I felt my jaw drop and I must have made some sort of involuntary yawp. Stoat demanded, "What?"

I pointed.

"What the fuck?" Stoat complained, dumping the van keys and his duct tape on top of my microwave. "Some asshole got rid of your dead dog. Big hairy deal."

But it was a big deal. It was huge. Somebody had been here, blessedly turned on the air-conditioning, and taken care of Schweitzer. Somebody was aware and maybe even cared that I was in some kind of trouble. Who could it be?

Justin! Had Justin gone to the police?

Eerily, as if he had heard me thinking, Stoat gave a laugh like a gunshot, explosive and brief. "No, it ain't Justin," he said curtly. "He's in the swamp. Feeding the gators. I took care of him."

Sitting in the living room with Chad and his father while they all sipped iced tea and talked, Amy very much saw Chad in the slim, quiet older man. Watching him, she imagined Chad as he might become when age had beaten him into a more refined, stronger if less shining kind of steel. She intuited that Ned—"Please call me Ned," he had told her with a shy smile—Chad's father could be counted on. Maybe that hadn't been the case in the past, but Amy believed people could change. Otherwise, what hope was there for the world?

"It's all right, Oliver." Amy patted the dog, who was sitting on her feet after trying to make friends with Meatloaf, who did not return the sentiment. "You just let him alone and he'll let you alone." Although smaller than Oliver, Meatloaf didn't seem to know it.

"That's right, Oliver." Chad spoke solemnly from across the room. "You listen to Amy."

She glanced at her husband, unsure whether he was being snide or serious, but the moment she looked at him, he looked away. Okay, so he was going through some kind of crisis that had driven him to his father for help, but she wished she knew what it was. Coming home, he hadn't hugged her or kissed her, which was no surprise. But she felt as if he wasn't as angry at her as before, and oddly, that concerned her. Chad seemed to be following his father's lead, unsure of himself. Where had his confidence gone?

He bit his lower lip, swallowed, and turned suddenly to look at her. For the past hour and a half, he had let his dad do most of the talking as Ned and Amy got to know each other and caught up on missing years. They had even talked about a heartache named Justin.

But now Ned seemed almost out of questions, and Amy felt sure Chad had something to say to her, yet felt hesitant. It was not like Chad to need help.

Would he welcome hers?

Amy took a chance. "Chad, what is it? What's got you spinning your tires?"

He swallowed hard, then said, "Us." He sat on the edge of his chair to lean toward her, his elbows on his knees and his big hands clutching each other. "It's just that, um . . ." He took a deep breath, then spoke rapidly, as if he needed momentum to get through this. "Amy, why don't we go away for a week or ten days, you and me, to try to get us back the way we used to be? We can go camping or something. Dad will take care of things here."

Amy felt a rush of joy, delight, tenderness—*oh, Chad, you're so sweet!*—and at the same time a surge of wrath, frustration, rage. *Men! He thinks this is all he has to do to fix everything?* Other contradictory emotions—a suspicion of sudden bright ideas, an attraction to restaurants, worries about the kids and cat and house, an expectation of change, a fear of change—all jostled Amy at the same time, rendering her incapable of an immediate response. Her mouth opened but no words came out.

Chad was starting to look upset. "Amy?"

With considerable effort she managed a single word. "Boggled," she whispered.

"Huh?"

"You're doing okay, son," Ned interposed. Lounging deep in the sofa, he spoke to Chad with the soothing wisdom of age. "At least she hasn't hit you yet. Most women would if you offered to take them camping for a second honeymoon."

True. To Amy, camping was pretty much housework redoubled, plus stinking fish to clean, but minus electricity and furniture.

"Oh!" Chad now looked more anxious than upset. "Amy, you call it. Where would *you* like to go?"

The hell of it was, she didn't know. She couldn't seem to imagine anything past staying at home, waiting for news of Justin. And her mouth still wasn't working right.

"No rush." Ned stretched, got up, and to Amy's surprise gathered the glassware and dishes they had used and headed for the kitchen sink. Over his shoulder he called, "It's not like you have to go tonight, or tomorrow for that matter." He left the room.

Amy managed another word. "Money?"

Chad burst out, "I've been stupid, complaining about money. Family is more important than money."

"Your job—"

"Our marriage is way more important."

"Justin?"

"Dad will man the Web site and the phones. Amy," Chad said plaintively, "before Kyle and Kayla come charging in here from school, could you at least tell me whether you *want* to—"

"Yes." Suddenly she could speak in complete sentences. "Yes, honey, of course I do."

Quinn spilled out the other contents of Mom's purse, which included a checkbook, a red Sharpie marker, a small flashlight shaped like Eeyore, some novelty pens, car keys, another key on a Hello Kitty ring, some wadded tissue, and her cell phone, which was turned off. Quinn said, "Mom never turns her phone off."

Forrest said, "I know."

Neither of their voices, Quinn noticed, was quite steady. He turned the phone on and checked the history. Mom's last phone calls were to him and his brother nearly a week before.

Wordlessly he passed the phone to Forrest, who looked at the data bleakly. Quinn started piling Mom's stuff back into the handbag. Forrest did likewise.

The shadows of the blue shack felt weighty now, ominous. Quinn wanted to say, "Let's look around," but fear of what they might find kept him silent. Beckoning his brother to follow, he set off. They checked out the small kitchen, then the small, dark bathroom with the two-by-fours blocking the window, then a bedroom neatly stacked with masculine clothing but clotted with masculine odors, and then the other bedroom, which they found oddly vacant except for an old-fashioned bed with a post at each corner, probably meant to support a canopy that wasn't there. And on the bed, nothing but a bare mattress and some shackles.

Ropes and handcuffs.

Fastened to the four posts of the bed.

Quinn stood and stared, unthinkable speculations knocking at doors in his mind that he would far rather have kept closed.

Almost as if in answer, Forrest burst out, "This is *not* for fun and games. There's urine on the mattress. And blood."

Quinn said, "It's definitely time to call the cops."

With business cards in hand for reference, Quinn phoned the Maypop County Sheriff's Office, asked for the deputy with whom he and Forrest had filed a Missing Persons report a few hours earlier, and was told he was in the field, unavailable. He left a message asking the deputy to call back, urgent. Next he tried the Maypop Borough Police and was told the officer handling his case had gone off duty. Again he left a callback message, urgent. Only the state police remained. Three strikes and he would be out. His hand shook as he pressed the tiny numbers on his cell phone. After asking for the trooper who was supposed to be his contact, he endured country music while he was put on hold. He had started drumming paradiddles on the wall to counteract the music when at last it stopped and the cop came on the line.

"Trooper Willet here."

"Yes. This is Quinn Leppo. We—"

"Who?"

"Quinn Leppo. My brother and I talked to you about our mother earlier today. We found her purse."

"She left her purse at home?"

"No. We found it in the neighbor's house, along with—"

"The neighbor's house?"

"The only place near hers. There's a bed in here—"

"What neighbor? Name?"

"We don't know! We're asking you to investigate whoever it is. The bed—"

"Were you invited in?"

"No! There's nobody home. I'm trying to tell you—"

"So you're trespassing and interfering with evidence."

"Officer, whoever lives here—"

"Is none of your business. I'm the investigator. The last thing I need is buttinsky civilians littering fingerprints all over the case. You and your brother exit that residence immediately, leaving everything the way you found it. That's an order."

"But—"

But Trooper Willet had terminated the call.

"Son of a bitch," Quinn said, snapping his phone shut with more than necessary force. "He said—"

"I know what he said," Forrest interjected. "I could hear him as if you had him on speaker."

He and his brother faced each other, exchanging a long look

with an unspoken question in it: now what? And Quinn felt tectonic plates shift in his world because he saw Forrest as never before: not his younger-sibling rival, but an equal, a strong ally, his brother on whom he could depend.

Quinn said, "That cop thinks this is a case, a puzzle for him to solve. He doesn't care whether Mom is alive or dead." Emotion sneaked up on him, causing his voice to break on the last fatal word.

Forrest simply nodded. "We stay. Look around. Find out who lives here. There's got to be an electric bill or something."

"And if Trooper Willet shows up?"

"If Trooper Willet shows up, that means he got his ass out from behind his desk and he has to take a look at this creepy place."

NINETEEN

I *took care of him*, Stoat had said. He meant he had killed Justin. The words staggered me like a blow, yet I could not comprehend or react. Instead of responding, I stood gawking at the place where Schweitzer's mortal remains should have been. Stoat must not have liked this, because he jabbed his duct-taped shotgun into the back of my duct-taped neck so hard I gasped with pain and felt something wet: my own blood.

"Now you listen, bitch." Stoat's rasping voice sounded as hard as the shotgun barrel. "You know I'm an orderly man. That means if I let you loose of this here duct tape, you follow orders. I aim to learn you the meaning of complete obedience, Miss Lee Anna. Say 'Yes, sir.'"

I could not think of a single wise thought ever generated by any philosopher, anytime, that seemed relevant to this situation. I said, "Yes, sir."

"Good." He yanked the duct tape off my neck so suddenly that I staggered with shock and pain. For a moment I stood swaying with my eyes closed, and when I opened them, Stoat stood too close in front of me, his favorite large, wickedly sharp knife in one hand, the shotgun in the other, and nothing had ever been as ugly as his distorted face. Nothing had ever smelled quite as sickening as his breath, and he grinned like a skull would. With all his rotten teeth showing he said, "I want some toast and two eggs over easy. If you break either of the yolks, I'll slit your throat."

"Yes, sir."

"Well, get moving!"

"Yes, sir."

He stood guard until I got out the things I needed: eggs, margarine, frying pan, spatula, bread for toast. The bread showed hints of green mold, but Stoat didn't have to know about that. He sat down at the table and propped his shotgun against it. "Don't break them yolks, now," he remarked, thumbing his knife's razor-sharp point and edge.

Talk about pressure. Two eggs over easy, what Pennsylvanians called dippy eggs. I'd cooked them a zillion times and the occasional broken yolk hadn't been the least bit important. Now it had become a matter of life or death.

Crack eggs against a flat surface, I'd heard somewhere, sometime, for a clean break and no jagged edges to tear the yolk.

I cracked the eggs on the stove top and managed to plop both of them into the hot frying pan without mishap.

Lounging with his booted feet on my kitchen table and his shotgun in his lap, Stoat added, "I might do it anyway. Slit your throat when you go to sleep."

This did not seem to require an answer. I kept my eyes on the frying pan and said nothing, but my mind jotted frantic memos. Offer coffee. Stay awake. Not tired anymore. Not.

Stoat demanded, "What you think, Miss Lee Anna? You like the idea of the knife?"

"No, sir."

"Neither did Justin, but that's the way I done him."

Sick, not just heartsick but all of me scared sick, must not let it show. Must not show emotion. Must not cry. Not. Cry.

With commendable steadiness I asked, "When?"

"Just before I found you."

Damn, it was plausible. Even though—had he asked where Justin was when he first came into the fishing shack, or hadn't he? I couldn't remember. The spatula shook in my hand as I lifted it to flip the eggs.

Focus, I coached myself. Concentrate. I quite thoroughly believed Stoat intended to kill me now that he was feeling better.

"You scared, Miss Lee Anna?" he taunted.

Without answering and without much finesse I flipped the eggs. Somehow, their yolks retained their integrity. Those eggs must have been laid by an honest hen, to whom I felt gratitude as I turned the burner off.

"Answer me, bitch. You scared?"

"Yes, sir."

Must not think about Justin. Must not cry.

I took a deep breath. With my back to Stoat, I reached for a cupboard door.

"Hey!" I heard the thunk of boots on the floor, and a nasty snick from the shotgun. I froze.

"I need a plate for your eggs," I said.

"Woman, you call me 'sir'!"

"Sir, I need to get a plate for your eggs, sir."

"Is that so, tricky bitch?"

"Yes, sir."

"Move slow."

Yes, sir. Whatever you say, Stoat, you goddamn effing goat with a goatee, sir. Moving as if I were trying not to awaken a sleeping baby, I got out the plate, slid the eggs onto it from the pan, then added stale and marginally moldy bread rendered edible by the toaster and a lot of margarine.

Placing the plate in front of Stoat, I wished my thoughts could poison the eggs.

I imagine he knew this and I could see he didn't care. He dug into his breakfast with evident satisfaction.

I sat down across the table from him. He stopped eating to glare. "I didn't say you could sit down."

I didn't move, but said dully, "Sir, request permission to sit down, sir."

Quick as a striking snake he deployed his shotgun as a club, and I stiffened and winced—not quite heartsick enough to be indifferent—but Stoat lowered his weapon and began to laugh like a kindly uncle. "Lee Anna, Lee Anna," he said, shaking his head and chuckling as he went on eating his eggs, "you're a piece of work. You must be hungry; fix yourself something."

This, too, this occasional humanity, was the real Stoat, making me feel bad for hating him so much. Yes, bad. With the back of my neck bleeding from constant contact with his shotgun barrel, nevertheless I felt like a bad little girl.

And making the victim feel bad, I realized in silent epiphany, was the whole point, the tipping point of torture. This was the unspoken understanding between the person with the club and the one on the floor: inflicting pain did not merely make the victim suffer physically; it made the victim feel what the shrinks call loss of self-esteem. Extreme loss, as exemplified by the way I felt at that moment: diminished by helplessness, unable to understand such punishment, but inclined, like a child, to accept blame. This was the strange dynamic between captor and captive, torturer and tortured, abductor and—Justin. Stockholm syndrome. Hanoi Hilton. Auschwitz. All cut from the same rotten old fruitcake.

Son of a bitch.

"I'm not hungry," I said, which because of the sickening circumstances was true.

. . .

Forrest yanked out a kitchen drawer and emptied it on the floor, making quite a bit of noise as an emotional release. It annoyed him that Quinn cringed, yelping, "What are you doing?"

"Ransacking." Forrest poked through the junk on the floor with the toe of one of his work boots, saw nothing of interest, and reached for the next drawer.

His older brother reached to stop him. "Don't!"

"Why not?" Overwrought feelings gifted Forrest with a rare, pellucid, very articulate moment. He stepped into the Suit's space, almost nose to nose. "Why the fricking hell not? We're trespassers, we've been ordered to leave, we're scofflaws. Why not do it right? Go turn on the damn air conditioner and then help me out. Mom was here. Whoever lives here probably has her. The fastest way to find anything with his name on it is to tear this place apart. Where's your balls, Quinn?"

"Not anywhere I'd want you to find them," Quinn retorted. "Would you try to be a little bit quiet? We can't turn on the AC. We need to keep an ear out in case the guy comes back."

"Oh, for God's sake, have some brass."

"Screw you. What do you plan to do if some gun-toting redneck walks in, kick him in the head?"

"That's pretty much what I'd like to do, yeah." Again, Forrest reached for a drawer, and again Quinn stopped him.

"On TV, don't they generally start by looking through the suspect's trash?"

"Only because that doesn't require a warrant." Admitting only tacitly that it was a good idea, Forrest strode to the kitchen trash and overturned it with a satisfying clatter of empty jars and cans. "Phew! Why no trash bag? And where's the junk mail?" The mess on the floor consisted almost exclusively of food containers along with a few soppy paper towels and napkins.

"Good question. Try to be a little bit quiet, would you? I'll check out the guy's computer." Quinn strode off.

A little bit quiet, my ass, Forrest thought. So vigorously that he worked up a sweat, he dumped all the kitchen drawers, then pillaged the countertop and cupboards, all without finding anything useful. Where the hell did this guy keep his papers and bills? Forrest hadn't seen anything that could serve as a desk in the living room or bedrooms.

Close enough behind him to make him jump, Quinn bleated, "I can't find any computer. What kind of person does not have a computer?"

Enjoying the novelty of being in a foul and masterful mood, Forrest shot back, "What do you think I am, an FBI profiler? Probably a gun-toting redneck. Come on." He headed for the living room, where he hurled hard rectangular cushions off the Spartan furniture, then overturned it. He found nothing of interest in or underneath any of it. Kneeling, he yanked open the TV stand and pulled out video after video, most of them Walt Disney productions, from *The Lion King* all the way back to *Pinocchio*.

"Jiminy Cricket," remarked Quinn, eyebrows raised, "no DVDs? This guy is stuck in the dark ages."

Forrest stood up with clenched fists. "Bedroom," he ordered between his teeth, and Quinn actually followed him in there. He started dumping dresser drawers onto the bed.

Peering at a shadowy corner of the hot and airless room, Quinn asked, "What's that?"

Forrest looked up from a pile of no-longer-white tube socks balled into pairs. By now his eyes had pretty much adjusted to the indoor gloom. Along with Quinn he studied a remarkably ugly gray metal furnishing bigger than a filing cabinet but not large enough to hang clothing in. "Beats me. Open it."

Quinn went over and tried to do so. "Locked."

"Look around for a key." Forrest kept emptying drawers, but with diminishing enthusiasm as he came across ripped jeans, T-shirts crusty under the armpits, graying underwear with stains that hadn't washed out.

"Where would you be if you were a key?" Quinn asked—rhetorically, Forrest hoped. Jeez, could it really be? The Suit, down on hands and knees checking the lower surfaces of furniture, ruining his expensive trousers?

Forrest pulled open the dresser's bottom drawer and yelped, jumping back as if the things in there were live snakes. "Quinn, come here!"

Just behind his shoulder Quinn drawled, "Whatsa matter, little brother, you scared of sex toys?"

"Startled me. Ick! What's this guy been *doing*?"

Somewhat to Forrest's mortification, Quinn stepped past him, took hold of the drawer, and dumped it. Riding crops and other whips, cane switches and leather straps, handcuffs, red thong underwear, and the like looked no less icky when displayed upon stained whitey tighties.

"Gross." Forrest stepped back. "Sick."

"Interesting," Quinn said. "I read someplace that the best way to hide anything small is to put it in a dildo, because nobody will want to touch it." He picked up one.

"Ew!" Forrest protested.

"You're wasting time. Check the vibrators."

"You check them. I—"

"Wait a minute." Quinn squeezed a rubbery phallic representation. "There's something in here." A moment later he found a slit in the item's hollow structure and extracted a small key.

"I cannot believe you did that." This was true. Forrest felt dazed, almost dizzy, as he followed his brother to the gray metal enigma in the corner.

"The key fits," Quinn reported as he opened it, spreading the double doors to reveal the contents. Boxes of ammunition filled a shelf at the top. Empty rifle racks occupied the middle.

"It's a gun safe," Forrest said, "but where are the guns?"

"And what are all these papers?" Quinn picked up a thick stack of documents from the bottom of the gun safe and leafed through them. "Jesus Christ. They're just the bastard's bills, stuff like that."

"Why would he hide them in a locked cabinet?"

"Paranoid."

"Well, who the hell is he?"

"His name appears to be Steven Stoat."

"Coffee?" I asked Stoat.

"Sure thing."

"It's just instant. In the microwave."

"Good enough." Rather messily enjoying his eggs, he was still in a benign mood, which had given me time to think and stiffen my own spine. Okay, Stoat the Goat claimed to have killed Justin, but why hadn't he said so before, when I had found Justin's Magic Marker note on the picnic table in the fishing shack? Had he been preoccupied by the snakebite? Or had he only recently fabricated Justin's death to torment me? This seemed quite possible. But even if Justin *was* dead, I was still alive and needed to keep living. If only Stoat would stay human for a few minutes, I had a request. But never disturb animals when they're eating, Mother had always told me. Patience might possibly mean survival. I had to wait.

I even waited until he was finished sipping his coffee but, with precise timing, slipped it in before he started to get up from the table. I looked up to speak to Stoat as nearly as I could like one human being to another. And in the most natural voice I could manage, I said, "Hey, boss, I'd like to go brush my teeth, okay?"

This was a baby step in the right direction, namely, the bathroom. What I really wanted, desperately, was a shower.

Being filthy was beyond unpleasant, almost unbearable. I could actually feel the yellow scum coating my teeth, the crud forming between my toes, and a disgusting crust developing behind my ears. Not to speak of the cuts, scabs, and blisters on the bottom of my bare feet.

Stoat gave me a long, expressionless look out of his one functioning eye. "You women and your teeth," he said finally, as if dental hygiene were on a par with lipstick. "No way am I letting you in that bathroom with the door shut, cuz there ain't no bars on the window."

"That's all right," I said, and the pitiful thing was, I meant it.

"No funny business, now," Stoat warned. "Me 'n' my shotgun *and* my buck knife are coming with you."

"Yes, sir." Standing up to lead the way, I added, "I expected nothing less of you, sir."

"Are you being a smart-ass, Lee Anna?"

"No, sir. Not at all."

Hefting his weapons in both hands, he stood in the bathroom doorway, blocking the door from closing, as I took my time brushing my teeth and flossing them and brushing them again, ostensibly paying no attention to Stoat but actually very aware of his growing boredom. When he yawned, I about-faced, stepped into the shower barefoot but otherwise fully clothed, slid the shower curtain closed, and turned the water on full blast. I had really good water pressure, and I did not even mind that at first it spurted out freezing cold.

"What the fuck!" Stoat swiped the shower curtain out of the way to get at me and was zinged in his swollen face by needles of water. He jumped back, and I closed the curtain again.

"I'm not going anywhere except right here in this shower, Mr. Stoat, sir," I sang out earnestly.

"You crazy bitch!" He sounded angry, but not enraged. I judged myself safe for the time being and shed my clothes like a lizard clawing its old skin off. Never before in my life had a shower felt so good, or perhaps so necessary. I soaped myself all over with my sudsy pink ball-of-mesh scrubber, twice. I shampooed and conditioned my hair. I made the mistake of thinking of Justin, which gave me a pang, so in order to counteract it I sang what I could remember of "Girls Just Want to Have Fun," and actually heard a snort of laughter from the blurry shotgun-laden presence right outside the shower curtain.

I would have stayed in the shower all day if I'd thought I could get away with it, but all blissful relief must end. To maintain my own morale, I kept singing, transitioning to "Achy Breaky Heart" as, spiderlike, I reached out from behind the shower curtain with one arm to snatch a towel.

"What the hell is the use of drying off?" Stoat asked. "You're gonna get back in them same wet clothes, ain't you?"

Aaak. I hadn't thought far enough ahead. Parading in front of Stoat wrapped in a towel would soooo not be a good idea. I stalled for time. "Just let me dry my hair."

"You goddamn get dressed and come out of there."

His tone bespoke a loss of patience. I goddamn got dressed and came out of there with my arms folded across my breasts to hide my tits; I never wore a bra, and now I might as well have been in a wet T-shirt contest.

Oddly, my modesty irritated Stoat. "What the fuck? You think I'm gonna rape you? You think you're attractive to me? Crazy bitch, I'd rather fuck a warthog. I'm a pedophile and proud of it. Ped-o-phile. Say it."

What a bizarre way to be reassured. "Pedophile," I mumbled, starting to shiver from cold in my wet clothes.

"Louder!"

Squaring my shoulders, I shouted, "Sir, you are a pedophile, sir!"

I suppose I was a bit feckless.

Stoat swung his shotgun at my head.

TWENTY

That man struck like a rattlesnake, although that comparison is unfair to the snake, because Stoat made no sound of warning before deploying his shotgun. But because he tried to reverse it to strike me with the butt, I was able to duck the blow and run.

But I was startled and frightened right out of my mind. Instead of running for the front door, which would have made more sense, I ran to my bedroom, where my dry clothes were, with some vague idea of locking Stoat out.

Just as I reached the door, he caught up with me and clubbed me on the back of the head, knocking me all the way down and half-unconscious. Rather than try to fight back, I curled sideways on the floor, knees to my chin, eyes squinched shut, and hands protecting my head. Something flat, probably the shotgun butt, smashed my hands. Something pointed, probably the metal-clad toe of a goddamn redneck cowboy boot, struck my ribs. Hard. Hurt. Then my spine. Really hard. Hurt even worse. Then my hip. I don't know why the hell I didn't scream, except out of mindless pride, as the blows sent me spinning across the linoleum floor like a hockey puck.

With what goal? That whimsical idea coaxed my eyes open to

see whither was I spinning. I caught a glimpse of a shadowy lair where Stoat's booted foot could not reach me, and with more instinct than thought, I uncurled to scoot under the bed like a coachwhip snake.

"Hey!" I heard a clatter as Stoat dropped his shotgun, felt his fingers trying to grab my fleeing ankles, and it was my turn to kick, hard. I think I connected nicely with one heel, and it seems to me that I hit him on the swollen side of his face. I felt him let go of me, howling. "Bitch!" he yelled. "Now look what you done. It's bleeding!"

He said a great deal more, of course, cursing me vehemently and brilliantly, mingling the scatological, the profane, and the obscene. Huddled under the bed with the dust bunnies sticking to my wet clothes, skin, and hair—so much for feeling clean again— I listened to his virtuoso performance with shock and awe.

A moment later the bedclothes were jerked away, and I got an unnerving view of his grotesquely distorted face, black-and-blue and now red with blood, as he got down on his hands and knees to peer at me, positioning himself to see me with his good eye. Luckily, because this room of my pink shack was so small, I'd tucked my full-sized bed into the corner, jammed against the wall, and now I'd jammed myself there also. Stoat couldn't reach me. Dripping red spots onto the linoleum, he did not look pleased. Indeed, the expression of his single slitty eye gave me new insight into the meaning of the word "ugly."

Rather too softly he told me, "You get your goddamn lard ass out from under there."

My only answer was not to move.

"I'm telling you, bitch, get out from under that bed and clean up this mess."

I almost smiled. Stoat, neat freak, unable to stand the mess his blood was making on the floor, what a crazy—yes, crazy.

Viscerally in that moment I understood for the first time that Stoat's obsession with tidiness was not a harmless quirk, but an extension of his need to control. Not just normal control: Stoat needed to control everything. Quite aside from any practical considerations of not wanting to go to jail, he had to control Justin even if it meant—

Goddess damn the pervert to hell.

Abruptly I asked him, "How did you kill Justin?" With the knife, he had said earlier, but I wanted to see what he'd say now.

"The way I'm going to kill you, asshole! With this gun." One way or the other Stoat was a liar, but he gave me no time to appreciate this. He shoved his shotgun under my bed. No doubt about it, Stoat couldn't reach me but his artillery could.

"Not a good idea," I said.

Paying no attention, he said louder, "And if you don't get your fat butt out from under there right now, I'm going to make it hurt."

"Whoever those people are across the road at your place, they'll hear a gunshot right away," I continued as if with sincere concern for his welfare. "Just like I did when you shot Schweitzer."

He started to edge the gun into position, but then, in a delayed reaction, he heard what I had said. I saw common sense kick him in the face. He demanded, "Are they still there?"

"How should I know?"

"Who are they? Cops?"

"How should I know that either?"

He swore himself silly, and if my position was undignified, well, so was his. I could almost see capital-C Control clashing against capital-R Reality within his underdeveloped mind.

Finally his eyes snapped back to me and he yelled, "I'll use a silencer! A pillow!"

"You expect me to hold it for you?"

Checkmate. I watched him take it in. It's pretty impossible for a person with only two hands to aim and fire a shotgun while pressing a pillow to the muzzle at the same time.

I added, "Besides, if you kill me, who's going to clean up the mess?" And now that he was no longer ordering me to move my lard ass, perversely I began to wriggle out from under the bed.

I did this because, having had his rant and rave, Stoat might be comparatively harmless for a while now, judging by my experience of him. Actually, I felt not at all sure he wouldn't still shoot me—or, as a more silent measure, knife me—but I couldn't stay under the bed forever. I scrambled out from under its foot, stood up, and brushed dust off myself. Parts of me, where Stoat had struck or kicked me, hurt considerably, but I ignored them.

Standing a few feet away from me, Stoat kept the shotgun aimed at me.

I looked at him and felt only annoyance, which I did not allow to show in my face. I said, "What does a person need to do around here to get into some dry clothes?"

That was a mistake, my letting him know what I wanted. Deep in his scrawny chest he chuckled. Then he ordered, "Clean up this mess."

Sure, whatever. I didn't want blood drying on my bedroom floor. But I didn't want to treat my bathroom towels like cleaning rags either. "I'll go get paper towels from the kitchen."

"No. Use these towels right here."

Something in his voice warned me that I'd pushed him far enough. So I did as he said. But the irony was, as I scrubbed on hands and knees to clean his blood off the floor, my own blood ran down from my lacerated scalp to drip on all the same places.

Because State Trooper Willet had ordered him and his brother to vacate what he now knew to be the Stoat premises, Quinn tried calling the Maypop Borough Police instead, and lucked out. The officer assigned to the Clymer/Leppo case had shown up for work. "I was just about to return your call, Mr. Leppo."

Sure you were, Quinn thought, but he kept acid out of his voice as he briefed the officer, telling him only that they had found their mother's purse at a neighbor's house and the man's name was Steven Stoat; was he known to the police?

"Steven Stoat, huh? Doesn't ring any bells, but let me bring him up on the computer. Hold on just a minute."

"He's running Stoat for us," Quinn whispered to Forrest. Some people liked to say yes and some people liked to say no; this cop seemed to be one of the former, happy to help.

Back on the line a moment later, the man sounded disappointed to report, "He's clean."

"No criminal history at all?" Quinn's voice shot up.

"Two speeding tickets and one DUI years ago. Nothing to flag him as a violent offender. Perhaps he and your mother simply went somewhere together."

"Leaving a dead dog on her living room carpet?"

"Well, that could be an unconnected incident."

What were the chances? With clenched teeth Quinn said, "It looks as if my mother might have been held here against her will."

"What makes you think that?"

"A bed with bloody handcuffs."

"I see." The police officer's voice rippled with innuendo.

"No, you don't see! It's a bare bed and the handcuffs are neither pink nor fuzzy! If you—"

"There's no need to shout, Mr. Leppo. I will be glad to put out a BOLO on Stoat as a person of interest in your mother's case."

"Fine. Thank you."

Concluding the call, Quinn looked at Forrest silently standing by in the messed-up bedroom. "Now what?"

"More of the same, I guess. Try the Sheriff's Office."

Quinn did so, to find that the deputy assigned to his mother's case was still unavailable. But on impulse he asked whether he could speak with Deputy Morales. A few moments later, Morales came on the phone sounding like an old family friend. "Quinn! How are you and Forrest? Did you sleep?"

"Some. Listen, Deputy, I know this isn't your case, but—"

"Please, call me Bernie. I am glad to hear from you. What is going on?"

So Quinn told him about the barricaded bathroom window and the weird bare bed with shackles and the sex toys and finding the key to the gun cabinet in a dildo. At this point, much to his own embarrassment Quinn suffered a jag of the giggles. He had already realized his need to talk was emotionally driven, but he hadn't realized he was cracking up. The only way to stop giggling was to cry. Damn everything. With tears burning at his eyes, he put the cell phone on speaker and passed it to Forrest. Then he folded to a seat on the bedroom's clothing-strewn floor, putting his arms around his legs and his head on his knees.

He could hear Bernie Morales saying, "It sounds like not very nice sex kinks. You found out who is this man?"

Forrest told him, "Steven Stoat."

"Stoat! I know Stoat. Pineapple face, cave chest, goat beard, big mouth like he eats the hot dog sideways, ugly like someone hit him in the face with a sack of nickels . . . no wonder he never got married."

Forrest asked, "How come you know him if he has no criminal history?"

"Oh, Stoat, everybody knows him. Kind of creepy, compulsive. At the Stoat family reunion he lines up the folding chairs with a ruler, all straight and the same distance apart. I pity the nephew who lives with him."

Quinn suddenly recovered. Forget the nephew; his thoughts were all for his mother. He raised his head and, loud enough for Bernie to hear him, he exclaimed, "It sounds like he must be the one who rearranged Mom's stuff!" Furniture lined up, crockery marching single file down the middle of the table.

Bernie said, "You back, Quinn? Yes, it sounds like Stoat, but what does that prove?"

"Nothing," Quinn muttered.

"Nothing," Forrest repeated into the phone for his brother. "So now what?"

"Me, I can do nothing. It is not my case. What will you two do?"

Forrest said, "I have no idea."

Quinn stood up and said, "There are more things here we need to look at."

He half expected Bernie to warn them about trespassing or staying out of it, letting the authorities take care of it. But Bernie did not respond like a cop. Instead, he said, "Stoat left nothing but ammunition in the gun cabinet?"

Forrest deployed his eyebrows and remained silent. Quinn said, "That's right."

"Then he has the guns. Keep a lookout. If he comes to the front door, you go out the back."

After concluding the call to Bernie Morales, Forrest eyed his brother, checking on him without comment, glad that Quinn had broken down first. Forrest knew his own turn could come at any minute.

Quinn saw him watching and demanded peevishly, *"What?"*

"Nothing. I need to get out of this sicko room." The sight of whips and leathers and dildos strewn on the bed made him queasy.

He badly wanted to get out of this entire shadowy blue shack, but apparently Quinn had something else in mind. Turning sharply, Forrest headed into the living room.

It felt marginally less like a sauna in there. Forrest stood watching, numb and uncomprehending, as Quinn shoved the sofa back together. Once he had done that, the only things strewn in that room were videotapes, Disney cartoons, all over the floor. Forrest stared down at them.

Walking up to stand beside him, Quinn said quietly, "Exactly. A guy who comes fully equipped for sadomasochism, watching *Bambi*?"

Forrest stiffened. No longer numb, he felt sick. Defying his own queasiness, he picked up the first tape that came to hand, stuck it in the VCR, then sat on the sofa, grabbed the remote from its place on an end table, aimed, and clicked. The TV glowed to life.

The video started to run. There were no polite preliminaries, no introduction, no scene-establishing sequence, and it was not *Bambi* or any other Disney classic. It was a home video showing a man and a boy naked. What the man was getting ready to do to the boy shocked Forrest so badly that he could not take in everything at once. As if the film were illuminated by a strobe light, he could take in only shards out of sequence. Pubic hair, body hair, chest hair. Hollow chest and skinny, sloppy physique, folds of belly skin. Big-knuckled ink-stained hands grabbing the boy. Forrest bit his lip and had to close his eyes for a moment. He remembered as if in a bad dream that the kid had dark eyes yet blond hair kinked into cornrows. The man, the pervert, the pedophile, liked kinks. Forrest opened his eyes and for the first time focused on the man's face, visible over the boy's head. It was a face as ugly as the deed, acne-scarred skin dark with beard stubble, small stony eyes glittering with gratification. From the boy's eyes flowed tears. The man grinned, and decaying teeth bristled from his mouth. In a raspy voice he urged, "Cry, baby boy, cry!"

"For God's sake, turn it off," begged Quinn from the other end of the sofa.

Forrest jumped up, tossed Quinn the remote, then ran to the bathroom, where he vomited. He had been forgetting to eat; there was not much for his stomach to puke except yellow bile, and it left a terrible taste in his mouth.

When he went back out, Quinn had the TV turned off.

"Wanna watch *Snow White and the Seven Dwarfs*?" Forrest tried to joke.

"No, thank you. Do you think that naked, nauseating old goat was Stoat?"

Forrest sat down, considering. "We don't know, do we? Was there anything in the background to give us a clue?"

"I don't remember, but I think the background was just a cloth drape. We could check—"

"No way am I looking at that sick tape again."

"What about the others? If they're the same kind of thing with the same guy—"

"You go right ahead and play them if you want, Quinn. I'll wait outside."

Quinn's only answer was not to answer and not to move. He sat on the opposite end of the sofa from Forrest, staring without focus. After a while he said as if talking aloud, "We have child porn. What help is that?"

"Huh?" Even to himself, Forrest sounded like a sulky teenager. He felt weak and faint and he didn't like it, although he wasn't about to admit it to his brother.

Quinn said, "How is it getting us any closer to finding Mom?"

Forrest thought, *God, I want my mommy*. The elemental force of the thought made him feel shaky all over. *I really do. I want Mom. Why the hell didn't I realize that before she disappeared?*

When he was able to talk, he said, "If Mom knew anything . . . if Stoat is a pedophile and she caught wind of it . . ."

"She would have called the cops."

"But she didn't. So . . ."

"So maybe he knew she wanted to call the cops? So he—what? Grabbed her?"

Worse than that, Forrest feared. Much worse than that. But he could say only, "Quinn, I've got a really bad feeling about this."

TWENTY-ONE

Down on my hands and knees, ruining my bathroom towels by wiping blood off the floor with them, I ignored my own blood dripping from my head, and I tried to bypass the pounding pain where Stoat had bashed my scalp with the shotgun butt, because I had a more serious problem: survival. Stoat held me captive. Making an annoyingly rapid recovery from his rattlesnake bite, he no longer really needed me. So how to stay alive?

I figured Stoat could still use some tender, if not very loving, care. In my experience there was no man alive who would not want to be fussed over, especially with part of his face turning black and falling off. I knew Stoat liked to order me around like a slave. And I knew he sometimes liked my big mouth. Could I make him comfortable and get him talking? Somehow pull a Scheherazade on him?

Huh. I'd never thought of the *Arabian Nights* in that way before, but Scheherazade was the archetypal victim of Stockholm syndrome, pleasing her captor with her storytelling skills, then joining with him in marriage, and that was supposed to be a happy ending? I sure as hell did not want to spend a thousand and one nights with Stoat the Goat, but any future after today was not my immediate worry.

By the time I stood up and gathered the bloodstained towels into my arms, I had thought of an opening gambit. On my way to the washing machine with Stoat following close behind me, I paused in the living room and turned on the TV. Moving into this isolated slice of Eden, I had treated myself to more satellite TV than I could really afford, almost certainly more than Stoat had.

Stoat halted, transfixed by the Animal Planet spectacle of a pack of African wild dogs disemboweling an impala. As I moved on toward the washing machine, he snapped, "Stop. Drop that stuff. Set."

Obligingly I plopped the armload of bloody towels on the carpet, handed Stoat the remote, and sat down. Shotgun handy, he sat down also, comfortably, on the sofa, and when Animal Planet cut to a commercial, he began surfing the channels. I swear the pupil of his one visible eye dilated when he found a noisy show featuring oversized men, "gladiators," in an eight-sided chain-link "cage" instead of a boxing ring, savagely fighting with their fists and feet. One kicked the other in the jaw. The other reeled, then retaliated with a wrestling clinch. An announcer kept up a stream of commentary while a large audience of surprisingly normal-looking people watched, yelling in excitement. This barbaric spectacle was apparently present-day and considered a sport. Stoat seemed fascinated. I found it difficult to plan my next move under the circumstances, but I tried.

After a while I stood up. Stoat, damn him, alerted instantly, grabbing his shotgun and barking, "Where you think you're going?"

"To the kitchen for some snacks."

He grunted assent but followed, watching me closely as I put together a couple of plates of Ritz crackers, sliced cheddar cheese, and stick pretzels. Back in the living room, I placed one plate on the coffee table for him, took the other for myself, and sat down again. My stomach, much more frightened than I allowed my mind to be, wanted nothing to do with food, but I methodically chewed and swallowed anyway, partly to keep up my physical strength and partly to foster the illusion I was trying to establish, that of a happy housewife watching TV with her guest.

In due time I set my plate aside and stood up again.

"*Now* what?" Stoat barked, turning away from the TV with evident frustration.

"Would you like something to drink? Those pretzels are salty."

"I'll show you salty if you keep interrupting," he muttered as once again he followed me to the kitchen, where I filled a couple of glasses with ice and Sierra Mist.

"Ain't you got no proper soda?" Stoat complained.

"If I'd known you were coming, I would have stocked up on beer," I said lightly. "What do you like to drink?"

"Root beer."

"Next best thing," I said with a blithe little laugh, back in the living room, delivering his drink and sitting down with my own. "Tell me," I prattled on, "if a lion, which is from Africa, fought a tiger, which is from India, which one do you think would win?"

He gave me a surprised look. "Now, that," he said, "is an interesting question." But he did not answer, fixated again on the TV screen. The fights, I had seen on the menu when he was surfing, would be on all day. If Stoat's interest did not wane, I had time.

After I finished my drink, I stood up.

"*What?*" Stoat didn't even look away from the TV.

"Bathroom. Potty break."

"Sit down. Hold it."

"I can't anymore. I've been holding it all day. Listen, Stoat—I promise I'll be right back. You don't really think I could climb out of that little window, do you?"

He made a show of studying the width of my hips. "No, I guess not," he drawled. "You ain't no skinny little kid." But then all humor left his voice. "Don't shut the door. If I hear it shut, I'll break it down. Go ahead."

Yes!

Maybe, actually, I could have fit through the bathroom window on a diagonal if I had tried, but I had no intention of doing so. I'd won victory enough; Stoat had let me out of his sight. And oh, what a relief it was to use the toilet without supervision. First, I nipped into my room and grabbed some dry clothes. Then, in the bathroom, I put on the dry things, including socks and sneakers, before I flushed the john. I even combed my hair. When I felt I was ready, I checked myself in the mirror. This time I had my guard up against a captive's irrational shame. I looked levelly back at my own bruised eyes in the mirror, pressed my lips together, and nodded.

When I reported back to my chair in the living room, Stoat, as I had hoped and expected, barely looked at me. He appeared not to notice either my dry clothes or my shoes. I made myself nibble some more cheese and crackers, leaning back in my chair, hiding, I hoped, any sign of how high my adrenaline was running.

It was the middle of the day. Cars passed occasionally. Strangers were still parked at Stoat's place; I'd checked on my way back to the living room from the bathroom. If Stoat had any sense, he wouldn't harm me once I got where people could see. To reach the front door, I would have to run straight past him, and he'd stop me before I could get there. But the back door . . . I measured the distance with my eyes. Much shorter. But farther from where Stoat sat.

Taking a deep breath, I stood up.

"What?" Stoat barely stirred from watching the "warriors" on TV, barely even sounded annoyed.

"I'm going to get some napkins."

"What the hell for?"

Already halfway to the kitchen, I catapulted into a run, darted to the back door. Quickly—I'm not sure I had ever moved faster in my life—I twisted the dead bolt and grabbed the doorknob—

It wouldn't turn.

I tried again, wrenching at that knob as if I wanted to tear it loose, but to no avail. I couldn't open the door.

Although the door was not locked, the latch wouldn't budge no matter how I turned the knob. I rattled it—

Behind me—not nearly far enough behind me—Stoat laughed. Laughed! The bastard, he'd been playing me all the time. He had probably disabled the doorknob while I had been taking my good old time in the bathroom. "Something wrong with the damn door, huh?" he drawled as one of his wiry arms clamped around me from behind, pressing my upper arms to my sides, and something dreadfully sharp nudged the front of my neck.

"Forrie." Quinn sat on the sofa next to his tough kid brother who was coming undone. "Like you said, this place is sicko. You want to get out of here, go somewhere, have something to eat?"

Forrest looked up at him wild-eyed and addressed a completely different, unspoken question. "If he killed her, then what's her purse doing here? Wouldn't he have gotten rid of the evidence?"

Quinn found he couldn't meet his brother's stricken gaze. He studied his own Italian leather shoes.

"Quinn?"

He had to clear his throat twice before he spoke. "According to TV, sometimes criminals keep items from the victim."

"You think that handbag is a trophy? A souvenir?" Forrest sounded squeaky, almost hysterical.

Quinn didn't trust his own voice to speak. He nodded.

"But he'd be crazy not to get rid of her ID!"

Quinn stood up and went around the sofa to where he had found Mom's purse in the first place, checking the floor for an object he had just hazily remembered. But Forrest had kicked stuff around so much that he didn't see it anywhere. He got down on his hands and knees to search under the end table and the sofa.

Forrest asked, "What are you looking for?"

"That pad of paper."

"Huh?"

"When I picked up Mom's bag, there was a tablet of cheap paper, the kind they give to kids in school, lying on top of it."

"On *top* of it?"

"Yes, as if it had been placed there for some reason."

Belly down on the thin carpet to peer under the sofa, Quinn heard rather than saw Forrie stand up and prowl around the room. After a moment he called, "Is this it?"

Quinn sat up to look. "Yes."

"It was facedown on the floor under some of the so-called movies."

Quinn got up from the floor; Forrest came over to him with his find; but as Forrest reached out to hand it to him, a loose sheet of yellowish paper fell out to drift downward like a feather.

As it landed on the floor, Quinn felt recognition hit him like a fist in his gut, punching a wordless cry out of him.

At the same time Forrie exclaimed, "That's Mom's hand-writing!"

Quinn grabbed the sheet of paper off the floor, but his hand shook so badly that he had to lay it on the back of the sofa to read it. Forrest crowded next to him. Standing shoulder to shoulder, neither of them made a sound as they read:

Dear Forrest and Quinn,

Dear sons, please remember life has not been kind lately so this news is not terrible to me. I have encountered a man who needs to kill me. He promises to do so as quickly and painlessly as he can. By the time you receive this, I should be dead. This is my last will and testament in which I divide all my belongings equally between you. There is much I want to say but cannot, except that I wish you long and wonderful lives.

With greatest love,

Mom

"Oh, my God," Quinn whispered, and for the first time in his life it was really a prayer. He could not seem to see properly, but he felt Forrest start to shake, then heard him making urgent noises that were not words. He turned to put his arms around his brother.

Forrest returned the hug for only a moment before he stiffened and said, choking, "No. No, or I'll lose it." He pulled away. "We've got to get out of here."

"Where?" Quinn barely managed the single word.

"I don't know. Anywhere. I can't stand this place. Come on!"

Robotically Quinn followed Forrest out the front door. Forrest dived into the driver's seat of the rental car and called, "Where are the keys?" Without giving Quinn time to respond, he all but screamed, "Where are the damn keys?"

Quinn pulled them out of his pocket and handed them over, then got into the passenger seat; blinded by tears, he felt in no condition to drive. But a grinding sound from the starter and the way the car lurched forward told him that Forrie was not likely to do any better.

"Whoa," Quinn managed to say, "take it easy," as the Chevy Aveo jolted and swerved onto the road. "Where are we going?"

"I don't know!" The car veered wildly.

"Forrie, pull over. You're going to wreck." Quinn grabbed the wheel with one hand and tried to clear his flooded eyes with the other so he could see to steer. He got them off the road, and Forrest put his foot on the brake; they were not going to die after all. The car rolled to a stop in front of a blur of fuchsia.

"Don't scream or I'll slit your throat," Stoat said, dead quiet in my ear.

He needn't have warned me. My fright reaction is to stiffen like a Barbie doll, and sometimes I hate myself for that. I couldn't have screamed if I wanted to. I could barely breathe.

"I'll do your skinny neck same way I done Justin." With his disgusting lips close to my ear and the smell of his frankly rank breath reaching my face, Stoat nattered on in a hoarse, almost hypnotic whisper. "It ain't as easy as they make it look on TV. It ain't like sawing a log. You got to put the point of the knife here—"

He demonstrated, reaching clear to the other side of my head to jab at the sensitive skin of my throat. I closed my eyes, but his voice went on. "And you got to stab it in deep, two, three inches." I felt the knife tip break the skin and thought crazily, he's giving me a hickey. The bastard's hugging me and giving me a knife hickey. How loverly. "Then you got to kind of pivot it in there, deep, so's you get the jugular and the windpipe and the carotid and whatever. It ain't just a cut, like this." He slid the knife blade across my throat, and I could feel the blood trickle. "You got to do it right."

To my utter surprise I opened my eyes, felt my mouth moving, and heard my own voice speak quite calmly. "You did that to Justin?"

"Sure thing."

"How did you make him hold still for you?"

"Well, I had to shoot him first."

"Oh, I see." I nodded as politely as if I felt no knife at my neck, then amended, "No, I don't see. If you shot him, why didn't you just finish him that way?"

"Because I like knives, Miss Lee Anna. I am fixing to do you the same way. Give me one good reason not to kill you right now."

I had been wondering the same thing since he'd finished eating his fried eggs and stopped acting sick, although the side of his face remained grotesquely swollen; I could feel it right now, plump and hot against my head.

"Answer the question, bitch!"

"Sir, because the twin jets of blood spurting from my carotid arteries would make one hell of a mess, sir."

"I'll take you out in the back woods and slit your throat like a deer."

"Sir, then I'll scream like a witch with her broom up her nose, sir."

I hoped to lighten him up. Sometimes I had known him to react to my "big mouth" with a flicker of transient kindness. But it was not my crude humor that saved me. It was the sound of a car scrunching through the sand and leaf litter to park in front of my house.

I felt Stoat go as rigid as I-bar while he and I remained in our position of weird, perverse intimacy.

"Shhhh," Stoat hissed in my ear, tightening his hug-hold on me, pressing the knife harder against my throat and me harder against him. "No noise or you're dead."

Sir, yes, sir.

Yet this might be my last, best chance of rescue. . . . I waited, my mind clutching at straws of possibility, expecting to hear the car turn off, then someone knock at the front door, maybe yell something so I'd have a clue who it was and a chance to do something. But no, not so. Moments passed, the mystery car kept running, and I didn't hear another sound. The silent strain between Stoat and me was reaching a crescendo. When the tension climaxed, he would kill me.

I closed my eyes, opened them again, clenched my teeth, then whispered to Stoat, "Aren't you curious to see who it is?"

His grip shifted; his head reared in wrath. "Shut up or—"

Before he could complete the threat, I slammed my head back as hard as I could into the injured side of his face.

I'd never been snakebitten, but I figured this would have to hurt enough to give me a chance, and it did. Stoat yelped like a kicked dog, all his limbs flew out in a spasm, and he dropped the knife. I heard it hit the kitchen floor as I was already sprinting toward the front door.

Speed boosted by adrenaline, I flipped the lock and the dead bolt, turned the knob—but it wouldn't open. Damn Stoat! However he had rigged the back door, he had done the same to the front. More in frustration than in any hope that I might be heard, I pounded my fists against the inside of the door, then regained some wit and scrambled to flip back the drapes and look out the front window. There sat that same stupid car that had been parked in front of Stoat's blue house. If—

If nothing. Nothing but blackness, because Stoat hit me very hard on the back of my head.

TWENTY-TWO

In the rental car, Forrest shoved Quinn's hand off the steering wheel, noticed tears in his brother's eyes, and started to sob even though there was no damn time for crying; tears made him angry at himself and at Quinn, who was being a pain, trying to take control as usual, reaching for the keys in the ignition. Forrest whacked his hand away but somehow in the process ended up bawling in his brother's arms, making too damn much undignified noise. But Quinn was weeping too, the Aveo's engine still chugging away, and the car's air conditioner droning. A blast of cool air from the dashboard helped Forrest to gear down from sobs to sniffles, pull away from Quinn, and find a paper napkin amid the fast-food debris that littered the car. He wiped his face, blew his nose, and said, "Shit."

"Shit and a half," Quinn agreed huskily. "Did you just hear some kind of a pounding noise?"

"No."

"Must have been in my head."

"Mine feels like it's about to explode."

"Yeah. And we need to go to the cops."

Dully Forrest studied the rental car's controls. Somehow the gearshift had ended up in park. He reached for it.

Quinn's hand stopped his. "You're in no condition to drive."

"Neither are you." Forrest didn't need to look at his brother to know this, or to know that if their eyes met, both of them would break down again. He stared up through the windshield at pink and green mimosa.

Quinn said, "We'll just have to call the cops, then."

Forrest nodded.

"You want to go inside?"

"Here?" The pink shack. Mom's house. And Forrest's gut quivered at the thought of Mom. "I—I don't know."

"Not as bad as the other place." Quinn still sounded shaky.

"Yeah, but—where's the note, man?"

"Huh?"

"The—" Forrest just barely managed to say it. "The letter Mom wrote us." They would need to show it to the police. "Where is it?"

"Oh, shit." Quinn took an audibly unsteady breath. "I left it—"

"Okay, okay. We gotta go back for it. I can drive that far." He reached for the gearshift again.

Quinn said, "Be careful, little brother."

Forrest was careful. As he drove the short distance, he heard his brother on the phone to the Sheriff's Office. "I'm sorry, I can't remember the name of the deputy assigned to our case." He didn't sound sorry, just thoroughly upset. "Listen, just put me through to a detective, okay?"

During the pause that followed, Forrest pulled up in front of the blue shack, where he idled the car for the sake of its air-conditioning.

". . . possible homicide," Quinn was saying. "We found a note from our mother." He summarized what it had said. "Yes, I'm sure it was written by our mother. I recognized her handwriting." His voice quivered. "No, I can't bring it in. You need to send somebody out here. You expect us to drive when we can't see straight? Anyway, there are things here you ought to see. State police? Fine. We'll wait here." He clicked the phone closed.

Forrest looked over at him, then wished he hadn't; Quinn had turned away, but he saw his shoulders shaking. Reaching out, Forrest took hold of his brother's arm below the shoulder and squeezed hard. "Suit." The affectionate insult might help. "It's not over yet."

"Fuck all, Forrie," Quinn managed to say, choking, "those phone calls of Mom's that we never returned—"

"I know."

"—what if she was trying to call us about something important?"

"Yeah, I know."

"Maybe if we'd called back . . ."

"Quinn, a guilt trip is not going to help. Stop it."

"But I feel so goddamn bad!"

"I know. Me too. But we gotta man up now."

Having very limited experience in being knocked unconscious, I could not at first figure out what was happening when I woke up sputtering. Horrified, I felt as if I were being drowned by what looked like a pooka, a shape-shifting water demon, to my blurred vision. Or some kind of evil monster bending over me and dumping cold water on my head. And cursing out of his grotesquely unbalanced half-purple face. Expletive, expletive, expletive, then "Lazy bitch, get the fuck up and make me some dinner!"

Oh. Stoat.

"Something hot, goddammit! I'm hungry."

Huh. Evidently the car in the front yard was no longer an issue. I wanted to ask who it was and whether they had gone away, but of course I could not. Without speaking, I began to struggle to sit up.

"I want me a real cooked meal now."

Huh. That was one of the more unlikely things for anyone to expect from me, but Stoat didn't know my track record. And if he still wanted me to cook for him, that meant I would live a few hours longer.

Wobbling to my feet, I weaved toward the kitchen. Stoat followed me with the shotgun in hand.

I had no problem considering my options, because there was only one substantial meal I really knew how to cook. Blinking, trying to focus on things that kept sliding apart into duplication, I rummaged in the freezer compartment of the fridge.

"Gimme some ice for my face," Stoat ordered.

Oh, poor baby, I'd hurt his ugly snakebit face. What about my aching, bleeding head? I said none of this, of course, just took him a plastic bag of frozen mixed vegetables.

"You call that ice?"

With an effort I moved my mouth and formed words. "Better than ice cubes."

But he pulled back and would not accept what I was offering in my outstretched hand. It would seem his obsessive sense of order was offended by the idea of applying chopped broccoli, cauliflower, and carrots to his face. "You damn well get me ice."

I draped the sack of veggies over my own head injury and got him ice. It took all my compromised strength to flex the plastic ice cube trays. Taking him the ice in a ziplock bag, I felt shaky all over.

To my surprise he was showing all his rotting, crooked teeth in a grin, and I heard him chuckling. Okay, so maybe I did look a bit goofy walking around with a pack of frozen veggies on my head.

My shakes went away when I realized Stoat was no longer immediately dangerous. I set out the pound of frozen ground turkey
I had located. I looked in cupboards and found a jar of tomato
sauce and a box of linguine. Close enough. I moved my unwilling
mouth again. "I could make spaghetti."

"Then do it!"

I found that when I filled a large pot with water, I had no
strength to lift it. Surely the gentleman of the house should have
taken care of that task for me. But I did not ask. Instead, I slopped
out most of the water, put the pot on the stove, turned the burner
on, then added more water by trudging back and forth to the sink
with a margarine tub like a one-woman bucket brigade, with California Blend on my head yet. Stoat gave occasional staccato
bursts of laughter. Betweentimes I could feel him watching me,
but I did not waste the energy to turn my head and look at him
sitting there at my kitchen table with his shotgun and his ice pack.
I salted the water, left it to boil, stuck the meat in the nuker to
thaw, and found another big pot to make the sauce in. Normally I
would have chopped an onion. In no way, shape, or form could
anything about this occasion be considered normal. Forget the
onion. I scraped and crumbled thawed meat into the second pot
and started it browning. Put the meat's frozen core back in the
nuker to thaw some more. Then I tried to open the jar of sauce.

Crap. I couldn't.

I simply did not have enough strength to twist that lid off. Too
punch-drunk. I tried again, my improvised ice pack slid off my
head to splat on the floor, and the jar slid on the countertop but
did not submit to me. Next I would knock it onto the floor, break
it, and then where would I be? I had only the one jar of sauce. I
knew I should ask Stoat to open it. And I knew damn well I
couldn't. No way.

He knew it too. He knew exactly the predicament I was in, and it tickled his—his grits, I suppose. Through the ringing in my ears I heard him laughing, laughing while cheering as if the spaghetti sauce and I were meeting in the octagon, the "cage." "C'mon, Lee Anna! You act like you can do anything. Super cow! No, make that sow! Hey, c'mon, super sow!" His laughter grew darker. "Open that damn jar or I will shove this shotgun right up your fat ass so it don't need no silencer."

As if my own weakness did not frighten me enough already?

Carefully fumbling, I managed to lift the damnable jar in both unsteady hands and take it to the sink, where I blasted its lid with hot water while I regarded it with malice. My back to Stoat, I gave it the evil eye I did not dare show him. I had been knocked out and was staggering around without even a big mouth to save me; if things got much worse, I'd be dying on the floor; and at this moment a pernicious inanimate object had turned stubborn on me? I hated it. I hated that spaghetti sauce jar with an irrational passion, transferring to it all my repressed feelings about Stoat. It was that contemptible jar taunting me, that nasty jar sniggering in triumph over me. Screw the thing! In a paroxysm of fury I seized it and wrung its neck.

The lid popped off.

Stoat crowed with laughter. "Attagirl, Lee Anna! You show it who's boss! Jesus, if you could see your own face!"

If I were not suddenly so weak again, I would have thrown it at him as I had once seen my mother throw a can of sliced beets at my father in a moment when he had pushed her too far. Aiming it like a football, she'd gotten a nice spiral on it so that clots of bloody red splashed the wall, the ceiling, the other wall, the floor—

"Well, get a move on!" Stoat interrupted my reverie.

The microwave dinged, cuing me to get out the rest of the meat and crumble it into the pan to brown. Hazily I became aware that the pot of water was boiling, and I put the spaghetti in there.

When the meat was browned, I dumped the sauce on top of it and stirred. I made my spaghetti sauce in a deep pot so it wouldn't splatter the whole stove. This was my sole claim to culinary genius. I turned to the cupboards—

Stoat barked, "What now?"

Cupboard alert, sir. I made an effort to remember the names of the items I needed and enunciate them clearly. "Colander, plate, fork."

"Sir!"

Terror energized me. "Sir, I need to get out a colander, a plate, and a fork for you to eat with, sir."

"What the hell is a colander?"

"Spaghetti drainer, sir."

"Well, why the hell didn't you say that?"

"Chronic undifferentiated vocabulary overuse, sir. Do you prefer your spaghetti al dente, sir?"

"Who the hell is Al Dante?"

Luckily I had no sense of humor left at all. Goddess only knows what would have happened if I had laughed at him. Flat-faced, I spooned out a strand of the spaghetti, which was actually linguine, and tasted it. Unfortunately it required several more minutes of cooking. "It's going to be a while," I remarked, adding, "sir."

Stoat menaced with the shotgun. "Hurry it up."

But there is no way to hurry linguine. I couldn't warp the space-time/pasta continuum just to placate Stoat. And I was wondering how to break this to him when I heard a distant, unexpected noise.

A siren.

Sounding progressively louder. Heading toward us.

Ambulance, fire truck, police car? There was no way to tell, and no particular reason to pay attention, yet I listened intently.

So did Stoat. I suppose I should have been relieved that something had distracted him from fussing about his dinner for the moment, but I felt only apprehension.

More so when the siren bleeped to a halt just short of passing my house.

Stoat threw down his ice pack, jumped up, reached me in two strides, and put the gun to my head.

TWENTY-THREE

By the time the first police car arrived, Quinn had led the way into the blue house, where he and Forrest had put their mother's purse and her letter back in their original positions. Quinn felt as taut as the wires on a snare drum, but he had himself under steely control now. And as far as he could see, so did his brother.

He glanced outside as the siren bleeped to a stop and the officer, a state trooper, got out of his cruiser. "It's Willet," he reported.

Sitting on the sofa, stony calm and quiet, Forrest nodded. Quinn stood in the shadows near the front window and watched as Willet swaggered over to the shack's crude wooden steps. Muscular, with no paunch, but a bit short for a cop, Willet showed every indication of having a Napoleon complex, from his extremely erect posture to his scowling face to his shining boots. He did not merely open the front door; he subjugated it, whamming into the shack without knocking. Nor did he bother with a greeting. "I ordered you people to clear these premises."

As calmly as possible Quinn said, "If we'd left, you wouldn't be here to look at evidence now."

"Which said same evidence is no damn good since you two done tampered with it."

"We haven't touched the bed with what may be our mother's blood on it." He tilted his head toward the room. "Go see."

"You don't tell me how to do my job!"

"Wouldn't dream of it," said Quinn, utterly toneless.

Willet glared at him. Quinn stared back with his heartbeat drumming in his ears but, he hoped, with no expression on his face. He didn't hear the second cruiser pull in, but Forrest got up and walked to the front window to see. "Somebody from the Sheriff's Office is here."

Immediately, Willet barged into the room with the bare bed and shackles. Wanting to get ahead of the other cop, probably.

Quinn wished the sheriff's deputy might be Bernie Morales. But in a moment he could see it wasn't; that would have been entirely too helpful, Quinn thought bitterly. The law officer who came in was the detective they'd met earlier, Deputy Kehm, a tall, rawboned, sad-eyed man with a bald head but a robust white walrus mustache that made his leathery face look very tan. "Quinn, Forrest," he greeted them, shaking hands. Quinn fretted over his use of their first names; was the cop being condescending or just friendly? "What's this about?"

Quinn led him to Mom's note, pulled it out, and watched him read it. Forrest put a tape into the VCR and turned it on. As it started to play, Quinn noticed it was not the same one as before, but contained much the same content, except that this one added bondage.

Kehm's head jerked up. "Jeez!" he exclaimed, staring. "Are all them tapes like that?"

"This is only the second one we've watched," said Forrest.

Quinn asked, "Is that old goat Stoat?"

"I don't know."

"The answer is yes," said a ponderous voice; Trooper Willet had reentered the room to watch the video from behind them.

"Yes, I recognize that man as Steven Stoat, which means we can issue a warrant for his arrest for sexual misconduct with a minor."

Quinn heard this and turned sharply. "To hell with his sex kinks!" The minor would be Stoat's so-called nephew Bernie had mentioned, and if he had lasted this long, he could wait. "What about issuing a warrant for the bastard on suspicion of kidnapping my mother?"

Trooper Willet faced him belligerently. "So you found her purse, so she was here in this house, that don't prove—"

"You need to see this," Kehm interrupted smoothly, handing him the letter.

After reading the sheet of tablet paper, Trooper Willet demanded of Quinn, "Where'd you find this?"

"On top of her purse."

"How do I know you didn't write it yourself and plant it?"

For the first time in his life Quinn actually saw red. A haze of that color obscured his vision as sheer rage suffused his body. As he tensed to attack Willet, he felt hands grabbing his arms hard enough to hold him back: Forrest and Deputy Kehm.

He heard Forrest tell Willet, not too steadily, "That's my mother's handwriting."

Kehm said pleasantly enough, "Willet, looks to me like we got a crime scene here. It's all yours. You take the videotapes and pursue the sex crimes charges. I'll follow up on this other angle."

Willet rumbled, "I told these two boys this morning to clear out of here. Now all the evidence is tainted."

"Not the tapes. No way they altered them."

"Okay, but I still ought to cuff them for trespassing, obstruction, and acting just plain stupid."

"No need. You want them out of here, I'll take them with me."

Quinn's vision started to clear, and he regained just enough sense to keep his mouth shut. Rather than yelp, *"Boys?"* at Willet, he stepped back. Forrest and Deputy Kehm let go of him.

Forrest told Trooper Willet with strained courtesy, "We'd like to have Mom's note after you're done with it."

Willet glowered at him and offered the note to Kehm, who held an evidence bag open to receive it. After closing and labeling this, he pocketed it, turned around, and winked one of his sad, hound-dog eyes at Forrest. His white walrus mustache made it impossible to tell whether he was smiling as he did so. He thrust his chin toward the front door, and without a word Quinn led the way out. Going down the three unpainted wooden steps was like a descent into hell, if only because of the heat and fiery light. Kehm opened the back doors of his cruiser for him and Forrest.

"You are not under arrest," he told them as they got in.

Quinn still didn't trust himself to say anything.

Forrest asked, "Then where are you taking us?"

"My office, so we can talk about your mother. You hungry? I'm hungry. Let's stop for something to eat. You like pulled pork barbecue? Chili dog?"

Friendly, Quinn decided. But what the hell was the use of "friendly" under the circumstances? Pulled pork barbecue, hell. They needed to find Mom.

"We need to eat," Forrest said as if hearing Quinn's thoughts, "so we can think halfway straight and stay on our feet. Thank you, Officer Kehm."

"Chicken soup? I know a place that's got good chicken soup."

This was not a melodramatic movie; this was real life and didn't deserve to be saddled with such a cliché. Quinn had to close his eyes and clench his teeth against his own frustration.

Forrest told Officer Kehm, "Whatever you want is fine with us."

238   NANCY SPRINGER

. . .

Within a few minutes after the twins came home from school, Ned felt confirmed in his good impression of Amy. Saying hello to Kyle and Kayla, he saw ten-year-olds who still looked somewhat like children, not fashion models, and thereby he saw a sensible mother. Talking with his grandchildren, he encountered kids who were mannerly yet full of life, and he gave credit to good parenting.

While pleased to meet him, the twins seemed not overly impressed that he was their newfound grandfather. "Now, if *Justin* came back," Kayla told him, "*that* would be something."

"Yes, it would."

"Justin is our brother. You know what happened to him?"

"Yes, I heard."

"He's probably dead," Kayla said, but not quite as if this were her personal conviction. More as if she wanted to see whether her new grandfather would respond with horror.

Ned said, "That's sensible to think under the circumstances. But I still hope he's alive and he'll come home."

"Okay."

Kyle took over the interrogation. "Listen, we heard you're a drunk. Are you a drunk? No offense."

"None taken. I used to be a drunk, but now I am a recovering alcoholic. Do you think your father would bring a drunk into the house?"

"No."

Kayla asked, "How did you stop drinking? Did you get religion?"

"Yes, kind of, in a nondenominational sort of way."

"Non what?"

"Nondenominational. Not Baptist or anything. More Zen, actually."

Kayla blinked and did not ask what Zen meant. Instead she asked, "Can me and Kyle play with Oliver?"

"Kyle and I," Amy corrected from the sofa.

Ned said, "Oliver would love that if it's okay with your mom."

It was okay. Oliver happily romped off into the backyard with the Bradley twins. Once they were out of the room, Ned told Amy and Chad, "They're a credit to you." Good kids, in Ned's experience, hardly ever came from bad families, although the opposite could be true, as he had proved by example. He'd had good parents. He'd had a good wife. The fact that Chad had turned out so well was a testament to the job his wonderful wife had done raising the boy after he, Ned, had turned into a drunken butt-head.

Of the twins, Amy said, "They can be a bit outspoken, but I don't want to squelch their honesty away. You handled them well."

"I'm glad you didn't shush them."

"Sometimes I have to."

"Not for me."

"No, not for you." She smiled, and Ned had to restrain himself from hugging her. Tacitly, he and she had just settled something between them. Without minding in the least, he had felt her watching him and judging him, assessing whether he could be trusted with the kids. He had also sensed that it was not in her nature to pass judgment and that she was now relieved to be done with it. She probably had no idea how greatly her acceptance warmed his heart.

Still holding the gun to my head, Stoat swore in a way that made cursing not just a vent for frustration but also a reinforcement of a threat, finishing off with, "You lard-ass uppity shit-tail damn stupid cow, how the hell did you call the cops on me?"

"I didn't!" Instead of speaking as calmly and firmly as I wanted to, I squeaked, "How could I?"

"You think I'm stupid? Who else—"

I managed to interrupt with articulate sincerity. "Mr. Stoat, sir, if I had called the cops, they would be *here* instead of—where are they? Your place?"

"I'm fixing to see. Move." His freak-show face as grim as his tone, he marched me the few steps to where he kept his duct tape. Ripping some off with his snaggleteeth, he stuck it none too gently over my mouth. "Sit." He prodded me into one of my kitchen chairs and duct-taped my hands behind me. Setting down his shotgun so he could immobilize me more quickly, he swaddled tape around my ankles and the legs of the chair. "Don't make a sound and don't move," he said harshly and, in my opinion, quite unnecessarily. I nodded meekly.

Satisfied that he had me under control, Stoat took his gun and strode into the living room. Nothing prevented me from turning my head to watch him. Crouching beside my picture window, he peeped behind the closed drapes at a sideward angle, hardly moving them at all. Then he started to curse again, rapid-fire, like an automatic weapon. I didn't think he was speaking to me. I suspected he generally swore aloud when life didn't suit him. "That fucking half-assed car is back down there," he complained between bursts of stronger language. "What the fuck's that all about?"

I wished I knew! Who in the world had driven into my front yard, and why? I wondered whether Stoat had seen anyone after conking me on the head. But even if my mouth had not been silenced by duct tape, I could not have asked him.

Peering out the window, Stoat swore some more. "Dickhead state trooper parked in front of my house. What the fuck the goddamn cops think they're doing? Jesus shit, here comes another one. Looks to be from the sheriff."

Deep in my aching guts I felt a sluggish stirring of the feathered thing with wings called hope. Dare I hope this sudden influx of law enforcement might have something to do with me?

"This is bizarre," said Stoat. "What the fuck do they want?"

Bizarre was the word, all right. Everything seemed so surreal that my faint fluttering of hope went still almost immediately, and the only thing I could think was that someone had found Justin's body.

Stoat craned his neck in an effort to see better—

And lost his balance, falling over and whacking his head on the corner of the windowsill. Just a few feet away from where Schweitzer had once lain, Stoat flopped to the carpeted floor and lay still. Knocked out.

I felt my mouth attempt to open beneath the duct tape, felt the skin stretch around my wide-open staring eyes; I was so astonished. Due to Stoat's bluster or his bravado or both, I had not realized Stoat was still feeling pretty damn weak from the snakebite.

Could he be—dead?

No, dammit, the bastard was not dead. He lay faceup, and I could see his greasy gray nose hair moving as he breathed. But he seemed to be out cold.

For all the good that did me when I sat firmly adhered to a kitchen chair. And when, of all the frustrating things, I knew there were police right down the road!

Immediately I tried to get free. I struggled to slip my hands out of their sticky binding, but I soon found that the duct tape was way stronger than I was. I tried to kick my legs free. Same problem. I tried to stand and walk while still taped to the chair, only to put myself in great danger of falling. Panting with effort, I sat still again, trying to think.

As my breathing eased, I could hear Stoat snoring. Snoring! The loathsome man lay sleeping like a baby on my living room floor.

I wanted to scream. I thought I would lose my scant remaining mind to sheer outrage.

Then another seething, bubbling sort of snoring sound turned my attention away from Stoat and toward the stove, where I saw a large pot boiling over.

The spaghetti! Or linguine, whatever. I had forgotten all about it. Not only would it overcook, but the sauce needed to be stirred or it would burn. In fact, I already smelled it scorching.

I felt a moment's concern, then rebelled against it. There went Stoat's dinner. Nyah, nyah. Served him right. Lying there taking a snooze.

A sensible woman would have felt relief that he was not threatening her for a few moments, but I had deteriorated way beyond being sensible. I hated him. I wanted to lie down and sleep too. Slumping in the chair as far as I could, I rested my chin on my collarbone and closed my eyes. Almost instantly I dozed off, for what might have been ten or fifteen minutes but seemed like a few seconds.

Then an intensely irritating shrill peeping sound awoke me. At first I could not think what it was other than just egregiously the last straw, the icing on my crappy cake, the cherry on top of my wretched captivity. Then, wincing at the clamor it made, I realized it was the smoke detector.

I looked. Smoke was starting to rise from something on the stove.

I looked at Stoat lying on the living room floor. He showed no signs of hearing the smoke detector. Maybe he was conked out or in a coma. Maybe he was deaf. Maybe he was dead after all.

Which would have been delightful under other circumstances. But right now, if the stove went on burning Stoat's dinner long enough, the house would catch on fire. With me in it. Unable to escape.

It was a definite "Oh, shit!" moment.

Despite the obvious fact that I could not move, somehow I had to get to that stove. My feet touched the floor in close proximity to the chair legs. I pressed my toes into the linoleum and shoved, but nothing much happened. I attempted a sort of seated hop. Nothing. Wisps of smoke wafted over my head now. If I could have opened my mouth, I would have screamed. I panicked, and somehow my panic enabled me to fling my entire body into levitation mode. Lo and behold, the chair and I moved a few inches, although not exactly in the direction I wanted.

I tried again, of course. And again, and again, I have no idea how many times, with varying degrees of success, although I could not correct or predict my heading. The chair and I scratched a wavering path across the linoleum in the general direction of the stove as the smoke in the kitchen fast-forwarded from wisps into clouds into a billowing overcast that hung only inches above my head. The panic that energized me now was fear of suffocation, asphyxiation, dying of smoke inhalation even before my house burst into flames. Damn Stoat and his damn spaghetti and his damn duct tape.

By the time I finally flumped my way to the stove, smoke settled like a kind of attack fog around my head, stinging my eyes, depriving me of proper breath, making me cough through the tape covering my mouth. And what the hell did I expect to do about it anyway, stuck in a chair with my hands behind me? I couldn't even see, let alone think. More frantic than ever, I ducked my head in an attempt to find better air, and in so doing I banged my nose against the stove knobs that turned the burners on and off, which gave me a thought.

I nudged one of the knobs with no effect, and the heat from the stove top singed my hair and nearly blistered my face, meaning it was probably way too late for my pitiful heroics to make any difference. By being a good Stoic I could have sacrificed myself and let an appropriately hellish inferno take Stoat along with me. But the survival instinct trumped philosophy. Slewing my head at an improbable, muscle-straining angle, I positioned my duct-taped mouth on the handle of one of the knobs, pressed against it until my teeth hurt, and attempted to turn it to the "off" position.

Attempted more than once. Heads are not trained in fine motor skills, let alone working through duct tape, so it was not easy. But I finally, clumsily, very nearly toppling into the stove, got one burner turned off. I leaned sideways and stretched my neck to reach the other, applied my muffled mouth again and turned it—not quite off, but it would have to do. With no strength left, unable to breathe properly or open my mouth to pant, feeling weak and queasy, I let fear advise me once more and did something desperate and counterintuitive. I deliberately tipped myself over onto the kitchen floor.

Ow. I banged my already-banged-up head pretty good.

But there was still some air down there. I could breathe again.

And I could let myself sag onto the linoleum. I could rest.

So that's what I did. With no idea whether I would ever get up again, I lay on the floor, let my legs hang from their bindings, closed my eyes, and relaxed. Despite the yammering of the smoke detector, I actually dozed, dreaming I was back in the swamp with Justin, walking through drippy Spanish moss that groped us and Spanish daggers that tried to neuter us and a variety of other insults. Justin struggled with tangled vines and I scratched mosquito bites and we had a great conversation about what we would eat when we got out of there. He wanted to gorge on Snickers bars. I just wanted to bury my head in a five-gallon tub of chocolate-chip cookie dough ice cream.

TWENTY-FOUR

Again Bernie drew missionary duty, driving the Leppo brothers back to Stoat's house, where they had left their car. He was hungry, and he should have been on his way home, but he did not mind, for the slanting late daylight gave him a mellow mood in harmony with the yellow halos it limned on the rows of soybeans in the fields, the tousle-headed pine trees, the cows strolling home—Bernie had always liked cows. He liked simple, humble things. He noticed that someone had erected a pole with crossbars from which hung white gourds, now rimmed in saffron by sundown light, for birds to nest in. Bernie decided he wanted to do the same in his backyard.

Forrest and Quinn saw none of this, he could tell, for they looked only at their own hands. Heads bowed as if grieving a death, they did not speak. Bernie knew some Americans preferred to keep their silences, but he could not stand it. "You hear bad news from Deputy Kehm?"

The older, taller one, Quinn, shifted his bleak gaze to Bernie for an ominous moment before he spoke. "Not from Kehm. Our mother left us a note that said she, um—"

"I hear about the note," said Bernie to spare Quinn, who seemed to be having difficulty going on. "But what Kehm say?"

"Nothing."

This sounded like Deputy Kehm. Everyone on the force knew his good ol' boy act was just that: an act. Really, Kehm cared about his food and his mustache but not much else.

"Nothing," Forrest echoed, "and that's what he expects us to do."

"Go back to the hotel, watch TV, and go to sleep?" Quinn sounded incredulous. "As if we could sleep? Isn't there any local TV or radio or someplace with computers—"

"We need to get the word out," Forrest explained.

"—or photocopiers where we can put together a poster—"

Bernie said, "Down in Panama City, maybe." Fifty miles away.

Neither of them seemed to hear him. "Not just posters. Organize a search." With every word Forrest sounded more fervid and more desperate. "With tracking dogs, helicopters—"

Quinn interrupted. "Bernie, is anybody staking out Stoat's house?"

"I don't know. But Kehm will check with the Stoat family to see if they know where he is."

"Do you think they will?"

"No," Bernie admitted.

"He's probably in California by now," said Forrest morosely.

Quinn muttered, "They still should stake out his house."

Bernie saw Stoat's skink-tail blue shack ahead, with the Leppo brothers' rental car parked in front. He offered his last, best advice. "For the posters, try the churches. They have offices."

"Open after business hours?" Quinn asked.

"No. But look in the phone book, call the preachers at home. Someone will help."

Almost in a whisper Forrest said, "It's no use, is it, Bernie?"

In all probability, Bernie knew, he was right, but no one with a heart would say so. "More use than to lie in bed looking at the ceiling." Bernie turned left, bumped over a culvert, and stopped in front of the bright blue shack, now embellished by even brighter CRIME SCENE DO NOT PASS tape. A large yellow X of the stuff sealed the front door.

"Thank you, Bernie. You're a friend." Quinn reached toward Bernie and shook his hand with sudden fervor before getting out of the cruiser.

Forrest said thank you and shook his hand too. Both gave him wan smiles as they waved and headed toward their rental car.

Bernie felt as if he should not leave them. But what could he do? He had no copy machine to make the posters, no tracking dog, no helicopter, only Tammy Lou, who was waiting for him at their *casa feliz*, their happy home. Bernie left.

A disturbing sensation of Stoatness awoke me, and I twisted around to look up from where I lay on the kitchen floor. Sure enough, looming over me, Stoat stood at the stove ravenously eating spaghetti sauce out of the pot with the big wooden spoon I had been using to stir it, which left smears of blood red on his face. When he sensed me staring up at him, he gave me a look of pure malice. "What the hell you think you're doing?"

The duct tape still sealing my mouth prevented me from voicing any of the several trenchant replies that came to mind.

"Goddamn spaghetti looks like Elmer's glue," Stoat said. "My dinner is ruined." He kicked at me as if ruining his supper had been my intention. But the effort made him almost lose his balance, and his pointed cowboy-boot toe harmlessly hit the kitchen chair. "Now there ain't no damn time to cook none. Git up."

I narrowed my eyes at him, trying to telegraph to him that he'd overlooked one important detail.

He railed, "I said git up! What the hell's the matter with

you—oh." Belated realization did not make him any less pissed off. He swore luridly as he got out his knife, and I could not help cringing at the sight of the long blade shining in the dim kitchen—why so dim? The answer took a moment to float into the mist of my mind: Stoat and I had slept for hours. Day was fading. An un-mistakably evening breeze reached me on the floor, and belatedly I realized the smoke had cleared; Stoat must have opened some windows. Come to think of it, the noise from the smoke detector had stopped.

Bending over, he cut me free of the chair, and very nearly sliced my legs in the process. Then, barely giving me time to flex my numb feet, he grabbed my elbow and hauled me up—I think he would have dislocated my shoulder if I hadn't managed to get my feet de-ployed. The muffler on my mouth kept my scream of pain from sounding like much. He sawed and ripped to remove the duct tape from my wrists. I whimpered when the weight of my nearly lifeless arms swung forward to hang from my traumatized shoulders. Stoat shook his mangy head in mild rebuke. "See, my extra bedroom don't seem so bad now, does it?" He meant being spread-eagled and hand-cuffed hands and feet, and fuck him with a salty dick, he was right.

Then, orderly creep that he was, he could not seem to help picking up the chair and positioning it neatly at the table where it belonged.

Once I had reacquainted myself with my hands, I ripped the tape off my own mouth. Ouch. But why, at this point, should any-thing *not* hurt?

"Where's your damn car keys?" Stoat growled close to my ear.

The words were clear enough, yet I couldn't seem to compre-hend them; maybe I had been hit on the head too many times. "Huh?"

He had not put his knife away. He lifted it slightly and glared.

"Huh, *sir*?" I blurted.

He gave me a look that said *Read my lips.*

"You want my car keys?" In order to look for them, I reached toward the kitchen light switch.

Stoat struck my hand away. "No damn lights! You want the cops to see?"

"Um, cops?"

"What the hell you think I want the car keys for?"

Ah. My weary and perhaps damaged brain began to function. "Are they still there?" Meaning at his house.

He railed, "How the hell should I know? I don't see no fucking cars, but there's fucking yellow cop tape out front. If I didn't feel so goddamn crappy, I'd kill you and steal your fucking car."

Either he did not feel strong enough to drive, or he did not feel strong enough to break my steering column and start my car with a screwdriver. If the former, he would kill me eventually. If the latter, he would kill me when I found the keys. That part, the murderous part, was so shockingly clear it worked like a jump start on my mind. I must be as helpful to Stoat as I could, as long as I helped him get tired and get nowhere.

With clarity as if my mental lights had switched on, I remembered where my car keys were. In my purse. Which, according to Justin, Stoat had stolen and taken to his house—but he didn't know I knew that. Meanwhile, the spare keys lay right there under his hatchet nose in the pink pottery bowl on my kitchen table, along with Scotch tape, rubber bands, a coupon cutter, a three-socket electrical outlet converter, emery boards, a lint roller, and various other household detritus, including a small stuffed aardvark that had belonged to Schweitzer.

Looming over me with his head weaving like a water moccasin ready to strike, Stoat hissed, "For the last time, where's your *keys?*"

"In my purse!" I chirped just like my mother at her most virtuous and helpful moments.

"And where's that?"

"Um, in the living room, I guess," I said, pretending not to know it was right where he had put it, at his house. If he didn't remember that, let him figure it out.

He grabbed me by the arm, yanked me forward, then stood behind me and nudged me in the middle of my back with the tip of his knife. "Walk."

I walked. We progressed past the kitchen table, where the pink pottery bowl was barely to be seen in the dusk, and after that, each step took us farther away from it. But I didn't congratulate myself much, because psychosis only knew what Stoat would do when we didn't find my purse.

I led him to the place where I ordinarily parked it, between sofa and armchair, then made what I hoped was a convincing show of peering into the shadows. "It's not there."

Stoat snapped, "Then where the hell—" He stopped, and I wished I could see his ugly face as he remembered. His tone changed when he said, "Oh, *fuck*."

Gee, wherever could it *be*? But I had the good sense to remain silent.

Stoat poked the knife tip harder into my back and growled, "You gotta have spare keys. Where's your spare keys?"

With what I considered fairly convincing innocence I said, "It should be easier to find my purse."

"Screw your fucking purse! I asked you, where's the spare keys?"

He terrified me so much that I babbled convincingly, "I, um, sir, I don't know!"

The sharp pressure against my back increased. "You dumb cow, *think*!"

As if I wasn't thinking? I had thought enough to know that if he found my car keys, he would probably kill me.

I squeaked, "Um, maybe, um, they could be in one of the boxes I haven't unpacked yet?"

Something slammed against my shoulders—his hard, constricting arm throwing me off-balance, jerking me back against him, as he switched his knife from my back to my throat. I felt the blade, razor-sharp, quivering there. Or maybe, as I vividly remembered his earlier lesson about the carotid and the windpipe and the jugular and so on, maybe I was the one quivering.

I felt his hot breath as he said, "Think harder, bitch."

He didn't say it, but I knew: I could tell him where the car keys were. Or I could die now instead of later.

TWENTY-FIVE

So depressed he didn't feel as if he could move, Forrest stood beside his brother, both of them watching as Bernie Morales drove away. Somehow the friendly cop's departure made him feel as if he'd been dumped to fend for himself, like an unwanted cat, a lost child—

I am not a child, he reminded himself, and he managed to speak, albeit vaguely. "Oh, well."

"Yeah." Quinn stirred, straightened, and turned to trudge toward the rental car. "I guess when we get back to the room, we'll try to ferret some do-gooders out of the phone book, like he said."

"You drive." Forrest pulled the keys out of his pocket and tossed them to his brother, knowing Quinn would feel marginally better behind the wheel. He got into the Aveo's passenger side. As Quinn started the little car, Forrest looked blankly out of his window. Flat landscape, bare lawn around the blue shack leading up to forest behind, weedy fields on each side, a few bushes with fluffy cluster blossoms, hard to tell what color in the sundown light, maybe rose or peach or white. Sunset clouds, all warm colors, reflecting in the windows of the chill blue house.

Quinn put the car in gear and pulled away.

Forrest felt himself jolt upright as if struck by a bolt of lightning. "Wait!"

"Huh?" Quinn hit the brakes.

Forrest said, "I saw something."

"What?"

"Not sure. Maybe nothing. A shadow. A movement. In the house."

"Are you sure?"

"I just said I'm not sure!" Surprised to find himself shouting, Forrest lowered the volume. "It's hard to tell, but I was looking at the windows and something made me think there's somebody in there."

"You want to go back and look?"

This did not deserve an answer. Forrest got out of the car, closing the door as quietly as he could, and started to head around the side of the blue shack. He heard Quinn turn off the car and glanced over his shoulder to see his brother following him.

As soon as he rounded the shack's corner and stepped into the backyard, Forrest saw a streamer of yellow police tape wafting in the evening breeze. An instant later he saw where it had come from. The X of tape that had sealed the back door was ripped aside. Someone had made entry.

He stopped to stare, blinking, frozen like a deer hit by headlights. Without needing to look, he knew his brother had halted by his side.

Close to his ear Quinn said softly, "Good call, Forrie."

Forrest nodded. Then, as if the movement of his head had freed up his working parts, he edged forward for a better look. Quinn, ever and annoyingly the older brother, stepped past him to peer in, then whispered, "There's a light on!"

"I can *see* that," Forrest muttered, fixated on the roller blind pulled down in the window of the back bedroom where he and Quinn had found the sex toys. The light within illuminated the window blind like a movie screen, and Forrest had not watched a moment before a quick, slim shadow crossed it. Forrest felt his heart pounding.

"There's somebody in there!" Quinn sounded breathless.

"Stoat?" Forrest whispered.

"I hope so! Let's get him!"

"He has guns. We need cops."

"No damn time!"

"We need *something*." Although he managed to hold his voice to a whisper, Forrest felt himself panting from the sheer danger of the moment. "Get the jack handle out of the car."

"He'll get away!"

"I got the back door; you got the front. Hurry up!"

Quinn gave a wordless, agonized gasp, turned, and ran back toward the car. Forrest stayed where he was.

The light in the bedroom suddenly died.

Forrest stiffened, trying to watch the back door he could now barely see in the twilight.

Something moved. Shadows? Wind. No. Forrest saw the back door opening.

There was no time to think, only to react. Forrest sprinted forward, ready to fight Stoat with his bare hands.

The slim person in the doorway startled so hard he let whatever he was carrying thump to the floor, then stood rigid in the doorway. Forrest saw his pale, youthful face seemingly floating in nightfall's shadows.

Quinn's voice said, "That's not Stoat."

Forrest said, "It's sure not," as his brother stood beside him, improvised weapon in hand.

"Who the hell are you?" the boy challenged.

"Who the hell are *you*?" Quinn returned sharply, all New Yorker.

But Forrest's eyes had adjusted to the dim evening light; he could see the boy's face in more detail, and he recognized him now, even though the kid's face was murky with dirt and scratches and his blond cornrows were gone. "Quinn," he said, "it's him. The one on the tapes."

"Quinn?" echoed the boy, his face transformed with excitement. "Quinn and Forrest?"

Justin had felt lower than a cockroach, sneaking out of the fishing shack while Miss Lee was asleep, but what else was new? Aside from the single day of freedom he had just spent, he could barely recall a time when he hadn't felt worthless. He accepted the soreness of his body, especially his bare feet, as what a piece of shit like him deserved. Limping up the weedy lane in the dark, he wasn't more than halfway back to the dirt road before he blundered into Spanish daggers and cut his shins. He could feel blood trickling down his legs as he stumbled on his way, and weirdly he felt better. Pain on the outside took away from pain on the inside.

I HAVE A PLAN, said the note he'd left, and he did. He planned to go hide out with his grandfather, his father's father, whom he'd liked the one time he'd met him. So the old guy was a drunk? Good. That and the way he'd stayed away most of Justin's life told Justin he didn't care too much, which was fine, because Justin wanted to be let alone. Not forever. Just until his bruises faded and his hair grew back and some other parts of him healed. Then maybe he could face—no, Christ, he didn't see how he could ever face his family, since he'd betrayed them by staying with Stoat when he should have, could have, told a teacher or somebody. . . . He couldn't explain why he hadn't spoken up, because he didn't understand it himself. But that was only one of the embarrassing questions he didn't want anybody asking him, only one of the reasons he didn't want to be in the news or on TV or, worst of all, testifying in a courtroom. He had bad dreams sometimes about being questioned by a stone-faced district attorney:

"What happened after you regained consciousness, Justin?"

And forced by the paranormal power of the law, Justin was compelled to say far too much truth: "Mr. Stoat told me to come up and sit in the front seat of the van and stop crying or he'd give me something to cry about. I wanted him to take me home, but I already knew it was no use. I said I had to go to the bathroom, thinking maybe he'd let me out of the van and I could run, but he told me he wasn't a fool. After we got to his place, then he let me go to the bathroom, but the window was all boarded up and there was no lock on the door."

"Go on."

"Um, he watched."

"Go on."

"He yanked all my clothes off and pushed me into the bathtub and told me to take a shower. I felt sick. I couldn't get the water temperature right. I was still messing with it when he came into the shower with me. He had all his clothes off too, and—I was so scared I just froze."

"What happened then?"

"He pushed me into the water and washed me all over with soap. He held on to me hard with one hand and—touched me—"

And then generally, before the worst of it, he woke up. But thinking this, already awake in the sodden chill of a swamp night, Justin made the nightmare stop by sheer force of will. *No. NO. I'm not telling. Never.*

When his sore bare feet found the sand road, he knew which

way to turn. Seeing the sun set had helped him to figure out which way was home. Not sweet home Alabama, but his more recent home, Stoat's home. Justin knew Lee would think he was crazy to head back there, but to him it felt right. Anyway, he needed shoes and socks and fresh clothes and some money—he knew where Stoat kept the jar full of spare change—and he would grab something to eat before he thumbed a ride in the back of somebody's pickup truck, got to a town, took a bus to Birmingham, where his grandfather lived. It wouldn't be too hard to do this and avoid Stoat. He would watch the house and let himself in when Stoat went to work or whatever.

On the sand road he forced himself into a painful jog trot. Through the constant background noise of insects he heard the unmistakable single-note wordless Johnny Cash song of a male gator, so low and powerful it made his back prickle. He heard the creaky complaint of a disturbed heron. Then he heard the distant thrum of an engine and the scrunch of tires on sand. Vehicle approaching. Nobody drove through the swamp at this time of night with any good intention; even if it was not Stoat, it had to be alligator poachers or drug dealers or some other kind of slime with a crime to hide. Instantly, without needing to think about it, Justin lengthened his stride to run off the road into the woods, crashing through brush like a deer. And seeing headlights between the trees now, afraid to be caught in their white beams, he dropped to the ground, or rather shallow water, behind palmettos. He did not care what he might disturb there, poisonous spiders, scorpions, snakes, whatever, because he was more afraid of Stoat than any of those things. He could not see the vehicle, but at least he felt pretty sure whoever was in it could not see him, because he kept his head down and he wore the old green baseball hat that Lee had found.

Good thing. The passing vehicle, with a coughing, wheezy engine, really sounded like Stoat's van.

But that may have been because he had Stoat on his mind, Justin told himself. After it had driven past and he could no longer hear it, he got back onto the road and on his way, running as long as he could, then slowing to a walk, then running again.

During the night he hid from two more vehicles, getting himself wet and grimy in the process. When daylight began to intrude on night's protective darkness, Justin thought it would be a good idea for him to get off the road, now that he had come close to the edge of swampland. Instead of sheets of scummy water, he saw a real creek meandering through forest that sometimes flooded, judging by the splayed trunks of the trees, but right now was dry. Almost as dry as his mouth. In a kind of mental dawning, an epiphany, Justin allowed himself to recognize that he was very thirsty.

The water in the creek ran clear. He could drink it.

Picking his way through the woods to get there, Justin discovered that he was also very weary, so fatigued that he wobbled on his feet. And when he crouched to drink, he very nearly toppled into the creek. Bracing himself with one hand, he managed to cup water in the other and slowly drink his fill. Then he would have liked to bathe, but he felt as if he might drown if he tried. So exhausted. Falling-down tired. Could barely keep his eyes open.

And no wonder, he realized foggily. When had he last slept? Not this past night, and not the one before either; then he had been hiding from Stoat in the river. And the two nights before that, he'd stayed awake to feed Lee.

Sheesh, thought Justin, yawning as if he would dislocate his jaw. Definitely it was time for a nap, if he could find a safe place.

Luck favored him. Farther up the creek bank he spotted an old, leaf-littered, and very likely forgotten wooden rowboat beached upside down. Justin waded along the edge of the creek so he could get to it without struggling through thorny vines. Once there, he used what felt like the last of his strength to tilt one side of it off the ground and peer at the bare earth underneath, checking for snakes or scorpions.

A few beetles scurried away and a few worms squirmed their way out of sight. Nothing he couldn't deal with under the circumstances.

Whispering, "Sweet!" Justin crawled underneath the rowboat and let it drop back to the ground so that it formed a carapace over him, a big high-domed wooden tortoise shell. Lying on soft, sandy earth in sheltered darkness felt heavenly. Closing his eyes, Justin told himself he would sleep just a few hours, until the heat of the day awoke him. . . .

Sweating, Justin awoke from sleep so deep he could not at first recall where he was, especially when it was so dark he couldn't see a thing. He explored with his hands, and his fingertips encountered wooden planks.

Duh. No wonder it was dark, under a rowboat; he remembered now. How long had he slept? His gut growled like a predator. He had to get home and find something to eat.

Crouching in the boat's dark belly, he pressed his shoulders against the thing and heaved. Flipping it like a road-killed armadillo, he stood straight up. But the darkness surrounding him remained. He felt a breeze cool his sweaty body, heard it soughing in trees all around him, then looked up between their boughs and glimpsed stars.

"Jesus," he said, incredulous, "it's nighttime again." Could be just after dark, could be late night, could be nearly morning. No way to tell. He'd wasted a whole day.

Which wouldn't have mattered if he had brought food with him. But he hadn't. He'd expected to reach home—well, Stoat's place, assuming he could elude Stoat—before he got really hungry.

But now he felt as if his guts had grown teeth and were gnawing him from inside.

"Hell," Justin muttered. "Damn everything." He wanted to get moving, he needed to get moving, hunger dogged him to get moving, but how could he, in the nighttime woods where he could feel the prickle vines winding around his bare ankles?

Wide-awake and fuming, too annoyed at himself to sit down, Justin stood waiting for his vision to adjust to the dark. After what felt like forever, he could see, minimally, shadowy trees and the shining water of the creek. He pulled the bill of his hat down to protect his eyes from twigs, then started to feel his way forward, each barefoot step an ordeal.

He wanted to reach the creek and wade along its bank back the way he had come, to the road. Just the first part, getting to the water, took seemingly hours of stumbling, as if the tree roots were clutching at his feet. Then, as he waded along the edge of the creek, some unknown object tripped him so that he fell into the water. He didn't mind, but he would have enjoyed his impromptu bath better if he had seen it coming.

Limping along the edge of the shadowy water, he bumped against some kind of a wooden structure and explored it with his hands for a while before he realized it was the bridge where the road crossed the creek. And even then, getting out of the water and onto the roadway was a feat accomplished by sheer blundering.

Finally he felt smooth sand beneath his sore feet again. He looked up, but could no longer see the stars. So he studied the faint sheen of the creek to make sure he was headed in the direction he wanted. Then he walked onward. His hunger had become, like his injuries, pain to be ignored.

After a while he urged himself into a lope. After another while he realized why he was able to do this. It was getting light out. He could see a little.

It was morning, but not Thursday anymore. Realizing it was Friday, Justin felt a little bit like Rip van Winkle.

He kept loping along the dirt road until the dawn turned to daylight, and far ahead he saw metallic glints sparkling between the trees: traffic. People going to work. He had almost reached the paved road. Looking down at himself, all dirty and damaged, he realized he could not let anyone see him that way. So, keeping his fragmentary glimpses of cars and pickup trucks within sight to guide him home, he headed into the woods again, woods with normal, narrow trees. He had put swampland behind him now. He was not too far from home.

Home? Like hell. He knew Stoat would kill him on sight, yet he was still thinking of Stoat's house as home and he knew this was crazy, which was just another reason why he couldn't tell anybody about himself yet. Because then the whole world would find out what a fucked-up mess he was.

The woods slowed him to a walk, and even though he could now see where he was going, he still got his skin ripped by the green thorny vines that twined everywhere; there was no avoiding them. Once the woods finally let go of him, he forced his overtaxed body into a trot through a cotton field, staying so far back from the road that nobody could recognize him even if they noticed him. The smudges of blood from his bleeding feet nearly matched the red clay.

Then he had to fight his way through woods again. Make that jungle so damn thick he ended up getting down on all fours to burrow under the green tangle like a fox. So his feet were grateful for the break, but his hands and knees were not. It felt like a very long time—hell, it *was* a long time—before he made it out of that mess. With the sun scorching him from high in the sky, he felt weak from heat and fatigue, hunger and thirst.

But he recognized the cow pasture he was in. Home—no,

Stoat's blue shack—was getting closer. The shack where his socks and shoes and spare clothes were, and some food, and money. That was all. Then he would buy a bus ticket or something, go to his grandfather.

He handled the cow pasture the same way he'd handled the cotton field, trotting straight across at a cautious distance from the road, meanwhile wondering whether he could possibly find something to eat. He was wavering and stumbling as he jogged. When he neared the far side, he saw a feeding trough. The next moment he was there as if he had flown, looking for anything edible. Dried corn would have been fine with him. Purina cow chow would have been even better. But he saw only wisps of hay and a few nuggets, some kind of kibble, scattered underneath. With shaking hands he tried to gather them—

"Hey!" a man's voice yelled from somewhere across the pasture. "What the hell you doing?"

The farmer! A friend of Stoat's. Justin ran without looking back, never knew how close or far away the man was. He did not dare give him a glimpse of his face. He sprinted past a house and two trailers to dive into the woods. But as soon as wax myrtle, yaupon, and palmetto hid him, he collapsed to the ground and had a kind of fit like a sick dog, convulsing and shaking hard, trying not to whimper and yip; he bit his lip till it bled. It took a while before he was able to get up and walk on.

Not run or jog. Walk. Even when he found the four-wheeler track he would follow the rest of the way through the woods, he couldn't get his wretchedly hungry body or his painful, bloody, plodding feet to move any faster. It was just about all he could do to stay upright and moving. When he finally saw the bright blue house through the trees, he could have cried.

Until he saw something was wrong. He stopped as if he'd hit a wall.

He knew without having to get any closer what that yellow stuff across the back door was. Police tape.

What the hell? Lee must have found a way out of the swamp, because it looked like she had gone and called the cops.

This was a good thing, he reminded himself, that Lee was safe. Lee was the best. She understood him better than anybody. He wished she would have let him stay with her and be her son. He knew she didn't mean any harm, calling cops to his house. But there they were. Now what the hell was he supposed to do?

Justin dropped to his hands and knees, at first in despair, then in caution. He crawled forward to have a closer look. Nearing the edge of the woods, he bellied down to combat crawl, peering at the back of the bright blue Stoat shack for any sign of movement. At a distance, across the road, he could see the front and side of Lee's bright pink shack too.

Maybe she was home and he could go over there and she would give him something to eat. She would. And she wouldn't shout at him or curse him or hit him for running away either.

Justin blinked, trying to get his thinking into focus. He had run away, but why? The night when they had bedded down on bunks in the fishing shack seemed as far away as something on *Star Trek*, as if the swamp were an alien planet. He had run because—because Lee wanted him to go back to his parents. Dad. Mom. Mythical beings he could barely remember as he lay in the sandy dirt just being tired and starved, even his thoughts almost too tired and starved to move. "Mom" was a blank, yet the word caused a hot ache in his chest that tugged him toward Lee.

His body responded, trying to get up. Get up. Go. Somebody was at home over there, opening the windows, he could see them opening. But over here it was only cops—

Duh. He couldn't go to Lee because Lee had called the cops. Because Lee was a good person, not messed up like him, and she wanted to do things right. She couldn't help it that Justin just wasn't ready.

Justin's body let go of all hope and sagged back into the sandy dirt at the verge of Stoat's backyard. He lay there without moving as the sun set and the day began to darken. He wanted to give up and sleep, but hunger tore at him like a wolf, insisting that he had to stay awake and do something. His own body, ordering him around.

From where he lay, he could see only the back and one side of the shack. But the place was so small he could tell nobody had turned on any lights inside. Not like he'd been watching for lights to come on, not like he still had brains enough for that, but all of a sudden he noticed there weren't any. Not even the blue flickering glow of a TV set. Could it be there was nobody in the house? Not even Stoat?

What were the chances that anybody was in there waiting in the dark? He could see that Stoat's van was not parked in its usual spot at the corner. As for cops, who cared anymore? Hunger made him reckless and willing to take the risk. He heaved himself to his feet in the bushes, waited a moment until a spinning sense of vertigo passed. Then he took a deep breath and stepped into the open.

He traversed the backyard quickly, noting that his feet hurt even worse than his gut; despite his hunger, socks and shoes had to come first. He ripped the yellow tape away from the back door, then pushed it open in the dark as he had done many times before. But even though he lived here, supposedly, he did not turn on a light yet. A sense of constant guilt had been beaten into him for the past couple of years, making him feel as if he must be sneaky. He found his way through the shack to the bedroom just by shuffling his feet. But in the bedroom they encountered obstacles. Clothing seemed to be strewn all over the floor. In order to find his shoes he needed to turn on the light.

He groped for the switch on the wall, found it, flipped it, then blinked in the blaze of the ceiling fixture, staring at the mess. The cops had really tossed the place. What the hell had they been looking for?

His clothing lay all over. Quickly he shucked off the filthy clothes he had been wearing for three days and found clean ones to put on. He felt too uneasy to shower; his dunk in the creek last night would have to do. He should have soaked his feet in soapy water, smeared them with antibiotics, and bandaged them, but that would have taken as much time as a shower. Instead, he found two pairs of cushy white cotton tube socks and put them on one over the other. He didn't see his comfortable old Chucks, so they were probably still under his side of the bed where they belonged. Stepping over piles of clothing, he went there, and yes! He found the floppy, forgiving shoes, and by lacing them loosely, he was able to put them on.

Dressed, he substituted one of his own baseball hats for the green relic Lee had found, turned off the bedroom light, then headed for the kitchen. He didn't need to turn on a light there, just open the refrigerator. He gulped some Mountain Dew straight from the two-liter bottle, then grabbed the loaf of bread, the pink salami, and some sliced cheese. But no matter how much his stomach howled and gnawed, sitting at the table to make a sandwich seemed out of the question. Carrying the food, Justin headed for the back door.

But the moment he opened it, he heard the panting breath and pounding feet of someone running toward him. He dropped his food and froze, trying to see who it was. Not Stoat, thank God. Young man—no, young men. Two of them now, barely visible, but he could hear their voices.

"Quinn, it's him. The one on the tapes."

Justin's mind seized upon nothing of this beyond the word "Quinn." In the fading light he saw nothing except the faces of the two young men, and he saw Lee in them, and he knew them; they were Lee's sons, Forrest and Quinn. He could not question how they had come to be there; it was simply a miracle. He named them like Adam naming creation. "Quinn and Forrest?" And a great sunrise of emotion suffused him.

TWENTY-SIX

"Um, car keys, the keys to my car," I babbled as Stoat pressed his way-too-sharp knife blade to my throat. I had three choices: tell him where the keys were and be killed, or not tell him where the keys were and be killed, or come up with some convincing prevarication to live a few hours longer. The survival instinct made me a time miser, hanging on to every minute no matter how miserable. I needed a lifesaver lie, stat.

Bless my control freak husband, he had made me a good liar.

The thought of Georg inspired me.

"I know where there's a key. I think I know," I prattled. "It's under, um, I remember my ex-husband put a spare somewhere on the underside of the car in one of those little magnetic boxes, you know the kind I mean? On the whatchacallit, undercarriage of the car."

Stoat's already tight grip constricted around my shoulders, his knife bit the skin of my neck, and he said several harsh things, concluding with, "*Where* on the undercarriage of the car, bitch?"

"I don't know. Not exactly. That's where *he* put them. It was his idea. I never—"

"Oh, shut up." Suddenly Stoat turned me loose, not so much

letting me go as unable to stand me anymore; he thrust me away from him, hard. I fell onto the sofa and decided to stay there.

Stoat raged, "You expect me to *crawl* under your bitty-ass stupid Yankee car to find the fucking key?"

At first I thought this was rhetorical, but he glowered at me as if he wanted a reply, so I said, "Sir, I expect nothing, sir."

"You're goddamn right. It's getting dark out there. I don't suppose you got a freaking flashlight?"

I did not. Practical equipment has never been my forte. I did not own any flashlight. . . . Wait a minute.

"There's a little one in my, um . . ." I could not help hesitating, terrorized, dreading to displease him.

"In your *what*?"

"In my purse, sir. A little LED light shaped like Eeyore."

"What the hell?"

"Kind of a—a blue donkey, sir . . ."

"Shut the fuck up. Just goddamn shut up, would you, and let me think."

I did as he said. I shut up, and from my seat on the sofa, I watched him think. In the darkening room he loomed over me, buck knife in hand, way too much like doom incarnate. I knew what he was thinking. He was considering his options. He could go to his house and get the car keys out of my purse, but meanwhile, what was he to do with me? Duct-tape me to the chair again? It seemed to me that he must be running out of duct tape. He could take me with him, walk me over there at gunpoint? Make that knife point? Either way, somebody might drive past, and I might make a break for it, try to get away, and it was too goddamn long of a walk. He wouldn't like that option. But the other one was to crawl under my car searching for a goddamn key box on its murky underside, with what illumination? And even supposing he could find a flashlight, maybe hike to his disabled van and get one out of the glove box, then what was he supposed to do with me meanwhile? Tie me up with something other than duct tape, like what, Schweitzer's leash? Or take me along, when he knew damn well I would try to escape?

Most people, when they are thinking, gaze off into space. Stoat did not. He stared straight at me, looking down his unlovely nose with his stony eyes—yes, I realized with a shock, eyes, plural. His second reptilian eye had reappeared, showing that his swelling was down. He had to be feeling better. Damn.

I didn't like his returning health. And I didn't like the way he was looking at me. Forget shutting up; I had to distract him. It was time to try that oldest of advice-column canards: Get Him Talking About Himself.

I cleared my throat and smiled as if I were on a first date. "Stoat," I ventured, "I know you're from around here. Do you have brothers or sisters close by?"

He gave me a flinty squint-eyed stare. "Why? You planning to leave them something in your will?"

"Just asking."

He relented. "Sure, I had sisters and brothers. Three of each."

"That's a big family. Were you poor?"

"We was sharecroppers. Course we was poor."

"But you had a good mother and father?" I asked with faked innocence, figuring otherwise.

"Of course." Shifting from one foot to the other, he sounded no more impatient than usual. "Ma and Pa were good, God-fearing people."

God-fearing. Interesting. "Was your mother the one who taught you how to keep everything so neat and tidy?"

Scowling, Stoat looked perplexed in his goatlike way. "I don't recall that in particular. Ma just kept me fed reasonable and clothes on my butt and she whupped me when I needed it." He grinned, apparently delighted by memories of parental violence. "Course Dad whupped harder."

"Were you scared of him?"

"Course I was! What the hell you getting at?"

Reminding myself that I was trying to prolong my life didn't keep my big mouth from doing its worst. I said earnestly, "Well, I was wondering if your God-fearing mother and father would want you around if they knew you were a faggot."

Stoat lurched toward me. "What the hell you talking about?"

"Why, what you did with Justin."

"Now, that's just sick, not knowing the difference between me and Justin and a pair of faggots!" Ranting, Stoat stood over me, bent to get in my face. "I'm a pedophile and Justin is just—just—innocent. Hey, Justin's a *virgin*, didja ever think of it that way?" Stoat spoke with such fervor that his spittle flew into my face. "Justin ain't fucked nothing. He just *got* fucked and fucked, but he never fucked *me*, so I ain't no faggot and if anybody thinks I am, they're crazier than you are, bitch."

Okay, I had succeeded in sticking it to Stoat before he killed me, but I didn't enjoy it much, watching his body language while I tensed to run if he raised the knife.

Nodding solemnly, I asked, "But would your mother think—"

"She wouldn't think nothing!" Stoat's voice shot up to a screech. "Why would she want to think! Her and Pa sent us to church when we was kids, but it wasn't their fault whatever we done once we was grown. They visited my brothers in prison, didn't they?"

"I wouldn't know," I said, ultrasoothing. "You never told me."

Stoat glowered at me uncertainly.

I went on. "But you did tell me you made it a point to remain celibate until your parents had passed away."

"That was just to spare their feelings! I wouldn't want to know all about what *they* did for sex, would I? Like, I think my father bruised my mother up some, and I know he used a whip, but that ain't *sick*, just embarrassing. I would never let them know I knew. Sex things ain't nothing to be ashamed of, but they should ought to be kept private."

"Of course. I absolutely agree." Then the imp of the perverse got into me again. Dying no longer looked so bad if I could put the screws to Stoat first. "So, are your brothers in prison for sex crimes?"

Saying that was like providing a spark to gas fumes; Stoat's explosion seemed to fill the room. Rearing to stand ramrod straight, he shouted a stream of obscenities and curses too dizzying to remember and too foul to repeat. "You stupid bitch!" was the mildest of it. "You think I got to be what I am because of my *brothers*? Screw that! Whatever I done in my life was on my own, with nobody's damn help, you dumb cow. . . ."

I think throughout the entire rant I did a pretty good job of sitting still and looking vaguely sympathetic, although I kind of curled my arms around myself to protect my tender underbelly in case of attack.

A valid instinct. Way too suddenly, in midobscenity, Stoat fell silent with his lips still moving. Mouth open, he hunched over like a giant fishhook to glare down at me. Then he closed his thin lips while his narrow flinty eyes remained open to stare at me. Eyes with no humanity in them, they might as well have belonged to an anaconda.

Very quietly he said, "Tricky bitch, what the fuck you up to, fucking with me?"

"You *know* us?" Quinn blurted, staring at the boy standing in the doorway of the blue shack, the victimized boy he had given hardly a thought in his desperation to find Mom.

"You know us?" Forrest echoed, sounding just as much taken aback.

"I know your mom." His voice had a pleasant huskiness, a burr.

He spoke quietly, but Quinn nearly shouted at him. "Where *is* she?"

"Isn't she right over there?" In the semidarkness, the boy gestured toward the pink shack. "Her house?"

"No!" Quinn could not help stepping forward as if in threat.

The boy reached inside the doorway for the switch to turn on the back porch light. Sixty watts, maybe, but to Quinn it seemed too bright; it showed too much, reminding him that this kid had been through a lot. Quinn saw his pale, bruised face, his wide eyes, his bitten lip, his childish mouth trembling—no, not just his mouth; he shook all over. He had been brave enough to turn on the light, but he quaked and swayed, clinging to the doorway's frame for support.

Quinn exclaimed, "We won't hurt you!"

He felt his brother shove past him, hurrying forward. "He's falling over." Forrest caught the kid by his shoulders and eased him to a seat on the slab of pavement outside the back door. He knelt beside him. "Are you going to faint? Head down between your knees."

The kid resisted. "I'll be all right when I eat." With one faltering hand he fumbled at the loaf of bread he had dropped.

Quinn stepped in, opening the bread bag and handing the boy a slice. Cheap soft white bread, about as much good as giving the kid a cube of sugar. Quinn found the salami and cheese, sat down on the ground with his long legs crossed, and started to put together a sandwich for the boy. "What's your name?"

"Justin," he said with his mouth full.

"Justin. Okay, Justin, take a breath and tell us how you know our mom."

He waited with strained patience while the boy swallowed bread and took more than one breath. Finally Justin said, "I lived here with my uncle Steve. Um, Stoat."

Quinn noted the past tense but said nothing.

"And?" Forrest coaxed.

"And Miss Lee Anna came over on Sunday." Quinn saw the boy's eyes dart as if looking for a place to hide from things he didn't want to say. "Unc—um, Stoat knocked her out and put her on a bed with handcuffs."

This would have been hard for Quinn to follow if he had not already seen that bed. God. That awful bed. Blood on the bare mattress, blood on the handcuffs. Mom's.

Quinn bit his lip to remain silent, but Forrest cried out, "*Why?*"

With raw pain in his voice Justin said, "Because of me." He ducked his head, hiding his face.

Quinn shoved the sandwich into his hands and said softly to his brother, "Forrie, don't interrupt. Let him tell it his way." He watched Justin eat and waited until the boy's head came back up before he asked, "Then what happened?"

Justin swallowed, then swallowed again, then said, "Tuesday it rained. So Tuesday night, he took her out to the swamp to kill her. And me, I figured, because—anyway, I snuck a baseball bat into the truck and when we got there I—I—I don't know why I didn't just kill him then and there. Anyway, I hit him on the head, and me and Lee, I mean your mother, we went into the river. . . ."

Unfathomable emotions rattled the boy's voice like a cage. As if he couldn't stand to listen, Forrest said, "Justin, take your time. Are you saying you saved Mom's life?"

Again, Justin gulped twice before answering. "I thought so. We ran off into the swamp and we about starved until last night—no, night before last—we found a shack with some food. Then it took me until tonight to get back here for more food and fresh clothes and some shoes because my feet are a mess." He stiffened as if remembering danger temporarily forgotten, and his husky voice grew tight. "I need to get away. If Stoat finds me here, I'm dead."

Quinn said, "We won't let anybody hurt you, Justin," surprised to realize how much he meant it. This soft-spoken, scared, gutsy, messed-up kid had walked right into his heart when he wasn't looking, high-top Chucks and all. Quinn had a pretty good idea that Justin had invaded Mom's heart similarly. And that Mom had somehow found out he was being sexually abused and had gotten herself in trouble trying to save him. According to Justin, they had both escaped from Stoat. But there was too much the boy wasn't saying. Where was Mom now?

Forrest surely had the same question, but he broached it indirectly. "Justin, when was the last time you saw Mom?"

"Right about this time last—no, a couple of nights ago."

"Okay." It wasn't really okay, Quinn knew, and he gave his brother points for keeping his voice gentle. "Where?"

"At the fishing shack in the swamp. Asleep."

"You left when she was asleep?"

Instead of answering, the kid dropped his sandwich to the ground as if he had lost all appetite. He sat staring into the night.

Quinn urged, "Justin, look at me."

He did, his eyes narrowed with nearly tangible pain; Quinn felt its impact. Justin burst out, "It's all my fault if Stoat got her. I didn't rub out my tracks, I left a trail he could see, I'm so fricking stupid, and that really did sound like his van. . . ." He had started to sweat and shake. "But she has to be all right! She has to be home!" Wildly he gestured in the direction of the pink shack. "She has to!"

"She's not," Quinn said, and despite his best effort to be gentle, the words sounded stony bleak.

"But she has to be!" Justin cried. "I saw somebody open the windows over there!"

Stoat grabbed his shotgun, and I saw my death in his anaconda eyes.

I screamed as I had never screamed before. Shrieking, I jumped up from the sofa and ran with vague ideas of barricading myself in my bedroom. But Stoat, already on his feet, caught me easily. I barely made it halfway across the living room before he grabbed me by the arm and flung me onto the floor as if he intended to stomp me into the carpet.

I kept screaming like a smoke detector going off; I couldn't stop. But I made up my mind that, anything Stoat did to me, he was going to have to face me down. Rolling onto my back, I looked straight up into his eyes, dead leaden things, hiding under the shadow of his brows.

Stoat ranted, "I'm getting out of here on foot if I got to, but first—"

With my big mouth at its most strident, I interrupted. "On *foot*? Stoat, you don't have to do that. The car keys are right on the kitchen table."

"What?"

"The car keys are in the pottery bowl on the kitchen table."

"Why the fuck didn't you tell me that in the first place?"

"Because you're not going to just take them and let me be, are you." This was a statement, not a question. The past few days had made a good Stoic of me. I met his glare with my own level stare, and maybe, just a little, I hoped the truth would be more than he could deal with.

No such luck. "I got to shut you up for good."

The Stoics were okay but they had no damn sense of humor. I

wanted to go out with some flair. Solemnly I reminded Stoat, "Don't shoot me. The cops over at your house might hear."

His mouth writhed like rattlesnakes, venomous, and I could actually see the blackened, dead part of his face start to open up in a sickening chasm as if to display his necrotic soul. Clutching his shotgun by its twin barrels, he lifted it. "I'm going to beat your tricky-ass brains out, you fucking ugly redhead bitch." He swung the shotgun butt high.

I am nothing if not crazy when it counts. "Stoat, wait a minute," I told him earnestly. "I'm concerned, and I think you need to seek medical attention."

The shotgun swung down, but in a disorganized way, as if I had messed up Stoat's aim and his impetus. I sat up, and the shotgun butt slammed into the carpet behind me. Stoat yelled, "What the fuck you talking about?"

I hoisted myself with my hands to get my feet under me. At the same time I cocked my head back to establish sincere eye contact. I said, "Parts of your face are falling off."

Stoat didn't say anything, but his mouth moved, twisting ugly as he swung his shotgun up like a golfer ready to tee off. My head being the metaphorical golf ball, I dived for an entirely different part of the carpet and screamed.

The shotgun butt swished over my head, but I kept right on screaming as I scuttled like an oversized cockroach under the coffee table. I grabbed the legs from below and held on hard. In that moment I comprehended to the bone why drowning people grasp at straws. With all the life energy in my body right down to my toes I shrieked, "Help! Somebody help me!"

"Shut the fuck up!" Stoat roared, swinging his shotgun-cum-club at the coffee table. Maybe he thought he could send it flying off me, but I hung on through the first impact and the second. And the third, for all the good it did me. That blow shattered the wood. Or the pressed processed chipboard or whatever the damn cheap thing was made of—Stoat's rifle butt struck like a bomb to send jagged hunks of it flying off me.

Trapped between him and the sofa, I rolled over on my back because, damn his septic guts, if he was going to kill me, he was going to do it to my face. He looked like a homicidal gargoyle, lifting his weapon, and I raised my arms in a futile gesture to defend myself, but at the same time my brain burped and words spurted from my mouth. "Stoat! You know Justin actually told me you're not a bad guy?"

He blinked, barking, "What?"

"Justin! Said! You're not a bad guy, and he'd be right if—there's a term the ancient Greek philosophers used. . . ."

"What the fuck you talking about?"

"He'd be right if you weren't such a consummate ontological asshole!" I ducked.

He struck so swiftly I got out no more than half a scream, fled no more than half an inch, before the butt of the shotgun smashed my upraised arm and bashed the side of my head. I felt no pain, just an odd inner snick, and I heard no whack of impact, not with my ears. My brain registered the bump, and I saw nothing that made any sense, just fireworks behind my eyelids, and then I heard, although I'm not sure it was real, the most clangorous crescendo of sound, crashing shouting yelling pounding bedlam. All my philosophies be damned, there was a hell after all, and it sure seemed as if I was going to it.

TWENTY-SEVEN

"I saw somebody open the windows over there!" Justin's words hung echoing in Forrest's mind for a moment after he had said them.

"When?" Forrest demanded.

"Around dark."

"Yesterday?" It must have been when they were burying Schweitzer.

"No! Today! Just a little while ago."

Quinn leaned forward from his seat on the ground. "Are you sure?"

"Sure I'm sure," Justin said with a country boy's innate patience. "I was hiding out back, wondering if it was safe to go inside, and I saw somebody over there open the windows."

Forrest felt Quinn's stare and turned to face his brother. He knew how Quinn felt, because he felt the same way: incredulous, afraid to hope. He shook his head. "It's too simple. Why would Mom—"

His words were snatched away by a loud, chilling scream.

It stopped his breath, a woman's scream of deathly terror, coming from the direction of the pink house.

Forrest had never heard anything like that scream, not even in a horror movie. Such extremity, the terror of the valley of the shadow of death, could not be faked. Its primal power catapulted him into a run toward the pink shack, run, run, the fastest he had ever run in his life, during which he heard that piercing scream again, twice; Forrest felt it like a stiletto stabbing his gut. Quite abstractly by comparison he noticed headlights bearing down on him as he pounded across the asphalt road, but the car swerved to miss him, then turned in at the pink shack. With those screams reverberating in his ears, Forrest couldn't think; not until the car stopped right in front of the pink shack, its high beams flooding the front door with much-needed light, did he realize it was his brother, Quinn, the quick thinker. And he had Justin with him. As Forrest sprinted across the front yard, he saw the kid leap out of the car's passenger side, but then limp as he tried to run.

Forrest saw Justin and his brother peripherally, his focus all on Mom's front door. Thinking his momentum would bust him right through it, he rammed it with his shoulder, but the door shrugged him off, made him mad. As Quinn and Justin ran up beside him, Forrest reared back and kicked in the door, right beside the knob, the way cops did on TV.

Those people, though, on TV, they always had guns to point and warnings to roar. Forrest had neither. When the door burst open, he retained just enough sense to flip on the indoor light switch, but then he stood frozen in helplessness at what he saw.

Justin shouted, "Uncle Steve, don't!"

Forrest would not have recognized the man as Steven Stoat. He saw a monster with a grotesquely lopsided, blackened, rotting face, with slits for eyes, a snarl for a mouth, a hollow-chested shambles of a body interrupted in the midst of swinging some sort of a club at—Forrest saw red hair and crimson blood, bruised skin and torn clothes, a face way too still: Mom. On the floor, hurt. Forrest could look at nothing else. Yet somehow he kept getting closer; his feet had carried him through the door and inside the house without his knowing he had moved.

Beside him Quinn yelled, "Forrie, he's got a gun!"

Forrest didn't really care about anything his brother had to say. He just wanted to get to Mom and make sure she—please, God, she had to be alive—but Quinn grabbed him by the arm and yanked so Forrest's head flew up. He saw Stoat fumbling with his club to point—

It wasn't just a club. It was a gun. Long. Big. To Forrest it seemed as big as a cannon.

And he had no weapon with which to fight back, not even a stone to throw. Quinn and Justin looked as helpless as Forrest felt. Quinn still had that stupid jack handle, but what was the use of it against a gun?

One, two, three, Forrest thought crazily. Three beer cans on a fence rail, three ducks in a shooting gallery. Stoat would take out him and Quinn and Justin just like that.

"Uncle Steve!" Justin screamed. "No, please don't!"

And Forrest yelled, "Mom!"

All I could see were remarkable special effects—lightning flashes, flaring supernovas, comets, and meteor showers—until the dazzling pain was done with my eyes.

Even then, what I saw was hard to interpret from where I lay bleeding on the floor. My main impression was of feet. Stoat's scuffed cowboy boots with their pointy toes turned toward the front of the house. Toward wing tips, work boots, and a pair of Chucks.

With horror as heavy as my love I recognized the three young men instantly. I knew them at once by a single look at their shocked bodies, arms outflung, silhouette targets against a surreal blue-white light blasting through the front door. Stoat would kill them, my sons, all three of them. Why were they here in my wretched pink shack for Stoat to murder? Close to my face I saw his shotgun butt freshly bloodied from clubbing me and his big-knuckled, frenzied hands repositioning the weapon so he could shoot them down, Quinn and Forrest and—and the one I loved like my own child—he would slaughter them like three calves on meat hooks.

And I lay stunned, injured, broken, helpless to prevent it.

I could not move.

"Mom!" cried one of my children.

I moved.

I had to, just like I'd had to get up at night when the babies cried; the summons shocked me with high voltage to the heart and could not be refused. Somehow I moved. I rolled to one side, flung my usable arm around Stoat's ankles, and rolled back with all the kinetic force in my badly compromised body in an attempt to yank his goddamn pointy cowboy-booted feet out from under him.

But the pain of moving made me faint at the same time as I heard the shotgun fire.

Justin felt as if time had pleated and he had somehow slipped across the folds, because once again he was just a little boy begging for his life, "Uncle Steve, no, please don't!" The man with the gun had once again loomed to fill the darkness of night, a deity of evil with death at his command, and the only hope of continued existence was to plead and promise, promise, promise to stay and never disobey and never tell the dark secret, never

ever. Shaking with terror, Justin knew he had disobeyed and now he must die. He saw his doom incarnate raising the shotgun toward his shoulder, and he cringed, on the point of closing his eyes—

He saw something trying to rise up from the shadows like a wounded bird trying to lift its wings.

Lee!

Time focused like a laser; everything Justin had ever been or could be was *now*, that moment as Lee rolled sideward with an arm swinging out like a scythe to snatch Stoat around his cowboy-booted ankles, attacking with all her wounded strength.

Stoat leveled his shotgun just as he staggered.

He started to topple.

The shotgun blasted fit to earthquake the house down. Justin did not just hear it fire; he felt it shake him to the bone, and bits of white ceiling snowed down on him from where the blast had struck. Yet he remained standing while Uncle Steve—while Stoat the Goat fell.

Justin did not wait until Stoat hit the floor, or the floor hit Stoat. He lunged to hit him at the same time and grab the shotgun when Stoat lost his grip.

Only the damn creepy strong pervert didn't lose his grip, didn't let go, not for an instant. Justin smelled his so-called uncle's hot and furious breath in his face as he tried to wrench the weapon away from him, but goddamn—no, there was no God and Stoat the pervert was still master, still stronger, still doom, getting the better of Justin—

Wait. Someone was helping. Justin saw someone hammering Stoat across the knuckles with a jack handle and somebody else wrestling Stoat's hard old arms away from the shotgun before he completed the thought, *Quinn, Forrest*. With the death weapon, the shotgun, in his possession, Justin stood up and stepped back while Stoat still lay sprawled on the floor.

Forrest and Quinn left him there, both of them hurrying to tend to their mother. Lee lay far too still, and standing there with the shotgun heavy in his grasp, Justin heard Quinn and Forrest saying to her, "Mom? *Mom?*" but he did not hear her answer. Unconscious? *Dead?* God, please not dead, and he wanted terribly to see whether she was breathing, to go to her like her sons, yet some dark instinct made him glance at Stoat still lying dazed on the floor—

No! Stoat was sitting up, and all in one quick motion he pulled his knife out of his pocket, opened the blade, lifted the weapon—

Justin did not wait to see whether Stoat intended to throw the knife at Quinn, at Forrest, at Lee, or at him. Without wasting time putting the shotgun to his shoulder, he aimed it and pulled hard on both triggers, God help them all, please let there be a round left in one of the barrels—

The concussion smothered the sound of his scream.

Stoat's chest exploded, spraying the room with red.

With the shotgun still hanging in his hands, Justin stood dazed by the din of the gunshot ringing and echoing in his mind, by the spectacle of his all-powerful captor splayed like roadkill before him, by a sense of all solid footing falling away from underneath his sore, sneakered feet. He balanced on a knife-edge of time. His future uncertain, fearsome, the specter of prison bars looming. His recent past gone in a burst of red. He had killed—

Killed Stoat?

"Is he dead?" Justin whispered to the shifting cosmos, shifting between man and boy, the man declaring, *Yes. Yes, it had to be done,* and the boy begging, *No, no, please, I didn't mean it, not Uncle Steve—*

Lee's voice said inside his head, *He is SO not your uncle.*

"He was going to throw the knife," Justin said a little bit louder. And what Stoat had done to Lee—would she be all right?

With a sense of tension stretching, then snapping, a bond breaking, Justin shifted his stare from Stoat to Lee and her sons. Forrest knelt beside his mother holding her hand and whispering to her, although she appeared not to hear him. Quinn stood at a window talking rapid-fire on his cell phone. ". . . already on their way? Good, but we need an ambulance also. My mother. Yes, she has a pulse and she's breathing but she's unconscious. No, I can't stay on the line. There are things I have to do." He snapped his phone shut.

Justin heard this without much comprehension, as if it were background noise, because his ears were still ringing and his mind clamoring. He watched without really seeing as Quinn lifted his mother's feet to place a sofa pillow underneath them, then ran to the bedroom and returned with a blanket, which he spread over her. "Trying to keep her from going into shock," he told his brother, his voice stretched thin.

Forrest turned on him, shrill. "Kind of late, aren't we? She moves down here all alone and we act like we don't care and now—" He choked, trying to control tears.

"Forrie, we can't help it that we're a pair of jerks too much like our father."

"But *Mom!*"

"I know. I wish—I want—I hope to God she'll be all right."

"She will. She's got to."

"Mom, stay with us, okay, please?" Quinn crouched by Lee Anna's head, stroked her hair, and said tenderly to her still, silent face, "Mom, we're idiots, we—" His voice hitched. "We need you."

"We love you," said Forrie, very low. "Hang in, Mom."

Mom. Justin heard the word profoundly, and something

free-floating within him began to connect, react, and magnify like yeast rising in homemade bread until its warm swelling filled him and displaced all else. He had no room in him for hesitation, none for shame or fear, and no need for a weapon. He let the shotgun drop to the floor with a thud. Startled by the noise, Quinn and Forrest looked at him.

"Could I borrow a phone, please?" asked Justin.

TWENTY-EIGHT

S upper, London broil with potatoes and asparagus, had been a strain for Amy, who had gotten out of the habit of cooking. But she had done her best not to let Chad know how stressed-out she felt, because she had made up her mind that Chad's reconciliation with his father could only be good for him and Kyle and Kayla. And maybe even for him and her—but, loading the dishwasher, she did not yet dare to hope, or even think about his idea of going away together—

The phone rang.

"I'll get it," Amy yelled, heading toward the kitchen. Kyle and Kayla knew better than to answer the phone when it might be about Justin, but Amy didn't want Chad and his dad, who were chatting in the living room, to be interrupted. "I'll get it," she repeated as she plucked the wireless from its cradle on the kitchen counter. "Hello?"

A youthful, husky male voice with a hint of burr in it said, "Mom?"

Amy's body knew that voice, responded to it, as vibrant as a tuning fork: *My child*. Yet her quibbling mind could not believe, only question. She whispered, "Justin?"

"Yeah, Mom, it's me."

Amy screamed, a lovely, musical scream of sheerest soul-piercing joy. "Justin!"

The conversation in the living room abruptly stopped.

Amy heard Justin say, "Listen, Mom, are you listening?"

At the same time she cried, "Justin, are you all right?"

Chad came running into the kitchen with his father lagging a bit behind. Ned stopped at a polite distance. Chad grabbed Amy, putting an arm around her. This seemed so natural to her that she barely noticed, even though it had not happened for months.

"Son, are you okay?" Chad yelled, although Amy still had the phone.

Justin said, "Not really. I just killed somebody."

Amy gasped. Chad demanded, "What is it?" Amy could not answer.

Justin kept speaking, his voice flat with shock. "I killed . . . him. You know, the one who took me. He had his knife out to throw. I killed him with the shotgun. I don't know whether I'm in trouble."

"Justin, where are you?" Chad demanded, his face next to Amy's, his mouth close to the receiver.

"Maypop."

"Maypop," Amy repeated for Chad. As her mind started to function, she clarified, "Justin, do you mean Maypop, Florida?" A small town they passed through on their way to Panama City.

"Yes."

"We can be there in an hour," she said to Chad.

But Justin was the one who responded. "Please. The police are coming for me. I hear the sirens. I'd better go."

Amy's voice rose an octave. "No, Justin, stay on the line!"

But only a click and silence answered her.

She tried to put the phone back in the cradle, dropped it instead, and clung to Chad for support, feeling his arms tight around her, so natural she decided to forget that comfort had ever been gone, withheld. His embrace strengthened her.

"Take a deep breath, honey," he said. Honey. And he sounded as if he needed a deep breath too.

"Oh, my God," Amy said against his shoulder. "Oh, my God, I can't believe it."

Without letting go of Chad, she was aware that Ned picked up the phone she had dropped, found the most recent number on its screen, and pressed the green Talk button. He listened, then shook his head.

"Justin shut the phone off?" Chad demanded hoarsely.

"Somebody did, or else somebody's using it."

Amy let go of Chad and stood not quite steadily on her own.

Ned said, "What are you waiting for, you two? Get going. I'll take care of things here."

Bernie Morales arrived first on the scene, in large part because he knew exactly where it was. As he got out of his cruiser in front of the pink house, a man opened the front door and beckoned to him urgently. "Bernie!" the man called. "Thank God!" and not until then did Bernie recognize him as Forrie Leppo. It was as if Forrest had been to war overnight, the past day had changed him so much. He looked steelier, sharper, like he'd been in combat. Even his voice had sharpened. "We need an ambulance!"

"Coming right behind me."

Without answering, Forrest disappeared from the door. Heading inside, Bernie put his mind in first-responder mode to memorize the moment like a movie still. Forrest on his knees beside a woman lying under a blanket on the floor: his mother? Bernie didn't ask, because he could see she was alive and being cared for, while the other person bleeding into the carpet looked very dead and that was a more serious matter. Bernie framed a mental snapshot of the guy's face—what the hell was wrong with it?—and the bloody mess where his chest had been and the potentially deadly knife close to his slack right hand. He leaned down to touch one of the man's wrists, checking the condition of the body—no pulse, but still warm. Then he straightened up and took in the rest of it: shotgun on the floor, boy sitting on the sofa looking stunned. Quinn sitting beside him, intent on a cell phone.

It was not Bernie's job to ask too many questions; that was for the detectives to do. He walked closer to Quinn and waited.

Quinn held up the cellular, one of those smartphones that might as well have been a computer. He presented the screen for Bernie to see. Bernie wondered why he was looking at a photo of Justin Bradley. He remembered the case, a heartbreaker across the state line in Alabama, boy abducted in broad daylight, not found yet.

Then he looked at the kid sitting next to Quinn. The kid faced up to look back at him, his eyes dazed, terrified.

Bernie said, "Holy shit."

"Justin Bradley, meet Deputy Morales," said Quinn.

"Stoat had me," said Justin Bradley hoarsely, looking at the body on the floor as if checking; was it still dead, or would it stand up and attack him?

"Stoat!" Bernie exclaimed. "Is that him?" He stared at the swollen, discolored face that had been ugly enough to start with.

The boy said all in a rush, "Yes. He was beating Lee, um, Miss Lee Anna with the shotgun. We got it away from him, but he was going to kill somebody with the knife. So I shot him."

"Bernie," Quinn said urgently, "Justin's parents are on their way, going crazy to have him back."

Another siren sounded, and more wheels pulled in, crunching the sand. Bernie parted the window drapes to look. "State police," he reported.

And the ambulance had arrived, apparently, because medics were swarming into the house with their equipment bags, pushing Forrest away so they could all crouch around the victim.

"I have to get back to Mom." Quinn sounded stretched pretty tight. "Bernie, Justin killed Stoat in self-defense. The creep was going to knife us. Does Justin have to stay here, or can he go to his parents?"

"Is he a minor?".

"Yes."

Sounding only a bit shaken up, Justin said, "Quinn, go on, take care of your mom. I'll be okay."

"Justin, you're the best." Getting up, hasty and awkward on his long legs, Quinn thrust his cell phone at Justin. "Call your folks back and have them talk with Deputy Morales. Bernie, do you think you can work something out here?"

More vehicles had pulled in, and Bernie caught a peripheral glimpse of his chief walking in the door. He knew better than to make any promises, although he badly wanted to. In Florida, the fact that the boy was underage did not mean he couldn't be questioned. But it did mean he could be released into his parents' custody if Bernie could keep him off the chief's radar long enough. "I'll see what I can do."

I had become so accustomed to things being surreal that waking up in a neck restraint under intensely white lights amid medical equipment and people wearing scrubs seemed like just another phenomenon in the Stoat experience. Pain, yes, pain in the head and one arm and various parts of my midriff, definitely Stoat-related pain. Firmly in Stoat-Stoic mode, I accepted that there would be more of the same, and I took in my view of the ceiling and people's heads without much curiosity until I saw a face, no, two faces almost hidden behind the others that jolted my heart even though I thought I must be mistaken, because it couldn't be Quinn in a dirty shirt and beard stubble, or Forrest with a pale, strained face instead of a smile.

Yet it was. My entire battered being knew, despite the objections of my brain; I experienced marrow-deep recognition to the extent that I snatched off my oxygen mask and tried to jump off the emergency room bed, screeching, "Forrie! Quinn!"

Many hands restrained me, and many voices told me to lie still, but I paid attention only to the sound of Quinn's voice telling me, "Chill, Mom," and Forrest saying, "Relax, Mom, we're right here," and then the touch of their hands, awkward and gentle. They stood beside my bed stroking my shoulder, my face. "You're in a hospital," Quinn said as if I were senile. "You got hurt."

"Of course I got hurt! Stoat—"

One of the medical professionals, a short, balding man in a white coat, interrupted. "Mrs. Leppo, do you remember how you were injured?"

"Stoat clobbered me with his shotgun butt, trying to kill me! Where is the bastard?"

Everyone ignored my question. "She remembers. That's good, isn't it, Doctor?" Forrest asked the medico.

"It would seem to indicate a lack of concussion."

"So she has no brain injury after all?"

"It's too soon to be sure. No two brain injuries manifest in quite the same way."

I considered that I had acted brain-injured for most of my life, so what difference did it make? "Where," I demanded more loudly, "is Stoat?"

Quinn iterated, "Chill, Mom."

And Forrest. "Relax, Mom. You don't have to worry about that Stoat dude anymore."

I was becoming almost as irritated at the pair of them as I was glad to see them. "Is Stoat in jail?"

Without replying, my sons looked at each other, consulting.

"He's *dead*?" Forget being stoical; I felt suspense in the most literal way, as if I might lift right off the table.

The doctor tried to intervene. "Now, Mrs. Leppo—"

"Yes," Quinn told me, "Stoat is dead."

"The cops killed him?"

"No. Justin did."

"Justin!" Implications hit me one after another, whacking my brain with almost the same dizzying effect as Stoat's shotgun butt. Justin was alive! Did his parents know? Justin had good reason to kill Stoat, but I knew him; he probably felt awful. Was he in trouble with the law? Or within himself? Who would help him? Would he have the good sense to call his parents? He was such a messed-up kid he might not. I had to do something.

"I have to get out of here." Again, I tried to sit up. Annoyingly, my sons helped hold me down.

Quinn said, "Mom, you're not going anywhere except to intensive care."

The doctor tried again. "Mrs. Leppo—"

"Clymer," I snapped at him. "My name is Clymer. Miss. I'm not married."

"She's upset about Justin." Forrest explained what he apparently considered my rudeness to the doctor.

"Damn straight I am!" I could not seem to stop becoming unhealthily wrought. "Where's Justin now?"

"We don't know, Mom. We left him at the house with the cops and came in the ambulance with you."

Cops?

I wanted a lot more answers, but the people in scrubs began to roll me away somewhere. To my astonishment, Quinn kissed my cheek. I felt the prickle of his chin stubble on my skin. "I love you, Mom."

This astonished me so much and felt so good that I floated in time for a moment in which there was no Georg, no divorce, no Stoat, and no victim of Stoat. I was loved.

Forrest prolonged the moment. "I love you, Mom." He squeezed my hand.

Then he had to let it go as nurses wheeled me off to an elevator. He and Quinn had to stay behind for some damn bureaucratic reason. But I felt only the warmth of their love all the way.

Maypop, Florida. Too damn apt. *I may pop to pieces,* Amy thought, because just the restraint of her seat belt felt unbearable. She felt swollen almost out of her skin by nebulous, shifting emotions, a cloud of anguished feelings that fogged her to her fingertips, even to her eyes, closing her in like the nightfall darkness pressing against the windows of the car.

Chad was driving, very much separated from her by his truck's large console. By making an effort, turning her head and focusing, Amy could see his backlit profile. He was not speeding as usual when he drove his beloved red Ram pickup, quite the opposite. On the flat, straight road between fields of soybeans he soldiered along at the speed limit or below it, extra careful in this perilous time, and Amy could see the muscles of his jaw working in his pale face.

Chad spoke, words struggling out of him as if he felt pinned under a great weight. "Would you try that phone number again?"

"Um, sure." He meant the number Justin had phoned from, which she had entered on her cell phone. Rummaging for the phone in her purse felt like searching a dark bog, in slow motion yet. What made the process even more surreal was that Chad showed no impatience. And when she finally found the cell and made the call, he showed no disappointment when she told him, "Not available."

He reached across the console toward her, but not long enough for her to reach out to him in return. He retracted. "Gotta keep both hands on the wheel," he muttered. "Not functioning real well."

"Me either." Amy couldn't verbalize further, but her fog of emotions felt as if it were condensing into liquid yet growing bigger than she was, vast, a sea, and she were a jellyfish about to be beached on an unknown land.

Chad, also, might have been feeling as if he was out of his depth, because he said, "Amy . . ." He hesitated, then spoke slowly. "Honey . . . things aren't going to get any easier."

Having Justin back, he meant. Their son was going to need a lot of help. "I know."

"Are we . . . are we on the same page?"

Amy felt like splattering her jellyfish self of anguish all over the interior of Chad's precious truck. Even calling her "honey," he still sounded as if he were talking about a working partnership, planning a job, and Amy needed so, so much more.

"That depends. Charles Stuart Bradley," she demanded, "do you love me?"

The truck swerved across the road's center line, then toward its dark edge, as if Chad were drunk. Amy thought he would curse, but he just took his foot off the gas, applied the brakes, and pulled over to the side of the road.

Still without speaking, he turned to her and reached for her over the console with both hands. This time he did not retract. He took hold of her firmly yet tenderly, and he kissed her—Amy had to close her eyes, dizzied by sheer hope. Chad's mouth did not try to dominate hers; his lips coaxed her to respond, and she did. It was the perfect kiss.

He laid his head on her shoulder and said gruffly, "God, yes, I love you."

"No more jellyfish," Amy murmured.

"Huh?"

"Never mind. I love you always, honey. Feel better?"

"Yes. Amy, sweetheart, you've been right all along and I was wrong."

"Shush. That *so* doesn't matter anymore. Let's go find our son."

Within moments after Chad got the truck back on the road, he asked Amy to try another phone call, and this time someone picked up: a sheriff's deputy named Morales.

Chad made it to the Maypop County Sheriff's Office by following the directions Amy relayed to him from Deputy Morales, who stayed on the line with them the whole time, coaching them and cautioning them to drive carefully. Chad felt he might not have made it without him. He felt as if he were carrying a tremendous weight made up mostly of his own overfull heart. He felt breathless and strained, sweating as if he were running a marathon. Which in a way he was, and he hadn't trained. For the past year he'd been lounging in a kind of emotional La-Z-Boy, and now here he was in a lather of desperate hope and fear and wanting his son and loving his wife and feeling unworthy and feeling—feeling so much he could have drowned in his own bellyful of blood, sweat, and tears.

Finally at the sheriff's office, Chad tried to park his big pickup neatly between the lines and failed, but for once he didn't make a second attempt to get it right. He jumped out and got around to the passenger side of his truck in time to help Amy get down; Chad kept meaning to install a step for her and kept forgetting. The way he felt right now, he hated himself for that one small neglected act.

He held his wife's hand as they started across the parking lot toward the double-wide trailer building occupied by the Maypop County Sheriff's Office, but they didn't get far.

A kid, looked like a teenager, jumped out of an old beater of a cruiser and sprinted to meet them, and Chad's heart riffed like a crazed drummer inside his chest, but he couldn't see the boy's face; Justin—please, it had to be Justin—kept his head down, his eyes shielded by the bill of a baseball cap.

Quite spontaneously, because his legs no longer seemed willing to support him, Chad got down on his knees.

He saw Justin's face.

Justin, yes! But—God, this wasn't the Justin he remembered. Justin had the hollow, haunted look of a war survivor aged and hardened beyond his years, yet at the same time he looked paradoxically, childishly young and hurt and vulnerable.

"Justin!" A mother's potent call. Amy ran to her lost child and wrapped him in her arms.

Justin said, "M-M-Mom," and broke into tears.

An instant later Chad got there to bear-hug both of them. He felt his son sobbing uncontrollably. And his wife. And, unashamedly, himself.

Justin had told himself and told himself that he was not going to bawl like a baby. But the instant he had seen his parents, the most potent upheaval of emotion ever in his life had overpowered him to shoot him straight into their arms, then turn him inside out while they held him, they kept holding him, standing strong and holding him together when he felt like he was nothing, nothing at all except tears.

It wasn't until Bernie Morales came and offered everyone a

box of tissues that he noticed Mom and Dad were crying too. They didn't act embarrassed, so why should he?

"I feel for you all in my heart." Bernie stretched out his arms in a fatherly sort of way, herding them toward the Sheriff's Office. "You come inside, we try to make this quick, get you out of here before the nosy people find out, yes?"

Oh, God, Justin realized, it wasn't over yet. It was going to be days before it was really over, maybe weeks, maybe—never.

Bernie took them inside to a room with a table, where Justin slumped in a chair with his face hidden under the bill of his cap. "Sweetie, take off your hat," said his mom, her voice so warm he realized she was kind of teasing.

"Sit up straight," said his dad the same way.

Somehow, just by being annoying parents, they helped him lift his head and face Bernie, who was turning on a tape recorder. "Justin, we talk just about today, okay?"

Okay. Whatever.

Bernie Morales recorded the date and Justin's name, then coached, "Start with what made you go into Liana Clymer's house."

"We heard her scream."

Bernie pretty much led him through it. All that his questions required of Justin was quick, simple answers. Somebody brought in cans of soda pop as if this were just a little get-together. But toward the end, Justin felt something fearsome and akin to Stoat trying to turn him inside out again. "I had to kill him," he blurted. "I didn't want to. Am I going to jail?"

"No, no, not if this is true." Bernie turned off the tape recorder and stood up. "Okay, I must go put this in writing for Justin to sign, and then we are done for today, okay?"

Once Bernie had left the room, Dad and Mom both got up,

came over to Justin, and hugged him again. His voice thick with emotion, Dad said, "Son, you're a hero."

"I don't feel like a hero. I feel bad."

Dad asked simply and gently, "Why?"

Justin barely managed to choke out part of it. "B-be-because I killed Unc—I mean Stoat."

"Unc?" Dad asked just as gently.

"Uncle Steve."

"You called him Uncle Steve."

"He told me to."

Dad's voice became only slightly harder. "So he made it like you were family."

"Yes, and—and—he wasn't bad to me sometimes, and—and I had to go and kill him!" *Don't goddamn cry*, Justin ordered himself. He was nearly crying but not quite. *Don't.*

There was a long moment of silence. Justin stiffened, expecting Dad to tell him Stoat deserved to be killed. But instead, Dad said, "Son, whatever you feel is how you feel. We all have a lot of sorting out to do."

Mom said, "I see a family therapist in our future."

Dad nodded, looked Justin straight in the eye, and said, "Speaking of family, let me make a phone call." He got out his cell phone.

Justin stared, struck by the sight of the BlackBerry yet oddly comforted. "Is that your same old—"

"Some things stay the same but some things change." Into the phone, his father said, "Hi, Dad, how is it going?"

Justin felt astonishment lift his head and his heart.

"Are Kyle and Kayla still up?"

"Grandpa?" Justin gasped.

Smiling with blessedly genuine warmth and ease, his father nodded at him. To the phone he said, "Listen, Dad, great news. You can tell them we found Justin."

Justin could hear the joyful noise on the phone from where he sat. Three voices, one old and two young, yelling and crying. And a dog barking.

"Grandpa's dog," Mom told Justin, very matter-of-fact.

"Yes, he's right here," Dad was saying into the cellular. "Howsabout you put the phone on speaker?" He did the same at his end, then handed his BlackBerry over to Justin with a grin, assuring Justin he would do just fine.

"Hi, squirts," he said, and in answer to the resultant clamor, "Yes, it's me. I've been in a dungeon. It's a long story. Grandpa?"

"Yes, Justin." The elderly voice sounded all choked up. Unbelievable, to have a grandfather who cared about him waiting for him at home.

"Hi, Grandpa."

"Justin, I'm so glad you're coming home, I can't see straight."

"Um, good, I guess." Trying to change the subject, Justin asked, "What's your dog's name?"

"Oliver."

Kayla yelled, "And he likes Meatloaf!"

"You feed him meat loaf?"

For some reason everyone started laughing, and Justin laughed along with them without knowing why.

TWENTY-NINE

Descartes should have spent some time in Maypop Medical. Thinking had nothing to do with the definition of existence; here it was hello, I had a bowel movement, therefore I am. I'm afraid I was not a patient patient. Because Stoat had smashed my forearm rather thoroughly, I required surgery to pin the bones back in place, which had to wait until the swelling went down, so between that and a hairline fracture of my skull and a bruised spleen from being kicked and a few cracked ribs, I was stuck in the hospital for five days in order to heal. But I think the most important healing that took place there occurred between me and my sons.

"Where's Schweitzer?" I remember asking none too lucidly. Those days I wasn't quite firmly in residence in my own body. My face, cut and bruised with blackened eyes, made me barely recognizable to myself. Some sort of intravenous lotus juice dripping into me all the time kept me a bit muddled.

My sons exchanged glances. Forrest asked cautiously, "You mean Schweitzer's body?"

"Yes."

"We buried him in the front yard."

"Oh. Good." I meant good, Schweitzer had not been taken

away by strangers or thrown into the garbage; Schweitzer had been interred by people who knew him and were fond of him. If I had tried to say any of this, I would have sounded like a maudlin drunk, so I dozed off—not an unusual occurrence. An image of a small grave in front of a pink house formed in my mind, but the pink house wasn't my cute pink shack anymore. Some unseen hands of my mind pulled it into goo like taffy, a bloody gory mess. I woke up.

"I can't live there anymore," I said to no one except myself, and it was true. With a swampy feeling I realized I could never again feel comfortable in the fuchsia shack surrounded by fuzzy-blossomed mimosa trees. Not even if I bought a sofa cover and put down a new carpet. Every day when darkness fell, it would be as if my mind were spraying Luminol, and I would see blood fluorescing like soul rot. Schweitzer's blood. My blood. And Stoat's. I had either a fainting memory or a disturbing dream of his hot blood splashing all over me as he died.

"I can't go back to that pink shack," I told my sons the next time I saw them.

"Come back up north with us, then," said Forrie. "We'll find you someplace to live where you won't run into Dad."

"Your father's okay." I must explain that aftermath is the stubble left after something is mowed down, and those days I was pretty much all aftermath of Stoat. I had lost all resentment of Georg; compared to Stoat, the man was an effing role model. Hacked down to the root emotions, cut off from embarrassment or inhibition, I felt like an open-backed hospital gown mentally as well as literally—a new experience to both me and my sons. They gawked at me.

"New sense of proportion," I explained, and the provenance of my remark led me to ask, "Have you heard from Justin?"

They hadn't, not directly, although they had their own inside source, a sheriff's deputy named Bernie Morales. Quinn had contacted him to get his cell phone back, then gone to see him for the same reason, and Bernie had not only provided the phone but also told him Justin was doing well. That Bernie had witnessed the boy's tearful, wholehearted reunion with his mom and dad. That Justin was not allowed to leave Maypop for a few days, so he and his parents had gone into seclusion to avoid the media.

"We could check the TV," Forrie said, meaning CNN.

"Nah. I've seen enough of Stoat to last me a lifetime." Having learned of the Justin Bradley connection, newscasters were all over the story, which included me. My sons told me there was a news posse parked outside the hospital waiting for me to appear. Quinn and Forrest were in collusion with the hospital staff to come and go through the laundry bay. They were my only visitors except for the police who had taken my statement.

Hearing my full story, Forrest had said with a stunned look, "My God, Mom." He had said it more than once. "I can't believe what you've been through. And what you did."

And Quinn had blurted, "It's no wonder Justin wouldn't quit until he'd found you."

I told my sons nothing of the absurd daydreams I was having about Justin. As soon as Justin felt well enough, he and I could start making megabucks doing TV interviews. Gee, what would I wear to talk with Piers Morgan, and how would I get my hair done? Maybe somebody would want to write a book, or even better, somebody would want to make a movie. Who would star as Justin and who would star as me? There would be big money, but Justin and I wouldn't argue about who got how much, not after what we'd been through together. We would be like heroes who had gone through war side by side, buddies for life.

Semper Fi. I wanted to see Justin, and find out how he was doing, and talk with him.

I had two sons who loved me. Yet I wanted Justin so much that I had to ask myself a few questions and come to some hard answers.

Luckily I did so in time. Before Justin and his parents came to visit.

They came by my hospital room on their way home to Alabama. I assumed Bernie Morales had sneaked them in through the laundry bay.

It was the day before I was due to be discharged. Forrie and Quinn were out at the pink shack packing my things into a storage container, and I was trying to ignore whatever was on daytime TV. I wondered whether zoos thought constant videos were good for caged monkeys.

Justin walked in.

I forgot TV was ever invented. Justin looked as if he had put on a year's growth in the week or so since I had seen him. He wore all new clothes; he stood solid; he walked tall. I almost didn't recognize him. Yet I knew him to the heart of my bones.

I gasped, "Justin!"

"Hi, Lee." So far Justin was the only person in the world who called me that, and the way he said it told me a lot. That, and the fact that he took my hand, leaned over my bed, and kissed me on the not-quite-so-beat-up side of my head.

Only my decision kept me from blushing like a sunset. "Justin," I ordered, "sit down, tell me everyth— Hello, are these your parents?" Because there in my room stood a good-looking, smiling man in a trucker hat and a pretty woman with a pot of pansies in her hands and her face all in bloom with gladness.

"Yes. Mom, Dad, this is Lee." He stood back as if displaying a prize exhibit. This is the crazy woman who knocked on Stoat's door and saw the right advertisement at the wrong time.

Dad shook my hand awkwardly and very gently. "I need to thank you so much I don't know what to say."

I protested, "But, Mr. Bradley—"

"Chad. Everybody calls me Chad."

"And I'm Amy," said Justin's mom, setting the pansies down to kiss me—not a typical feminine air kiss, but a motherly kiss on the cheek. "Thank you for giving us our son back."

"But Justin's the one who saved *my* life. Twice. No, three times."

"Bull." Justin came forward to take possession of me once again. "You and Forrest and Quinn—"

He became bashful. I covered for him. "Sit down, all of you. Please."

They did, pulling chairs close to my bedside while I kept my big mouth going. "The other children?" I asked Amy. "The twins? How—"

"We've been on the phone to them *and their grandfather* every day." I wondered why she put such a special stress on "grandfather," and smiled at Chad as she said it. "They're waiting at home like it's Christmas. We finally get to take Justin home today."

"We've been hiding out in a motel," Justin told me. "I had to stay to explain to the cops about Stoat and stuff."

I saw my chance to maybe help. "Do you miss Stoat much?"

Justin opened his mouth without speaking. Chad asked, "You're joking, right?"

"No, not at all. Justin, do you miss him?"

"I—I'm not sure. I mean, I killed him. I had to. But then I felt bad."

"Of course you did," I said. "Stoat had a kind of creepy charm, and you lived with him for two years. You couldn't *not* like him a little. I did."

"But at the end—"

"I know. So I hated him too." I rolled my eyes, mocking myself. "Human feelings are wacko. A person can feel two or three or half a dozen ways all at the same time."

Justin only ducked his head, but Chad sat bolt upright and exclaimed, "That was me for the past year."

Although I had no idea what he was talking about, I nodded. "Me too."

Justin surprised me by asking, "Lee, are you going to be okay?"

"Sure. I'll be out of here tomorrow."

"Good! I bet you'll be glad to get home," said Justin eagerly. "You know, I never noticed the inside of your house. I like the mimosa trees, though."

And his mother turned to look straight at me. Her eyes met mine. Not demanding, not pleading, just asking: did I understand what was really going on here, about the mixed emotions Justin could not yet control or even comprehend?

I nodded. Yes. Yes, I did understand. I had some very mixed feelings myself. It's not that I wasn't tempted.

But he was *her* son.

"No, actually, Justin," I said quite simply and easily, "I don't want to live there anymore. I'm going back up north."

He stared at me, startled, maybe even stricken. *"What?"*

"I'm going to stay with my sons for a while, until the busted parts of me get better—"

"And then you'll be back?"

"No." I made it sound like no big deal when the truth was I wanted him for my surrogate son almost as badly as he wanted me for his surrogate mom. But now that he had his real mom back, the right thing for me to do was get out of her way.

And out of Justin's.

If I really cared about him, I had to want the best for him. Sure, I dreamed of forming a lifetime bond based on our mutual experience of Steven Stoat. But Justin was young. He shouldn't build a career based on memories of Stoat the Goat, for God's sake, no matter how lucrative it might be. Far from it. He should forget the bastard, as much as possible, and move on, and have a life.

"No," I said, "once I feel better, I'll find someplace to live near my old friends and my family. You know, I was kind of running away from home when I moved down here."

He was having a little trouble speaking. "But I was looking forward to visiting you all the time."

I doubt he realized how much he wanted to come back to re-visit familiar misery, seeing the blue shack across the road from mine, turning away from the hard work of recovery, feeling more comfortable in his passive past.

I must never let him know how much of an understanding I shared with him. He wanted understanding too much for his own good.

Forcing myself to sound like any obtuse and well-meaning adult, I said, "Well, you can come see me once I find a place to stay. I'm sure we'll keep in touch."

"Um, sure, of course." He and his mother and father stood up at the same time. He didn't kiss me or come near me again, just said, "Thanks for everything, Lee."

"No, Justin, thank *you*."

No longer looking at me, he shrugged and stood back. But Chad warmly shook my hand, and Amy hugged me and kissed me. And everything Justin's parents couldn't say to me showed in their eyes as they left my room with their son.

Quinn and Forrest came in shortly afterward to find me staring moodily at a pot of pansies. Forrie asked, "What's the matter, Mom?"

"I hate good-byes."

"Justin was here?"

"Yes, and I rode away into the sunset."

"Well, then that's where we live. So hello." He and Quinn both grinned at me.

My sons. My *family*.

I smiled in response to them. Actually, I think I beamed. "You're right, you two. Hello."

Nancy Springer has written fifty novels for adults, young adults, and children, in genres that include mythic fantasy, contemporary fiction, magical realism, horror, and mystery—although she did not realize she wrote mystery until she won the Edgar Allan Poe Award from the Mystery Writers of America two years in succession. Most recently she has ventured into adult suspense, such as *Drawn into Darkness*.

Born in New Jersey, Nancy Springer lived for many decades in Gettysburg, Pennsylvania, of Civil War fame, raising two children, writing, horseback riding, fishing, and bird-watching. In 2007 she surprised her friends and herself by moving with her second husband to an isolated area of the Florida Panhandle, where the bird-watching is spectacular and where, when fishing, she occasionally catches an alligator.

CONNECT ONLINE

nancyspringer.com
facebook.com/nancyspringerauthor
twitter.com/nancyspringer

Read on for an excerpt from
Nancy Springer's "darkly riveting"* and
"fast-paced, edge-of-your-seat"** suspense novel

DARK LIE

Now available in print and e-book
from New American Library

*Wendy Corsi Staub, author of *Nightwatcher* and *Sleepwalker*

**Heather Gudenkauf, *New York Times* bestselling author of
The Weight of Silence and *These Things Hidden*

As usual, I had to tell myself I wasn't doing anything wrong. Every other minute of the week I lived for my husband and his business, my elderly mother and father, family values, et cetera. Surely I could be allowed my bittersweet secret on Saturday afternoons. If my husband ever found out . . . But I'd told him no lies. I'd told him I was going to the mall, and there I was.

I stood at the window of the plus-size store, pretending to scan the display of boxy blazers with matching elastic-waist skirts. Despite my uneasy conscience, I felt pretty sure that, in my old brown car coat and my favorite dress with its full blue corduroy skirt, I looked like any other overweight, middle-aged housewife in search of clothing that would disguise her thunder thighs.

Middle-aged? I was only in my thirties. But an "affliction," as my parents called it, had roughened my face, scarred my skin, stiffened my joints, and made me look and feel a decade older. It was just lupus, and I'd met other people with lupus who danced through it, but my case had attacked like the wolf after which it was named. And the steroids my doctors had prescribed gave me chipmunk cheeks and hippopotamus hips. Actually I could have used some new clothes, if only for retail therapy.

But instead of really studying the plus-size fashions, I watched the reflections in the display window's glass. That way, I could surreptitiously look down the mall.

There were not as many shoppers as usual on a Saturday because this was the first sunny, warm day after a miserable Ohio winter. Anybody with good sense was out digging in the garden or flying a kite. But I continued to watch and hope, because the spring formals were coming up and the mall was having a well-promoted Prom Time sale, so maybe—

"Dorrie!" Somebody behind me called my name. "Dorrie, hi!"

"Oh, hi." Turning, I forced a smile. The speaker was an overly perky woman from church. Fulcrum is not such a small town—we have a branch campus of University of Ohio—but it's still a one-mall town, and in that mall on a Saturday afternoon I could expect to meet people I knew.

"Sam let you out of his sight?" teased the woman, an annoyingly skinny redhead who worked as a teller at the People's Bank of Fulcrum. "All by yourself?"

I made myself keep smiling, although I wasn't amused. Sam was a nice guy, no worse than her husband or anybody else's. Like most of them, he was not much to look at, just another standard-issue male with a big blunt pink face as plain as a pencil eraser, and hands that were clever when it came to machinery but klutzy when it came to romantic caresses. Like most of them, he didn't dance or ask for directions, he left his wet towels on the bathroom floor, he required full-time care and feeding. But as husbands went, Sam was as good as most and better than some. Didn't drink or fool around, did his best within his limits to make me happy. Not his fault if I wasn't.

I tried to reply lightly. "Yeppers. Sam let me out all by myself."

"What's he doing? It's such a beautiful day. I hope he went golfing."

"No, he's at the machine shop." As usual. Right out of college Sam had taken a management job at Performance Parts & Gears, and now, only eleven years of shrewd hard work later, he owned and operated the place. Sam made good money, but he paid the price in long hours and penny-pinching and headaches. I would have loved to have gone on a cruise to Bermuda, Alaska, Panama, anywhere, but Sam couldn't leave the shop that long, or so he said.

"He's there almost twenty-four/seven, isn't he?" What was that edge in the redhead's voice? Sarcasm? Envy? Disapproval? "And so are you, aren't you, Dorrie?" True, although my helping out in the office was supposed to have been temporary, until Sam could afford to hire somebody. Which he could now, but he didn't want to spend the money. The redhead burbled, "Working with the hubby—I don't know how you do it. I'd go insane."

I stiffened. "Not at all." But if anyone knew how much I lived in a secret world of memories and daydreams . . .

I changed the subject. "Want to see what I bought?" I held up my plastic shopping bag. As usual, I'd purchased something light-weight I could carry around so I'd blend into the mall ambience.

The redhead peeked at my purchase du jour. "Wire baskets? Graph paper? For Sam?"

"Baskets for Sam's desk. Graph paper for me. In case I go back to teaching."

"Really! Is that what you're planning—?"

I cut her off. "I'm not sure." Actually I'd gone into teaching only to appease my parents, and was surprised to find I was good at it and I liked it, if it weren't for the administration, and some of the parents I had to deal with, plus the grading system and the politics. . . . I didn't really want to go back. But I felt I had to do something with myself. Life stretched ahead far too empty. Some churches might have social activities other than the occasional covered-dish supper, but not mine. Some bodies might enjoy yoga or Zumba or a membership in the gym, but not mine. Some husbands might take their wives on interesting business trips or vacations, or bring them flowers for no reason, or have long, soul-searching conversations with them, but not mine. Sam and I used to talk, but not so much lately. Maybe if we had been able to have children, things would be different, but—

"But what about your health problems? Will you be able to hold a job?"

Annoyed, I glanced at my wrist as if I had to be somewhere. Except there was no watch there. I never wore a watch to the mall on Saturdays. Didn't want to notice or care how much time I spent there. My wrist showed me only a display of irregular white splotches, unpigmented skin, caused by lupus.

"Two hairs past a freckle," teased the redhead.

Pertinacious woman, did she have to notice everything? I showed my teeth in what I hoped passed for a grin as she consulted her own wristwatch and told me with digital precision, "It's two thirty-seven."

"Um, thanks."

And at that moment I felt my face forget all about its polite smile as a movement far down the mall caught my eye. The lilt of a certain walk amid hundreds of walkers. Barely more than a hint at the distance, but my heart beat like butterfly wings. I'd know that coltish stride anywhere.

"Um, excuse me," I told the redhead, hurrying off.

Limping, rather. Lupus made every movement painful, but if I let it slow me down, it would get even worse. At least today I wasn't having the knock-me-flatter-than-roadkill fatigue. It was a good day. Actually, a wonderful day now that I had spotted the person I had come to see.

Not to talk to. Just to see. Secretly.

There. I caught sight of her more plainly now: a slim teenage girl striding along, her dark eyes shining as she laughed with her friends. A boy kept glancing at her; was he in love with her? He ought to be. The whole world ought to love this delicate girl with her sleek dark hair pulled back from an Alice in Wonderland brow, her small head poised high on a balletic neck. Capering, she broke free of the group for a moment to skitter like a spooked filly—no, she was lovelier than a filly, I decided as she circled back to the others. She was a deer playing in a cow pasture, set apart from the other teenage Ohio corn-fed stock by every fawnlike, long-boned move, every lovely feature of her fair-skinned face.

Juliet.

Juliet Dawn Phillips.

My daughter.

Who didn't know me.

Whom I was not supposed to know. Whom I had given up for adoption sixteen years ago.

When I'd married Sam, we'd thought we'd have children. We'd bought a house, big and rugged, kind of like Sam, to accommodate all our dream children. More children than most people. Maybe four or five or six.

It hadn't happened. Lupus had happened instead.

Sam and I had been married for ten years now, and it had taken about eight of those to diagnose the lupus. My parents had muttered darkly of STDs at first, behind Sam's back. Doctors had postulated hypochondria or depression. Even Sam had believed it was all in my head or, rather, my hormones, some kind of woman thing, and what I needed was a family. But it was my irregular menstrual cycle and my inability to conceive that had made the doctors stop murmuring vaguely of chronic fatigue syndrome, Lyme disease, possible lead poisoning, or whatever, and finally order the blood tests that had confirmed the lupus.

For ten years now it had been just me and Sam, Performance Parts & Gears, and our house—lavishing my frustrated maternal instincts on the house, I had made it a warm and welcoming place, as much unlike my parents' home as possible.

Welcoming, but empty. Barring miracles, Juliet was the only child I would ever have.

Hiding behind a MALL INFORMATION sign, I gazed at her and let the sight of her transport me into the memories that seemed more real and alive than my weekdays, my husband and his forever work, my married life:

Me, Dorrie, age sixteen, and I am balletically slender with my long dark hair pulled back from my Alice in Wonderland brow, but I do not realize I am beautiful until Blake tells me so.

My parents will not let me crimp my hair, put makeup on my face, or wear jeans, ever, for they wish to save my soul. But they are not unkind. They have let me put aside the prayer bonnet except for Sundays, and they hope this will help me make friends at school and avoid being jeered at as before. Always after school my mother is waiting with cookies warm from the oven. We talk little but she often prepares the meals I like best, hamburgers or spaghetti, as if to tell me something she cannot say.

Evenings I spend at home. Mother and Father will not let me go to the amusement park or the video arcade. They won't let me date, or stay out after dark, or talk on the phone unsupervised, but they try in their ways to make me happy despite the many restrictions. My father is interested to hear what I have learned in school, and my mother keeps offering more cookies. Yet for some reason I remain thin.

Blake Roman is one of the older boys at my school in Appletree, Ohio, my hometown, which—although I do not know this—I am soon to leave, never to return. If Blake is aware of my parents' rules at all, he bypasses them entirely. He doesn't ask for my phone number. He doesn't ask for a date. He doesn't even say hi to me before the day he joins me as I walk home from school, takes the books from my arms, and places them on a park bench. He says, "I know your name. You're Candor Birch. I'm going to call you Candy. You're going to be my Candy."

My parents call me Candor, and everyone else calls me Dorrie. Once an aunt tried to call me Candy. My parents stopped inviting her to the house.

I have not particularly noticed Blake before. He is ordinary looking. But the moment he speaks to me, his voice transfixes me. Unlike him, his voice has black, black hair and a handsome passionate Latin face. His voice possesses such princely power that the simple words he is saying sound wonderful, romantic. His gaze, like his voice, issues out of his ordinary-looking face, out of his brown eyes, with a force of focus that is—more than powerful, more than princely. The authority and intensity in that boy's gaze—I recognize it. I've seen it in all the masterful leading men in the only movies my parents will let me watch, the old classics. Rock Hudson. Humphrey Bogart. Alan Ladd.

Blake says, "I know who you are. Candy. You are beautiful like Cinderella. My Candy. I love you." Right there on the sidewalk in the full stark March daylight he takes my face between his strong hands and touches his lips to mine, softly, tenderly, his touch radiating throughout my body to linger there as a physical memory. It is Clark Gable sweeping away Vivien Leigh, it is John Wayne grabbing Maureen O'Hara, it is Spencer Tracy putting the moves on Katharine Hepburn. It is a perfect, perfect kiss, and it is my first.

The memory played back in my mind as clearly as a DVD. But as Juliet and her friends drifted down the mall, I paused the video in order to follow, feeding upon the sight of her.

Luck, careful snooping, and a talkative teenage neighbor had let me know Juliet spent some of her Saturday afternoons at the mall. About half, but a fifty percent chance of seeing her was good enough for me. I had missed Juliet's childhood and puberty entirely. My parents had led me to believe that she had been adopted by an anonymous couple far, far away, in California or someplace, and I would never see her beyond a single look at her in the delivery room. I carried that memory like a snapshot in my mind: the strong bloodstained baby, arched and stiff with indignation, lying on my belly with her tiny fists battling the air. The nurse who had placed her there said, "You've given someone a beautiful daughter for Christmas." It was Christmas Day 1995.

Peace on earth and goodwill for me that year had been my parents pretending my baby daughter had never happened, encouraging me to go on with my life while upholding the same pretense. Which I had tried to do. Having no idea my little girl was right here in Fulcrum with me.

Fifteen years later—a bit more than a year ago—I'd found out accidentally, from the bureaucrat who'd taken my application to renew my teaching certificate. "Small world," he had remarked to me across his desk in the Department of Education building in Columbus. "I know Don Phillips. He and I went to law school together. How are he and Pearl doing?" Faced with my blank look, he'd added, "According to the transcripts your college faxed to me, Phillips paid your bills. We're talking about the same Don Phillips, right? District attorney, lives in Fulcrum?"

I don't remember what I said, but I'm good at being vaguely agreeable.

"Is he your uncle or something, paying your tuition?"

I had no idea. News to me.

But I'd always wondered why my parents had sent me to college, uncomplaining about the expense, when they were the type to scold about "money up a puppy's rectum"—honestly, those are the exact words they used—if I broke an orange juice glass while washing the dishes.

Driving back to Fulcrum from Columbus, with my hands clenched tighter and tighter on the steering wheel, I had headed straight for my parents' brown shingled house.

I suppose I ought to call it a Cape Cod, but it lacked the implied coziness and charm. It was just small, that's all. Rife with restriction, like the people who lived in it.

Walking into the entry, where plastic covered a rag rug that covered the carpet that covered the floor, I saw Dad in the living room, watching *Jeopardy!*; he waved but did not look at me. I headed in the opposite direction and found Mom in the kitchen, a sterile white place with no nonsense or fridge magnets, just as the other rooms held no whimsy or dust catchers, just as Mom wore no personality or jewelry except her wedding ring, ever.

Standing at the kitchen sink, Mom was cutting up whole raw chickens, undoubtedly purchased in bulk at a bargain price. Immobilizing a plump chicken leg over the index finger of her left hand, Mom wielded her favorite old wooden-handled butcher knife, neatly severing the drumstick from the thigh as she sliced unerringly through the joint. I shuddered. Big sharp knives always gave me a sick feeling in the pit of my stomach. I didn't know why.

"'Lo, Mom." I heard the tension in my own voice.

But nodding back at me, Mom seemed relaxed enough, her gray hair smoothed back under a crocheted prayer bonnet instead of a starched linen one. My mom was fifty-five, but she looked seventy. Being born old seems to run in my family.

Of course she asked me whether I would like some freshly baked "hermits," applesauce-and-honey pastry cut into bars, and I declined because always and forever I was dieting. Quite truthfully I told her that I wished I could still gobble her warm-from-the-oven baked goodies the way I used to. Sitting at the kitchen table, I made small talk for a few minutes, then said, "Mom, I need to get in touch with the adoption agency from, you know, back when I was a teenager. . . ."

Mom dropped her knife into the sink with a clatter and swiveled to look at me as if I'd morphed into a warthog. Foreseeing such a reaction, I'd rehearsed an explanation.

"The doctor says I should, because of the lupus," I told her levelly. It's easy to lie to your parents when they've trained you to hide your true feelings, to live a lie. "The baby may have inherited a predisposition for autoimmune disorders from me. So the adoptive parents need to be notified. Which agency was it?"

Mom told me, "You'll do no such thing."

"You don't want me to do what's right?" I don't think I'd ever argued with her so coolly. I was able to do it because at that moment, having spent hours thinking about what she and my father had done, I hated her.

And maybe she sensed something deep underneath the calm words. She left her work to sit at the table facing me, wiping her hands with a dish towel, faltering, "If your affliction . . . If God sees fit to punish . . . God's will . . ."

"I just want to inform the agency," I lied. "But if you won't tell me the name of the agency, then I'll have to try to find the child and notify her myself. It's not so hard anymore, you know, on the Internet. I—"

Mom interrupted. "There was no agency."

"No agency? But you always said 'the adoption agency' this, 'the adoption agency—'"

"It was a private adoption. You can't notify any agency or trace it on your whatchacallit, computer. So just put any such nonsense

out of your mind, Candor Verity." Her use of my full name signaled the finality of this pronouncement.

Candor? Verity? She and Dad had named me Truth, Truth,
yet they had been lying to me for years.

"You are not to speak of it again." Broomstick straight and
rigid, Mom stood up and marched to the sink, where she picked
up her knife to dismember another chicken.

I wanted to grab the big butcher knife away from her and stab
her right in the—but the thought, the impulse, frightened me even
more than the sight of the knife did. I got up and left the house.

Over the next few days I had found out what I needed to know
from public records and news archives on the Internet. Don and
Pearl Phillips had a single child, a daughter, Juliet Dawn Phillips.
Her birth date: Christmas Day 1995. And yes, she was adopted. A
gubernatorial hopeful who touted right-to-life and family values,
Donald Phillips had made public reference several times to the
blessed adoption process that had given him and his wife their
beloved daughter. He hadn't gone into detail about the private
adoption, which, from what I had just learned about where my
college tuition money had come from, had probably skirted the
edges of legality. While he hadn't exactly bought a baby, my parents had certainly made lemonade in the shade.

So that was what I learned last year . . . but even now, on a
sunny Saturday afternoon in the Greater Fulcrum Shopping
Mall, I still clenched my teeth just thinking how my parents had
shamed me for getting pregnant, snatched me away from the only
home I had ever known, arranged for the disposal of my baby, and
then "let" me attend U of Ohio right here at Fulcrum, still under
the parental thumb.

"Hypocrites," I whispered through my teeth as I accelerated
past a Hallmark store and a jewelry store, anger lengthening my

stiff, painful strides. "Lying hypocrites." I hoped Juliet was planning to go to a real college and have a career—

It looked like Juliet and her friends were heading for the food court.

Yes. Swerving like a flock of starlings, they swarmed the taco stand. I sat down on one end of a mall bench, forgetting my anger, once again intent on just watching. Juliet stood hugging herself, rubbing her bare arms with her hands. The child was underdressed for the weather; what were her adoptive parents thinking, to let her out of the house in that skimpy top, with her sleek little belly bare? Didn't they care whether she caught pneumonia or, even worse, boys?

Didn't they realize she might make the same mistake—

No, my dreaming mind took over. It hadn't been a mistake and it couldn't happen to Juliet because there was not, would never be, and never had been another boy like Blake.

I am sixteen and living a fairy tale. I have been a good, good girl for years and now it is all happening, I am Cinderella and Snow White and Sleeping Beauty all awakening as one, and Blake is my miracle prince. Every day in school he gazes into my eyes and gives me the most special flower, a white rose folded out of notebook paper, with a red candy nestled deep inside. Hiding in a stall of the girls' room, I suck on the cherry candy as I unfold the rose to read Blake's secret message to me. His angular printing sprawls all over the paper; each line seems to dive off the edge of a cliff. "My sweet, sweet Candy," he writes, "I am going to open you and suck your sugar." I have no specific idea what this means, but it warms my whole body with the most wonderful feeling. "I am going to taste you with my mouth and my tongue. Meet me in the back stairwell at beginning of lunch period. I am starving for you, my love."

A girl I barely know stops me in the hallway. "Listen, stupid, stay away from Blake Roman," she tells me, hard-eyed. "Where do you think he learned those slick moves of his?"

What I perceive as her jealousy sets me aglow with joyful defiance. Missing lunch, I meet Blake in the back stairwell, because I am like a heroine in one of the romance novels I read on the sly; I have been swept away. I am caught in a kind of carnal rapture. In the shadows under the last flight of stairs, Blake starts to pull my top up. "But someone might see us," I whisper.

"Yes," he agrees, "and that makes me hungry like a wolf. I need you. Do you love me?"

"Yes!"

"Then you will do this for me." Expertly he lifts my bra to bare my small breasts. He is so sure of every move, so masterful that I know he is more than my prince; he is my love angel, born knowing how to do these things just for me. I obey him as I have always obeyed those with author-ity: God, the preacher, the teacher, my parents . . . no, I try not to think of my parents. I sense clearly enough that what I am doing is so deeply forbidden that I cannot even imagine what would be my punishment. But my parents' authority has been superseded by a more compelling one, Blake's, because nothing, nothing in my life or my dreams, has ever felt so wide-eyed spine-curling shocking electrically good as what he does to me.

"I'll be waiting for you right here after school," Blake whispers as he twitches my bra back where it belongs, "and we'll go somewhere and I'll unfold you like a white flower, my Candy, my love."

Sitting there in the mall, I realized I'd better stop playing that particular memory or it would show in my face. I refocused on Juliet. She and her friends had settled at one of the sticky plastic tables in the food court, and right beside it was another table, empty. Back-to-back with Juliet's chair stood an empty chair. I stared at it.

No. I had promised myself I would keep my distance. I knew in my heart that my being here constituted questionable mental hygiene, that there was something unhealthy about the way I was acting. Imagine if anyone were to find me scouring the Internet—the Fulcrum Area High School home page, the Phillips family Web site, Facebook, MySpace—imagine if anyone were to find the downloaded pictures of Juliet that I kept in a scrapbook hidden under my mattress. Imagine if anyone had seen me trying to get my first sight of her, watching summer band practice with binoculars from my car. Anybody would think I was sick, pitiful, even a bit psycho—and now I wanted to sit close to her to eavesdrop on what she was saying? No. Maybe someday, somehow, I would hear the sound of her voice, but not today.

Maybe someday, somehow, we would talk face-to-face. Often, trying to fall asleep at night, I fantasized about a revelation, a reunion, how she would embrace me and I would whisper "Daughter" and she would reply "Mother" and we both would cry. But that was a wish-fulfillment fantasy, nothing more. In my real life it was enough—it was going to have to be enough—to attend Youth Symphony concerts and see her playing all the flute solos, to drive past her high school (I couldn't drive past her house; it was in a gated community), to watch her talking with her friends as she ate her burrito.

I hadn't gone places with friends when I was her age. I'd been a shy nobody, unfashionably dressed in the modest tops and skirts, some of them home sewn, that my mother had provided. Worse than being the only girl in my school who wore kneesocks instead of panty hose, I was too well behaved. I was hopelessly uncool.

Blake hadn't had friends either. He'd worn slim black jeans instead of saggy pants, black boots instead of Converse sneakers. Other boys had stayed away from him and that seemed to be the way he liked it. Rebel. Loner. A misfit, like me.

But it looked to me as if Juliet was normal. Popular, even. She and all her friends were laughing about something. I wondered what was so funny. Were they being mean, laughing at someone, or was it the good kind of laughter, warm laughter? I wondered what Juliet was like, really. Did she go "awww" over puppies and kittens and lop-eared bunnies? Did she give her adoptive mom and dad a hard time? Did she dream about horses? Was she smart, a good student? Did she cuddle babies? What kind of music did she listen to?

She stuck something into one of her nostrils, some sort of gimmick—maybe from the party store?—that flashed like a tiny sapphire blue strobe. The kids laughed so hard a blond girl nearly choked on her soda.

I smiled, feeling an odd, aching pride. My daughter, clowning around? I'd never been like that.

She removed the blue flasher from her nose and placed it into one of her ears, then stood up to stick it into her navel. She posed like a fashion model. Perhaps some ribald things were said. Juliet grinned at one of the boys, put the tip of her thumb to her teeth, and gestured subtly with her fingers. The boy slumped in his seat amid howling and hooting. Whatever the exchange of insults had been, apparently Juliet had won.

I tried not to beam too obviously. *My daughter.*

Juliet looked at her wristwatch, removed the sapphire strobe from her navel, exchanged a couple of good-bye hugs with her girlfriends, and walked away while the others stayed where they were. Juliet had to go somewhere, evidently. I wondered where. Some sort of lesson? Flute? Gymnastics? Voice? Had she inherited my love of singing harmony?

At a distance, I followed her out of the main mall entrance to the front lot where everybody parked; the back lot got used only at Christmastime. Standing on the mall apron, in the shadow of one of the pink concrete pillars holding up the portico, I watched as Juliet walked into the sunshine. Sashayed, rather. Or skylarked. Always that balletic lift in her step. Sunlit, her long, dark hair shimmered almost golden as she strode toward the red and white checkerboard MINI Cooper her parents had given her.

There didn't happen to be anyone else going or coming at the time. Not that anyone would have noticed me anyway, just another housewife waiting for her husband to bring the car around.

Wait, there was one other person out here. As Juliet strode across the parking lot, a middle-aged man limped toward her, leaning heavily on a thick wooden cane. Disabled. From his other hand, the one not gripping the cane, hung several heavily pendulous plastic shopping bags.

He spoke to Juliet, and I saw her smile and nod. She followed him to a neutral-colored van. Watching, I felt my chest swell warm, warm as she opened the side door for him. Yes, my daughter was a nice girl, yes, my daughter had a good heart, helping a handicapped man. She took the heavy plastic bags from him, turned, and leaned far into the van to place them where he wanted them.

And the man stood up straight, swung his cane like a club, and struck her with it, hard, on the back of the head. She fell into the van. He threw the cane in on top of her, shoved her dangling feet inside, and closed the sliding door with a slam. Then he walked briskly around the front of the van, climbed into the driver's seat, started the engine, and drove away.